I0772406

DESCENDENT

Ian Halloway

Book One of the Apostate Series

Bad French Media LLC

Cover and interior design by Bad French Media LLC
Back cover photo by Bad French Media LLC

Publication Data
Names: Halloway, Ian, author.
Title: Descendent / by Ian Halloway
Description: Springfield, MO : Bad French Media 2022
Identifiers: LCCN 2022947576 | ISBN 979-8-9865645-0-0
Subjects: Fantasy Fiction / Adventure

ISBN 979-8-9865645-0-0
Printed in the United States of America
10 9 8 7 6 5 4 3 2

For E. and J.

Contents

Part One: Continuance

Part Two: Anathema

Part Three: Megiddo

Clavis

Acknowledgements

Part One: Continuance

CHAPTER 1

"I liked that one." Eva's eyes narrowed as Jude's finger toggled through the channels. "And you know the rule. We don't change the Great One."

Jude smiled as he backpedaled the switch to find the song still playing, the sweet voice singing about her lucky star. "Sorry, babe, just nervous. I wasn't thinking."

Peering out the windshield, there was no indication of a need for Jude to be nervous. Light traffic, blue skies, and plenty of time to make the appointment. But the expression on his face showed his preoccupation.

Eva smiled and sang, "I just turn around and you're by my side," right along with the music, horribly off pitch. Her screeching always made him smile. Seeing the look on his face, she playfully hit him. "This is my job. No need to worry. You don't feel bad. Nothing hurts. And none of the doctors have said anything you need to worry about."

Jude nodded. "I know. You know how I get. I just need someone to tell me every now and then." He gazed out at the horizon, scanning.

Eva's hands tightened on the wheel. "You see anything out there?" she asked, afraid of the answer.

"Yeah, I see them almost every day now."

Eva forced a smile for him. "Well, that's why I'm

driving." She started singing, "I got you, babe." Eva's not-so-spot-on Sonny Bono brought Jude back to the present, long enough for him to turn the channel.

Jude thought there really wasn't anything worse than a doctor's appointment in which you don't know the outcome. He would give anything to just know. He would welcome a well-placed fruit-sized tumor. At least then he would have an answer.

CHAPTER 2

Jude and Eva sat in the waiting room of Dr. Puriel, MD, PhD. The pretty receptionist introduced herself as Rebecca and asked if there was anything she could get them while they waited.

Jude was happy they had the room to themselves. Of course, to him, it didn't seem like there would be too many people running around batshit crazy, but someone was paying for the sweet office.

Eva was looking at her phone, clearly finding the most enjoyable way of killing time. Jude watched her, still amazed at how strong she had been through all this. He was just about to say that very thing when Rebecca coughed.

"The doctor will see you now, Mr. Travers."

Eva turned to him and smiled, and the moment was gone.

Dr. Puriel was the perfect mix of handsome and age. If he were any younger, he would have been too intimidating.

"Mr. Travers. Mrs. Travers. It's very good to meet you." His handshake was firm and well-practiced. However, his it didn't match the coolness of his face. Dr. Puriel hesitated, and for a moment, he studied Eva, as if trying to place her face. Failing, he gestured to the chairs in front of his desk. The chairs were well-worn, puffed red leather, like something straight out of a Victorian movie. He removed a pad of paper from the top drawer and sat at his desk.

He looked at Jude but said nothing.

"We have seen every doctor my health insurance will pay for," Jude said, trying to draw a smile from the sober-looking Dr. Puriel. "And so, with no answers from them, the last one suggested coming to see a psychologist. You came highly recommended."

Dr. Puriel scribbled his notes, making no sign of even hearing the compliment. He glanced up from his notebook, suddenly realizing Jude had stopped talking, and coldly said, "Mr. Travers, I have reviewed your complete medical record, every scan, every nurse's notes. But the reason I am good at my job is I do not rely solely on the work of others."

"Listen, doc, I don't think I can stand another battery of exams and tests," Jude interrupted. Just the thought of redoing the past five months chilled him.

Dr. Puriel stared. When Jude had gotten the hint that the interruption was unwelcome, the doctor softened. "I see no reason to rehash the same exams that have been double-checked already. But I will administer different tests to probe your mind, Mr. Travers." Dr. Puriel's eyes narrowed. "Also, let us be clear, you will do whatever tests I deem appropriate, or you will leave."

Jude nodded. "Sorry, doc. I'm just nervous."

"Mr. Travers, please understand that I feel for you. But I can assure you, there's an answer to what you're experiencing. All questions have an answer, it's just about whether we can truly understand it when it comes."

Eva tried to clear the air. "We are just so grateful you could see us so soon. I think the waiting and not knowing is driving him crazy." Eva caught herself and glanced at Jude, who looked back and smiled.

Dr. Puriel nodded at Eva, seeing the strain in her face. "This is understandable."

"Can I ask you what type of experience you have in this area?" Jude had done his online research of the doctor but wanted to ask the question anyway.

"If you are asking if I have ever dealt with the extremely emotionally and mentally disturbed, the answer is yes, often. If your question is have I ever come across a patient with your symptoms, then I would have to say no. In a tragic sense, Mr. Travers, you are unique in this area."

Jude stifled a smart comment. He was too tired to find any levity at this point.

"I would like to begin today. First off, please tell me exactly when you noticed your first symptoms."

CHAPTER 3

Six months prior.

"What else do we need from the store?" Jude searched around for his keys, trying to get out of the house before he was asked to do any more chores. He caught his image in the mirror above the sofa. A quick check, he thought, just to make sure he was presentable to the outside world. He was generally happy with what he saw. There were a few more white hairs around his temples than he had remembered, but Eva said she loved them. He shrugged, just happy he still had a good mop of dark hair on his head.

Eva stopped what she was doing to respond to his question. She watched her husband admiring himself and smiled at his vanity. "You have the list, sexy," Eva said as she smiled at his blushing. "Just get whatever is on there. You should probably check with Max to see if he needs anything."

Jude nodded and went to the bottom to the stairs. "Max," Jude yelled up toward Max's room. He didn't even have to think about where his son could be found. Max would be in his room, glued to his Playstation 6. "I'm going to the store. Is there anything you need?"

No answer. Typical. Jude chose not to yell louder. He went up the stairs and walked into Max's room. The room was lit only by the string of led lights that ringed his room. They cast an odd green color. Jude had been correct. His 18-year-old son was glued to the screen with headphones on, shutting out the world. "Max?"

Max was entranced by the goings on of the game. His dark hair matched his dad's, but he wore it with more control than his father. Jude always thought it was comical that Max would get ready to stay in his room, but Max said he always like to be prepared to go out. "You never know who is going to call," he would say, to which Jude would just shrug. Max smiled as his dad entered the room, giving Jude the idea that maybe he had heard him the whole time. Max's deep blue eyes darted from the screen to Jude. "Yeah?" he said in a false exasperated tone. Jude knew he was trying to bait him. Jude bit.

"Oh, please, good sir, don't let me disturb you. I would hate to think I am taking up too much of your time." Jude looked around the room that was in a general state of disorder. "I know you're right in the middle of cleaning this sty. I'm going to the store. Is there something you would like me to get, maybe something to keep your energy up? We wouldn't want you to faint from exhaustion."

Max smiled as they danced a familiar dance. "No worries, Dad. I can always pause." Pushing a button, Max stood up. Jude couldn't get used to the fact that his son was now taller than him. "Let me see. What do I want?" Max drew it out, seeing how much more he could needle his father. "I guess I can always go for a frozen pizza and a beer?"

Jude rolled his eyes. "Hilarious. Seriously, make a decision. I need to get out of here before I'm asked to do more shit. In fact, why aren't you helping your mom out?"

Max had his stock answer ready to fire. Unknown

to Jude, he had already been asked this question by Eva. "Studying for finals."

Jude's eyes narrowed. "Really?" Jude looked at the screen. A character in a swirling white robe was standing in front of a fiery gate, a staff held aloft in one hand, a sword in the other. "I guess I missed this part of AP American History. Is this the Battle of Bunker Hill or the Watergate scandal?"

Max scoffed. "Sheesh. Done with that stuff. I only have a religious studies final." Max smiled. "If you really think about it, this game is actually helping me understand man's struggle with himself and his existential dread. I mean, when my time comes, I just hope I'm ready to make the right decision, you know?" Max dramatically gazed off into the distance.

Jude clapped at the performance, proud of how full of shit his son was. "Delightful word of the day, but figuring out your existential dread is for your thirties. Please finish up and go help your mom. She has a hair up her ass. It's all hands on deck today."

"Hair up my what?" Eva, holding a hoard of Max's clothes, grinned at Jude, knowing he would owe her a back rub for that comment.

Jude jumped at the sound of his wife. No matter how many times she did it, he was always amazed at how soundlessly she could move. Seeing her smile, he wisely didn't answer her question and turned to leave. "Last chance, Max. Anything from the store?"

"Surprise me, Dad." Max smiled and waited until his father and mother were out of view before sitting back down and pressing the play button.

Eva followed Jude down the stairs, dropped what she had been holding, and embraced him from behind. "Cut him a break. He's eighteen. College starts in the fall. Eventually, we'll be missing these days."

Jude turned. He gazed deeply into Eva's blue eyes. Same as Max's. "Of course you're right. I am fortunate to have you in my life to keep me on track." He went in for a kiss.

Eva gave him a quick kiss, but pulled back. "Don't think you're off the hook for your little comment back there. Now, get your ass to the store." She spanked him as he turned toward the front door.

Getting in the truck, Jude relished the perfect December day. The sunshine was deceiving as the wind cut sharp against his skin. Jude quickly settled into his seat. He allowed the engine to warm a little as he found the perfect station on his phone. Soon, Willie's blue eyes were crying in the rain, and he was off.

The Travers family lived outside the small town of Springfield, Missouri, an unassuming little metropolitan. Eva didn't like living in cities, so they had always chosen to live on the outskirts. They had lived in their little house for the entirety of Max's life and had come to love their little home. While they lived out in the county, they weren't too far from modern conveniences. Still, Jude loved the fact that he passed farms and forest groves on his way into town. In his mind, he was a country person, even though he lived in a subdivision that had not yet gobbled up all the existing farmland. He hoped the undevelopment would last.

He had done this trip countless times over the years—gas, groceries, or some other random errand—but the routine never bothered him. He liked to roll down the windows, even in the Missouri winters, and drive, singing as loud as he wished. He always jumped at the opportunity to get out, play his music, all without compromise or argument.

On this perfect winter day, the world would change for

Jude. This was the day he began to see it.

It started as a minor flaw in his vision. As he drove over the James River, he looked out over one field and saw a blemish just at the horizon. It just caught his eye, and he turned back to the road, dismissing it as a distant tractor or shed.

Getting farther down the road, the city began and the scenery changed, but at the horizon line, he saw it again. He came to a stoplight and really took a good look at what it was. Later, when he was asked to describe it, he would say it seemed like a warp in his vision, as if someone had taken their thumb and smudged the horizon.

Now, confirming he was seeing something odd, Jude rubbed his eyes. He glanced back. The warp was still there, but smaller this time. This satisfied Jude. It was probably stress-induced or an eye floater. He toddled on with his day.

FIVE MONTHS PRIOR

Eva tried to remain calm. "Just set up an appointment with Dr. Ray. It's no big deal. She will check you over and give you some eyedrops or something," Eva said as Jude seemed more and more panicked.

Over the past few weeks, the warps had been getting worse. Sometimes, it was just one in the distance, but more often than not, there were four or more of varying sizes. Some would appear much closer then vanish.

It didn't take long for Jude to realize this wasn't an issue with his vision when the warps would remain static. Still, to be cautious, he had his eyes checked. The eye doctor found nothing out of sorts.

Jude dreaded what he had to say next. "I already saw Dr. Ray." Jude winced. The optometrist told him to immediately see his general doctor, saying things like "MRI" and "just to make sure." Jude hadn't shared this information with Eva. Denial was a powerful drug.

Eva's brow scrunched. Furious he had been keeping things from her, she knew it would be better to remain calm and simply asked, "Oh, good, and what did she say?"

Seeing how his wife was taking this revelation made him feel worse. Dr. Ray had said nothing good. But he couldn't say that, so he started with the seemingly positive. "Mostly nothing, but she checked my blood and did a quick scan. She doesn't think there's any cancer or tumor worries. So, I feel much better about that." He turned away from her to leave the room.

Seeing him trying to escape, she asked, "What else?"

Stopping dead, Jude responded, "That was about all she could confirm."

Eva wasn't having any more of this. "Enough, Jude. Quit holding out on me. You are no good at it. You're too honest." She softened her tone. "What else did she say?"

Jude hesitated. "Well . . . what she couldn't confirm is the bigger problem. She was actually hoping for some sort of benign tumor," Jude said with a laugh. Seeing no amusement in her eyes, he coughed. "Because, you see, it's better for her to have AN answer than what she has now, which is a mystery. Apparently, doctors don't like mysteries when it comes to their patients."

Quickly, Eva said, "What's next?"

"Oh," Jude continued nonchalantly, "she wants me to see a neurologist to rule out some brain issues. A battery of tests that will take a great deal of my time and bodily fluids." Jude turned serious. "Look, Eva, I meant to tell you. While there is no reason to assume the worst, this may not turn out to be pleasant. You know how Ray is, no sugarcoating. If it is neurological and my symptoms are getting worse, there may not be a good outcome."

"Why didn't you tell me? I would have gone with you." Eva and Jude always went to their doctors' appointments together. They both were a little neurotic when it came to doctors, and they put each other at ease. One listened and got the details while the other freaked out. This had been their arrangement for years. Eva felt hurt by being left out.

Jude knew he had hurt her. Something told him this wasn't going to be a good outcome, and he wanted to soften the blow. He obviously had miscalculated. "I would have, honestly. Here on out, you're there. I knew Ray was going to say either tumor or something worse. I didn't want you to hear it that way. If it was terminal, I wanted to have a few normal nights before the gnashing of teeth and rending of clothes began."

Eva laughed at his visual. He always made her laugh. She looked at her husband, his dark features and perfect face that showed the wrinkles of many years of laughter. She also saw his dark eyes and the terror that hid behind them. She needed to ease off. "I get it. But here on out, you and me. Promise?"

He breathed in deep and smiled. "Promise."

ONE MONTH PRIOR

"Jude, I don't really know what to say." Dr. Freeman kept peering down at his file. The bald spot on his head allowed a clear view of the roadmap of veins and arteries that made up the top of his scalp. He looked as if he had been a neurologist since before Missouri was admitted into the Union. Jude had been told he was the best, but that was something that gave little comfort.

Jude stared out the large window overlooking the St. Stephen's Center for Neurology. The antiseptic smell of the building permeated even the inner sanctum of the doctor's office. Jude thought he would eventually get used to the smell, but weeks and weeks later, it still stung his nostrils. Spring had entrenched itself outside. Young green leaves grew on the oaks, their yellow dust still coating every surface they could find. There were fourteen warps today. Two of them inside the office. It made enjoying a nice spring day impossible. He looked at his reflection in the window. Seeing his face even in the weak reflection showed him how much the stress was showing. Eva pulled at Jude's hand, snapping his attention back to Dr. Freeman.

Dr. Freeman continued. "I bet you feel like a pincushion at this point." Jude could tell he had learned his people skills in some sort of two-hour seminar. He was probably more concerned about the type of bagel they served. On any account, he desperately needed a refresher.

"More like a research monkey, Doc." Jude glanced over at Eva. She gave him the smile he needed.

"All for your betterment, Jude," Dr. Freeman said in his typically dry manner.

"No doubt, but I've had so many different hands up my ass, I think I may have to get remarried." Eva laughed, knowing he needed the audience.

Smiling, Dr. Freeman continued, "Which is why it is very distressing to tell you we can find nothing physically wrong with you. All functions are normal."

Eva, always painting a rosy picture, said, "That's wonderful, though, Dr. Freeman, right?"

Dr. Freeman jumped at the chance to take on a positive

tone. "Yes, of course. From a medical standpoint, there is no reason you shouldn't live a long and normal life. But what is disturbing is that the scans confirm what you have been saying. You truly believe you are seeing…" Dr. Freeman glanced at his notes, "warps."

Jude expected this. There had been hints that some of those on the medical team thought he was malingering. Jude, not being a complete idiot, couldn't fault them for trying to go down every road. "Yes, warps. I am glad my brain is seeing what I am seeing. What's next, Doc?"

Dr. Freeman shifted in his seat. "I think the next part is to examine your mind."

Jude breathed in deep. "You think I'm crazy."

"Jude, I don't know what to think." Dr. Freeman's earnestness was clear. "I have pulled what's left of my hair out about this. If we want to rule out all issues, we must now explore your mental stability."

Jude turned to Eva. Eva had a flashback of the times she'd caught Jude staring wildly into the distance. She had never seen the look before, and it frightened her that her strong husband maybe going mad. Jude said, "I'm losing it," bringing her back to Dr. Freeman's office.

Freeman said, "Jude, please, remain calm."

"How can I do that?" Jude pleaded, looking from Freeman, to Eva, to the warp that materialized two feet away. "You've said there's no procedure or medicine that will fix me. I'll just slip into insanity and drag my family down with me. Now is not a time for me to be calm."

"Jude, please," Eva pleaded.

Freeman waited until he had Jude's attention. "I am not a psychiatrist, but I know you need to focus on the fact that you know what's going on. Having self-awareness of your condition is a positive step that should give you hope. People who are 'losing it' don't know they are losing it."

Jude's muscles eased, and he sat deeper into the couch next to Eva. Hope was dimming. He was willing to reach for any glimmer. "Okay. That's something."

"Exactly." Dr. Freeman relaxed, seeing Jude wasn't going to lose it in his office. "I have contacted the very best in this area. He has agreed to meet with you."

Seeing Jude was occupied staring at something, Eva asked, "And who is that?"

Dr. Freeman glanced quickly at his notes. "Dr. Abe Puriel. Actually, when we suspected this was the road we would have to go down, a member of his staff approached one of my doctors, and they got to talking about your case. When I made the call to him, he was very willing to meet with you as soon as possible."

Eva squeezed Jude's hand tight. "See, everything is going to be all right." She looked into his eyes and saw the terror recede. "You're stuck with me for a while, old man. We'll go see if this doctor can help you find some of your marbles."

Jude laughed. "Okay, Doc, when can I see this guy?"

"You have an appointment in a month."

CHAPTER 4

Puriel heard the last sentence and let it hang there for a while before he began. "Okay, Mr. Travers."

"Call me Jude."

Puriel's eyes squinted, and Jude couldn't tell if he was happy with the informality.

"As you wish, Jude. And I assume you want me to call you Eva?"

"That would be fine." Eva had been in a trance during Jude's retelling of his last six months. She had heard it countless times, lived through it herself, but the fear seemed to grow with each retelling.

"Jude, how many of these warps do you see now?"

Immediately, Jude said, "Twenty-four."

He arched an eyebrow. "And you say they are static, how close is the closest one you see?"

Without looking, Jude replied instantly, "Behind you and to your right. In the corner of the office."

Puriel did not glance back to the corner. "And have you ever approached these warps?"

Jude stumbled, "Ye . . . yes. I did once before all the tests, then a few times during the examinations."

"Can you describe if the warp feels like anything?"

Jude pursed his lips, considering how to form the

description. "It's always been difficult for me to really explain. When I try to touch a warp, my hand also begins to warp. It starts with the fingers, then my entire hand twists and contorts."

"But do you feel anything?"

"Not the first few times I did it. It was just like an optical illusion."

"And that has changed over time?"

Jude peered down at his hand. "When I began to see fifteen or twenty warps at a time, I noticed when I would touch one, I would feel an odd sensation."

"Meaning?"

Jude chose his words carefully. "It's like a warming. Like I put my hand in sunlight. It's actually pleasant."

"Then why do you seem disturbed by this?"

"Well, it's like something in my mind tells me not to let go. The feeling is so comforting. So satisfying."

Eva saw Jude looking at the back corner of the room. "Four days ago, I found him standing in the living room with his arm outstretched. I asked him what he was doing and . . . well, it's like he didn't even recognize me. It freaked me out. I ran to him, and when I touched him. . ." Eva's voice trailed off, and she glanced back to Puriel.

Sensing there was more, Dr. Puriel said, "Please, Eva. Continue."

"I reached him. Looked at him staring into space. His eyes were fixed on something." She shook her head. "There was no pain, no worry. The lines on his face had eased. It had been a while since I had seen him like that." She paused and looked at Jude, who had turned back to her. "Doctor, when I touched his arm, it snapped him out of it. But in that moment, two things happened. First, for the smallest of moments, I think I felt what he is talking about. It was like seeing the sun break out on a cloudy day."

"And the second?"

Eva's face, which had been brightened by the memory, suddenly turned dark. "All that happiness, all that contentment I saw in his face, washed away. It was like I broke him. I still feel terrible about taking that away."

Jude smiled wistfully at his wife and turned back to Dr. Puriel. "I've been able to stop myself from trying again. I'm not here to freak anyone out, and if Max came home. . . Well, this has been hard on him as well."

Dr. Puriel nodded. "When one suffers, their loved ones suffer along with them." Jude nodded without comment, thinking Puriel must have gotten that off a poster somewhere. "When was the last time you tried to touch a warp?"

"That last time Eva saw me. I would say that was eight or nine days ago. Honestly, now that I am seeing more and more warps, I'm also concerned about what the effect of touching one would be."

Puriel asked Jude, "I understand your reluctance. I may feel the same way. But I am going to need to see this for myself."

"Now?"

"What better time than the present?"

Jude sighed, then got to his feet and walked over to the corner of the office.

"I am going to record this. I hope you don't mind. I think it will be essential to my personal research." Dr. Puriel retrieved a smart phone from his coat pocket and held it up to Jude.

"No problem, but just know the other doctors said none of their recordings showed anything unusual. Just me standing there, arms out."

"Yes, I understand. I want to see it myself."

Eva moved uncomfortably in her chair. "Jude?" she said urgently.

Jude gestured back towards Eva. "Doc, do you think my wife can go get a cup of coffee or something. She doesn't do well with this."

Dr. Puriel nodded and pressed a button on his office phone. "Rebecca, please take Mrs. Travers to the coffee shop around the corner." Dr. Puriel smiled at Eva and motioned to the door.

"I won't be long, Jude. If you need anything, just text."

"No worries." Jude smiled. "I'll see you soon."

With a brief glance at Dr. Puriel, Eva turned and left the room.

CHAPTER 5

As he put some monitors on Jude, Dr. Puriel told him to describe everything he was seeing and doing, knowing there would soon be a moment where he couldn't. Jude got up from his chair and approached the corner of the office. Dr. Puriel pushed the record button on his phone. "Let the record show it is three-forty p.m. We are with patient Jude Travers."

"So, I'm about three feet from the warp."

"And how big is it? What is its shape?"

"I would say it's about two feet tall and kinda has the shape of one of those yoga balls my wife sits on. It's not sitting on the ground. It's about four feet off the ground."

"It is hovering off the ground?"

"Yeah, but I don't want you to think it's hovering like a helicopter or bird. It's making no motion, as if it's part of the wall. What it looks like? Take all the surrounding colors—the carpet of your floor, the brown bookcase, the books in the case—and smear the colors in a twisting pattern that dissolves into black."

Dr. Puriel frowned. "Black? I've never read that you have mentioned this in your prior statements."

Jude nodded. "As the warps have gotten bigger, they've started forming a black place in the middle. In this warp, it's about the size of a baseball."

Dr. Puriel took some notes. "Please continue."

"As I get closer, I begin to feel something odd. Like goosebumps running up and down my spine."

"Keep getting closer and talking." Dr. Puriel came up close to Jude and stuck his hand out in the area of where Jude described the warp was. He felt nothing.

Jude was now engrossed by the warp and hadn't even noticed the doctor had moved. "As I get closer, the lights glow around the black baseball." Jude's fingers were stretching out with yearning. "I'm almost there. My fingers feel warm. I can usually still talk for a moment after I get there. It's always the weirdest sensation, like being in the ocean. You know how it pushes you away, then draws you back in? It's the same thing here. I feel some pushback, then all of a sudden. . ." With a quick gasp, Jude stepped forward, and both his hands seized the warp. "I'm there. I got it."

"Quickly, what is going on?"

"My hands are playing in light. All the colors. I feel . . . good. Like first waking up after a long nap. Or Christmas morning when you were a kid." Jude's words slurred, as if he'd had too much to drink. His eyes, which had gotten dreamy, perked up. "My hands. My hands."

"Yes, what about your hands?"

"They are sinking into the warp, about to touch the baseball. I'm touching it." Jude's eyes got watery. A smile crept across his face.

"What do you see?" Dr. Puriel asked urgently. But it was no good. Jude was lost in the warp, and Dr. Puriel knew his voice was being drowned out by whatever Jude was experiencing. "Let the record show it is now three-forty-five p.m. Patient Travers is lost in some sort of trance. His vitals are within normal rates. But there was a spike in his heart rate just prior to him touching the warp."

FIFTEEN MINUTES LATER.

"Let the record show it is now four p.m., and Mr. Travers generally remains unchanged. The last reports have stated he can remain in this position for over an hour. For our purposes here, I will . . ." Dr. Puriel's voice trailed off as he watched Jude move. Jude moved his hands apart and in front of him, as if he were trying to get a car to stop. The health monitor began to beep, showing Jude's heart rate was now at one-hundred-and-twenty beats per minute.

"Patient's heart rate has now spiked to one-twenty from sixty-eight for no apparent cause." Another beep, and the heart rate jumped to one-thirty-nine. "I am also seeing the look on the patient's face has altered. He now seems as if he's in some distress."

Dr. Puriel turned off the video and strode behind Jude. "Jude, I am going to bring you back." With that, Dr. Puriel placed his hands on either side of Jude's head and closed his eyes.

CHAPTER 6

"So, are you going to go back?" Marshall asked. Marshall Dunlop had been Jude's friend since they fought each other in the fourth grade (a disagreement over three-on-three basketball which resulted in a black eye, a loose tooth, and a trip to Principal Harrison's office). Since that time, they had been in many small-town scrapes and adventures. They saw each other as family. Marshall's wife, Amy, set Jude up with Eva, and the four had been close ever since.

Jude leaned back in the well-worn seat of the booth. "I don't know, man. Seemed to me like a bunch of bullshit." Jude took a long drink from his glass. "I have to say, I am seeing less of them now, but they're still around."

Besides Eva, Marshall was the only person Jude confided in. He knew he couldn't tell anyone the complete truth, not even Max. Jude never questioned that Marshall would believe him, and he didn't let him down.

"Well, that is something. Sounds like you're running out of options, old man." Marshall said with a smile. "By the way, Amy and I wanted you guys to come over for dinner this weekend. It's been a while. It may do you some good."

Jude nodded and glanced around the bar. He and Marshall had been coming here well before they'd turned twenty-one, when their IDs said they were Ron Westly and

Harold Patter. The owner at the time hadn't been too pleased when they returned for their respective twenty-first birthdays using their actual names, but she got over it. Jude remembered when the place had been called "The Red Room" and catered to the young and unassuming. Since that time, it had gone through several name changes and was currently "The Springfield Tap House," which specialized in some sort of craft beer that tasted like lawn clippings. Jude and Marshall stuck to pitchers of Bud.

"Something was different today." Jude took his eyes away from the warp partially obscuring the barback, who was standing around doing nothing. "I don't remember much after I touch one, but I've always felt … I don't know, good, I guess, after I do." Jude finished his glass and poured another. "This time was different."

"How so?"

Jude looked at his full glass. "Terror. I don't know what. Don't know why, but I still feel it now. Running up and down my spine. Terror."

Marshall gave a big sigh. "Well . . . that sucks."

Jude laughed. "Yeah. Thanks for the insight. I'm so happy to have you in my life to tell me how much it sucks."

Marshall ran with it. "I mean, Jay, your life has been pretty sweet until now. But it seems like the clouds have opened up—and hallelujah! It's raining nothing but shit."

"Thanks for the recap."

"How I haven't found you hanging in your closet is beyond me."

"Please, I wouldn't make it so tidy."

"You're right." Marshall looked around the bar and thought of all the times he'd had with his friend, a friend who might have been slowly losing it. "You need a break. A road trip. Just me and you. Get out of the office and doc exams. Wind in our faces. We'll bring tents and see some cool shit."

"Ah, two weeks of crapping in buckets, fighting off rashes, and gas station sandwiches. Sounds great."

Jude was many things, but an outdoorsman was not one of them.

"Then you choose the place. I'll pay for everything."

Jude suddenly grabbed his chest and began gasping for air.

"What the fuck, Jude!" Marshall stood up. "What going on!"

Jude started laughing. "I'm sorry, I thought I died for a moment. Did you say you would pay for everything?"

"You're an asshole." Marshall sat back down, slightly embarrassed at his reaction, hoping Jude didn't read too much into it. "Why do you think it was different this time?"

Jude shrugged. "It may have been that I hadn't tried grabbing one in a while. Don't know. Not really looking forward to doing it again." He ran his fingers through his hair in frustration. "I've got to get a hold of this shit, man. For Eva. For Max."

As the words left his mouth, a warp opened up in the middle of the table. The edges of it swirled with lights, and in the middle, was the black orb, larger than he'd seen before. It breathed in front of him, pulsing with life. The light became so bright, Jude's eyes became fixed on the orb. His vision dimmed.

Panicked, Marshall rose, moved to the other side of the booth, and grabbed Jude's shoulders. To everyone else in the bar, nothing was out of place, but Marshall had seen these looks on Jude's face before. "Jay! Come on, man. You okay?"

Some onlookers noticed the fearful tone of his voice. Some wondered what was going on. One got their phone out and started recording.

"Jay. Come on. Come back!"

Jude's hands shot out, and stood fixed, outstretched, as if trying to stop an oncoming bus. His mouth opened agape. With his eyes wide, staring into nothing, people were coming over to offer help.

"Should I call nine-one-one?"

"Your buddy need some help?"

"Is he having a stroke?"

Marshall turned away from his friend. "No, no, he's fine. He just needs some time. He'll be okay."

His words did not calm the crowd, whose attention was now being held by the sound coming from Jude.

It began low, guttural, but grew in intensity. It was just a sound, with no form, but it soon became clear the sound was in fact a word spoken over and over again.

"Please please please please please please please please please."

While loud, it was said not as a command, but a prayer.

***

Both of Jude's hands were now inside the black orb. His normal vision had been replaced. He no longer saw the bar, that much he knew, nor could he turn his head. The booth had dissolved in the swirling lights, and now all he could see was the gray space.

Not in a room, but not outside. He stood on a gray floor that expanded into the horizon. He seemed surrounded by darker swirling gray clouds, churning over and over. Later, when trying to explain it to Eva, he found the sameness of his surroundings made it difficult for him to determine the dimensions of the area he was in. The clouds could have been ten feet away or a thousand. He would describe it more in terms of what he felt. A feeling of not belonging.

"Marshall? Anyone!" he screamed into the vastness. He moved his eyes to the ground. Even though the ground was a perfect unbroken gray, he could sense he was moving forward. "Anyone, please!"

Jude could feel a wind press against his face as he moved forward toward nothing.

***

Marshall reached out his hands, placed them on Jude's shoulders, and shook him like a rag doll, shattering the gray world, bringing Jude back to the bar.

Jude blinked and looked around at the people staring at him, their phones still out.

"What happened?" he asked Marshall. Jude looked behind his friend and saw that the large picture window hung in shatters and people outside were shaking broken glass off their jackets and hats.

One of them shouted, "What the fuck was that?" Others answered in mumbles and drunken grunts.

Marshall pulled Jude out of the booth. "Let's get going." He turned to the bartender, who stared dumbfounded at the broken glass. "Money is on the table." The bartender nodded without looking at Marshall.

"Marshall, what happened?" Jude didn't feel drunk, but his words were slightly slurred.

As they walked out the door, Jude glanced at the broken glass that had fanned out beyond the window. "Just get in the car. I'll get you home."

CHAPTER 7

"Max! Please pay attention."

The late spring day shone outside the window. Max's eyes were fixated on anything other than school. Shook from his daydreaming, Max gave his attention back to Mr. Helms, his fourth period Religious Studies teacher. "I'm sorry."

"I'm glad you're sorry," Mr. Helms said playfully, rolling his eyes. Turning back to the entire class, she said, "Please give your attention to today's speaker. She's a professor at Missouri State University in world religions. Actually, one of the youngest professors in her field. A prodigy if you will; and she has been kind enough to give us some of her time. You at least can act like you're paying attention." The last comment brought a smile to only Mr. Helms, who thought himself quite humorous. Seeing no smiles, he coughed and said, "Without further ado, please welcome Dr. Angie Chiseler." A light applause scattered the room.

When Dr. Angie Chiseler entered, it was as if she had brought life-giving air with her. At least to the males in the class. Usually, the Religious Studies classes were used to guest speakers that ranged from pale-faced priests who had the charisma of slugs, or old Sunday school teachers who went by names like Marge and Bertha. Dr. Chiseler happily looked nothing like either. With tan skin as if she just came from the beach and a dazzling smile, she greeted the class with an air of confidence only the very attractive have. She walked with the authority and confidence of an accomplished and wise professor, but her long auburn hair was tied back into a ponytail, giving her a youthful, disarming appearance.

Sadly for Max, he didn't notice. While Dr. Chiseler was turning heads, Max was already back in his head. His thoughts drifted back to his father, as they always did these days. Young men typically daydreamed about the hidden secrets of Friday nights or the small flirtations that always gave their pulse a jump. But now, no matter how hard he tried not to, Max thought about his father and all that was going on. Every night now, he would look into his mother's eyes and see the concern, the worry. Despite all the "it will be fine" and "tomorrow's another day" expressions, he still laid wide awake at night. He was convinced if he could just see the world through his father's eyes, he would understand everything that was going on. He thought that thought, prayed that prayer, until exhaustion took him.

"What do you think?"

Max turned back from the window to see Dr. Chiseler standing above him. He first noticed her scent. Like fresh rain on wildflowers. It was feminine and ensnaring. The fragrance hit his nose and settled into his brain. Then her eyes met his. Her odd green, flecked with gold. His face flashed hot and panicked. He stammered, "Um … I'm sorry, what was the question?"

Exhausted, Mr. Helms heaved a large sigh. "Max, please pay attention."

Dr. Chiseler smiled kindly at Max, and without looking at Mr. Helms, said, "It's quite all right. I was young once." This drew a few laughs, as it seemed Dr. Chiseler was all of twenty-two years old. With flowing auburn hair and a body not yet touched by time, it was hard to imagine anyone thinking of her as old. "What I asked, Max, is some people believe religions were created to answer the unanswerable. To give early humans direction in a directionless world." She brought her hands above her head and dramatically said, "To bring order to the chaos." More laughs.

It didn't take long for Max to become mesmerized. He smiled sheepishly. "So, man created God in his own image?"

Dr. Chiseler smiled widely. "Perfect statement. What are your thoughts?"

Max frowned. He certainly didn't want to say something stupid. He panicked. "I don't know. Maybe."

She seemed satisfied with his non-answer. "Maybe indeed." Dr. Chiseler turned back to the class and picked up the dog-eared Bible that Mr. Helms always had sitting at the corner of his desk. "This is as good an any segue into my topic." She clicked a button on her laptop, and the PowerPoint came to life on the screen behind her. "I would hazard a guess that most, if not all, of you were raised as some sort of Christian. Am I right?" All the students looked around and nodded. No one seemed to object to her statement. Satisfied, she moved to the next slide and read it out loud to the class. "Your religion isn't real." She was happy to see some eyes widen. She waved the bible in the air. "Interesting read here. Any of you actually read it cover to cover?" There were a few nods. "My job at the MSU is to explore ancient beliefs and faiths. Try to figure out why people created these little myths in the first place. Now, for today's lesson, I'm not going to try to dissect the entire Bible here. But maybe explore a few areas that may be thought provoking to you here. If any of you have any questions, please hold them to the end." She looked at an eager girl in the back who seemed like she was about to have a conniption. Dr. Chiseler was used to this reaction and carried on with her lesson.

"Most of you are aware of Moses and his role in the whole bible story. There have been countless movies about it, so I'm going to assume I do not need to retell it. After the whole leaving Egypt and the Ten Commandments, does anyone here know where the Jews went?"

"The promised land?" said Billy Jacobs from the front row, with a touch on uncertainty. He was desperate to be right, but more desperate not to be wrong in front of the pretty guest speaker.

Dr. Chiseler awarded his answer with a smile and a nod. "I couldn't have wished for a better answer. Thank you." Billy beamed and blushed. "I will ask, though, promised by whom?"

"God," was the answer given by a few students.

"Which god?"

This answer seemed to confuse the students. The eager girl waved her hand excitedly in the air.

"You're right, maybe that was a confusing question. Let's just say the land was promised to the Jews by their god and press on. But what does this really mean? Was this 'promised land' an empty utopia just waiting for a wandering band of Jews to happen by? Of course not. The land their god promised had already been inhabited by a great deal of people. Mothers and fathers and little children running around living their lives. And they prayed to different gods than the Jews. So many different gods. Gods for dancing and for fortune. Some were goat shaped. Some had bull horns." The images she showed on the screen flashed before the students. Images of gods carved on stone and little statutes of figurines. She stopped in front of Max. "Let me ask you, Max. What do you think these people…" she pointed at the slides, "thought about Moses and the Jews taking their land? Do you think once they found out Moses's god had promised their land to them, they were okay with it?"

Max was relieved to get a softball question. "I would think they didn't agree. These people…"

Dr. Chiseler interrupted, "Canaanites, is what the Bible calls them."

Max had heard the word before. "These Canaanites probably thought their gods had wanted them to keep their land."

Dr. Chiseler smiled. "Oh, what to do then? One god says yes, but another says no. What do you think happened?" she asked Chase Martin, who sat next to Amie Houghs, the eager girl who kept trying to answer the questions.

"Who, me?" Chase had tried his best to hide all year and had done a pretty good job of it. Seeing Dr. Chiseler nod, he thought a moment, then said, "I would assume they fought. And since I've never heard of the Canaanites, they lost."

Dr. Chiseler did not appreciate Chase's glib nature. "Actually, it was way more than that. Moses told his general, a man named Joshua, to go into the land, and murder and pillage every Canaanite village and town. He was ordered to wipe the land clear of any living thing that could be tied to the Canaanites. I think in today's society, we would call that genocide." She sighed and added, "But I guess you were right in the end, young man. The Canaanites lost."

Sophie Jenkins blurted out, "So, God ordered a genocide? Is that what you're saying?"

"Not what I'm saying. Not at all. It's what this book is saying." She lifted the Bible again. "We all know history is written by the victors. And the early church fathers knew they had to justify the slaughter of a whole group of people. Even back then, these men were skilled marketers. You needed a good hook to sell a new god. A powerful god works, a god who murders babies in their crib, not so much." She paused, and an image of Noah's ark appeared behind her. "Does anyone here know how the writers of the Bible accomplished the sanitization of murder? No one? It's a good one. You are all familiar with Noah and the flood." Everyone nodded, enraptured by Dr. Chiseler. "Good. What isn't covered by the various movies is what happens after Noah lands safely. Usually, the movies end with a rainbow and we are left to assume everyone begins to hump like rabbits." Laughter spread at the image she created. Dr. Chiseler gave a quick apologetic look to Mr. Helms, who merely nodded his head. "What isn't discussed is Noah's son, Ham. Yes, that was his name. So, the story goes that Noah planted grape vines and made wine. Being unfamiliar with its effects, Noah got really drunk, tore off his clothes, and danced around naked ... or something like that. The next morning, Noah's sons went to pick up their passed-out father, and Ham, his second born, gazed at Noah's naked body. We are left to speculate what exactly Ham saw or did. It remains unclear why this was some huge problem, but the writers of the Bible decided it was so bad, Noah cursed him and cast him out." She watched the students. While intrigued by the story, she could tell they didn't know where she was going with this. "So, Ham left his father and brothers behind, and populated a new land. The Bible says this curse was passed from Ham to his son, Canaan, and all his descendants." Realization dawned on Max and some of the other students. "You see, the writers of the Bible made it okay to root for the Jew's genocide of Canaanites because they were all just descendants of Ham, who was cursed by Noah, so they were subhuman anyway."

"Is that true, though?" Chase asked.

Dr. Chiseler looked at the boy and thought there might be hope for him yet. "That the Canaanites were descendants of one man named Ham? No, not at all. These people didn't call themselves Canaanites. They went by hundreds of different names and had no connection to Noah or Ham or any of that. But it is true the writers of the Bible needed a justification for a bloodthirsty god who would command his people to commit unspeakable acts." She could see some were uncomfortable with her tone. "I know what I'm saying can be distressing. All I ask is your think for yourself. Do the reading. Do the research. Not just Joshua, but look at the entire line of early kings. King Saul and his absolute paranoia. Kings David and Solomon and their odd proclivities. All in the name of their god. All of them flawed humans this book glorifies and sanitizes. This theme of covering their asses goes right through and past the New Testament, but that's for another day."

Encouraged by the others who just blurted out questions, Amie couldn't remain silent any longer. "What is the point of this?" She wanted to say more. Usually, when she spoke out, she would have the support of her fellow Baptists. But now, she knew the room was not hostile toward Dr. Chiseler.

Answering her question without acknowledging her, Dr. Chiseler said, "One could argue that there isn't much difference between the Israelites of old and the current Israelis. What do today's Israelis want? Their promised land. But promised by whom? Their god. And they will stop at nothing to keep it. Expand it. Are they still fighting Joshua's war? Still following Moses's orders? Maybe." Dr. Chiseler turned to

Amie's raised hand. "Yes, you have something to say?" Mr. Helms held his breath. He knew what was coming.

"Sounds to me the moment you go to college, people like you try to destroy God. I mean, what the heck is that? They are the chosen people and they're only wanting to keep what is rightfully theirs." Amie was always sure of herself—and always professed her faith loudly for all to hear. She was typically quiet when they were going through the Islam section, and only made a few potshot comments in the Eastern Religions section. But she always made sure Mr. Helms, and the class, knew her opinion (which was probably shared by most in Springfield, the true buckle of the Bible Belt).

Dr. Chiseler's smile didn't break. "I always enjoy a lively debate. Chosen people, huh? Chosen by whom?"

Without pause, Amie shouted, "By God. They are his people."

"You don't put much stock in the beliefs of others, do you?" Dr. Chiseler responded. "I would think the people who are already there would take issue with your God's zoning plan. And to answer your quibble about education, you think god is being destroyed by education?" She addressed the class, "If there is anything you take away from any of this, please…" she paused to hammer her point home, "please, question any deity who cannot hold up to some simple questioning, especially those with as much blood on their hands as Jehovah."

Amie's anger flared. "This is not education. This is heresy. This discussion is trying to lead people off the path. Mr. Helms, how could you allow this person to come in here and preach this nonsense? I think my father will have something to say about this."

Mr. Helms didn't know what exactly to say. He had run afoul with parents before and didn't need any more headaches.

Especially for just over forty-thousand a year. He looked at Dr. Chiseler and saw a woman who didn't have anyone to come to her defense. "Amie, please be respectful to our speaker. She is not forcing you to believe anything."

Dr. Chiseler remained unfazed by Amie's tantrum and accusation, as if she had been accused of worse things. She continued to address the class. "But that is the point. Whose path? The path Sunday school teachers talk about has been well trodden, and you should ask yourself what kind of people forged it before you go down it."

Amie tilted her head, pushing on through. "In all your ways, acknowledge Him, and He will make your paths straight." It was common for Amie to fall back on epithets found on various Hobby Lobby home decor.

Dr. Chiseler nodded, considering Amie for a moment. "You cannot travel the path until you have become the path itself." Amie grimaced, trying to figure out where in the Bible Dr. Chiseler was quoting. Dr. Chiseler continued, "Some have said if Christ were here today, there is one thing he wouldn't be, and that's a Christian."

Amie responded, "You see. It's that kind of talk that—"

"Mark Twain," Max said, cutting Amie off mid-sentence. Dr. Chiseler turned her gaze to Max. He could feel her green eyes bore into him, and he lost a second. He stammered, "Mark Twain said that." Dr. Chiseler smiled. "My dad is a fan." He glanced down to break their connection and hopefully vanish back into the background.

Dr. Chiseler considered Max for a moment longer, then peeked at her watch. "You know, I see my time is running out. Let's leave it at this." Turning to Amie, she said sarcastically, "Stay on your path, young lady. I am sure you have chosen the right one."

Feeling a sense of victory, Amie huffed, "I have."

Dr. Chiseler turned around and said, "No need to waste your time looking for any other ways forward. They are not for you." Before Amie could even register whether she had been insulted, the bell rang, and the students filed out.

Max grabbed his bag and started toward the door. As the boys filed past, they gave Dr. Chiseler one last look to keep them throughout the day. She didn't register their gawking, but before Max was past, she reached out and stopped him with a touch on his arm.

"Too bad I didn't get your opinion, Max. Maybe the next time we meet, you'll have an answer. I would be interested in what you have to say."

Max was struck a little dumb, but if he were ever going to play it cool, now was the time. "Anytime, Doctor. I think the subject is fascinating." He tried his best to sound truly interested in the subject. Tried to sound more mature.

With a giggle, she nodded at Max as he left the room.

CHAPTER 8

Seeing that all the students were gone, Mr. Helms let out a big breath. There would be calls from pissed parents, but in the end, he didn't think anything was said that would cause him being fired. He was wondering if he would have allowed the discussion in the first place had he known the specifics of it and chastising his cowardice when he realized the answer. "Well, that was interesting."

Dr. Chiseler smiled at him. "Regretting taking my offer, aren't you?"

Yes, he thought, but said, "Not at all. You have an open invitation in my class." He watched her bend over and pick up some notes that had fallen to the ground. His heart skipped ever so slightly.

She could sense where his eyes were but did not react, simply said, "That is why I love coming and talking to high schoolers. They are always so certain. I believe it is one of the last times in our lives when we're actually certain of anything."

Mr. Helms smiled at the concept and nodded in agreement. "You're right. I don't think I have had much conviction about anything in quite some time. I guess when they get to you, they start to question everything."

She shrugged. "Only the smart ones. I am sure you can understand there are more Amies in this world than needed." Dr. Chiseler got her bags together. "On the other hand, you have some bright spots in your class."

Mr. Helms grinned with some pride. Not that he could take too much credit, but it was always nice to hear a compliment about his students. "I try to encourage them. Even the Pentecostals of the group. And lordy, there are plenty of them." He motioned back toward Amie's desk with a knowing look. "They mean well, I guess."

Dr. Chiseler wasn't looking at Mr. Helms. She was focused on making sure she had everything. She then said, "Do they? I am not so certain. So much energy and time wasted on such drivel. But I guess to each their own." She gestured back at Max's desk. "I was impressed with that Max kid. Not many eighteen-year-olds know Twain. What's his story?"

Mr. Helms looked back at Max's empty seat. "Max Travers is a great kid. No drugs, no fights, does his work. One of those who makes my job easy. I hear he's going to Missouri State in the fall, so you may run into him."

Dr. Chiseler frowned. "I wasn't expecting you to give such a glowing assessment. It seemed like you were coming down on him pretty hard."

Mr. Helms nodded. "That's the thing. Great kid, but I've had to stay on him recently. He's been having a hard time of it at home. I've been trying to right the ship, so to say." Mr. Helms stopped himself from going any further. Dr. Chiseler noticed. "Anyway, Angie, I really thank you so much for sharing your time and expertise with the kids. I could tell they really enjoyed it. Most of them anyway. I'm sure your ears will burning for a while now."

Dr. Chiseler nodded. "No problem. Anytime at all." She started out the room but stopped and turned. "Actually, Keith, you have given me a thought. Let me leave you my cell number."

At the way she said his name, Mr. Helms blushed, the

weight of his forty-five years and his wedding ring becoming just ever so heavier. "Your cell number?" he stammered.

With a girlish smile, she said, "Of course. Call it women's intuition, but I believe I may have caused some stirring in this class. If any of your students…" she paused ever so slightly, "or you, want to discuss these issues…" She handed him a business card. "I sleep in, so tell them if they have any existential crises, hold off on that shit 'till after eleven."

Mr. Helms laughed nervously. "Okay, Angie. I'll tell'em."

"See that you do." All the flirtation left her voice.

CHAPTER 9

"I tried to get him out of there as fast as I could, honest, but I'm afraid there may be some videos online by the end of the day." Eva sat and listened to Marshall recount the event in the bar. She told Jude to go upstairs and rest, and he didn't fight her.

"So, you think Jude busted the window with what . . . his mind?"

"No. I don't know." Marshall gathered his thoughts for a moment. "It was obvious Jude and the broken window were related, but I can't say how. He started making this sound. It started low, then it got louder and louder, until he was shrieking. I ran over to him and started shaking him, and when I touched him. . ." Marshall stopped.

"What did you feel?"

Marshall glanced down at his hands and said, "Fear. I felt fear. Alone. Cold. Lost."

"And then the window broke?"

He shook his head. "No, it wasn't like that. When I was shaking him and he was screaming, I felt the whole room churn." Eva stared at him, not understanding. "It was like a wave ripped through the room, from the very back, then out the window. And the window just disintegrated. Not like a rock hit it, but like whatever makes up glass just fell apart. Like, on a molecular level. It just wasn't glass anymore, and whatever it was shot out onto the street."

Eva only nodded at Marshall as she sat on the couch, trying to find another question to ask. The thought of the silence and the eventual *what are we going to do about this?* terrified her. The sound of the car door slamming outside saved her.

"That's Max. Put on a smile, Marshall. We don't need to heap any more of this on him yet."

Agreeing, Marshall took another sip of coffee and checked his phone.

Max opened the front door and saw his mother and Marshall, noticing right away his father was not in the room. "Hey."

"Hey, Max," Marshall said as he kept his eyes on his phone. "How was school?"

"Fine. Where's Dad?"

"Oh," Eva said casually, "upstairs, getting dressed. He spilled something on himself and wanted to put on a clean shirt."

Accepting her lie, Max turned to go to his room.

Marshall rose from his chair. "I gotta get going. I'm sure Amy is convinced I'm drunk in a ditch somewhere." He collected his coat and turned before he left. "Seriously, anything he needs, just call."

After Marshall left, she allowed herself a few tears. And as she cooked dinner for her troubled husband and naïve son, she shed a few more. After they had dried, she went upstairs to check on Jude. Seeing him laying down on their bed, lights off, seemed odd.

"How are you feeling?" She entered the room softly, not wanting to overly disturb him.

He spoke loud and clear in the dim light. "It is the funniest thing. I know something terrible is happening to me, I can sense it in my bones, but no matter what, physically, I feel fine."

"Well, that's something, right?"

Jude shrugged. "The problem is my mind. It's like I've been staying awake on caffeine for days. I feel stretched. Weary." Eva sat next to him on the bed and rubbed his back. There wasn't anything she could say to comfort him, she knew that. But she would be next to him, at least.

"No matter what. I'm here next to you." Jude nodded at her statement. "Rest up. I'll get dinner together."

Later that night, the family was sitting around the dinner table.

"Why are we eating in here? Is the queen coming?" Max said as he stared at his phone.

"I thought it would be nice to actually look at each other while we eat," Eva said.

"Creepy."

Jude scoffed. "It's not creepy, Max. It's a pleasant change of pace. Now, honey, which fork is the tater tot fork?" Jude smiled at his wife, knowing she was trying her best to keep the night as light as she could.

"Whoa! What is this shit?" Max exclaimed.

Eva's eyes widened. "Language, Max."

"Screw that. Have you seen this?" Max turned his phone to his father, and Jude saw the footage he'd known would get out. All he could see was Marshall shaking him and then the glass breaking.

"Yeah. I had a minor episode today. I'd been hoping you wouldn't see it, but here's to hoping." Jude took a long drink from his glass of wine.

Eva looked back at her plate, not wanting to give the video any thought. "It's nothing to be concerned about, Max. Your father is being treated by the very best. I'm sure everything is going to be okay."

"THE FUCKING GLASS DISINTEGRATED," astonishment mixed with fear tinged Max's words.

Eva threw down her fork. "Goddammit, Max. Language, please."

"You mean, 'not at the dinner table,'" Max said, dripping with mockery.

No one spoke further. Jude tried to eat some more. He wasn't hungry in the slightest, but he couldn't just sit there and stare at the warp at the other end of the table. Eva moved the food around with her fork and gazed at her plate through watery eyes. Max didn't even pretend. He was glued to the comment section, just waiting for someone to identify his father.

Jude knew he would have to break the silence, but minutes slugged on and he didn't know where to begin. There was nothing he could really say to make anyone feel any better. He breathed in to say something, but was stopped by his phone ringing. The sound of it made him and Eva jump. Looking down at it, Jude did not recognize the number. Could it be a reporter? Co-workers asking if he was the one in the video?

Jude answered the phone. "Yes?" A few pauses, then Jude's brow furrowed. "Oh, yes." He looked at Eva. "Hello, Dr. Puriel. How can I help you? Yep. Oh, you saw. Uh-huh. Tomorrow? Sure, I can make it. She'll drop me off. Yeah, I don't like driving anymore. I'm sure she will have no problem with that. Okay. Tomorrow then."

"What did he say?" Eva asked.

"Sounded pretty clear to me," Max said, still reading

the comments on the video that had now gained five thousand likes.

"Yeah, the doctor wants to see me tomorrow at ten. He said he needs to run through some exercises with me. He also asked if you wouldn't mind coming along."

Eva's terror level was already too high, but she remained calm. "As long as you are okay with me being there."

"Of course. Remember, you're right next to me."

Max's phone chirped with the sound of a new text. Eva glanced at her son, but had trained herself not to ask who it was. She wanted no more arguments tonight.

Max read the text and grimaced. "I've got to go. I have homework."

Jude nodded, happy to have avoided a long conversation, but sad he felt happy about that. "Just take your plate back. What is your homework in?"

"Shit—I mean, stuff. In AP Chem and Religious Studies." Max grabbed his plate and left the uncomfortable dinner behind him

After the large amount of leftovers were put away and the dishes were in the machine, Jude and Eva sat down and worked on finishing the bottle of red.

"When Marshall brought you in here, you were white as a sheet and I had no idea what to think. I'm glad you're feeling better."

"I was just worn out." Jude finished his glass. "Man, it's been a hell of a shitty year."

She'd held her tongue for as long as she could and blurted, "I still think there's a connection."

Jude, knowing exactly what she was talking about, shook his head. "I have told every doctor. They say that even if this was post-traumatic stress, it wouldn't manifest in seeing swirling orbs. Or shattering glass from ten feet away."

Carefully, she asked, "Are we going to talk about that?" Eva desperately wanted to, but didn't want to press him too much.

"I couldn't tell Marshall. I put too much weight on him as it is. It's best if we keep this as much in the family as possible. When I touched the orb, the bar dissolved around me. It was replaced by something out of a nightmare. I was in some sort of gray wasteland." Jude, seeing Eva's furrowed brow, tried to think of a better way of describing where he'd been. He jumped and excitedly said, "Hey, remember that time we went to go spend Christmas with your friend?" He thought for a moment. "Ally? In Colorado?" Eva nodded. "That snowstorm in Kansas that swirled and turned the world white? That's what this place looked like. All gray, but undulating and alive. I was moving through the grayness, but it was more than that. I was being pulled like a piece of metal to a magnet."

The imagery frightened Eva, but she had to ask, "Pulled by what? To what?"

Jude shrugged. "I never got that far. I freaked out and pleaded with all that was holy to let me go. And…" he snapped his fingers, "I was back in the bar. Marshall shaking me like I owed him money."

Eva let out a breath. "Well, your prayer was answered."

Jude huffed. "I don't feel like God's angels were looking over me. It was more like I still had enough of 'me' to pull back." He poured a last glass of the wine and sadly peered at his glass. "I don't think that will last much longer."

"Don't say that," Eva scolded. "Never say that." She grabbed his face and turned it to where they were eye to eye. "Never. I expect you to be as strong as I know you are."

Realizing the wine had loosened the lock on some of

his darkest thoughts, Jude backed off. "It's the wine. I'm being stupid. Sorry. I'll just avoid getting in these situations until the doctors can figure this shit out."

"Language please."

Jude smiled, put his glass down, and kissed his wife.

***

The glow of Max's phone shined bright in his dark room. He read the text again before responding: "Max, get back to me so we can talk about your dad."

"Who is this?"

"We met in your religion class."

Max stopped and thought, what class? Finally, it hit him.

"The professor?"

"You got it. Call me Angie."

Max wasn't stupid. He knew it was unusual for a twenty-something woman to be texting him. But he was still curious.

"Okay?"

"I got your number from Helms. Can I call you?"

Max knew texting was safer. No real pressure to carry a conversation. But he remembered what Dr. Chiseler looked like, and that thought overruled any hesitation he had.

"Sure."

Max's phone rang.

"Hey."

"Evening, Max. Look, I know this is highly unusual for me to be calling you, and if it makes you uncomfortable, just tell me now and I will hang up."

"No, um…ma'am. I just don't know why you would

want to talk to me."

"I can assure you, Max, it is for nothing inappropriate. If you would like, I can call your mom or something and we can all talk together if that is better."

The small fantasy that had been growing in Max's head evaporated, which Max was sad about. "No. No need for that. If Mr. Helms gave you my number, I have no problem."

"Great! Well, let me tell you why I called. Like I said in class, while I am a professor of world religions, my actual focus has been ancient religions and beliefs."

"Like Old Testament?"

"A little of that, sure, but I have been more interested in what came in the beginning. Dawn of time stuff. I talked to Mr. Helms, and he said you have a very good mind and he thinks you may be interested in an internship I'm offering over the summer."

Max, who took religious studies for an easy A, rolled his eyes. Unenthusiastically, Max responded, "Oh, wow. Uh…I don't really know."

There was a brief pause in which Max hoped Dr. Chiseler would fill with, *That's okay, just thought I would ask.*

Instead, she said, "What's the problem, Max? You sound as if I just asked to borrow one-hundred dollars."

Max smiled. "It's not that I'm not thankful. But I don't think I'm going to major in religion when I go to college."

Dr. Chiseler laughed. "Jesus, Max, I'm not saying you have to become a priest or anything. I can offer you three hours of college credits and a fun experience. Free, of course."

Max felt like the conversation was slipping from him. "Wait. You said you wanted to talk about my dad. What does this have to do with an internship?"

"Honestly? I know you have been having a hard time

of late. You're smart, you're determined, and you haven't been having a good year. When I was your age, I also experienced troubles. My grades started slipping. I detached from my friends. I was always unhappy. Depressed. Then, seemly from out of nowhere, someone offered a hand up."

Max was intrigued. "Yeah? Then what happened?"

"I think you can guess. Someone taking an interest in my life, my problems, made a vast difference in my life. Helped me on my path, as your friend Amie would say. And I swore if I had an opportunity to do the same for someone, I would."

"Sounds like you got lucky. Sounds nice." Max had been hoping for someone to throw him a lifesaver and thought that maybe this was it.

Dr. Chiseler paused. "Yes. So, how about it? A summer internship where you'll delve into the mystic arts of long forgotten cultures?"

"Dr. Chiseler."

"Angie."

"Angie, you didn't answer my question. What does this have to do with my dad?"

"Your dad and his predicament, how it affected your life, is going to be a central factor in our studies. I promise you, Max, you'll be able to apply what we learn to the world around you. It won't be a waste of time."

Predicament? Max wondered at the word. Wondered what Angie really knew. Max had been daydreaming and praying for a way forward. The strain on the family, the constant cloud hanging over all their heads—anything to reach his dad. Now, he thought, God may have finally answered.

"Angie, you have a deal. I'm in. When do we start?"

On the other end of the line, Angie smiled at how excitedly Max had jumped at the opportunity. "I don't think there's a better time than now. First, why don't you tell me all you know about what happened to your dad a year ago?"

Max rolled his eyes. He had told this story so many times to so many different people, he hated recounting it. But he wanted to start out with Angie on the right foot. Why not one more time?

"You mean the night of the shooting?

CHAPTER 10

Jude and Eva sat in Dr. Puriel's office, looking around at the items hanging on the walls. Various degrees and ribboned proclamations hung in frames with a script so ornate, it would be indecipherable to Max.

On other walls, there was the calming, nondescript art one usually finds in a doctor's office. Splotches of paint here and there, forming rings or waves of undulating color. The largest painting hung behind his desk, and surprisingly looked exactly like those Magic Eye 3-D pictures that had littered the malls in the nineties. Jude laughed to himself..

"Careful, Jude. If you see anything other than a sailboat, I'm going to have to have you committed." Jude turned to see who was speaking, finding a short, overweight man in a brown suit with a pleasant face standing next to Dr. Puriel.

Jude smiled at the comment, clearly meant to break any tension. "I was just admiring Dr. Puriel's sense of humor. I don't think we've met?"

Puriel stepped forward to introduce the squat man. "No. I'm sorry. I should have told you when we spoke yesterday. This is Dr. Kiel."

"Call me Dan," he said pleasantly.

Without noticing the interruption, Puriel continued. "I have asked Dr. Kiel to attend our future sessions. I have worked with him for many years and believe he will offer some insights. You have no problem with this?"

Jude shook his head.

"Don't worry, Jude, I only charge you if I fix you. And I'll give you a free mug."

Jude smiled. Dan had been cut from a different cloth than Dr. Puriel. Jude also liked how Dan's informality seemed to annoy Puriel. "No, any help is great. This is my wife, Eva."

Dan smiled and gave Eva a slight bow, extending his hand. "It is also lovely to meet you, Mrs. Travers. I know this can be just as hard on you as it is on Jude." Eva took Dan's hand, and for a fleeting moment, their eyes locked. Jude noticed nothing, but Eva became very uncomfortable and retracted her hand with a stiff smile.

"Nice to meet you too." Her tone was hollow.

The two men took seats opposite Jude and Eva. Puriel turned on his recorder.

"Session two with patient Travers. I am joined by Dr. Dan Kiel, who is sitting in with the permission of Mr. Travers and Mrs. Eva Travers." Puriel set the recorder down on the table between him and Jude.

"Jude, if I may, I would like to ask you some questions to start." Dan looked at Jude in a calming nature. "Nothing you haven't talked about before, but something I would like to hear firsthand."

"Sure, Dan. Ask away."

"Wonderful. I know these phenomena began about six months ago, but I want to take you back about a year. I think you can now guess what I want to talk about?"

"The shooting?"

"Exactly. Can you tell me what happened?"

Jude rolled his eyes. He was rather tired of talking

about it. He glanced at Eva, who gave him a reassuring nod. "Sure. Like you said, it was about a year ago. It was late at night."

"Here in Springfield?"

"Yes. Eva asked me to go to the store and pick up some things for breakfast the next day. It had to be about eight-thirty. The sun was already down. I jumped into the truck, and off I went. I got to our usual store, and they were out of something Max liked, so we went down to try the next place."

"You said we?"

"What?"

"You said, 'We went down to.' Who was with you?"

"Max."

"Your son."

"Yes. He came with me. He had just broken up with some girl and wanted to get out of the house."

"Did you ask him to come with you or did he ask you?"

Jude thought for a moment. "You're right, I thought he needed to get out and asked him. At first, he said no, but then I bribed him with buying him a surprise from the store."

"What kind of surprise?"

"Oh, that's just what we say when we buy him a snack or something like that. It's what we used to say to him when he was a baby. It's like an inside joke."

Dan chuckled. "My mom said the same thing." He patted his belly, "Better be careful you don't give him too many surprises."

Jude smiled. "So, as we were going to the next store, I saw I was low on gas and turned into the nearest gas station. Max had a soccer game the next day, so I thought I would kill two birds. As I was filling up at the pump, I heard a few pops from inside the station."

"And did you look over there?"

"Yes."

"What did you see?"

"I saw a commotion from inside the store. People were running out. I heard more pops, then I saw a man running out. There were more pops, and I saw like a security guard or a cop chasing after him."

"And where did he run?"

"Yeah, like I said, he was running out of the store, and he was running right at me."

Dan's eyes got wide. "That must have been scary?"

"No shit. Scared the hell out of me. Especially with Max there."

"When you saw him coming at you, what did you do?"

"I yelled for Max to get down and I tried to jump into the car. Then I heard him yell, 'Give me your fucking car.' I turned, and he was right on top of me. I held my hands out, hoping to calm him down. To talk him down."

"Then what happened?"

Jude had a hard time thinking about this moment. His whole life had been sitting in the passenger seat of his truck. "Yeah, so I turned around. This guy wanted my keys and had a gun leveled at me." Lost in the story again, Jude's face turned beet red.

Dan noticed. "It's all over now. You got this. Just this one more time." He rose and sat between Eva and Jude. Dan put his arm around him and said, "It's okay to be sad. It's okay to be angry. It was a hard thing to live through. I just need to hear it. Once it's done, it's done."

Jude nodded his head in thanks. "I just still feel so angry and scared. My son was crouched in the corner of the truck, and this asshole could have taken that all away from me. I couldn't just stand there and let any of that happen." Dan gave him a moment longer. Jude swallowed hard. "Anyway, I stepped forward, blocking this guy from my door, and heard three more popping sounds. I flinched. My son yelled for me. And then the man fell against me. The weight of him knocked me down. Knocked the wind out of me. The officer came from behind and pulled him away from me. My shirt was covered in blood."

"But it wasn't yours."

"No. It took me a hard minute to realize the bullets came from the officer's gun and killed the shitbag before he could shoot me. The blood was his."

"So, other than being knocked down and a ruined shirt . . ."

"Yeah, I came away from the entire ordeal without injury. But, man, I shook all over. They said it was shock. Had me lie down with my feet up and a blanket." Jude laughed about how twenty minutes after the whole thing, Max sat next to him, playing on his phone. He'd found out later Max been frantically texting his friends.

"So, in the end, you were lucky."

"Well, luckier than the asshole who shot two people."

Dan nodded. "And when you started experiencing these problems, you were asked about this incident."

"Extensively."

"And they gave you some medication for possible PTSD?"

"Yep. I was up to try anything, but ultimately, they didn't work. I don't really feel like this incident 'haunts' me or anything. It just happened, and I continued on with my life. A little wiser now, possibly."

Dan asked. "Wiser how?" Puriel leaned closer,

seemingly also interested in the answer to this question. Jude was about to say something, then reconsidered and glanced at Eva. They locked eyes, communicating only as a husband and wife could. Turning back to Dan, Jude shrugged. "Oh, I don't know. I guess next time I'll just go to the next station."

Dan laughed. Puriel did not.

Puriel cleared his throat. "I think now would be a good time for us to discuss what happened yesterday at the bar. Dr. Kiel and I have reviewed various uploaded videos and have an idea of what people saw, but we are interested in what you saw."

Jude spent the next five minutes recapping what had happened. They both asked questions about the nature of the warp, how big it was, how it appeared out of nowhere. And then, finally, about the gray place.

Dan pursed his lips. "Do you know what you were talking about right before the warp appeared?"

Jude thought about it and shook his head. He glanced around the office, and for the first time in quite some time, didn't see any warps in the same room as him. Without a word, he stood up and went to the window. Looking out over the parking lot from the twelfth floor, he only saw a few warps in the far distance. "On the way over to your office, I saw some in the road as we were driving, but they seem to have receded. Thank Christ for small wonders."

Puriel wrote something down in his notebook. "Why don't you tell me more about this gray place? You said you felt movement toward something but couldn't see what it was."

"Right."

Dan continued Dr. Puriel's thought. "But you clearly remember feeling under threat. Like you were in danger?"

"No," Jude started. "More like I knew I was someplace

I should not be, and that I was going to get lost and never find my way home. I didn't feel the gray place itself was threatening, but I feared losing . . . I guess, everything."

Puriel asked, "Did you feel you were alone? Or did you sense any presence with you in the grayness?"

Jude looked at the Magic Eye print above the desk. It became somewhere for him to focus his gaze when he didn't want to go eye to eye with these men and their unending questions.

"No, I was alone. Imagine yourself standing on the beach looking out at the ocean, but the water is gray, the sand is gray, the sky is gray, and there's nothing around you in any direction. Now, imagine yourself being pulled from the beach, being drawn over the water, deeper and deeper into the ocean, not knowing when it will stop. That's what it felt like. That's what I saw."

Jude looked up to the print again, desperate for the men not to see the fear in his eyes.

"One day, Jude, I hope to fully understand what you are going through." Dan put his hand on Jude's shoulder. "Trust us, son. We'll get to the root of it." Dan gave Eva a smile, which she did not return.

Puriel peered at his watch. "Jude, I think this is enough for today. I am going to prescribe a medication you have not taken before. Dr. Kiel and I think it may be of some help." Dr. Puriel stood up, went over to his desk, and sent a quick message to Rebecca out front. "Rebecca will have the prescription for you. It is a complicated compound medication, something you won't find at a Walgreens, but don't worry, we always keep it in stock."

Jude was relieved the session was over. Exhausted, he didn't want to answer any more, remember any more. "Thanks,

Doc. When should we meet again?"

Eva, who had kept silent, finally spoke. "Wait a minute. What medication are you giving him? He has been pumped with enough drugs to kill a horse already."

Puriel shifted his weight and looked at Eva. "It's called Alatyrsium. It's a compound depressant that should help with sleep and some possible imbalances in Jude's mind." Puriel, as he was talking, saw Eva whip out her phone and begin researching the drug.

Eva chewed her lip. "Is that with a 'y'?"

Puriel nodded.

As Eva was busy researching, Dan answered Jude's question. "We think it's best for us to keep our calendar open for you. We'll call you when we think it's necessary, but anytime something unusual . . ." Jude smirked, "well, something more unusual happens, call us and we will see you."

Seeing Eva was satisfied, Jude answered, "Good enough for me. Let's hope these meds work and our next meeting is sometime away." Jude got up, shook Dan's hand, and nodded at Dr. Puriel who was now on the phone. Eva said nothing, stood up with her husband, and they both walked out of the office.

CHAPTER 11

Dan moved over to the couch where Jude had been sitting and sat down. He unbuttoned his pants and let out a large groan while placing his socked feet on the table. "Well, well, this is getting interesting."

Puriel put down his notepad, shut his eyes, and squeezed the bridge of his nose. "What are we going to do with this one, Dan?"

Dan didn't answer the question. "What did you give him to take?"

"Why do you care?"

"I am always interested in the whole drama of the thing. The showmanship so to say. Was it sugar water with cocaine? Seltzer and amphetamine?"

"No. Nothing so exciting. I thought I would try something to help him sleep long and deep. Dreamless. You didn't answer my question."

"Nope, I didn't. I have my theories."

"Care to share them?"

Dan smiled and lit a cigarette. "You know it is not in my nature to share." Dan saw a tired look in Puriel's eyes. "What? Pissed I treat these people as my friends and not test subjects?" He let out a large plume of bluish smoke. "Or pissed you have to work with me?"

"You know I think it's always important to maintain

professionalism. What if Travers walked back in now and saw you sprawled out like this was a frat house?"

Dan scoffed. "Fuck. Who cares? He isn't long for this world anyway. Way I see it, either you get him or he is lost. I really have no stake in this game."

Dr. Puriel had feared he would not have Dan's full cooperation for this very fact. Of course, Dan was right. Jude was always a good man, even more so now.

"That isn't the point." Dr. Puriel's voice turned heated. "That is NEVER the point. I help you when they are going to be yours. You help me with mine. The POINT, my fat little friend, is we maintain the Continuance. Fuck with that at your own peril." At his last point, Dr. Puriel sounded like a judge handing down a final sentence. "Anyway. You might have fooled Jude with your little show, but your silver tongue fell flat with Eva."

Dan grimaced. "I see what you were talking about. There's something about her, isn't there? Familiar. Unusual. It's like she is actually here with us, isn't it?"

Puriel was glad to see Dan could sense it as well. "While Eva Travers presents an interesting side note, she's not the problem here. I don't believe she should be our focus this time around."

Dan took another long drag. "Clearly, the key is Max."

"Agree."

"But there is no way there's some fucking eighteen-year-old kid pulling Jude through! Unless someone sent another damn messiah down. How can a child be doing this? And so quickly." With that, Dan rubbed his cigarette out on the couch, then quickly lit another one before Dr. Puriel could protest. He was talking now, so he was pretty sure he could have gotten away with murder.

"Well, I don't know if I would call a year quick. I have seen people pulled within six months before."

Dan coughed up some smoke. "Not in the modern era. No fucking way. Back when we started this shit and it was less than perfect, pulling people was easier. Admit it. We haven't had an extraction in under eighteen months in centuries."

Puriel didn't like the implications of what Dan was saying, but he had to admit Dan usually knew what he was talking about. Revelations like this suited Dan's devious mind. "You're right."

"Damn right." Dan liked to hear Puriel admit it. "What we have to figure out is how this kid is doing it. If he is getting help, who is helping him? And most importantly, why they are helping him?" Dan considered his cigarette for a moment. "Someone has to go make a house call." Then quickly added, "Not it!"

Puriel didn't rise to Dan's impishness. He knew someone would have to do a home visit and figure out exactly what was going on. It wouldn't be him or Dan. "I assume you have no problem if I send one of my people for that task?"

"Like I said, I have no stake in this game. Who were you thinking?" Dan glanced at Puriel. "Just curious."

Without answering, Dr. Puriel picked up his desk phone. "Rebecca? Yes, please connect me with Sham. Yes, I will wait."

Dan retrieved a cell phone from his pocket and dialed a number. "Jay? Hey, it's Dan. Doing great, thank you. How's tricks? Uh huh. Really? Reeeaally?" Dan smiled at Dr. Puriel. "Sounds fun. Anyway, if you can delicately extricate yourself from that mess, I'm going to need you to do a home visit. Yeah. Uh-huh. Yeah, Puriel has a possible extraction going on. Can you meet up with Shammy? I'll text you the address. What?

Springfield, Missouri. Yes, that's in the United States. Awesome. Have fun. What? Oh, yeah, Shammy should take the lead, but you can take any leftovers." Dan laughed. "You fucking tomcat! Later."

Dan put the phone back into his pocket and watched Puriel on the phone. "Damn, what are you guys dealing with over there? Waiting for an operator to connect you?" Dan laughed to himself.

Puriel was about to say something, but before he could, the call went through. "Sham? Am I bothering you? Well, I really don't care if I am. I need you in Springfield, Missouri." Puriel rolled his eyes. "Yes, it's unavoidable. They are sending Jeqon. No, you are taking the lead. Just find out what's going on. I'll send a memo with the details. Thank you." Puriel hung up the phone.

Dan laughed out loud. "Did you say you were going to 'send a memo'? Jesus Christ, what century are you from?"

Puriel didn't rise to his comment. "I thought you didn't have any interest in this case?"

"I said I didn't have a stake. Which is true. But I am interested. Something odd is going on here, and it may affect my interests in the long run."

Puriel nodded, knowing he couldn't prevent Dan in this area. "Well, I don't know about you, but I have had my fill of your company today. If there is nothing else, the door is right behind you."

Dan got up, gave a deep, sarcastic bow, and turned to leave, but before he got to the door, he said, "Last thing. You know Travers is in too deep. You are going to have to tell him. When will that be so I can be here?"

Puriel stared at his longtime companion, amazed, even after so many centuries, he was little more than a child. "I will have Rebecca contact you when it happens. But it will be soon."

With that, Dr. Puriel was alone in his office.

CHAPTER 12

The internship had been very trying. Max had to give up a normal summer filled with days at the lake, pools, and menial jobs. Since he was a graduate and would go to Missouri State in the fall, it seemed like people were always inviting him to a "last" road trip or "last" camping trip where you might have your "last" chance at Kelly Newburn or Hannah Hargrove.

For the first weeks, Max had regretted his decision. There were no pools or hammocks for him. Every day, he went to the office of Professor Angie Chiseler. There were some people taking summer classes, but the campus was unusually sparse. He found her office to be brightly lit with various images of deities adorned on the walls. She spent the first day introducing him to them, giving them each names, where they were from, what powers they used to have. Then she pointed him to his desk where she already had various materials for him to review. He spent his afternoons not relaxing or enjoying himself, but with videos about the ruins of Gobekli Tepe or Newgrange. When he completed a video, Angie had articles about Rudra and Gilgamesh or some other deity ready to go. After each session, she would sit with him and discuss what it was he learned. She never chastised him if he didn't get the work done and was always eager to hear his thoughts on the various topics. Still, he thought he'd made a huge mistake.

It was at the end of the first month when Angie could sense his frustration coming to a climax. "Max, you have to have a rudimentary understanding of some of the topics we are going to explore. You must learn to crawl before you can run."

She had said this to him a few times before. It didn't make him feel any better. "You keep saying that. I don't know, I just thought it would be different."

She frowned. "Different how?"

Max shrugged. "Like, not just reviewing old work. Can't I do this shit at home on YouTube? I mean, really, what am I doing here?" He motioned around the room. "Shouldn't I be doing something a little more active or at least helping you break some new ground or something?"

Angie smiled and ran her hand through his hair. "I think I get what you are saying." He blushed at her touch. Angie walked over to her desk and grabbed her backpack. "Come on. Let's get out of here."

"Where are we going?"

She stared at him questioningly. "If we are going to break new ground, we need a different workspace." He quickly grabbed his things, and they walked out together. The summer heat was oppressive the moment they stepped out of the building. He followed behind her as she nodded to the students they passed. She had her hair back in a ponytail and was dressed in a manner that did not give off any hint that she was a professor and not just any other student. She turned to him and waited for him catch up. "Max, I am happy you have chosen to spend this much time with me. I was worried I was going to have to work by myself this whole summer." She put her arm through his as they continued to walk.

Max, feeling a lump in his throat, was embarrassed he had just been complaining about his predicament. "I know I was bitching back there, but I just want to be of some use to you." The honesty of the statement surprised even Max. A cool breeze hit them, and all of a sudden, Max couldn't think of any place he would rather be.

Angie didn't comment but squeezed his arm. They walked across campus and went down a little alley that led to a two-story home that had been converted into a coffee shop. Max looked up at the hand painted sign that shouted, "The Dragonfly," in purple letters.

"I've never been here," he said as he watched people milling about their day through the large glass windows.

"Good," she said. "New experiences begin now, I guess. I found this little place when I first moved here and just fell in love with it. I have an in with the owner, so we have a study room on the second floor all ready to go."

They walked into the coffee shop, and Angie pointed to one the servers. She gestured to her and Max, showed two fingers, then pointed upstairs. The server nodded as they walked past. The stairs creaked under Max's feet as he followed Angie up. She came to a closed purple door and opened it, revealing an intimate room with a large round table and large soft leather chairs. Angie motioned him into the room while she placed a "Do Not Disturb" sign on the outside doorknob. Max sat in the closest chair and breathed in the mixed smell of leather and coffee. Angie retrieved a large binder from her backpack and placed it on the table in front of Max. With a smile, she invited him to look.

He read the cover which said <u>The Epic of Moloch and Astarte</u>. "I've heard these names before." He ruffled through some pages, stopping at a picture of a bullheaded god. He showed the picture to Angie.

She nodded, happy to see he was paying attention.

"They are Canaanite gods. I thought you would be interested in reading this. Take a break from all the factoids." She motioned to the title page again.

Max turned again to the page and saw it was being written by a Dr. Angela Chiseler. Max smiled. "I didn't know you were writing a book?"

"Well, if you want to make the big bucks in teaching, you always have to be writing. This is more of a compendium of stories I'm translating and interpreting."

Max thumbed through the pages, noting the amount of work that had gone into the massive number of two-sided pages. "I think it will take me the rest of the year to finish reading this. What are the stories like?"

"Just what you said. Stories. Myths that have been passed down from fathers to sons and daughters for generations. Each generation has put their fingerprint on the stories, but the roots remain."

"Why did you choose these two to focus a book on?"

Angie smiled wistfully. "There is something very special about these stories. Canaanite gods who keep showing back up throughout history. They seem to sashay through time itself. You can see them and their influence in so many other cultures. They were there for the Israelites' takeover of the Middle East. They watched their believers scatter in the shadow of King David and King Solomon. And yet, after all that and centuries of history, they are still here. They're clearly what I am calling "proto gods"—gods with qualities that have been copied by so many other traditions, most other deities are basically derivative. Moloch, the destroyer, and Astarte, the giver of life. How many more nuts and bolts do you need for a belief system?"

Max flipped through the pages and saw illustrations of

wise lords, goblets and swords with runes written upon them, and people on their knees, praying before glowing boxes. He got excited. Maybe all his reading this summer wouldn't be confined to archeologists digging in the dirt.

"May I read this?"

"Why do you think I am giving it to you? I think if we are going to unlock the mysteries of why people believe what they believe, we should begin at the beginning. I think Astarte and Moloch are good places to start." Motioning to the room, she continued, "And this will be the place for us to do this. I want your opinion about the work. Now that you have some working knowledge, you're ready to give me an educated opinion."

And that was how the next weeks unfolded. Gone were the days spent in her cramped office. In their little sanctum above the bustling coffee shop, he began to review the stories in her book. In addition to the new assignment, the long conversations with Angie made things easier. She didn't care that he hadn't memorized every detail of the Hindu Vedas or knew the dates associated with the prehistoric Olmecs. She knew enough for them both. He always felt like an equal in her eyes.

As time passed, she would ask him to stop his reading and apply what they were learning to his own goals. His own aspirations. They would meet at The Dragonfly and spend hours discussing topics that ranged from the trivial to the profound. She would also ask him questions about her manuscript, about what he thought about the various stories and if they made sense to him. It always made him blush that she honestly wanted his opinions.

Of course, the fact that Angie was a beauty didn't hurt. A few times, his friends had come into the shop and had seen them engaged in heavy conversations. He couldn't deny that he enjoyed the messages he would get from them throughout the day.

Max found it funny. When he first met Angie, she'd seemed older and unobtainable, but as they'd talked and she'd shared stories about her past and her thoughts, she'd seemed younger. By the end of June, she was his friend. By the end of July, he had fallen in love with her.

One thing that prevented any overt expression of affection from him was he knew he was here on a mission: his father. He'd been hoping he would see something in any of the readings or studies that would help him. But so far, nothing.

It was on a warm August day, when the internship was almost ending, that he finally asked. It was just like any of the other summer afternoons in their private room. A blueberry muffin sat in front of him untouched. "Why don't you help me with my dad? We have been pussyfooting around the topic all summer. Every time I bring it up, you have another assignment you say will help. One rabbit hole after another. Don't you see it's my father I have come here to ask you about." Max could feel the heat rushing to his face. He didn't enjoy talking to her in this way. Even though she had never given him any invitation, his heart held on to hope. "I didn't agree to lose a summer discussing shit like Zoroastrianism for nothing. You said you could help me with my father."

Angie glanced up from her cup of coffee and reflexively looked at the door, making sure it was secured. She tucked her hair behind her ear. "Max, you may not know it, but all you have been learning has been to see if you are ready." She stopped talking when she heard a server walk past. She then peered down at her watch.

Max snapped, "No. You will not play me that way. Say

there is some ultimate goal that will help my dad and then look at your watch and ghost me for a few days."

Angie smiled. "Max, I wasn't doing that. I was just checking how much daylight we had left. Do you want to get out of here? I think there's something I want to show you. Something that will ease your mind and answer some of your questions."

Even though her words were innocent, some part of Max's mind had turned a few of her phrases around, and he blushed at the thought.

If she noticed, she didn't let on. "I just don't want you to be late for anything."

"No. No," Max stuttered. "I don't have any plans."

"Good. Grab your stuff. I'll drive and we'll get your car later." In a fluid motion, she stood, waiting for him to move. His movements were awkward, knocking over the coffee mug and almost tripping trying to get up. She giggled and said in fake exhaustion, "Come on, Max."

Giving a head nod to some people on his way out, Max followed her into the summer light.

About ten minutes later, they arrived at an old two-story house in the middle of town. They said little to each other on the drive. His mind had been filled with conflicting thoughts fighting for dominance. She'd also seemed preoccupied.

As they pulled into a driveway, she said, "Well, here she is. Home sweet home."

"This is your place?"

"Well, for a while. I don't like apartments and the university pays me pretty well, so why not choose something I like?"

Getting out of the car, Max took in a better view of

the house. It was right out of Main Street USA. Large white porch, screen door, about fifteen wind chimes. Angie retrieved a duffle bag from the back of her car. "There's nothing I like better than sitting on a large porch and watching the world go by."

"The wind chimes are a nice touch." Max looked at each one. Some had brass bells, some wood pipes, but each was different.

"I spent a few years collecting those. I get one from each of my little work trips." She pointed to one of the simpler ones. "This is my newest. I got in Hatra in Iraq when I was studying Mandaeism." Max gave her a look. "It is an old gnostic religion. It's supposed to chime only when I have an unwelcome visitor." She smiled, turned to Max, and rang the wind chime. It did not make a sound. Laughing, she said, "I guess you passed the test. Let's go in."

Max sat in an oversized chair while Angie went into the kitchen. "Do you want something to drink?"

"Sure. Water's fine."

A few moments later, she returned holding a bottle of wine and two glasses.

She came back into the room and considered Max a moment. "I'm sorry, Max. I don't have bottled water. I have this or tap water."

Max swallowed hard. "No, this is fine." She continued to the opposite chair and poured the wine.

"I know you are underage for this country, but honestly, for what we are going to be talking about, I think you're going to need a drink."

Not wanting to sound like an infant, he said, "This isn't my first drink. My mom and dad have let me drink wine before."

She handed him his glass and motioned for him to drink. The wine was strong, spicy. He had snuck many drinks in the past and had tasted communion wine since he was seven, but he had tasted nothing like this. It was wine, but he could tell there were flavors other than fermented grapes. It coated his dry throat nicely. He gave a slight grimace when the tannins hit his tongue.

Finishing her first swallow, she said, "This is one of my favorites. Hard to find so I have it shipped to me."

Feeling uncomfortable and trying to think of something to say, Max asked, "From where?"

"Anyway, Max. You are now in my house. I have given you alcohol. You're smart enough to know this would be greatly frowned upon by outsiders, yes?"

Max didn't play dumb. "I would assume so."

"Good. I have opened myself up to scandal and ridicule. Your friends and the whole town have seen us hang out all summer."

Max nodded but didn't understand where she was going.

"What I am trying to say is I have much to lose by teaching you. I am putting myself out there. You can easily call me a nut, turn around and destroy me. When I tell you something, you know I have everything to lose. Learn from me or don't. I am completely at your mercy."

Max took another drink. "Angie, you have never steered me wrong. I won't start doubting you now."

She leaned back, comfortable in the fact that she had gained his complete trust and fealty.

"One thing I hope you have noticed in all our studies is that all religions or beliefs have certain similarities."

Max nodded. "Sure. Like flood stories, demi-god-like

saviors, and rules to live your life by."

"Exactly. Have you ever wondered why that is?"

"I always thought it was humanity's attempt to explain the world around them. Like, 'why is there thunder?' Because Thor, or Zeus, or something like that." Max enjoyed the mental image and realized the wine was beginning to work its magic.

She smiled and refilled their glasses.

"Perfect. Like you said in class, man creates god to allow him to get up in the morning. To keep him moving. To allow him the peace of sleep. There is a beautiful order to the chaos. And man has, through his countless generations, told and retold different stories to keep each other sane."

Max shifted in his seat. This was a subject they'd reviewed to exhaustion. But this time, he knew she was leading him somewhere different.

Angie continued. "There is one story, however, that seems to be present in all beliefs. It begins the same, then it alters, then it joins up again. Like, imagine seven different roads all going along their own paths, but at one point, they merge into one. This is what I have found out. I don't care what god, or gods, or sun, or goat, or woman, or man you worship, in the end, all beliefs end in the same place."

"And what is that place?" Max asked uneasily.

"Death, Max." She took another drink. "We all die. We are meant to die. It is part of the plan. And that is our commonality. Beliefs bicker all about what happens after, but the human condition of mortality binds us all."

"Some people believe nothing happens, that we just die and that's it."

"There are two truths," she said. "We all die. And no one living knows what that is like."

Max's head was swimming with alcohol in the August

heat. He made no comment about her statement. It was too hot. She was too pretty. The conversation was too heavy. Feeling the need to say something, he gave the perfect young man's response. "Yeah, I guess."

"But, Max, what if I told you I knew what death was like?" She watched him for his reaction, hoping he wouldn't run right out the door.

Max grimaced, not understanding what she was saying. "Like, you found a story you like best?"

"Not a story." She took a deep inhale. "I know what happens when you die."

Max did love listening to her. He noticed the sundress she wore brought out the color of her hair hanging loosely against her. The concern for what she was saying was overpowered by his attraction to her. "I want to know what you know."

"I have already begun to show you. I've studied this my entire life. Astarte wasn't just a goddess of life, but a teacher of men. Her lessons stretch through the generations. Once I teach you what I have learned, you will understand your father. You will know what he knows."

All sleepiness was wiped away and he stood up straight. "What are you saying?"

"Max, I am telling you once you understand death, its nature, once you know its name, you can control it, dictate to it. You will learn to reverse it." She stopped and looked Max's wide eyes. "What I am saying Max is that you can bring your father back."

CHAPTER 13

"Good afternoon, sir. Passport please?" The customs agent had had a long day already, but she maintained a professional manner. She now glanced up to see who she was waiting on. What she saw gave her pause. Standing six-foot-three, lean, with long brown hair, the man handed her his documents. She couldn't help but give a girlish smile.

"Thank you, Mr…uhhh…" she looked at the name and gave a hail Mary shot of pronunciation, "Siel?"

"Yes. Perfect, like the animal."

"And how long do you plan on staying in the United States?"

He peered at his watch. "Oh, not long."

"Here on business?"

"Yes."

"And may I ask what business that is?"

The man regarded her for a moment. "I'm here to prevent the loss of someone's soul."

Before she could register whether he was kidding or not, another man, blonde and just as handsome, barged in behind him. "Sham! Don't kid. They don't take kindly to that type of stuff. Do ya, ma'am?" He gave her his documents. "My business partner and I are in your beautiful country to see about expanding our business."

"And what business is that?"

"Why, isn't it obvious?" The men looked at each other. "We're male models. Sham only does hand stuff, and don't you doubt it, he's great. I, myself, will do anything."

The agent nodded and inspected the second man's passport. "That makes sense, Mr…huh. It just says Jeqon?"

"That's right. I'm like my country's version of Drake or Beyonce." Jeqon looked around as if he were going to impart a secret. "I'm mononymous, but don't hold that against me." With a wink and smile, he diffused any uncomfortableness the agent may have felt.

The agent didn't know what Jeqon was talking about, but it sounded dirty, and she had already had a long day. With a chuckle, she said, "All right. You two, please enjoy your stay in our country." She stamped their visas and directed them out.

Not saying another word, the men walked out of the airport. Once outside, Sham moved over to the Uber line.

Jeqon scowled and shook his head. "Jesus, Sham, couldn't you have sprung for your own car?"

Sham didn't turn. "I won't be here long. Didn't see the need. And why are you here? I thought we would meet up in Springfield."

Jeqon scoffed. "You people are cheap as hell. As for your question, I was bored. So, I thought, should I wait in Springfield for my best friend Sham? Or should I meet him at the airport so we can have a cool road trip together?" Jeqon put his arm around Sham and looked out into the distance. "Think of the adventures we could have from here to there? Maybe you'll finally lose your virginity along the way, huh, big guy?" Jeqon saw his physical touching was not appreciated from the look in Sham's eyes, so he withdrew and put his hands up. "Man, I don't want to start any interdimensional war. I mean, we haven't seen each other since…when?"

"Mididi," Sham said, the one word dripping with contempt.

Jeqon stepped back, remembering. "Yes. I knew it was something with a funny name. Anyway, I got the call, heard your name, remembered the outstanding work we both did, respectively, in Mididi, and guessed you'd be coming in through O'Hare." Sham stared at Jeqon, waiting for him to stop talking and explain what he wanted. "Anyway, come with me. We sprung for a car."

Knowing there was no realistic way to avoid his company, Sham picked up his bag and followed Jeqon out to the lots.

Sham caught up. "I know you know, and maybe I don't have to say this out loud, but it is important for me to tell you. This is our case. I'm taking the lead. You're merely to observe. I am making all strategic decisions."

Jeqon said sarcastically, "Yeah, yeah. You're the boss. I get it. I'm here to make sure the job gets done right." He smiled. "But I have to insist I'm in charge of the playlist."

They turned a corner, and Jeqon stopped at the car. Sham rolled his eyes. "What is this?"

Jeqon looked at him, honestly hurt. "What is this? What is this?"

Sham didn't see what the confusion was. "Yes. What the hell is this thing?" Sham glanced down at the car with disinterest. It sat low to the ground and had curves and lines that screamed speed. It was not the type of car that would go unnoticed.

Jeqon, in a matter-of-fact tone, said, "This, my good man, is a Hellcat with a 6.2-liter High-Output HEMI V8."

Sham was not impressed. "It's orange."

Jeqon looked at the car to see what the problem was. "Actually, it's called Go Mango."

"Don't you think we should have a little bit lower of a profile? We don't really know what we're driving into, and maybe…," Sham said, as if addressing a child.

Jeqon hit his head up against the car, and cut Sham off with a sharp, "Fine." A quick flash, and the car changed colors. "You know, I could have gotten the Demon, but I thought that was a little too much on the nose."

Sham quickly scanned the area to ensure no one had seen. Turning back to the car he smiled at his small victory. "Blue. Sensible."

Jeqon got into the car. "It's called Frostbite, dick."

"Odd name." Sham smiled as he felt his phone buzz.

"Who is it?"

Sham ignored the question and answered the phone. "Hello? Yes. I just arrived." He turned to Jeqon. "Yes, he is here. Uh huh. I made it clear." Jeqon rolled his eyes. "Oh, unless this penis on wheels breaks down, I would say we could be there in…" Sham glanced at the pocket watch he pulled out of his pocket, "eight hours. What? It is September the fifteenth. Yes, we will be there well before the sixteenth. Yes. I understand." Sham put the phone back into his pocket. "We need to get to Springfield, Missouri. ASAP."

Jeqon shrugged. "I knew that much. What are the details? You know, so I know my boundaries."

Sham typically avoided giving the specifics of his assignments but felt it was better to tell him. Jeqon was unpredictable at best. A straight up bastard at worst.

"A young man named Max Travers is attempting an extraction. I am to stop him without harm," he said the last part with a clear warning.

Jeqon scrunched his nose. "How young is 'young man'?"

"Eighteen years old. He turns nineteen tomorrow."

Jeqon smiled. "Wow, that is young." He paused as he got the Hellcat out on the road, pointing it south. "That can't be it."

Sham matter-of-factly asked, "Why do you say that?"

It was now Jeqon who looked at Sham as if he were an idiot. "No way in hell that an eighteen-year-old is doing this alone. It would take decades to have even the basic knowledge to come close to pull something like this off. Someone is helping him. But who?"

Sham sighed. "You are right. I have also been charged with determining who is assisting Max Travers. If I find they pose a threat to the Continuance, I am to mitigate that problem."

"And my role?"

"Observer," Sham said coldly.

Jeqon scoffed. "Come on, Sham, don't keep me on the bench." Sham didn't seem to understand the idiom. "I mean, you know no one can 'mitigate' like I can. I stand on my record."

Sham gazed out the window as they left the parking lot and entered the highway. "I have no problem doing my duty. As a Watcher, I serve at the whims of my superiors."

Jeqon shook his head. "No, no, I never said you did. What I'm saying is you do it because you have to. Because you are ordered to. However, I do it because I want to. Just promise me if you identify an 'issue,' you consider me to be your slice and dice man."

Sham saw on opportunity to make his road trip with Jeqon a little more bearable. Jeqon served the Thirteenth Gate, while Sham's fealty was with the First. They were diametrically opposed to one another. But on this mission, the were bedfellows. "Will you promise to conduct yourself in a manner of a proper observer?"

Jeqon answered excitedly, "Of course."

"Then I will consider it."

Jey gave a yell. "Fuck yeah." He pressed a button on his phone, and "Runnin' with the Devil" blared out of the speakers.

Sham rolled his eyes like an exhausted parent.

CHAPTER 14

"Jude. You are dead."

Jude sat in Dr. Puriel's office still staring out the window. The past few weeks had been terrible. At first, the medication seemed to help. But it turned him into a zombie, just sleeping or shambling around the house. The worst part was he would accidentally stumble into a warp and be back in the gray place. But he also had horrifying nightmares he was back in the gray place. It became impossible to know if he was dreaming the terror or actually experiencing it.

Last night was the worst, and the reason he was meeting again with Dr. Puriel and Dan. In the middle of the night, Eva awoke to find Jude standing over her. It was unclear if he was sleepwalking or in a warp trance (a phrase they had come up with). She turned on the light and saw his face was frozen in terror, eyes wide, mouth agape. She instantly tried to break whatever was holding him. He had confided in her his greatest fear was going into the warp and not coming back. The thought chilled her.

"Jude! Goddammit, WAKE UP!" She screamed louder and louder. Seeing no other option, Eva balled up her fist and decked him across the face with all her might. As she did, the room around her twisted and turned, like the walls themselves were made of silly putty and being stretched. The windows shattered. The lightbulbs burst. Jude looked into Eva's eyes and recognized her. They held each other, their breathing rapid at first, slowing to match the other's. She gazed up at her husband, kissed him, and said, "We'll deal with this in the morning. Let's try to get back to bed." He nodded, keeping to himself that he would not be sleeping anymore this night. Nowadays, sleep and wakefulness held the same fear.

It took Jude just a moment to realize what Dr. Puriel had said. He understood the words, but the meaning eluded him.

With some acceptance, he said, "I'm dying." He sighed, almost with some relief. "Well, I can't say I haven't prepared myself for this. All the crazy shit that has been going on. Honestly, I thought on day one it was going to be some crazy tumor that had wrapped around my brain and was going to punch my ticket." He looked at Dan, who had a warm smile on his face. "Actually, fuck it, it IS a relief. I'm tired of being tired. And what this has done to Eva and Max."

Dan kept smiling at Jude, but said in a singsong manner, "He's not getting it."

Dr. Puriel said, "Shut it. Give him a little more time. Mr. Travers, please listen to me. You are not dying. You are, in fact, dead." Jude turned back to Dan, who continued to smile, but now added a nod of agreement.

"I don't understand."

"This is my favorite part," Dan said without hiding an ounce of glee.

Dr. Puriel, ignoring Dan, continued. "I will help you understand. That night at the gas station, with the robber and the shooting..." Jude nodded, "you were in fact shot. Protecting Max, you stood between him and Max and ultimately took three bullets. You died right there that night."

"Instantly. He was a hell of a shot. You didn't even have time to look over at Max," added Dan.

At the sound of his son's name, Jude's anger flared. "Max! What the hell are you talking about? I'm fine. Max is fine." The weather outside, which had been mild and sunny, suddenly darkened, and thunder rumbled in the distance.

"Enough, Dan. Remember, this is my job." At the admonishment, Dan's smile wavered, and he sat back in his chair.

"You're saying I'm dead. I've been dead for over a year, and…" he paused, "and what? What am I then?"

Dr. Puriel put up his hands to get Jude to calm himself. "I will explain. As I said, you died that night at the gas station. Your son is fine. Eva is fine."

"Of course Eva is fine. She's sitting outside in the lobby waiting for me. We drove here today. We are going to catch something for lunch after we're finished with this dog and pony show."

Dr. Puriel peered down at his hands and studied them while waiting for Jude to stop talking. "When someone dies, especially if it is before their natural time, there is a system in place. That system is called the Continuance. One day, we are going to have to make a decision about you, and we want you to have every opportunity to prove your standing."

Jude was listening, but a thousand questions cluttered his thinking.

"Look," Dan began, "have you ever had a close call with death? Like a near miss in traffic, or like that time in sixth grade you almost drowned in the Dunlop's pool on the fourth of July?" Jude nodded, not even caring how Dan knew about that. "Remember how you felt. That shiver of just gazing death, lightly touching her lips." Dan spoke as if he were describing a lover. "See, there are many moments where you almost bite it. But you can't live your life if you do nothing but dwell on it, so your mind just lets you keep going. Understand?"

"Yeah, I guess."

Dr. Puriel continued. "Well, that touch is supposed to teach you to be more careful. To appreciate life and its fragility. But sometimes, that near miss is actually a hit."

"Like three slugs to the chest." Dan couldn't help himself.

"Anyway. When that happens, the Continuance takes over, and in your mind, you just keep going. Living, learning, making decisions. And when you come to the time you were supposed to die, we make a final assessment."

"Assessment about what?"

"An assessment about the value of your life," Dr. Puriel said.

Jude looked around the office and out the window and noticed the dark clouds were mounting again. Lightening flashed.

"So, this is some sort of purgatory before going to heaven or hell? That's what you are saying? That I am dead, and this is some sort of waiting area, where you guys are some sort of angels who are going to weigh my soul?" Jude glanced back and forth between Dan and Dr. Puriel. Dan's smile returned, but he said nothing.

Exhausted, Dr. Puriel stated, "No. This isn't purgatory."

"This is heaven?" Jude thought for a moment, then added, "Honestly, I'm cool with that. Except for the warps, I have all I need here."

"No, this isn't heaven. And no, this isn't hell. Those concepts are far too simple to describe what is going on." Dr. Puriel settled into his seat. "Okay, imagine Existence itself being one large entity. Humans, trees, stars, other life forms going about their day on some distant planet. They are all a part of Existence. The more complicated creatures require a great deal of energy. There is quite a bit of investment in each of you, and from time to time, we do an assessment to ensure the energy being expended is going to good use."

Dr. Puriel retrieved a pipe from his pocket and started packing it. "If that person is assessed as worthy, it goes on."

"On to where? Like heaven?"

Dr. Puriel thought about his answer for a moment. "Imagine this place around you," he gestured out the window and all around the office, "is like Grand Central Station. People arrive here and wait to see what their destination is going to be. There are thirteen different Gates in this place, so there are thirteen different destinations. Mortals come from the Fourth Gate. I came from the First." Dr. Puriel could see Jude wasn't following.

Dan rolled his eyes. "Christ, let me do it," he said as he spread his arms out. "All of this. All of it. Is so much more than you can possibly realize or comprehend. You can probably grasp that you are one, infinitesimally insignificant being, who was floating on a speck of a rock in a vast universe." He waited for Jude to nod in agreement. "In reality, your endless universe is just one of many in the whirlwind that is Existence itself. You are a micron, on a speck, floating on a fleck. Now, to give some order to this chaos, Existence has divided itself into thirteen different realms that are shuttered behind thirteen different Gates. Gates that we," he motioned to Dr. Puriel, "maintain."

Dr. Puriel interjected, "Don't get too hung up on where each Gate leads. For you, it isn't really that important. The point is to move on. Always forward. Many times, it is to a better place, but no matter what, your energy is moved on."

Jude narrowed his eyes. "What do you mean it isn't really that important where I am going? I think that is the most important question I could ever have answered. It's great that," Jude gave his best Dr. Puriel impression, "'many times it is to a better place,' but surprisingly, I don't find that of any comfort. What if I am one of the lucky few it is not better for?"

Dr. Puriel tried to skate by without adding anymore terror but knew he would have to answer the question. "If a person is assessed negatively, their energy is sent to the Thirteenth Gate to be repurposed for other projects."

"Repurposed?" Jude said accusingly. "People are thrown away so someone can…can…what, build a sidewalk, plant a tree?"

Dr. Puriel shook his head. "I'm sorry, Jude. I am trying to be as open as I can be. Trust me, for your race, humans, the standard for forward movement is quite low. As you progress, the standards will change, but they will always be fair. There is only so much energy in the Existence. We much make certain each atom is being used in a productive manner. The moment it's not, Existence steps in to correct the problem."

Jude was dumbfounded. "How can God judge this way?"

Dan laughed. "Please."

"Shut up, Dan," said Dr. Puriel. "It's a good question." Turning back to Jude, he continued, "Dan and I adjudicate each life. We place a value on the individual worth. That is why we are here, to make sure there are no mistakes."

"Who put you in charge?" Jude was incredulous. "Who the hell put two psychologists in charge?"

Dr. Puriel rolled his eyes. "Jude, we are not psychologists. This," he motioned to his office, "is a little ruse we have to use to probe different issues. My name is Puriel, and his name," pointing to Dan, "is Dokiel. One of our many titles are Arbiters of the Continuance. Prior to the Continuance, we were a type of…" he looked at Dokiel, trying to find the best way to explain it, "high ranking soldier, I guess would be a good way of saying it. I worked for the beings behind the First Gate, and Dokiel worked for the Thirteenth Gate. But one day," Dr. Puriel snapped his fingers, "we both found ourselves here. As to who put us in charge, your guess is as good as ours. We came into the Continuance at the same time, and more or less, we just understand what we are to do here."

Jude started to relax, amazed by what he was hearing. "So, I die, and there are no final answers, just more questions?"

"Well, if this comforts you, you are nowhere near done. You say death, but really, this is just a decision-making process." Puriel was happy Jude was starting to accept the truth of it.

"And you two were sent here to help people on their path or journey? Like guardian angels?" Jude looked at them hopefully.

Puriel, in a serious tone, answered shortly, "No."

Confused, Jude asked, "Then…" Jude paused and looked to the still smiling Dokiel, "what are you?"

"I—" Puriel started.

"We!" Dokiel interrupted.

Puriel nodded. "Yes. We are the final arbiters of your value. We represent two separate factions that are necessarily codependent." Jude seemed confused. "Okay, I hate to simplify things, but let's just say I am the good guy and Dan is the bad guy."

"Hold up. That is complete horseshit." Dokiel stood up and faced Puriel.

Puriel's tone was weary. "Time is a factor here. I am just

trying to get this part of it moving along."

Dokiel turned to Jude. "My man. Ever owned a car? Yes, of course you have. You know how now and then the tires wear out?" Jude nodded, but he had pulled back from Dokiel, almost sensing the wickedness. Jude had always liked Dan, but now he felt he had been clearly deceived. "Now, do you change those tires and get new ones? Of course, of course. It wouldn't be responsible not to. You want your car to run safely, right? Yes, of course you do. Now, does it make you evil if you replace the tires?"

"I am a tire in this question?"

"Well, right now, you're more of a tire with a slow leak. We are here to see if you can be patched up. That is our job. Somebody has to do it."

Puriel said, "A terrible analogy."

"But he gets the point. Good. Evil. Up. Down. Dawn. Dusk. They must exist to give definition to the other."

"But why would you relish throwing me away?" Jude asked.

Puriel waited for Dokiel to answer.

Dokiel put his smile back on. "Because, sonny, there are a lot of things you can do with a worn-out tire." Jude recoiled at the menace in his voice. Jude sprang up off the couch and ran to the office door. Neither moved to stop him.

"Eva!" he screamed as he flung the door open. The waiting area had vanished. The paintings, the desks, Eva. What replaced the waiting room, and, in fact, the entire world, was the gray void. Jude closed the doctor's door behind him and ran in the void, shouting for his wife. He could feel the wind hitting him, but there were no other features he could make out. After running for what seemed like hours, he collapsed on the floor and began to sob.

Puriel turned to Dan. "That is enough with you!"
He then went to his door and peered at his watch, knowing,
to Jude in the void, time was going by much differently. He
opened the door, and saw Jude right outside, sitting on the
ground. "Jude, please come back. There is nothing out there for
you." Jude, not seeing any other option, and knowing Puriel's
office was preferable to the nothingness, got up defiantly and
walked back in. Dokiel slumped back into the chair. Jude was
at least heartened to know it seemed Puriel was running this
show.

"So, is it time for my judgement? I'm to be thrown
away, right? That's what the warps have been all about. Why
they cause me nothing but fear."

Puriel gave Jude a pat on the shoulder and motioned
for him to sit. He then retrieved a glass from the side table
and filled it with a thin brownish liquid. He handed it to Jude.
"Please drink."

Looking suspiciously at the glass, he asked, "What is
it?"

"Scotch."

Jude smiled and drank deep while Puriel continued.
"Everything in the Continuance is real. Not living real, but real
enough. The women. The sunshine. The drink. It isn't a trick.
This past year, you acted exactly in the manner you would have
if you had lived. And Eva reacted in the exact way she would
have, and your son the same. It is a nearly perfect system. The
added growth done in the Continuance has saved many people
from being thrown away too hastily, which is bad for everyone.
It has also allowed some people to show their true colors, and
they were taken out before they could do anymore damage.
However, most people move forward."

Jude drank again. "And me?"

Puriel smiled. "I am happy to note you are well on your way to being…uh…well, promoted. You keep doing what you're doing and things will be fine. You're good, Jude."

Jude exhaled and said a small prayer, but then stopped. "Who should I pray to? It seems odd now."

"Pray to who you want," said Puriel gently.

"I'm a fan of Ahriman. Lusty devil that one was. Those Persians knew how to party," interjected Dokiel.

"The decision we make for you is unquestionable, based upon all the facts. Dokiel and I have a difficult relationship, but we have never disagreed regarding an outcome. So, choose a prayer that makes you happy and say it proudly."

Jude made a small prayer. No matter what Puriel said, he felt he was in a desperate situation and needed help.

After he stopped, he looked at Puriel. "You said the Continuance is nearly perfect. You also said that I am 'well on my way' to being moved forward. And that time is a factor. Why do I feel like I have only heard half of the story?"

Dokiel scoffed. "I would be surprised if you've heard a sixteenth of the shit you're in."

CHAPTER 15

Sweat dripped from Max's brow as his face contorted in concentration.

"Hold on! Hold on! You're almost there!" Angie shouted. "Can't you see it? You got it. You got it."

And then it was all over. Max slumped back into his seat, exhausted, panting.

Angie stood opposite him. "What the fuck was that, Max?" Sweat drenched her clothes. "What was that?" she asked again angrily.

Max opened his eyes in response to her tone. "I'm trying my best! Don't stand there and yell at me like that," he said, matching her anger.

Angie's icy glare held for a moment, then melted when she said, "I'm sorry, Max. I just want this so much for you. And you are so close." She sat back down on the couch and fanned herself. "You have been working very hard this past month. I just get overly excited when I see such progress."

Max sheepishly smiled. "I know. Just give me more time."

"What did you see this time? I could see most of it but give me the details."

Max took a long drink of ice water before he spoke. His throat was dry and rough, as if he had been screaming for the past hour. "I was back in the gray zone. I spoke the appropriate chants you taught me."

"Did you get the hand movements right? Remember that is just as important."

Max held his tongue. He knew she was trying to help him, but sometimes, he thought she was expecting too much for him in such a short time. He sat there panting in their private room at The Dragonfly, recalling how this magic shit all began.

***

"Let me tell you the nature of magic." She eased into the conversation, constantly waiting for him to run out of her house. He nodded and held out his empty glass, and she obligingly filled it a third time. She was surprised with how well he had taken to the shift in their relationship. She looked down at her sundress and knew her appearance, and the alcohol, probably made him more open to new thoughts.

After taking another drink, he asked, "I am more interested in what you just said about bringing my dad back from the dead."

"I'll get there." Seeing he was firmly on the hook, she began. "Long, long ago, before what was called the Rekindling, this world was filled with wonders. Some of these were objects that could do amazing things. You have heard of some, but they passed into only legend and myth. Stones that could give life. Rings that gave power. Blades that could not be defeated. These stories, while now just that, have their roots. It is the knowledge of these items, how they work, how they are made, that was taken from us."

"What do you mean 'us'?"

"I mean humanity. Mortals." She got up and sat close to him. Their knees touched. He could feel the warmth of her skin against his. "It was decided in our mortal realm, knowledge of magic would be sealed off. It's there," she pointed to his head, "but it has been taken from you." She could see she was confusing him. She waited a few moments before proceeding. "What we understand as our history, mankind's early history, has been fucked with. Altered. We cannot really hope to understand what we have lost, but what is important is that you and I understand that knowledge has been stolen from us."

He heard her words but was focused on how close she was to him. "Why would they, whoever they are, do that? And who are 'they'?"

Angie shrugged. "I have no idea, nor do I understand their reason, but I can tell you this, all that knowledge, all that information, is just there, waiting to be grasped. They couldn't destroy it, but they could seal it away. Once you tap into that knowledge, you can do amazing things. Anyone can, they just need the knowhow."

Max inspected the room for anything out of the ordinary, like odd pictures of witches or statutes of horned beasts. All he saw was a completely normal living room. "And are you saying you can unlock my mind?" he asked as he finished looking around.

She watched his eyes and smiled. "Disappointed, Max? No large black cauldron or bottles with eyes of newt or dead man's toes." Her smiled disarmed him. "Max, I am a professor. I work on facts and knowledge, not superstition and rumor. I am not saying I can move mountains, but there are certain methods I can employ to reach the land of the dead. I'm less a witch, more an operator who can connect you to the afterlife. What I can do will seem magical. And I believe it is, but it is the extent of my powers, so to say."

"I think you're saying you're like a medium."

She grimaced at the word. "No. I hate the association. Those cold reading charlatans are frauds. Every last one of them. I will admit, I started my studies with them and their history, but it was a dead-end. They really only knew how to separate people from their money. What I am offering is a real experience in which we can pull your father from the dead and you can speak to him, one last time. I think that's something you might be interested in. Am I right?"

Max considered her words. They sounded insane. But he had worked with her for weeks now and didn't think she was crazy. Actually, he thought she was brilliant. He thought about what he would say to his dad. He really didn't have anything to lose. She wasn't asking for anything from him other than his faith.

"I'm in."

***

When Angie had showed Max the summoning prayers of Astarte in her manuscript, doubt blossomed in his mind that maybe this was all bullshit. There were special prayers and hand motions to summon a lost loved one. They were intricate and complicated. He felt foolish at first even practicing. He'd constantly looked at the door to the room, hoping no one would burst in and see him, sitting on the floor, making odd hand gestures. She'd noticed his embarrassment and had assured him no one would come in and he needed to concentrate. It was about his twentieth attempt, when he first saw the gray zone, that he knew he was on to something. Any remaining doubt evaporated.

"Yes. Hand over hand, saying the prayers over and over. I felt the wind hitting my face. It was pleasant at first, like a sea breeze, but then, like you said, the wind became hot and smelled acrid. Like burnt pennies." Max took another drink of his coffee, trying to get the memory of the taste out of his mouth. "Then I felt my muscles harden, like they were pulling a weight at the end of a rope. Then, in the distance, I saw something making a beeline right for me. And then—"

Excitedly, Angie cut him off. "This is the part I don't understand. What happened? You were almost there!"

Max didn't quite know how to explain. "Honestly, it felt like I got decked in the face. And then it all came crashing down. Like I let go of the rope."

Angie nodded that she understood, but inwardly, she resented being so close and failing. She had a nagging feeling in the back of her head that something was amiss. Something she had not foreseen. Defeated, she asked, "Anything else you can remember?"

Max held back, embarrassed to say anything more. He wanted to avoid mentioning his mother in front of a hot twenty-two-year-old. He was still hoping these sessions were going to turn into something more adult.

Sensing hesitation, Angie turned. "Max?" His eyes turned to hers. "Tell me what else."

"It's stupid. But, at the moment I felt the punch, I felt my mom. I could smell her perfume and…I don't know, I knew it was her. But how is that possible? She is here, alive, probably sitting at home humming and folding laundry. How can she be there?" Max couldn't help but think about what he had been learning. Astarte had been very clear in her writing that what Angie and Max were trying to do was filled with danger. Phrases like "forfeiting the soul" and "eternal damnation" had glared at him as he'd read. Angie had explained she had been the one who'd translated those passages and was well aware of them. She reminded him of how the Bible says you shouldn't eat meat and dairy in the same meal, so he was probably going to hell anyway because of his mom's lasagna.

Angie affected a motherly look of concern, held out her arms, and enveloped him in a deep hug, pressing her body against his. "Please remember what you have learned. What is the Continuance?"

Max breathed in her smell, a mixture of perfume and sweat. "The Continuance is a fabrication and a lie meant to deceive and trap the spirit."

"What else?"

"The Continuance, and the demons who control it, lie to the souls of the dead. They will use every type of trick and scheme to keep us from reaching the departed. They will stop at nothing to reach their goals."

"Which are?" She sounded like a teacher trying to get her students to recite the alphabet.

Jude had recited his many times. She'd told him having this knowledge dug deep into his being would protect him from being fooled and keep him on track. "To prevent souls from reaching what is beyond death. From reaching the true end."

"That's right. Trust me, Max, your mom is fine, sitting cozy at your house right now. Probably still planning your birthday party, am I right?" Max smiled and nodded. "The Continuance has its safeguards meant to even ward people like you and me from messing with it. But we need to push through. Right on to the end. And then we will free your father."

The thought exhilarated Max. "And I will be able to

speak to him, correct, before he moves on?" He had asked several times, but he just wanted it to be true so badly, and was worried of being duped.

"That's the plan, Max. I don't know how long you will get, but do your part and you will set him free." She looked at her phone and saw the time. "I don't think we should make another attempt today. We both know tomorrow is the big day."

Max nodded. Through his studies with Angie, he knew it was his bond with his father that was the most important factor to reconnecting with him. Max had never let his father go, no matter how painful it was for Max. He'd never found the "peace" the various counselors, psychologists, and his own mother talked about. Tomorrow was Max's birthday, and according to Astarte, this would be his best chance to freeing his father from the trap of the Continuance. The moment he sparked into the world, the moment his father first held him, was a bond too great for even the Continuance to deny. Especially now that Max was armed with the knowledge and correct prayers.

"Do you know what you are going to say to him?" She hadn't asked him this question before. She'd felt it was too personal and had wanted him focused on the task.

This question had plagued Max's thoughts since the middle of August when the whole Continuance concept went from a grand story to a reality.

"I'm going to say I'm sorry."

Angie gave an understanding squeeze of his shoulders. "You know he will forgive you. You didn't know. How could you have known you would have played a part in his death?"

The words, blunt to hear, confirmed all he had been telling himself. "I know he will forgive me." Max teared up. "He has to."

Angie helped him up and gave him a long kiss. "Early happy birthday, Max. It's going to be a good day. Eat your cake with your family, then come to my house, come to me. And at the end of the night, you will get the forgiveness you so desperately need."

He held her close. "I never asked what you are getting out of this. All this time, all this effort to help me, I feel like I've been doing nothing but taking and taking. It would make me feel better if I knew you were getting something out of this as well."

She kissed him again. "It is sweet you think of me that way. Don't worry about me. I am getting more than you know. The more people extracted from the Continuance, the weaker the trap becomes. My hope is that one day, the whole thing collapses. And then, we will all be free. If I can lend a hand in that and help you out at the same time, that's a life well spent. I'll see you tomorrow." As he turned to leave, she slapped him on the butt for good measure. He smiled and closed the door behind him.

CHAPTER 16

Puriel glared at Dokiel with a look that clearly meant let me handle this.

"You're correct, Jude," Puriel started. "The Continuance is nearly perfect. However, every now and then, we experience a problem. The same problem you are going through right now. There is a reason your Continuance is . . . let's see . . .a good word for it would be corrupted. When someone from the world of the living refuses to let someone go, it ties the dead to the world of the living. This isn't uncommon actually, and over time, with acceptance, the bond weakens and allows the Continuance to run flawlessly. And it isn't that unusual for the bond to remain because of an inability to let the dead rest. When that happens, the person in the Continuance will see warps. It would be only now and then, and usually, the subject dismisses it as a trick of light."

"Why didn't that happen to me? They have gotten worse. I can barely live, if that is what I am doing," said Jude.

"That is what I am getting at. Rarely, the bond between two people can be fortified, or strengthened, by a third party." Jude didn't understand. "There are some people among the living who are talented in reaching into the Continuance. Sending and getting messages. They use the bond between the living and the dead to do this."

"So, what you are saying is some sort of charlatan medium is using…I would guess Max or Eva, to get a message to me? That doesn't sound like a tragedy," noted Jude.

"And it wouldn't be. The Continuance can withstand a modicum of meddling."

Dokiel couldn't stand being silent anymore. "This," he gestured to the gray void, the only thing visible out the office window, "isn't some medium, or shaman, or voodoo priest. Someone is trying to extract you from the Continuance, and neither you nor I want that to happen."

"I don't know what that means."

Puriel stepped forward. "An extraction is literally what it sounds like. Someone in the living world is using one of your loved ones to try to pull you from the Continuance."

"But what does that mean?"

Puriel continued. "For you? It means you will be trapped forever in the world of the living, never moving on, never finding rest. The gray zone you see around you is the space between the living and this place. The things you feel in the void, the fear, the loneliness, you would feel forever on the other side in the world of the living. You would forever haunt the living, a twisted and tortured form of what you once were."

"A ghost?"

"Simply, yes. A ghost. Not all ghost stories are real, but some do exist. The living should not be fascinated by ghosts. They should see them for what they are: a source of lamentation and sorrow. It is not an eternal existence I wouldn't even wish on Dokiel."

Dokiel bowed at the backhanded compliment and added, "And for us? Losing a being to an extraction weakens the Continuance. Imagine going down the highway at eighty-five miles an hour and then slamming the car into reverse. Too many times and you're up shit creek."

Puriel rolled his eyes. "What is with you and car metaphors?" He looked back at Jude, "He is correct, though. We cannot lose too many people to an extraction. Everything in Existence is about balance. Extractions are such a huge imbalance, they can throw everything into chaos. I do not use that word lightly. I am talking about Existence itself twisting and exploding inward and outward. Like your bedroom last night. Or the glass in the bar—but on a universal scale."

"Wait a minute. All that just for me?"

Dokiel scoffed again. "Jesus, this isn't about you. It's never about you. If it were just you and you alone being extracted, I wouldn't be here at all. There are far more interesting Continuances going on right now."

"Dokiel, any more outbursts and you can sit this one out. No one is stopping you. I am more than capable of this myself." Puriel turned back to Jude. "My friend here does make a point, Jude. This isn't all about you. Let's say you are given a job, a job you love that gives you meaning, and you can only make five mistakes. As long as you don't make these five mistakes, you keep the job."

"Am I like the fifth mistake?"

"No. I'm not saying that. But if you had this job for an eternity, you would do anything to prevent even one mistake, correct?" Jude agreed. "I don't really know how many extractions the Continuance can withstand, but Dokiel and I do everything we can to prevent even one. We have lost many, and at a substantial cost. We treat each one as if it is our last."

"I understand. I don't want to shamble around rattling chains forever. What are we doing to prevent this extraction?"

"We have lucked out so far. Your bond with Eva is something we haven't seen before, but now is not the time to explore that question. We should just be thankful it has allowed her to act here on your behalf strongly. We believe it is her influence that has kept you grounded these past months. Therefore, we feel the problem is your son, Max."

"My son is not the problem." Anger spiked in his words.

"That was poorly worded. We feel it is Max's bond that is being manipulated. We are unsure yet by whom, but we have sent messengers from the world of the living to stop whoever it is. But it must be done by the sixteenth of September."

Jude blinked and thought for a moment. "Max's birthday?"

"Yes, the day of a child's birth is historically the first and strongest bond with a father. The manipulator obviously knows this. All these warps have been Max's attempts to pierce your Continuance. Obviously, he's been getting better and better as time has gone by. Dokiel and I feel if we do nothing, you'd be extracted in his next attempt."

"And these messengers you have sent, they will not hurt Max?"

Puriel glanced quickly at Dokiel. "Certainly not. Max will be safe."

Dokiel interjected. "The manipulator, on the other hand, will be dealt with."

"Do you know anything about this person?"

Puriel shook his head. "No. He or she has stayed hidden successfully. Whoever it is is well-practiced and clearly needs to be eliminated."

"I ask again. What can we do? Just sit here?"

Puriel sat next to Jude. "Partially. We are waiting for our people to tell us when it is done. But to seal the problem and cut the cord to Max, we are going to allow you to send one message to him. Something he needs to hear. Something that will allow him to let you go. Can you think of something like that?"

Jude sat back and thought. He went through the events of Max's life in his mind. First steps, arguments, vacations. Jude remembered the time he taught Max how to tie a tie for his first school dance. His face when Hannah broke his heart. His face.

Jude then remembered Max's face the night of the shooting. The terror, the fear. He was supposed to protect him. Did He?

"What happened to the shooter the night I died?"

"You stood in the way of his escape. He needed those keys, and you refused. You also refused to get out of his way. He shot you three times, emptying his gun. By the time you hit the ground, the officer had already put four of his slugs into the robber's back," Puriel answered.

"And Max saw the whole thing?"

"Yes."

Jude considered it for a moment longer. "I know what I want to say to my son."

CHAPTER 17

Shamsiel hadn't realized something was wrong with his little road trip with Jeqon until they hit St. Louis. Southern Illinois all looked the same. Shitty little towns broke the tedium of the landscape dominated by farmlands. Thinking back, the problem he and Jeqon were having could have begun as early as Bloomington and he just hadn't noticed. But now that he saw the Gateway Arch, Sham knew something was terribly wrong.

It dawned on Jeqon at the same time. "Is that the Arch?"

Sham nodded as they crossed the Mississippi River. "Yes."

Jeqon wasn't familiar with all landmarks, but he knew something was wrong. "How many Arches does St. Louis have?"

Sham watched as they approached the Arch. "Turn off here." Jeqon didn't question the command and took the first exit in Missouri. "It only has one. This is the second time we have passed it." He took a deep breath and recounted their trip. They hadn't taken any wrong turns or gotten off on any odd exit. They should have been deep into Missouri. He pointed Jeqon to a church parking lot near the Arch. "Park here. I need to check something." Getting out of the car, they walked up to the large structure that dominated the landscape. Sham glanced at his pocket watch. "It doesn't make any sense. By my watch, we should be nearing Springfield."

Jeqon only shrugged as he followed Sham to stand right before the metal Arch. Jeqon looked at the late morning sun as it gleamed off one side of the metal plates. He peered back into the downtown area and saw the shadow cast on the ground. "What are you doing?" he asked as Sham began waving his hands in the air and muttering into the late morning air.

Sham didn't answer him. Instead, he spoke louder for Jeqon to hear. "Nothing under the sun is hidden from me. I command you reveal your shape and nature," he said over and over, all while performing precise hand motions in front of himself. A flash of heat radiated from the Arch and pushed them both back. Sham held two fists out and turned to Jeqon. "It is fighting me. A little help would be appreciated."

Jeqon smiled. "Happy to help." He began his hand motions and said, "What is hidden cannot hide from me. I command the shadows and the crevices, reveal your shape and nature." Working together, the wind stopped and they both saw the Arch flash red. Black twisting vines appeared all along the sides. In the space below the arch, a large flaming hexagram appeared. Instead of lines, the hexagram was composed of fiery letters outlining its purpose. Jeqon looked about and saw all the tourists were oblivious to what was happening.

Sham studied the words for a moment. The language was familiar, but disconcerting. He placed one finger in the air and traced. A new word that would have been unpronounceable to any of the oblivious onlookers blazed in front of Sham. A moment later, he sent it to join the words of the hexagram. The moment the word touched the others, the shape flashed a brilliant white and fell to the ground in ashes.

Sham watched as the vines withered and died at the base of the Arch.

Jeqon smiled at Sham as he turned to say something but stopped and noticed something was still amiss. Sham glanced up and saw the sun moving quickly across the sky. The people around them sped up and moved at an unnatural rate. The world spun around the two Watchers as if they were the only two in existence. If they had been mortal, it would have been nauseating. The night sky appeared, and the moon did its dance quickly across the blackness. In another moment, the sun reappeared and blazed in morning glory. It streaked overhead, then settled in a position clearly far past noon. The people around them returned to normal and life carried on. The whole ordeal lasted thirty seconds.

Sham checked his pocket watch. The hands had spun forward. What had been ten-thirty a.m. now showed seven at night. Putting the watch back, he said, "Back to the car. Now."

Getting back into the car, Jeqon peeled out of the parking lot and found the entrance ramp back to the highway that would take them to Springfield. It wasn't until they cleared St. Louis that Jeqon finally spoke. "What the hell is going on?"

Sham had spent the last silent moments trying to answer that same question. "Clearly, we have underestimated what we are dealing with. This isn't a typical case."

Jeqon furrowed his brow. "No shit, Sherlock. I haven't seen a protection ward that large and powerful in eons. I can't even imagine the focus and power it would have taken to create it. Hell, it was strong enough to work on you and me, and I don't know about you, but I am not easily duped."

Sham looked at the mile markers and did a quick calculation. "Nor am I. I believe Max Travers is in well over his head and dealing with people and forces he has no concept of.

He is in great danger."

"Fuck yeah," Jeqon swore as he pressed the gas. "I thought this was going to be a cakewalk. This just got a ton more interesting." He pushed the car even further, easily breaking all speed limits.

Sham stared at the road, hoping he wouldn't be too late.

***

"Ten-thirty? Cutting it kind of close, Shammy."

Sham didn't rise to the challenge. Thankfully, there were no more wards or delays from St. Louis to Springfield. They even lucked out on light traffic. Chicago to Springfield should have only taken eight hours. They should have arrived a whole day early. It was the night of the sixteenth of September, and they were just now pulling in front of the target residence. Someone had gone to great lengths to slow their travel. Sham was nearly certain he would meet that someone tonight.

"Whoever is in there, they have played you for a fool." Jeqon said.

"Played us both for fools," Sham corrected. He looked at the two-story home. It seemed unassuming at first, but then he noticed the details that would be missed by mortal eyes. The runes hiding in plain sight: the design of the paver stones, the arrangement of the bricks that made up the porch, even the pattern in the drapes. All were wards meant to keep the unwanted away. No one came to this house the owner didn't want.

"She has really done a number on this house. Man, oh, man. You really have to have some appreciation for the detail, don't you, Shammy?" Jeqon inspected some of the specific inscriptions on the stones and saw someone of his kind wouldn't be able to pass. "Looks like you are on your own, buddy. I envy you." He smiled at Sham. "You know what's in there, don't you?"

Sham nodded. It was a witch, clearly. But not any run of the mill hag, but a necromancer; a witch skilled in raising and communing with the dead. "Not exactly who. Not what form it has taken, but the ward that delayed us alone was a clear sign of what we're dealing with." Sham considered the next moves. "I thought we had gotten them all," he said more to himself.

Jeqon shook his head. "You had hoped we had gotten them all. Necromancers are like sand in the carpet. Once the knowledge of raising the dead was released into this world, it was always going to impossible to get rid of. They are going to pop up from time to time. But this one is well-practiced."

Sham had had enough of his commentary. "Stay close to the car. I will go get the kid and deal with the witch. It has been made clear to me the kid is my first priority." He paused to let that sink in to Jeqon. "If the necromancer gets past me, please detain it." Sham noticed Jeqon nodding too eagerly. "And I mean detain it. I have questions that need to be answered. I don't need your ministrations to make that difficult."

Jeqon's excitement deflated, but then he asked, "And after that, after you have asked all your questions, I can get all Malleus Maleficarum on her ass?"

Sham smiled at how simple his companion was. Like a puppy with a new bone. "Yes."

Pleased, Jeqon sat in the car and tried to find the best set list for witch interrogation. Sham got out of the car.

He carefully approached the house. He had to be careful, but he also had to move quickly. If Max was still alive, he may not be for much longer. He cast his fingers out, and a white mist erupted from the tips. The mist twisted itself into ropes and looked like it was testing the way forward. When the rope encountered a dangerous path, the mist would back off and find Sham a new one. Eventually, the safest passage to the front door was illuminated to Sham, and he moved forward. Before he stepped on the porch, he sent a quick message to Puriel.

"Going in now. It's a necromancer."

He stepped onto the porch and saw a simple wind chime began to swing, back and forth, but thankfully made no sound. Praising his luck, he checked the handle. Seeing it was unlocked, he entered the house.

CHAPTER 18

The incense burned Max's nose. The room was stuffy. Sweat began to bead on his skin, but he made no complaint. When he'd first arrived, Angie had greeted him with another long kiss and had taken his hand and led him downstairs. Once there, she'd shed her clothes and stood before him naked. The small pendant she always had around her neck, nestled between her breasts, was the only thing she wore.

"This is our one chance, Max. Let's make it count." She smiled and glanced down at his pants. "Pull out all the stops. Don't you agree?"

Max did not need to be told twice. Max knew many of Astarte's spells involved a fair amount of nudity. He didn't really understand the mechanics, but doing magic in the buff seemed an essential element. He quickly stripped down and found himself naked and sitting before a stone alter, with Angie sitting on the other side, sweat beading down both their bodies. He tried not to stare at her and quickly looked around the basement. He hadn't ever been in here before, and it seemed very much like he'd expected. Strange glyphs carved into the stone foundation, giving some meaning he couldn't decipher. Woodcarvings hung on the wall, showing scenes of people gathered, performing rituals of their own. He wondered if the scene he and Angie were about to play out would be worthy of such art.

Angie watched as he looked around the room yet still stole glances at her. She was happy a little bit of skin seemed to put Max in the right mindset. Smiling, she said, "Concentrate, Max." She handed him a goblet, and he took a long drink of her wine. Max shut his eyes. She told him to begin.

Max began to say the words he had committed to memory and said countless times. Angie assured him her translation of Astarte's words were accurate, and he couldn't fault her. It had worked before, so tonight shouldn't be any different. "Cocytus, open your waters to me. Flow over me. Bring me to my father." His eyes closed as he said the words over and over again. His hands, together as if in prayer, parted and reached forward, then pulled back into a prayer. The words and the movements fell into a rhythm. Angie watched as her student performed the ritual perfectly. Seeing him now and how quickly he rose to the challenges she put before him, she knew there was something very special about him, something that drew him to her. She knew it was fate.

Sweat poured from Max's brow. Once he opened his eyes, the basement was gone and he found himself in the gray place again. The otherworldly nature of the void unsettled him, but he felt Angie's presence, and that heartened him to get the job done. The first prayers had gotten him into the void. Now that he was there, the second ritual would begin. Once he had gained his bearings, he began. The hand motions were simple, but they had to be in time with the prayers. "Come to me. Bring to me what was lost that I cannot find. Bring to me what was taken." He said it over and over while bringing hand over hand, as if he were pulling a rope. It was effortless at first, but soon, he found his muscles flexing, straining, pulling a great weight toward him. The air quickly turned from sweet to sour.

The strain almost became too much. He slowed the prayer as he struggled against the weight. Finally, he could see something coming in the distance. It began first as a figure, but then grew into the form of a man. Max had never gotten this far before. The excitement gave him his second wind, and he began to pull faster. He couldn't see the figure's face, but he called out, "Dad?" Whoever the person was, they seemed to be dancing or flailing about. Max slowed his pulling, but the person didn't slow their pace toward Max. When Max saw the face it left no doubt that this was his father, but he seemed hunched and twisted, moving as if in agony. The unnatural movements sickened him.

Max's eyes widened as he began to take in the entire picture. "Angie," he yelled into the void, "something isn't right."

Jude came closer. It was him, but it was not the man Max had expected. He'd hoped for the man who'd played catch with him in the backyard. Who'd taught him how to start a bonfire and change a tire. But Max knew this version of Jude. He was all too familiar with it. This was the Jude Max had last seen, twisting and bleeding from gunshot wounds. His blood drenched his shirt and dripped down his arms to his hands. Max could see his father's face was contorted, and he was yelling something.

"Dad! It's me! It's Max. Please look at me!"

Jude just stared at the ground, his body clenched in fear and agony. Max stopped pulling. He had stopped the chants, but his father's bleeding and mangled corpse still came toward him. Max tried to remember some of the rituals he had read about banishing a spirit, but couldn't remember them. "Sweet Jesus, something has gone wrong. Angie!" he yelled. "I can't stop. Help me with the counters. I can't remember them." Incense flashed strong in his nostrils, and Max felt Angie's presence even more. He waited a moment, hoping something would happen, but nothing changed. Fear began to grow in his mind. "Angie, stop this now!"

Her voice rang out over the expanse, as if a voice from the heavens. "Max. Stay calm. This all a part of the trick. I told you it would be hard. Just stick to the plan." He tried to find comfort in her words and voice, but his eyes were glued to father's tortured form. He was losing all hope. The incense filled his lungs, cloyingly sweet, and began to turn his stomach. He couldn't deny she had prepared him, told him about all the possible deceptions the Continuance would use to protect itself, but this didn't feel right to him. Desperately, he looked around, hoping something would happen, anything, to help. All he saw was the void and his struggling father.

Amid the confusion and terror, deep inside his mind, a white spot of clarity began to grow. At first, he didn't sense it, but a nagging sensation gnawed at him. Closing his eyes, he reached into his mind. He could sense it, something calm in the storm that raged. He stretched out toward it. There was a flash behind his eyes. Knowledge dawned on him. He had been fooled. He didn't know why she had deceived him, but in the end, it didn't matter. A pair of red lips and a little nudity was all it had taken for him to become duped. Max hated what he had done.

Astarte's writings had warned him. Warnings about what he and Angie were doing, about the consequences of what they were attempting. When he'd asked her, Angie had waved them away with a smile and a kiss, and he'd never questioned her. He felt like a child, allowing his emotions and hormones to cloud his mind. She'd known exactly what strings to pull, and he'd danced for her. And now, his father was paying the price.

He opened his eyes to the sight of Jude, mangled and torn, and it cleaved through Max. He chastised himself. Why couldn't he have just let his father rest in peace? Realizing his grief was now causing more pain, he screamed out, "Oh, Dad. I'm sorry!" He repeated his regret as tears flowed. His father came closer and closer. He could hear the gasps and grunts of fear and pain. "Forgive me!" Max reached out to his father in attempt to give some comfort, but found Jude was always right out of reach. Jude had stopped, but Max realized the world was moving around him in the void. The incense intensified once again, and Max could feel he and Jude were both being pulled out of the void. Max knew it was Angie. Max would reenter the world alive and well, but his father would emerge not as the man he loved, but as this shambling corpse. A tortured specter. Max knew, as he felt the tug moving him backward, all was lost.

Time was endless in the gray void. As Max and Jude were pulled farther back, Max could see his father's features becoming more translucent, his moans becoming more muted. This gave no comfort. Max knew his father's torture would last for eons, silently and out of sight. What remained of Jude's screams filled the void and Max's mind. Even if Jude could understand anything Max had said, Max couldn't find the right words. He didn't know how to tell his father he had given up.

At Max's lowest point, when all was lost, another sound joined the din. Something in the distance, somewhere far behind them. The moment Max heard it, both he and Jude stopped moving, and the smell of the burned herbs vanished. The sound grew louder, until Max realized what it was. Wind chimes. As if the chimes were caught up in a hurricane. They were menacing, but oddly comforting. Max could no longer feel Angie's presence. She had been replaced by another being.

Another moment later, a figure appeared. Max's eyes had gotten so used to the grayness, the light that shone from this new person blinded him. Max closed his eyes, but could feel the warmth of the light on his face. Relief flowed over him. He breathed it in and was at peace. He opened his eyes and saw a man, bathed in light, standing next to him and his dad in the gray void. The man looked at Max and gave him a grim smile, as if Max were a child who had been caught doing something naughty. Before Max could say anything, the man threw his hand out. Light emitted from each finger and pierced the void.

The words came from the man, but his lips did not move. "I purify you from this trespass into this realm. I dispel your sorrow. I change your darkness to light. I will allow you to reenter." With the sound of the last word still hanging in the air, Max felt the rope snap. Air rushed from behind him. Max's father's face, only feet from Max, stopped contorting.

The fear and pain that had been there just a moment before was erased. Blood no longer stained his clothes. Color returned to his skin. Jude was no longer a twisted and tortured soul, but the man Max remembered.

Jude locked eyes with his son. This was the man Max had been hoping to see. "Hiya, kid," Jude said.

Before Max could respond, the light the man had created coalesced behind Jude and formed a swirling orb, like a warp of light in the void. Then Jude started to recede backwards. Max ran up to his father and turned to the glowing being to protest, but before he could say anything, Jude reached out and put his hand on Max's face. "It is my time. You have to let me go Max." He removed his hand and began to drift away. "It wasn't your fault. None of it was. Remember, I'm your biggest fan. In this world, and the next."

Tears streamed down Max's face. He'd heard more than

he could have hoped for. He'd heard what he'd needed to hear. "I love you, Dad."

Jude smiled. "And I love you." He continued to smile at his son as they moved farther and farther apart in the void. He smiled even after he couldn't see him any longer. Max could feel himself being pulled back. Before the gray void disappeared, the smell of incense flared up for just a moment.

With a pop, Max opened his eyes. He was back in Angie's basement, sitting naked on the cold floor. The incense had been snuffed out, and the alter and candles had been knocked down and lay broken on the floor. Max looked around hurriedly. He did not see Angie, but saw a tall, muscular brown-haired man holding a bathrobe in front of himself and averting his eyes.

He cleared his throat. "Time to get dressed, son. Don't you think?"

Max, realizing how ridiculous he must have looked, quickly got into the robe. He tied the belt around himself tight. Max scrambled and grabbed his clothes. He didn't quite know what to say. Thankfully, the man spoke first.

"You were messing with things you should not have been messing with, son." Sham could see on Max's face the shame that was growing. "I do not presume to know everything that has been happening in this little nowhere town, but I do know you are way out of your element."

Max recognized the voice as the same man who'd saved him and his dad in the void. The clarity he'd gained in the void remained. "I'm not going to pretend I understand exactly what happened. But I know one thing is exceedingly clear: my father and I owe you, don't we? Big time."

Sham nodded. "I agree. Big time."

Max shimmied his pants back on. "May I ask who you

are? I'm—"

"Maxwell Travers. I know you." Sham inspected the rest of the room, making sure he noted everything he needed. "I am Shamsiel, leader of the 365 legions." Max gave a confused look as he put his head through his shirt. "It doesn't matter. That was a long time ago. Call me Sham."

He didn't want to ask because he never wanted to see her again, but he had to. "Where did Angie go? She isn't still here, is she?"

Sham put a reassuring hand on Max's shoulder, sensing his fear. "She vanished. I am assuming she had some sort of proximity warning I was unaware of." Inwardly, Sham chastised himself for being so rusty. "So, you say she was calling herself Angie? I am sorry if the timing seems odd, but I am going to need you to tell me the complete story." He put a hand out to motion Max to the nearby couch.

"Where to begin…" Max said.
Sham seemed confused at the statement. "At the beginning, of course." Max nodded and told Sham all he knew. The more he said, the more he realized how ridiculous the entire affair sounded to him. About his father, about meeting Angie, the internship, the magical rituals and spells. He thought Sham would ridicule him and his story, but he only said, "You and your father are very fortunate."

Telling the story had exhausted Max, but he asked, "Why is that?"

Sham was uncertain as to how much to tell Max. If he were to tell him the truth, the boy wouldn't sleep again. "It doesn't matter. Come here. I am going to give you one last gift, then we are going to call it a day." Max slowly walked toward Sham. Sham placed his hands on either side of Max's head and said, "After this cruelty is seen and said, erase these thoughts from his heart and head." Max's eyes closed. "Happy Birthday, Max." Light erupted from between Sham's hands.

CHAPTER 19

Jude removed the glass from his lips and placed it on the table in front of him. The smoky flavor of the scotch continued to slightly burn its way down this throat. Coughing, he realized he was a little confused. He didn't consider himself a day drinker.

"Calm down there, buddy. You're going to make us think you've never had good scotch before." Dan lifted his glass to Dr. Puriel.

Dr. Puriel laughed. "Maybe it is a little early to be drinking." He looked out at the window. Jude followed his gaze. It was a beautiful day. "But hell, it's not often we get to give splendid news, Jude." Jude was still confused. Dr. Puriel hit a button on his phone. "Rebecca, please bring in Mrs. Travers." He turned to Jude. "I think she would like to celebrate with us, don't you think?"

Jude turned back to the door and watched his wife come in. She smiled, sat down next to him, and squeezed his hand. She entered with a look of worry, but seeing the glasses, she was more confused. "What did I miss?" She smiled in response to the cheery looks from both doctors.

Dan said, "No scotch for you, Eva. Someone has to drive Jude home. But you can celebrate tonight." He nodded at

Jude. "Tell her."

She turned to her husband excitedly. Jude stammered, "They just said I was cured. And…" Jude glanced around the room and out the window, and saw no warps, "they're right. I don't see anything out there anymore!" The truth of it stopped him, and he embraced his wife. Eva put her arms around her husband and squeezed hard.

Dr. Puriel looked quickly from Eva to Jude. "It was a simple vitamin imbalance. Can't believe no one saw it before, but the medications he has been taking rectified it." Many times, people believed something because they wanted to believe. With that in mind, he threw them both a little lie, hoping they would swallow it. It would make his life easier if they did.

To Dr. Puriel's relief, Jude got up and hugged Dan. Dan laughed and stole a quick glance at Dr. Puriel. Jude then turned and shook Dr. Puriel's hand. "Thank you so much. I really can't believe it. I was so worried when you called me in this morning. You don't know what this means to me. I have my life back. You two have given me everything."

Dan tried to give Eva a hug, but she smoothly offered a handshake instead. The slight was not unnoticed by him, but he chose to ignore it. "Now, you two have spent enough time in doctors' offices, go out there and raise a little hell for both of us, would you."

His demeanor caused Eva to give a small laugh, and Jude smiled. Dr. Puriel inwardly groaned at the display.

Dr. Puriel nodded. "Agree. Enough doctors' visits." He began to walk them to the door. "You will probably have more questions, but they can wait for another day." When they got to the door, he grabbed Jude's arm and said, "You have your entire life ahead of you, no more worries. Please enjoy it."

You didn't have to tell Jude twice. He had reached his absolute limit on medical visits and was chomping at the bit to leave. But before he left, he said again, "Thank you, Doc." Dr. Puriel nodded.

After the Travers left, Dokiel sat down and poured the rest of Jude's drink into his glass. "Not bad, but that was very close. It is going to cost someone hours and hours in paperwork. Not me, mind you, but someone." He drank and took a draw on his already lit cigarette.

Puriel leaned against the closed door. Dokiel was right. It had been too close. "The result is all that matters. A little reset of his memory, and now he is back on track."

"What about Max? We aren't going to have to do this again anytime soon, are we?"

Puriel walked back to his desk. The walls of the office began to change. The fake diplomas and certifications disappeared, replaced with various odds and ends Puriel had collected over the centuries. He adjusted some glass paperweights that encased various flowers. "I will let Shamsiel and his people fix that one. It will take more effort, but they will get it done. I am hoping this is the last we'll hear of the young Max Travers."

Dokiel drained his glass and got up to leave. "Well, I'm off. I have spent too much time with people I have no hope of getting. I don't want anything to start rubbing off on me." He brushed off both shoulders. "I think I will spend some time with that Florida millionaire. He thinks he's still in prison." He chortled to himself and turned.

Before he left, Puriel asked, "Shamsiel said the necromancer got away, and when he left the house, Jeqon was gone. I would hope whatever information he retrieves is shared with everyone."

Dokiel frowned. "I am sure he will. I will look into it. Good work. 'Til next time."

"Yeah. Next time."

***

Jeqon thought El Paso in September was always dismal. While the rest of the country was settling in for a long winter, El Paso was enjoying ninety degrees and sunny, with no hint of any relief in sight. Of course, Jeqon had been to places even hotter. Places where fat under skin crackled.

"These fucking animals have no idea how good they have it," he said to himself.

Jeqon had to admit, this little bitch was very good at what she did, for a lower order of being. She had managed to escape Sham and slip by him back in Missouri. But no matter how cunning she was, Jeqon lived for this shit.

He was promised the leftovers, and he would not be denied his treat.

He had been here a few days, had sampled some of the local flavor, a wonderful mix of old-world Mexico and new world redneck. So much variety. But he was here on business, and on the third night, he got her.

Always the consummate professional, Jeqon made sure her bindings were secure and the soundproofing wards would hold. Then he began. Of all his talents, flaying was his favorite. The trick was finding the right instruments. Steel, no matter how sharp or how thin you pound it, would always be too thick, and gold, while thin, doesn't keep an edge, especially when there is a struggle.

Long ago, Jeqon found that obsidian worked best. With that blade, you could remove just the slightest layer of skin.

You know you had it right when the blood didn't spurt, but just appeared in the tissue, like a sponge taking in water.

Jeqon liked the witch's looks, so he began with her calves. Only a fool would start with a more tender section of skin, like the fingertips or groin. You had to build the pain, ratcheting it up. The screams were exquisite.

He sat in his carousel red Hellcat, remembering the smells from the last night. He liked to give his pets a few hours of stewing before he began again. She hadn't offered up any information, but he never asked any questions the first few weeks. He was thinking he might say something to her around Christmas. Jeqon had a flair for the dramatic.

He went back into the abandoned factory, opened a set of doors to the basement, and walked in. The light was out. He cursed himself.

He tried to turn, but it was too late. Light erupted, and he found himself lifted into the air. As he came down, his body was rent apart, hitting the floor in five different pieces.

"Watcher!" The witch stood above him, naked and bleeding. "Before your head dies, where are your keys?"

Part Two: Anathema

CHAPTER 1

Seeing the road clear of traffic ahead, she pressed the clutch down and put the car into fourth, letting those horses run. She would have never really considered herself a "gearhead," but she couldn't deny the joy of having a car as mean as she felt.

She watched the road sign fly past and laughed at how her life was now mirroring a Marty Robbins' song. She laughed and sang loudly into the night. It felt good to get the hell out of El Paso.

But unlike the song, she would not be returning. She knew she had to get as much distance between her and the rotting and ruined body of the Watcher. He would have friends. And they would eventually miss him. She furrowed her brow, trying to remember his name. Had he even told her? It had happened so fast, the torture made her memory fuzzy.

The last clear memory was seeing him leaning against his red car. The way he stood, it was clear to her that he wanted her to notice him. Ashamedly, she remembered how attracted she was to him. Chiseled face, pure blond hair, easy smile. She had been in El Paso a few days and had just started to trust it was safe to venture out. She couldn't stay away from people for too long. She'd never been able to. She was not the type of creature who hid away in caves or lived on the outskirts. She needed people, needed companionship. It kept her young. And him standing there, preening against his muscle car, had been a tall glass of water on a hot day. Only now, she realized his looks, his stance, even his scent, had all been a ruse meant for her.

The next clear memory was being bound and gagged. She'd strained against her restraints, but hadn't been able to move more than an inch. She remembered raising her head, peering out through swollen eyes, and seeing his perfect face. She saw no rage or hatred. He'd never said a single word. Just smiled and went along his business.

She remembered the drawings he had made on the cement floor. Various pentagrams and whirls, the odd glyphs from dead languages, dotting the floor around her. From the iconography, she'd figured out three things. One, he was a Watcher. A type of demon with unpredictable powers sent to the mortal realm to do the bidding of celestial beings. Two, she'd recognized some of the glyphs associated torture and hellfire, so he'd clearly been sent from the Thirteenth Gate. And three, no one had been coming to save her. If she had done nothing, she wouldn't have lived to see the next night.

She wasn't used to the sensation of fear. It had been so long since she'd last had the opportunity to feel it. Now, in the car, racing northward with the window's down, she allowed the sensation to finally leave her. She had forgiven herself for getting caught, but at the time, she'd cursed herself for being so lax. Being completely honest with herself, she knew she was out of practice. Usually, her activities did not cause any notice. This time, with Max, she'd known she'd pushed it too far. Even so, she'd had no idea the response would be so swift.

She remembered the events of this past summer with some fondness. Young man in distress. Simple. Gullible. But a good boy. Honest and trusting. Strong mind with a talent. Fine traits. She'd been drawn to Max. Fate had pushed them together, and while she couldn't understand the exact nature of how, she knew Max was special. That had been proven on September sixteenth, the night of the ritual. Someone looking in from the outside would have seen her and her efforts that night as an absolute failure. But they would be wrong.

She'd gained more than she had lost. That was…so long as she could live through the next couple nights. Admittingly, the extraction was a failure. No doubt in that. And while weakening and ultimately undoing the Continuance was a major goal, it hadn't been the only game she was playing that night.

She'd had her doubts it would happen, even right up to the end, but then it did. Someone (it had to be one of the Arbiters) opened the gateway between the worlds to allow Jude Travers to communicate with Max. So sweet and touching. Why Existence allowed this was unknown to her, but it had, and that was all she'd needed.

An illuminated road sign caught her eye, bringing her back from her musings. In large orange paint, it screamed out, "Welcome to Truth or Consequences, New Mexico. Population 6,145. 'Your Choice, Your Destiny.'" She could have mused for hours on the irony of the sign, but her mind needed to be focused on more important matters.

"Perfect," she said to no one. Her voice sounded hollow in the silence of the car. She'd wanted to find a little place to hole up for a while and see if her plans were still on track. Seeing the vacancy sign lit at the Sierra Grande Lodge & Spa, she turned into the nearest space and shut down the car. Stepping out, she checked the various wards she'd written on the vehicle, ensuring they still held. They were invisible to the untrained, but they shimmered under the green neon lights of the lodge. Satisfied with her work, she turned and went into the lobby.

A young man dressed in a beige bellhop uniform greeted her from the front desk. "Good evening, ma'am. Welcome to the Sierra Grande. Would you like a room?"

She returned his smile. "That would be great."

Not seeing any luggage, he asked her, "Any special preferences?"

She thought about the question for a moment. He was asking about smoking versus non-smoking or handicap accessible rooms. None of these mattered to her, but she needed a room where she would be undisturbed.

Putting on a sheepish smile, she said, "Actually yes, uh…" she looked at this name tag, "Alec. I am meeting a friend here, and we…" she blushed, "would like a room away from other guests. We don't want to disturb." She gave him a smile.

To her satisfaction, the images that came to Alec's mind were clearly written on his face. Looking at his computer to avoid any eye contact, he said, "Yes, ma'am. I think we can accommodate that. Most of the rooms are empty, it being the off season and all." A few keystrokes, and he asked, "Can I have your name?"

Knowing it would be best to shed the name Angie Chiseler, she chose a name that was closer to home, but a little modernized to throw off her scent. "Estelle Star." She said it without really thinking about it and realized she had chosen a name that clearly defined her as a porn star, a stripper, or both. She winced and admitted to herself she was still out of practice.

Alec smiled at the name. As long as she paid for the entire night, and not only an hour, he didn't care what she did in that room, "All right, Ms. Star, here are your room cards. I assume you may need two. You are in room fourteen, at the very end. But please, you and your guest, feel free to use our natural hot springs spa located in the interior courtyard." He kept his eyes on hers, but blushed at the thought of her in a bikini—or something less. He stammered, "It is kinda what we are known for."

Ms. Star was used to being seen as on object. Hell, she had lost count on the amount of times she'd used her looks to her advantage. But tonight, she was in no mood. She wanted to paint the walls with Alec's gray matter. Tear his balls off, throw them in the natural hot springs, and watch them boil. It was unknown if Alec could sense how much danger he was in, but he backed off and put his eyes to the floor. She calmed herself. She did not need any more attention. She thanked him for the room, took the room cards, and left to find room fourteen.

CHAPTER 2

Circa 1240 BCE:

Puriel eased back into the large leather couch and closed his eyes. The flames in the fireplace gave a pleasing light and cast the room in warmth. Leather-bound books, filled with tales from far away, scented the room. "Vltava" by Smetana played softly in the background. It was one of Puriel's favorites, and he allowed the music to take him down the river. Puriel thought about Vonnegut and his idea that music was the only real evidence of God.

The Continuance was an odd place for a being like Puriel. On the mortal Earth, it was somewhere around the thirteenth century BCE. The time of Ramesses, Theseus, and the rise of the Olmecs. But here, the Continuance allowed Puriel to enjoy whatever time period he liked. On this day in his office, it looked more like 1910. Not that Puriel was a Luddite. He enjoyed some of the modern conveniences but tried to avoid any pointless distractions.

A loud knock sounded around the office. Distractions, thought Puriel.

"Yes?"

Dokiel appeared, squat and fat, and wearing some sort of odd robes.

Puriel eased back into his couch and closed his eyes

again.

"What are you doing here, Dokiel? And why are you dressed like that?"

Dokiel shook his robes as if to air out his body. "You know, this job generally sucks. But you somehow find a way to make it suck even more. I was in the Continuance of some lower courtier of Emperor Di Zhi. The Shang Dynasty has been pretty swinging, but this guy is just the worst." Dokiel laughed. "They are just getting their Bronze Age on, so I try not to hold too much against the little buggers, but this guy is a nightmare in any era."

"Sounds like he's going to be one of yours."

"Oh yeah. I don't fully understand why the waiting period for this asshole. He kills his own wife and infant son, gets executed, the Continuance kicks in. Then, guess what?"

Puriel didn't glance over.

"He goes and kills his new wife in the Continuance." Dokiel chortled. "I mean, come on. This whole thing is a colossal waste of time." He gestured around the room.

Puriel didn't completely disagree. "It is not for us to question the wisdom, only to ensure the system keeps running."

Dokiel disregarded Puriel's boy scout response. He looked around the office and picked up a few items from the nearest table: a pipe, a snow globe, and a snuffbox. "What the fuck is this shit?"

"Those are my things. Keep your hands off them please."

"Of all the time periods, in all existence, of all places, you choose . . . what? 221 Baker Street? What the hell?"

Puriel got up and made sure his items were back in their places. "I do not have to explain myself to you.

Unlike you, I don't care to meddle in the lives of those in the Continuance. I only enter one if I am needed. I do not share your voyeuristic need to watch."

In relation to the entire span of existence, Puriel and Dokiel's assignment of the Continuance had begun quite recently. Neither of them understood the whole need for the Continuance, only that Existence wanted it, and they were to guard against the wrong ones moving forward or the right ones being lost. To Puriel, it was simple work. To Dokiel, who enjoyed complicating matters, it was simpleton work.

"I am assuming you are here to discuss the most recent decree?" Puriel asked as he switched the music from orchestral to Foo Fighters.

Dokiel shouted, "That is exactly why I'm here. I thought we had the ground rules settled. No one directly moves on or out. No extractions. And secure ALL Gates from trespassers."

When the Continuance began, Puriel and Dokiel were placed in it to keep it running. There are thirteen different Gates that surround the Continuance. Each Gate leads to a different realm of existence and purpose. Existence was phenomenally vast and while the thirteen realms always existed, it was determined all of the intermingling between them had to be stopped. The Continuance was put in place to bring order and separate the realms. Dokiel and Puriel were to make sure the Gates were only opened when needed.

From the inflection in Dokiel's voice, Puriel knew it was his last statement that had frustrated Dokiel most. They had been instructed the lower form beings from the "living" realms, what was known as the Fourth Gate, were to be kept separate, but they also needed to make sure other beings did not intrude on the "living." Exceptions were made to this rule, but Existence hadn't made any in quite some time. Until recently.

"What can I say, compadre? Apparently, the living need some adjustment, and the powers that be want the First Gate open so they can assist in that."

"You mean meddle." Dokiel sat down in a huff. "This job is glorified babysitting as it is. Now that these Gates are to be left open, why the hell am I even here! Let these humans fend for themselves."

"Obviously, they cannot, or at least, they need some guidance. Maybe one unified god is better than thirty? Maybe one deity keeps the mortals in check? I don't know." Puriel shrugged.

Dokiel lifted his hands in the air. "What the hell else do they need? I was just getting used to the gods. Hell, they had one for everything. Good crops, big breasts, larger dick. What else do you need in life?"

"I am not a great study, but they are evolving, and maybe there is something more to existence than wine festivals and sex."

Dokiel scoffed. "Well, I am a great study of wine festivals and sex, and I am telling you, they are delightful."

"Enough. The decree was clear. 'Keep the First and Fourth Gate open. Do not molest travelers.' Clear as day to me."

Dokiel paused a moment. "And you have no concerns? I think this whole 'Continuance' thing was kinda thrown together anyway. Was the system we had before so terrible? Don't you miss the days of just strutting around, tempting left and right?" Puriel gave him a grimace. "Well, for you, making sure people gave to the poor or shit like that?"

Puriel exhaled. "You do not need to be reminded of how it was. Souls being harvested behind the Thirteenth Gate wrongfully. Shattered spirits being moved on. There was too much chaos. Too much wasted energy and effort. It was havoc."

Dokiel did remember and couldn't really argue with him. The old way was definitely majorly flawed, but he wasn't certain the new system was the answer to the problems.

Both he and Puriel worked for Existence itself and answered to it, but they were creatures who were natural adversaries. When they'd been placed in the Continuance and ordered to run it, they gained the titles of "Arbiters," but deep down, Dokiel missed the old days and the old titles he used to use. He was Commander of the Thirteenth Gate, and not many outranked him. Nowadays, Dokiel felt more and more like a glorified middleman for Existence. That feeling was reinforced with the new order. And Puriel's apathy with it put Dokiel on edge.

He shrugged at Puriel's nonchalance. "What option do I have?" said Dokiel, standing to leave.

"None, which is why we shouldn't worry about it." Puriel had gotten used to these little tantrums Dokiel would throw every now and then. It was best to let him bitch and moan. He usually tired himself out and left.

Dokiel turned to look at Puriel but stopped himself from speaking. A thought came to him—a thought that soothed his worry that Existence was playing him for a fool. "Well, as you say. I just wanted to run this by you, but I guess there's nothing to worry about. I'm just being stupid."

Puriel did not disagree with him. "Are you sure you won't stay for a drink?"

To Puriel's relief, Dokiel shook his head. "I am going back. That guy is going to be executed a second time, and then I will take him."

CHAPTER 3

Dokiel watched as they led away the condemned man to be strangled by the awaiting executioners. Dokiel usually would have enjoyed the proceedings, a little drama playing out just for him, but things were different today. He had much on his mind. The idea that had formed in his head in Puriel's office had now blossomed into a full plan.

"You asked for me?" A slender blonde woman sat down next to him. Looking completely out of place in Ancient China, Sariel stood out in the crowd. Her Greek clothing could not hide her beautiful physique. The odd sight of her disturbed the assembled people, who began whispering and pointing at Dokiel's companion. Usually, Dokiel would be pissed about Sariel's disturbance, but he knew this Continuance was at an end. These people would soon fade into nothingness.

"Sariel, I need something from you. Something that is…let's say, off script."

"I have no problem with that." Sariel was intrigued. She was dutybound to follow Dokiel. She didn't wholeheartedly resent working for him (she knew she had made mistakes in the past and was lucky to even exist), but the monotony of being an underling in the Continuance was frustrating. In her mind, she agreed with the view that they were all glorified nannies, and she wanted more.

"You will need to understand, if you are caught, it will not end well for you, nor will I be able to help you."

"And if I succeed?"

Dokiel thought about what motivated Sariel. "You are here because of the choices you made." The reason Sariel was serving in the Continuance under Dokiel was well documented. Sariel had a penchant for mortal women. And as a demon, fornication with mortals was forbidden. The offspring of mortals and demons were troublesome at best, world crushing at worst. But she couldn't keep herself away from mortals, no matter the circumstances. "The creatures created by your lust are legendary. Their use in stripping souls has given them a purpose, but, every now and then, they still run amok in the mortal realm, and that is something Existence just can't have. You should feel very fortunate it was decided to spare you and put you away in the Continuance at the time of the Rekindling. It is a perfect place for you." Dokiel looked at Sariel, daring her to argue. "Even you know your proclivities need to be put in check."

Sariel nodded and watched as the local people gathering around her and Dokiel, still giving them a wide berth.

Dokiel smiled. "Don't worry, I believe forgiveness is divine. I am ready to do that for you. You accomplish what I ask, and I will see it as an atonement for your transgressions. I will ensure you move on from this place." Dokiel gestured to the surrounding village, but she knew he meant the Continuance.

Sariel did not try to hide her excitement. To be out of the Continuance. To be free. "Done," was all she said.

"Good. Now that the terms are set, let's collect this little bugger. We can talk along the way about what I would like for you to do for me."

As they walked, the townspeople scattered at Sariel's presence. It did not matter what alarm they raised, Dokiel saw at the horizon, the gray was starting to take over. As the gray rushed forward, people, houses, goats, everything dusted away into the swirling void. A moment later, nothing surrounded Dokiel and Sariel except the void and a hovering orb. The orb hovered in the air in front of Dokiel. He reached out, grabbed the orb, and peered into it.

"Greetings, little man. You have been judged." The screams inside were muffled but pleasant to Dokiel's ears. He knew this was just day one of this little man's torment, but he always enjoyed the first screams most. "Oh, and if you haven't guessed yet, you didn't win."

The orb would keep the man in anguish for centuries, as the energy that made him was slowly leeched off and repurposed for other projects in the Existence. Torment, true torment, shredded the soul, and that gave off an enormous amount of energy. Eventually, over eons of time, the little man would fade away into nothing and be blipped out of Existence, but not before every electron had been harvested.

Sariel walked alongside Dokiel as he put the orb in his pocket and asked, "What do you look like to him?"

Dokiel thought a second, remembering what time period he was in and where he was, but just shrugged. "Really, these little localities at this time in China have so many different beliefs, it is hard to keep track. But if I had to guess, I would assume I appear as some sort of fire ghost or something like that. Anyway, let's talk."

It would have taken them no time to reach the Thirteenth Gate, but Dokiel was stretching time in the void, knowing Puriel and his ilk would not be listening.

"I got an order earlier. We, both sides, are to keep the First and Fourth Gate open and are not to bother those coming and going." Dokiel looked for any reaction from Sariel.

"And that makes you uncomfortable?"

"I don't like not knowing. Particularly when people will be pissing in my own backyard and I am being told I have to sit there and smile."

"Well, what can you do about it?"

"And that is where you come in. Something big is going on in the mortal realm, Earth specifically, and I want my best person on the ground. Look around, keep me in the know."

Sariel glared at Dokiel with suspicion. "If you wanted to know what was going on, a spy if you will, you can just make a call down to our brethren in that realm." She changed her tone. "I am totally in, but I want to know what I am really doing down there."

Dokiel nodded. "The powers that be are going to be making some big moves. A new age is coming. Probably a fresh set of gods. Prophets are going to be involved, and I want you to be in the middle of it. There is going to be a new scale, and I would like you to put your thumb on it. For the greater good. I don't think the Continuance thing is going to keep, and to hedge our bets, I think it would be best for us to continue to collect as many souls as we can."

Sariel smiled. "Do I have any parameters? Any particular way you would like this done?"

"I do. I don't want you directly involved. I plan on you being down there for as long as we can get away with. You will draw too much notice if you start magicking here and there, so keep a low profile. You are going to find a vessel for the Thirteenth. A champion, if you will. An ace up our sleeve to use when we may need it most. I need you to find a young woman." Dokiel paused, trying to find the best words. "I need you to find a girl, as innocent as a dream. A girl who needs help. Desperate. A girl who has nothing to lose. I want you to help her. Give her assistance. Be at her beck and call. Teach her our ways. Instruct her on how to turn the mind and the heart. Anything she asks, do it."

"Anything?" Sariel was worried about the implications.

"Yes. We need our own. . ." Dokiel couldn't come up with the perfect word, "I don't know what I would call her . . . Ubermenschen?"

"But a woman?"

"Of course. I have a sense about these things. This whole thing," Dokiel gestured to everything around him, "will rise or fall in the hands of a woman. I just need it to be my woman. Also, finding a girl who is desperate and in distress shouldn't be too hard in this time period. Hell, most of those on Earth think women are little more than currency to barter for." Dokiel stopped, grabbed Sariel's face, and stared directly into her eyes. "But to assist you, I will give you this gift." A red flame leapt from Dokiel's forehead and slammed into Sariel's eye. Before she could be blown back by the force, he held her fast as the flame extinguished. He let her go and she opened her eyes. Her deceptively beautiful blue eyes flashed red with flame, then returned. "There, you are now taking a tiny part of me with you. I have given you singleness of purpose. With this, you will find her. And when you find her, you will recognize her." The last he said not to comfort or encourage, but as a deadly command.

Sariel pulled away from Dokiel. For a moment, she was blinded, her vision replaced by fire. Then, it was gone, and she saw Dokiel smiling at her. She liked the freedom of the assignment but knew meddling in the affairs of Existence could cause her to end up in a little black orb, screaming her lungs out inside someone's pocket. The thought of being leeched did not sit well with her. "I need to know you have my back on this mission. I understand if I fuck up it's on me, but if I need something from you, I want you to be there."

Dokiel had hoped not to have to make too many promises, but begrudgingly said, "You will have my support, off the books, for your mission. If there is anything I can do or get to you, I will."

They arrived at the Thirteenth Gate, and Dokiel, with no flourish or other word to the screaming human soul, chucked the orb over and continued to walk on.

"Is there anything else you want me to know before I leave on this mission? Maybe a hint of where to start looking for this champion?"

"Follow your heart. You have created some of the greatest children of the Pit. The stuff of nightmares. I trust you. Well, at least, I distrust you less than anyone else I know." Dokiel retrieved a box from his pocket and handed it to Sariel. The box had various seals which had been placed to protect its contents. "I want you to give this to the woman you choose."

Sariel rolled her eyes at the seals and the continued mystery of this whole thing. Dokiel and his dramatics, she thought. "Am I getting married to her?"

"It will be clear when you are to give it to her." Dokiel leaned close to Sariel and whispered in her ear. Sariel's eyes went wide. "Understand?" Sariel nodded. "Good. I am giving it to you now before you leave this place. Sending it to you in the middle of the mission would draw too much attention."

Sariel gave a salute and put the box in her pocket.

Dokiel took her hand, and in an instant, they were before the Fourth Gate, which was wide open.

"You must leave now. If you make it back, I will shower you with wonders and glory. If you don't, you don't."

Sariel nodded and clasped Dokiel's hands. "Make it official, boss."

"I, Dokiel, Commander and Arbiter of the Continuance, Guardian of the Thirteenth Gate, charge you with this commandment I seal into your being. Failing me is to fail the abyss." With that, Dokiel released his grip on Sariel, but for a moment, his handprint lingered on Sariel's body. The commandment had been given and sealed.

Sariel turned and left for the world of the living.

CHAPTER 4

Estelle Star slid the bolt closed on the door of room fourteen. The room's motif was southwestern with paintings of desert scenes with lonely tumbleweeds and bull skulls. Tacky maybe, but it was clean, and Alec had been right, there was no one in any of the adjacent rooms. She would need some privacy.

It had been a long road from El Paso. Weariness had begun to creep into her bones. She took a moment and sat on the corner of the bed to collect her thoughts. She looked around the window and various thresholds, inspected for any cracks or even chips of paint. If she were going to protect herself, she needed to ensure a good work surface. After a moment, she reached into her bag to retrieve her materials and began warding the room. Her well-practiced hands worked quickly. She smudged the walls, windows, and doorsills with precise symbols and words with meanings that had been lost to most mortals. The smell of burned sage, cedar, and sweet grass mixed poorly with the antiseptic scent of the room. A few minutes later, with a fine sheen of sweat on her brow, she stood back and admired her handiwork. No prying eyes tonight, she thought, only the eyes she would invite.

Putting away her smudge sticks, she retrieved a bottle of wine from her bag. She peered into it, checking to see how much she had left. She had used so much with Max, and when they were interrupted, she cold only take the one bottle she had with her in the basement. The ingredients were impossible to find in the States. She had ordered the various components, but they would now be sitting unused back in Springfield. Seeing that the bottle was more empty than full, Astarte knew she had to be careful. The wine had kept her safe since she had been on her own. It fortified her and without it she was a sitting duck.

She drew the hexagram on the floor with some sand she had gotten from outside, and then drew two circles encircling the star. It was hasty and not usually up to her standards, but she just needed to make a short call, and it would suffice. She drank a swallow from the bottle and called forth, "ana 'astadeik ya Sagar tueal nashni."

The room remained quiet, but she knew it would take a moment. It always did. Sagar didn't like to be disturbed, but he had never failed her. He loved her, and she could count on that. Finally, the lights in the motel room dimmed, then pulsed brightly. The sand of the hexagram began to rise then swirl in the air. A swirling without wind or sound. She sat back and waited patiently, hoping there would be no intruders from outside.

The sand fell back to the ground, making a form she was most familiar with, the family crest of her friend. She had seen it on countless letters back in the day.

A voice, without a body, emitted from the symbol. "Now what!"

She smiled at the exasperation in his voice. "Thank you for coming, Sagar. I really needed someone to talk to."

With a slight pause, the voice said, "From what I hear, you need more than that, Astarte." She instinctively looked at her wards when her true name was said aloud. "You have been busy, and it has been noticed."

Astarte toyed with the pendant around her neck, said a small prayer, and took another drink from the bottle. The sand on the ground heaved up, forming a familiar face, then head, and continued to form a full figure of a man. Complete with the robes she had last seen him in, Sagar stood complete and solid before her. He had left his corporeal body long ago. What stood before her was an outline of his soul or atman. By today's standards, he would be considered short, but no matter what era, he had handsome features. Sagar was her oldest confidant. He adored her, called her his Mohini, which in his culture, was a woman who ensnared your heart and life. And even though she could never bring herself to return his affection, she trusted in his love for her. He had proven countless times she could count on his heart. He would never lead her astray.

His face turned to look at her and stretched his mouth, as if waking from a long sleep. "Yep. It's serious. It has been a while since you have conjured my whole body." He glanced around the room and grimaced. "Where the hell are you?"

"Truth and Consequences, New Mexico."

"Date?"

"September 30th."

"So, let us recap. You started out with nothing, a scrawny girl basically living in a cave, then rose to some of the highest heights—and zip! Bam! Boom!—over four-thousand years later, you are hiding out in the Georgia O'Keeffe room of some rundown motel in a cleverly named town."

"That's the sum of it." She knew she would have to endure his chiding. It was all a part of the dance.

Sagar continued. "And then you make a call to your long-departed friend, hoping he can…what? Help?"

"I just needed to talk some things through with you.

You have always given good counsel, no matter if you have a beating heart or not. There is not one being in the multiverse I would put my trust in more than you." She smiled, hoping he would still respond to flattery.

It worked. Sagar smiled. "Well, you think that because you are wise. You have learned something over your years." He turned more serious. "Maybe we should begin with what I have heard and you can fill in the gaps. It would also be good for you to know what is known."

From the tone in his voice, she knew he didn't have great news. "What is it you have heard?"

"Someone," he paused and smiled, "and they don't know who yet, almost pulled off another extraction a few weeks ago. This one was unusual due to the complexity and effort it required. While there have been more successful extractions recently, they were typically souls no one would miss and involved people who had…let's say, issues. Rapist, death row inmates, people of that sort who clung to life so hard, it was probably inevitable they would attempt to pierce the Continuance. This latest attempt, though, was with an innocent. A well-connected innocent, and his extraction would have caused too much of a rift."

Astarte interrupted. "Did you hear why Jude Travers was such a special case?"

Sagar shook his head, clearly pissed at the interruption. "No. Honestly, there was nothing special about Jude Travers. Just some guy who got shot. It was his son, Max, who was the problem."

Astarte thought about the feeling of being drawn to him. She still couldn't think of why, but she was beginning to see she had missed the signs over the past summer. "Any details about Max then?"

"I was just getting to that, if you would let me speak."
Seeing her sheepish smile, Sagar continued again. "There
is some confusion, but it seems Max was supposed to be
watched."

She interrupted again. "What do you mean 'supposed
to be watched'? I did kill a Watcher in El Paso."

"No," Sagar said with urgency. "Stop interrupting! Not
watched by a Watcher. He was supposed to be watched over. I
don't know the Guardian's name, that isn't information I would
be privy too, but I do know Max was supposed to be guarded.
But something went wrong. You should not have been able to
get so close to him. Actually, you were lucky. If they had been
doing their job, you would have ended up a pile of ash."

The information hit Astarte. Of all the bad luck she had
endured over the centuries, this topped it. She'd set out to find
a broken child, someone she could manipulate, someone to
use, to move closer to her goal. Orphans were not hard to find.
Why had she settled for Max?

Sagar took a quiet tone. "Astarte, you know what this
means?"

She nodded.

"If you are quick, you can stay ahead of them, but I am
sorry. The Memitim, once released, always catch their quarry.
They are the dark deeds. They are retribution incarnate. You
have been marked for extinction."

Astarte tried to remember all she knew about the
Memitim. She knew they had a single purpose: to kill. They
were controlled only by Existence and sent out for two
purposes: kill anyone endangering those deemed blessed
(apparently Max Travers), or kill someone who has lost their
Guardian's protection. And they never failed. It was written
on the bones of Existence. If they were to somehow fail, reality

itself would rip apart.

She breathed in deep and put those concerns to the side for now. "What else have you heard?"

Sagar sensed she didn't want to discuss her impending doom. "How about a bit of good news?"

Astarte looked hopeful. "Yes please. I would take anything after that news."

"If you would have been successful with the extraction of Jude Travers, you may have accomplished what you have always wanted." Sagar said this with not one ounce of happiness.

She smiled. The thought of the Memitim hunting her had almost floored her, but this information almost made it worth it. She knew she must have been close, but had never imagined she'd been that close.

Sagar continued. "That information is not being shared even with the Arbiters of the Continuance. Travers would have unbalanced the whole structure. So, now all you have to do is . . ."

Astarte grimaced. "Find an equally powered soul, extract them from the Continuance, all before the Memitim hands me my guts to eat?"

"Exactly!" Sagar said brightly.

Even though she knew her odds were non-existent, being so close to her goal warmed her. "It's all I have ever wanted."

Sagar breathed deep. "I know. I have never understood this path you have chosen. I only hope if you are able to rend asunder the Continuance, you find peace. Will you finally rest, my love?"

The question caught her off guard. She tried not to daydream too much about her goals. "Without the

Continuance, will I find peace?" She paused for a moment. "Imagine no more Gates. No more barriers. No void. It would be as it was always meant to be. Immortals and mortals living in each other's realms. The mind, the body, the spirit, all freed. No human limitations. We would know Existence, and more importantly, It would know us." She breathed in deep. "Yes, if I bring this about, I will lay my bones down and rest."

Sagar saw her words were true. A flicker of peace flashed in her eyes. "It is nice to dream, isn't it, my love? I find that between our talks, that is all I can really do. Dream about what isn't. About what could be."

Astarte was brought out of her thoughts by the news she had not yet relayed to Sagar. "Well, let's keep dreams aside for now. Do you have more information?"

Sagar glowered at her incredulously. "You want more! Jesus, woman, I thought I did pretty good for a simple atman."

Astarte laughed. "I just wanted to make sure I didn't interrupt you anymore than I already have. I have news that may help me out with my current problems."

Sagar was intrigued. "And what could that be?"

Astarte continued. "When I was in the void with Max, things were going quite well. Then I heard my proximity warning chimes. I could tell something celestial was coming for us in the mortal realm, so I would need to escape. I was too vulnerable, too exposed in the void." She smiled at Sagar. "However, before my egress, I left a little gift, just on the off chance."

Sagar bit. "On the off chance of what?"

"Max had been whining on and on about how guilty he was over Jude's death, that I thought, just maybe, Existence would take pity on him and allow Max and Jude to talk to one another." Sagar's eyes went wide. "Someone in the Continuance opened the Gates to allow them to talk. It was just wide enough for me to send a message."

Sagar, shocked, said, "And?"

"I believe I got through to an old friend."

It took Sagar only a moment to realize who Astarte was taking about, and he scoffed. "Old friend, my decaying ass. Inviting her back into your life is nothing but asking for ruin. You might as well just stay in Wherethefuck, New Mexico and let the Memitim have you. You'll at least save on gas money."

She'd known he would react this way. Jealousy was a bitch and not one of Sagar's better traits.

Astarte put up her hands to calm her friend. She needed him placated if her plan was going to work. "If the Memitim are after me, and I am this close to taking down the Continuance, then I have nothing to lose. I need an overpowered friend. She fills me up. I need a jolt, and she can give me that. And besides, I love her." She knew saying it to Sagar might hurt his feelings, but she would not hide her feelings from her friend.

"You are a fool, Astarte. God keep you, but you are a fool."

She shrugged off the insult, as friends did.

"Don't you remember how you first met her?"

CHAPTER 5

A selected excerpt from the unpublished manuscript: <u>A Brave New Bible</u> from Professor Angela Chiseler, PhD in Religious Studies and Theology.

Joshua 1-6:

Joshua, who Moses picked as his successor, took command of the Israelites. Moses, before abandoning his people to go live the good life with his wife, commanded Joshua to enter the land of Canaan. Moses told Joshua there was no reason the people of Canaan should have any rights to the land and he had decided that land all belonged to the Israelites. He commanded Joshua to kill any manner of persons he found in that land. Moses was very clear that Joshua was to show no mercy to any person he found in Canaan. Any signs of the people of Canaan should be eradicated.

Joshua and his men took the golden Ark of the Covenant (which still contained the broken pieces of the ten commandments from when Moses threw his tantrum after seeing everyone having a good time) across the River Jordan. Once they were all across the river, Joshua, following the command of the what some had called Mad Moses, had all the men circumcise themselves, then sent those men as spies to the nearest town of Jericho.

Once there, his spies threatened the life of a whore (more than likely a regular woman but calling her a whore fit with the Israelite narrative). This woman assisted them in their activities. What became of the whore is unknown, but if they kept to the word of their lord, she didn't make it through the night.

Soon after reporting the information to Joshua, he commanded the city of Jericho blocked off and destroyed the town. His men did as commanded and set the entire town to the blade. The screams of women and children mixed and rose in the cold night air.

***

The barker in the street shouted over the din of the street bazaar, "Repent, for He has sent His prophet, a new king to burn down His enemies. For we are but dogs to Him. No! Less than! We are fleas on wretched curs, and we will be wiped away like Jericho." No one listened to him, and Sariel couldn't understand why. She had been on Earth for a good amount of years, yet she had not learned why these mortals acted the way they did.

She had her suspicions. Wasn't it easier not to heed the barker and just continue to go on with one's life: consuming, pissing, shitting, fucking, then dying? That was the best some of these people could hope for. So maybe it was ignorance. Because Sariel knew the barker was saying nothing but the truth of what was to come.

When she'd first arrived, she'd spent her time in the Shang, thinking that starting where she'd left Dokiel could prove fruitful. She found plenty of frightened, desperate young women, but none of them gleamed. Sariel was convinced the right one would make herself known.

She moved through parts of Asia and the Indus Valley, looking for the one. With the Gates opened, she could sense the presence of immortals and other demons, so she kept her actions under the radar as best as she could.

She had traveled through old Akkadia, and found herself in thriving Ebla, and that was when she first heard the news and knew her time to find the champion was coming to an end. She had heard that one of these mortals was calling himself king and demanding all follow him and his gods. That in and of itself was no news. These humans had just learned how to melt metal together. Of course the one of the first things they made was something to kill each other with.

These early humans were very clannish, and for some reason, hated all the other clans. They were always warring over whose multi-breasted, cow-headed god was right. If she had just been here for leisure, it would have been quite enjoyable watching the squealing apes murder each other for nothing.

But then, she had heard something odd. Something different.

Apparently, this king was to destroy all the cities of Canaan. The reason seemed simplistic: because Canaanites were "bad," and this joker and his team were "good." Sariel rolled her eyes at the stupidity of it until she heard about Jericho. Not really much of a city, more like a military fort, but the reports were clear, it had been brought down by the blowing of a horn.

Sariel gave the mortals some credit. Their stories were intriguing, and the little morality plays entertained the children in the markets, but the issue regarding the horn had given her pause.

The man who was relaying the story claimed to have been a witness, someone who would snuck out of Jericho just before the ground opened up and swallowed the city.

When he had stopped talking, Sariel asked him, "Did you see the horn?"

The man looked wild-eyed at Sariel. Most people discounted him as a liar and fool. Seeing Sariel's sincerity, he answered, "The horn was like nothing I have seen. Not a shofar or even a trumpet. It was like a thick snake, with red and black bands, that was over three cubits."

"And how did it sound?"

"I will never forget. It wasn't bright like any horn I had heard. It was a pulsing, reverberating sound that grew and grew, and droned on and on until Earth opened up and took Jericho for itself."

Sariel knew the horn. The man had described Yadki, a literal instrument of destruction. Sariel had seen it in action a few times in the past, and it was always wielded by Numereji, a being similar to herself, just working for the other side. If this new "king" had Yadki, someone from the First Gate was lending him assistance, putting their finger on the scale.

Sariel had left the wild man and Ebla behind and continued her mission, finding herself in the town of Gibeon, listening to the barker in the street. It amazed her how even after a few short days the story was being embellished. Now, it was men on pure white steeds, racing in circles around the walls, all of them blowing silver horns, until finally the walls crashed down, allowing this king and his men to go a-raping.

Sariel guessed Gibeon would be on this king's list. Gibeon was a beautiful mixture of non-believers and pagans alike. Sariel knew someone wanted these old gods wiped off the map. Pity. But it was what it was, and what better place to find someone desperate and in despair than in a doomed city?

Sariel found her way to a shrine of Moloch, who Sariel had met personally and had always felt was a decent guy, if not a little full of himself. There was some sort of trial taking place outside the doors.

Sariel got a good view of what was happening. She saw a collection of the town's elders sitting at a table. In front of them was a heap of a human. It was hard to tell from the wounds, but Sariel guessed the person used to be a girl. From the looks of the bloodied stones that surrounded her, she did not have much longer to live. The oldest man stood up from the table, picked up a stone, and walked over to the beaten girl.

"People," he announced to the assembled crowd, "we could not figure out why Moloch had abandoned us. The most devout of us," he gestured to the elders, "have investigated this matter to answer your questions. Why would Moloch leave us to this slave king? What can be done to appease him and gain back his favor?" The crowd agreed they shared these questions. "We have found the answer for you. And she sits here, bleeding in front of you." Shouts rang out from the crowd. The old man nodded. "Yes, some of your suspicions were correct. Our priestess has been corrupted by this young girl." Hissing and spitting commenced from the crowd. The beaten girl just sat there as the crowd grew more convinced. "Lotan, please step forward before final judgement is given."

Sariel saw a beady-eyed young man with stringy brown hair come forward. Lotan looked at the beaten girl who sat next to him and smiled.

"Lotan, can you please tell the people what you saw?"

Lotan nodded. "Two days ago, I was giving sacrifices in the temple, and I saw Ishat," he pointed to the beaten girl, "fornicating with the high priestess." The crowd erupted with shouts.

Weakly, Ishat shook her head. The old man turned back to her. "You deny this, girl?"

The crowd silenced and listened. "No, but Lotan isn't telling the wh—" The crowd erupted again at her confession and began to chant, asking for justice.

The old man allowed the chant to swell, then, with a hand, silenced the din. "I am this girl's father. And by my hand, I will deliver justice."

He raised his hand, and the stone came down hard on Ishat's skull, bursting it open and laying bare the tissue within. Sariel noticed the girl had not flinched once.

The crowd, happy with a little late afternoon bloodshed, dispersed, except Lotan, who was ogling the partially nude, completely dead body of Ishat. Eventually, he apparently got enough mental images to last him and skulked off. The elders went back into the shrine. Sariel, intrigued, followed.

Inside the shrine, the elders were standing over the body of a young woman struggling against her restraints. Some of her skin on her arm had been flayed open. From the stink of the smoke, Sariel could tell they had been burning this woman's blood in some feeble attempt to appease Moloch (who she knew for a fact, wasn't listening).

She overheard the elders saying, "And what if this doesn't work? We don't have the time to wait and see. Joshua and his bastard demons from out of Egypt will arrive and it will be too late." They all seemed to nod and agree. Another added, "This witch and her profanity should be given to Moloch. He will rain fire down upon the slave king and scatter his forces back whence they came." A resounding cheer rose. The girl turned her head and looked at Sariel.

Sariel's vision went red. The girl was bathed in a plume of flame that spun around her and twisted in fury. Then it was gone. Sariel was knocked back at the power of the spell ending. A searing sensation arose on her forearms, and she saw Dokiel's handprints flash. The pain subsided, but the prints lingered for some time. Sariel, composing herself, got the message. Loud and clear. She had found her champion. She held herself back to see how the girl would handle herself.

She looked nothing like anyone from Gibeon. Not like any woman Sariel had ever seen in her travels. Her hair was long and auburn, her skin was tanned, but lighter than those from this area. Sariel suspected the mother of this girl had been raped by some foreign marauder. It could only explain the oddity of this girl. For these differences, this girl never stood a chance with these people. And, if she had a taste for women and not men, she was doomed.

The girl's eyes were defiant. Green eyes mixed with gold flecks. Again, another oddity. While these men clearly didn't outright fear this girl, they also took precaution in dealing with her. Sariel knew if this girl had real power, her gaze alone would have torn the flesh from these men.

Before they could say another word, she spoke, "I know what you fools want. You think my blood will appease the great king." She glanced up to the horned idol that stood above the alter. "You do not know his heart, nor his deepest lusts. You want to slaughter his female vessel like a pig before him. To what end? Especially when he has spoken to me. The blood of Ishat has satiated his hunger, and he has revealed himself to me."

The elders stepped back while Sariel enjoyed the show.

Confused on how to proceed, they asked, "Then what would you have us do?" The question brought on other beseeches. She allowed them to plead for a moment, then held her hand up, demanding silence.

"Release me. Now." The guards, without looking at the elders, cut the restraints. She massaged her wrists and said, "Leave this Joshua to me. I will go out to him. He will not destroy this town. Moloch will not allow it."

The mood changed from fear, to confusion, to joy. Sariel knew they were just happy to have any plan. This had cost the elders nothing. They were going to kill her anyway. She either succeeded and saved the town, or she didn't and died anyway at Joshua's hands. They had nothing to lose. The elders bowed and scraped before her as they left her alone in the shrine.

Sariel kept to the back to see what the priestess would do next. She watched the priestess walk outside the temple and bark some orders. Quickly, men carefully carried Ishat's body and placed it on the alter. After they left, the priestess put a blanket over Ishat's body and said a small prayer. Then the girl found an offering cup near the alter, filled it with wine from a bottle, and drank heavily. Filling it up again, she sat down and hung her head.

"Don't know how you're going to pull it off?" Sariel asked as she stepped forward.

The priestess straightened at the sound of Sariel's voice, but didn't turn, just took another drink.

"I know exactly what I am going to do. I am not doing shit for these people. When this man comes with his armies, all these people are going to die, and that is fine by me. I hope it is slow and painful, just like they did with her." She gestured to the body.

"From what I hear, you will get your wish. Joshua and his band don't see you as other humans, but as fungus that needs to be ripped from the world. The only thing they will leave standing are the corpses they skewer into the walls. You included, my dear."

She shrugged, not caring. "Everyone dies."

"That's true." Sariel waited a moment. "But what if I tell you that you could be the exception?"

She laughed. "Look, stranger, it has been a long day. I put on probably my last show to save my skin for a few days. If you are selling salvation, I am not interested."

Sariel smiled. "If we are talking about saving your skin, then yes. But I am certainly not talking about any other type of salvation."

She considered her words carefully, finished her drink, and shrugged again. "I have nothing to lose. How can you save me?"

Sariel knew the first part of her mission was done. She held out her hand and grasped the girl's wrist. "My name is Sariel. I am at your service and will do anything I can to support you." As Sariel spoke, Dokiel's handprints flashed on her forearms. The girl found them warm to the touch.

"Are you one of Moloch's minions?" she asked, frightened at the thought that all this Moloch shit might be real.

Laughing, Sariel calmed the girl down. "No. I am not with Moloch. I am with you. I have been sent to offer aid and counsel and instruction to you." Sariel placed her hand on the torn flesh of the priestess's arm. A quick flash, and the skin was mended.

The priestess inspected her arm and let the words sink in. She heaved a sigh of relief, thinking, for the first time in weeks, she may not be doomed. The girl threw her arms around Sariel and squeezed, offering a prayer of thanks.

"Enough of that. I am here. But I still have no idea what to call you?"

The girl looked at Sariel. "Names are a funny thing. Little scraps of words we assign meaning to. I have been called many things, some pleasant, some not." She paused and gazed at the temple. "My mother was not the most loving of women. But she did try to teach me what she knew about Moloch and the different rites. Looking the way I do, she knew I would have to cut a path for myself if I were to survive, as she had done for many years as the Priestess of Moloch. However, after a series of droughts, the town council had her stoned right in the same spot Ishat died today. I still remember the moment right before she died. Just before the final stone smashed her face in, she pointed to me. She knew what she was doing. The council took it as a dying sign and gave me my mother's title. Astarte. I believe that will serve as my name."

Sariel considered the name and smiled. "So be it. We have some work to do."

CHAPTER 6

A selected excerpt from the unpublished manuscript:
<u>A Brave New Bible</u> from Professor Angela Chiseler, PhD in
Religious Studies and Theology.

Joshua 9:1-21:

After Joshua obliterated Jericho, the blood had only whet his appetite. He gave thanks to his God for his men's victory, and they turned their eyes to the next town of Ai. Again, spies were sent, trust was gained, and information was gathered. Sadly, for the people of Ai, Joshua made sure no information about Jericho's annihilation had reached their ears.

Joshua had received a complaint that the female spoils of war in Jericho were needlessly destroyed and a new tactic was put into place. Joshua's men, posing as peaceful emissaries, entered the gates of Ai. They were greeted with a grand feast that went long into the night.

When the festivities quieted, the Israelites opened the gates of Ai and allowed Joshua's army in. Those women were separated according to their beauty and spoiled. However, Moses's command stood. By the next night, they put all Canaanites to the knife.

By now, word had traveled all over the land regarding

Joshua and his army of brigands. The people of Gibeon knew they would soon share the same fate. The elders of Gibeon sent a great deceiver as a representative to Joshua.

This chiseler met with Joshua and secured his promise to leave Gibeon in peace. A peace for which Gibeon would pay a great price.

***

Standing alone in the tent's antechamber, Astarte was nervous. She had put her long hair back and adorned herself with bracelets and other fineries as Sariel had instructed. Before she left, she chastised Sariel once again for not going with her.

"You could be my assistant or slave or something like that. I think it would be more believable if I didn't go in there alone."

But Sariel explained it was a task she must do herself. If Sariel were recognized, they would both dead before Astarte said a word.

"Anyway, I have taught you what you need to know."

Astarte rolled her eyes. "You have taught me shit. I already knew how to lie. I am a woman of my age. Lying is natural."

"You know how to lie to fucking rubes in the desert." Astarte looked confused at the term, and Sariel huffed. "Lying to fools is easy. What I have taught you is how to confound and deceive someone who has been chosen."

"Chosen by whom?"

Sariel didn't like answering questions, but she followed Dokiel's orders. "I don't know who, but I know Joshua is more than a mere mortal animal. Which is why I cannot go with you. He may have people watching out for him. People who would recognize me."

Astarte gazed at herself one last time in the mirror and doubted. "I thought you were going to teach me magic or some spell or give me a potion. What kind of immortal being are you?"

Sariel sighed. "In time. I can't teach you anything as complicated as that in the span of a week. I am not some roadside magician doing tricks for coin. I can, and will, show you how to draw up the realms and create wonderful magics. You will harness the energy of Existence itself. But not today. I need to see how you do on your own. Using your skills and persuasion. If you can't accomplish this simple task, how the hell do you think you can do more?" Sariel did not wait for an answer. "Anyways, I suspect Joshua has been granted certain favors and cannot be harmed or magically manipulated at this time. So, it is for you and you alone to pull off this trick. What have I been saying this entire time?"

Astarte, having heard this over and over, rolled her eyes. "A good trick is magic."

"Exactly. If you can deceive and ensnare Joshua and leave his tent unscathed, then you will be the greatest chiseler since Zeus got women to get it on with a swan." That brought a laugh from Astarte. "And most importantly, please remember if this works, you kill two birds. One, you live to see many more days. And two, avengement. The punishment that will be heaped upon Gibeon will last for generations."

Astarte remembered how those words made her feel. Now, standing before the silk drapes of the tent, she smiled again at the idea. However, she swallowed hard at the prospect that these could be her last moments.

The flap opened, and a man gestured for her to come

inside.

The interior of the tent was spacious and well adored, but it was still clearly a battlefield tent. Soldiers stood in groups, reviewing maps and discussing troop movements in hushed tones. In the time since Jericho, Sariel had surmised Joshua was wiping out certain towns his deity had deemed unworthy to clear the land of Canaan for Joshua's people.

The men would occasionally look up from their discussions and watch as Astarte was led forward. They stared at her as if she were some barnyard animal that had wandered in for dinner, with amusement and bewilderment at the same time. She kept her eyes forward, concentrating on her goal. At the end of the tent sat a long table, roughhewn and set with a simple foods and plates, not with the finery she had been expecting. The men sat at this table were obviously high-ranking commanders, judging by their scars and the intensity of their scowls. They were not amused by her presence in the least.

She stopped behind her escort in front of the table. "Joshua," he said. A man in the middle of the table glanced up and nodded to her escort. Astarte looked at him and made some quick calculations. Younger, middle-aged (obviously not the oldest at the table), a few scars, about a head taller than her. Grim. Handsome. Clothes were well made, but well worn. They were made for hard marches and long days. Not finery. "This is the emissary who has come to speak to you."

Joshua looked from the speaker to Astarte and made his own mental calculations. Astarte was happy to see his eyes pause at the right places. Any hope she had of getting out of there alive had dimmed since most of the glances she had been getting were not just unfriendly, but downright murderous. A handsome man sitting next to Joshua leaned over and said some words into Joshua's ear, causing a smile to spread on both of their faces.

She had decided to wait to speak, and so the two stared at each other silently for enough time that the din of the other men in the tent had quieted as more and more people looked on.

Finally, he spoke.

"And what is the emissary's name?" He continued to look at Astarte, but it was unclear who he was addressing.

"She didn't give me a name," said her escort.

"Does she have something to hide?" Joshua said. No one answered.

Astarte began to cry. "Forgive me, I am clearly out of sorts. I have had much misfortune on my journey to see you. I am not the emissary. At least, I am not supposed to be," she said awkwardly.

Joshua's face, seeing her tears, softened slightly. His friend sitting next to him did not soften. "Please explain," Joshua said in a commanding tone.

Astarte took a steadying inhale, centered herself, and began her tale. "I was traveling with my father. He was to speak for our people, but we were waylaid by bandits on the road through Canaan. They struck my father down, and his retinue. They fought bravely, but they were outmatched. My father bought me time to escape, and his one wish was for me to complete his mission. I do not wish to sully your tent with my presence, but merely to plea my people's case."

For this part, she could thank Sariel, who had discovered Joshua had been sent into Canaan a few years before to do reconnaissance. While there, he had stopped the raping of a woman by a band of thugs. He had been injured in the fight, and the woman and her father took him in and

nurtured him back to health. Before he left, he'd promised
to return the kindness to that family. Joshua had kept this
incident secret from all but his god, Sariel had been assured.
Astarte and Sariel had carefully orchestrated every detail to
be perfect. The color of her clothes, the scent she used on her
body, even the type of smile. Somehow, Sariel knew these
details that would best ensnare the young leader.

Joshua's handsome friend (who Astarte had realized
was the only person not sporting a beard) tried to say
something to him, but he pushed him away. "I am sorry for all
your troubles. May He hold your father in his arms and give
you peace." The tension finally lifted, and the onlookers got on
with their business. "I can help you complete your task. Please
tell me what I need to hear. But first, name?"

"Herrana, Daughter of Aprax, Counselor of Gibeon."

"Well met, Herrana. And what have you come to tell
me?"

Astarte smiled at Joshua's emerging kindness. "I am
here to seal an agreement of goodwill and commerce between
our peoples."

"And where is Gibeon?"

"It is an island in the sea." She smiled and looked at the
men at the table. No one questioned her statement.

Joshua's clean-shaven friend asked, "And how do you
speak our tongue? Forgive me, Joshua, but I had to ask."

She was ready for this question. "My people have
been following the triumph of Joshua and his people since
your escape from Egypt. We make it our duty to try to foster
communication with all peoples." The friend didn't seem
convinced, but he didn't follow up with any more questions.
She was unsure whether Joshua had bought that, but he filled
a glass of wine and asked her to continue. "Gibeon offers our

hand of friendship to you, Joshua, and your people, with hope we can strengthen our ties."

"I only have aggression against the children of Canaan. I would think with what happened with your father, this would make you happy?"

"It does, but my people have dealt with warlords before, and on one day, they may say peace, but the next, they are at our door with flame. All I want is your word that we won't taste the end of your blade, or Gibeon women won't be pierced by any of your swords."

Her meaning wasn't lost on those at the table, who rose in argument, defending the honor of their troops. Joshua said nothing, knowing the reality of war and the atrocities that occur even under the best circumstances.

Astarte focused only on Joshua while the others yelled at her, saying she should be cast out and questioning why a woman had even been allowed to enter.

Joshua raised his hand and shouted, "Enough!" With that, the men settled and looked to their leader for his final word. He stood up, walked to the back of tent, opened a panel, and walked through. Before the flap closed, Astarte saw a large gold crate. The assembled men fell to their knees and beseeched their god. Astarte just stood there.

A moment later, Joshua was back. "I give my word, Gibeon is not to be harmed. Please tell your people we welcome their assistance in the future.'"

"Thank you, Joshua. You are merciful."

Joshua gave a dismissive nod and sat back in his chair. The men continued their discussions, and Astarte casually backed out of the tent. Thrilled her plan had worked, she exited the tent and turned to leave.

Her way out was blocked by Joshua's friend with all

the questions. He seemed like an honest man, but his eyes showed cunning. "I must say, young lady, that was quite a show you put on there. I especially like the weeping and the tragic story. Most men are suckers for a good tale, but the horrible circumstances you endured, so specific."

She acted like she didn't register the sarcasm. "It has been a harrowing journey. I must get back to my people to celebrate the good news." She attempted to get around him.

He stepped in front of her. "And mourn your father?"

Inwardly, she grimaced, knowing she should have led with that. She recovered quickly. "That goes without saying. But accomplishing his final task is my way of mourning him."

He stepped aside and led the way out. "I will walk with you to make sure you reach the edge of the encampment safely."

"That won't be necessary, my lord."

The man looked around, seeing if anyone had heard. "'My lord'?" Seeing no onlookers, he added, "You need to do a better study of Joshua's people. I am surprised you didn't slip up inside the tent. If you had, your little plan would have failed."

Astarte said nothing and continued to walk.

He walked with her and explained. "Joshua doesn't claim to be a king, or a lord, or anything. He is an ordinary man who has been asked to do extraordinary things. To him and his followers, there is only one lord." He paused to ensure she was listening. "Claiming otherwise is heresy."

She nodded that she understood. She gazed at him, and his suspicious eyes had relaxed. She didn't know why, but she felt as if he were more of a friend than an enemy. "And you think the same?"

He scoffed. "Oh no. While having only one god may

make things simpler, it just isn't my way." His frankness surprised her. He stood as tall as any man in the camp, but he did have a distinct look about him. He stood out among Joshua's people.

She saw the edge of camp. "You have me at a disadvantage. You know my name, but you have yet to give me yours."

He gently pulled her arm to stop her and bowed. "Let me fix that now. I am Sagar, an advisor of sorts to Joshua. And no, I am not one of his people, but he is a smart man. Maybe simple and ordinary, but he knows useful knowledge can exist outside of one's beliefs."

She smiled at his bow and continued to walk. He did not follow her, but instead shouted, "I know where Gibeon is."

She stopped and turned. Before she could say anything, he waved off any response. "Stop. I don't want to hear any more lies." She looked around to check her surroundings. Maybe she could kill him and still get out of here alive. He could already read her like a book. "I am sure you could kill me, but that will be most pointless. I don't know if you will believe me, but your secret is safe with me." He smiled wide as he walked up to her. He was not menacing. It was an honest smile.

Still, honest smiles could hide the coldest of blades. This truth, she knew more than most. "You say you advise Joshua, yet you would let him be deceived? How could you expect me to trust you?"

"A good counselor knows when to give and when to not give counsel." Seeing her confusion, he added, "I will keep your trust for three reasons. One, I did try to warn him, but was silenced. It is my job to advise, not to force people to listen. Second, his magic box apparently answered his prayer, which means either you confounded his god, or his god knows what you are doing and is okay with it. And three, I have never agreed with his bloodthirsty god's plans of conquest. Did you know even the goats and bulls are to be murdered? Can you imagine?"

A loud cheer rose from the middle of the encampment. Cheers in praise of their god. Drinking and merriment broke out, and as people ran by, they heard the last of the whores of Ai had died. Apparently, the men had been taking bets.

Sagar shrugged. "Ai had ten-thousand people in it. Our spies told us more than half of them were women, children, and the elderly. They held out a long time, but if the plan worked," he paused as he saw men laughing, "not even the rats of Ai survived."

After a moment had passed, she asked, "So, where does this leave me?"

"I hope your lie leaves you and your people in peace. If I can have a small hand is saving some souls, I'll do it."

Astarte's eyes narrowed. She had seen how he had been ogling her. She had been counting on it in the first place. "You're doing this for no other reason?"

He smiled and said, "Well, maybe I have been in army camps too long, but when I first saw you, I thought, look at this innocent face, so pure, so alluring. But then I heard you speak and listened to what you said. Such complete bullshit, but in your hands, you turned it into art. You showed great courage in there. I was transfixed. Trust me, I have seen many great hucksters and grifters, and they wouldn't have lasted five minutes in there. And a woman to boot." If he were attempting to make her blush, he was failing. She knew to be weary of men and their compliments. "You are young and just starting out in this life, but if you can keep your head attached to your neck, you just may end up ruling us all. You are what my people call a Mohini, and while you may lead some to their doom, it will be a beautiful ride." He took her hand and kissed the top of it gently. "My duty lies with Joshua, but, over time, I believe my heart could lie with you." He again took her hand and kissed it.

At this, she blushed. He could have had her arrested thirty times over by now but had only shown her affection. He looked up at her, happy to see her smile. Sagar then placed something into her hand. She looked down at her palm and saw he had put a pendant on a delicate gold chain.

"Let's call it a token of my esteem. If you ever need me, send it to me and I will come running, Herrana…or?" He smiled expectantly. She knew he knew.

Fastening the chain around her neck, realizing her fate was already in his hands, she said, "Call me Astarte. Thank you for your confidence and counsel. Don't come searching for me in Gibeon. I am done with that town."

He nodded his head. "Astarte, Joshua will find out eventually that Gibeon is about a three days' ride east of here. He will keep his word, no one will be harmed, but they will pay for the deception."

She shrugged, showing a lack of care. "I figured as much. I think I will need to ply my trade elsewhere." They had reached her carriage. She hopped in, and finally said to him, "May your gods keep you well."

He gently bowed his head and said, "I will be seeing you again, Astarte, my personal Mohini. Women like you cannot be missed in this world."

CHAPTER 7

Sagar and Astarte talked through most of the night in the little New Mexico motel, some about her current predicament, but most of their time was spent reminiscing over well-worn stories of their past adventures.

"I swear, you should have seen his face." Sagar laughed. "He looked around this little shitty town and said, 'this is Gibeon?'" Astarte laughed with him, of course having heard all this before. "But he was true to his word. He didn't harm one person. Of course, he turned Gibeon into a slave town for about five generations. I am sure you shed a hundred tears for them." Sagar said sarcastically. Sagar saw Astarte laugh and was happy his attempts to keep the mood light were somewhat successful. He knew the Memitim could not be very far from Astarte's thoughts.

Astarte listened to her friend talk, and he did love to talk, especially since he had been silent for so long. She knew he had a lot of catching up to do. The smile she wore was for her friend, but inside, she was tormented by the fact that she was so close to her goal, but she would more than likely never make it. This would render her struggles meaningless, and that terrified her. She listened to the old stories, some of which she had played a part. David and Goliath's sword. King Saul and the Witch of Endor. When she saw Sagar had finally talked himself out, she presented her idea.

"I think I might have my way out of this Memitim problem. Now, more than ever, I need to get to Sariel. I can only hope she got my message."

"Explain."

"I need to recover something I…" she chose her words carefully, "lost many years ago. Sariel will help me find it. At least, as long as she got my message. And if I do, then not only will the Memitim be a nonissue, it will help me bring down the Continuance."

"And what is this item?"

Astarte looked around at her wards that still glowed around the room. She still didn't trust they would hold. "I can't say out loud. If anyone were listening, it could be put beyond my reach."

Sagar nodded, trusting Astarte was a master on this subject. "How can I help?"

"If Sariel got my message, and if she was able to break her bonds, and if she is waiting just on the other side, breaking her out will take considerable power. I need a focus point. A spot that will ease my work. Can you help me with that?"

"That is a lot of 'ifs.'" Sagar knew what she wanted. She wanted ley lines. Ley lines were invisible lines that spanned the world. While they were invisible to most mortals, the lines still held influence in this world. Many great and horrible actions had occurred on the nexuses of ley lines. On these nexuses, heavy magic could be constructed. This was what Astarte wanted. Of course, the trick was finding these intersections. Detection of the ley lines was well suited to atmans like Sagar. Sagar wondered if this was the sole reason she called him forth, but pushed that idea out of his mind. It didn't matter to him. He would have done anything for her. Without a second thought, Sagar closed his eyes and splayed his fingers on both hands. A thin, warm light emitted from each finger and shot out beyond the room. Some lines twisted together and changed colors. Astarte was hoping this wouldn't take long. The longer the wait, the farther she would have to travel.

"Got one," Sagar opened his eyes. Astarte was relieved. "How far?"

"Not very. Mission San Miguel, about two-hundred miles north. If it is Sariel you want to talk to, and you want it to remain private, you will need to do a desecration. You got the juice for that?"

Desecrations could be exhausting, especially for longstanding wards that would have to be undone. Astarte looked at what remained in her bottle and weighed her options. Without confidence, she said, "Yes, I can do it. And with that location, the signal will be clear as a bell."

Hearing the weariness in her voice, Sagar asked, if only for his sake, "The only reason they are after you is because of the Continuance. Why don't you just stop? Why does it fall to you?"

Knowing Sagar would ask this question (because he always did, eventually), she rose from the bed, and stamped her feet to get the blood flowing again. "I was chosen."

"Just because you were fed a story four-thousand years ago doesn't mean you have to keep on going."

Astarte closed her eyes, feeling the weariness settle in. "The Continuance isn't just a sorting area for the saved and the damned. That is the package that has been sold. Its primary function is to separate the immortal from the mortal, the natural from the supernatural. Before the Continuance, people could actually speak and interact with their gods. They came here and lived among us, destroyed things for us, created things with us. It was messy and terrible and beautiful and horrible all at the same time."

"So," Sagar interrupted, "that's what you want? Petulant demigods demanding fealty? True curses and incantations to vex souls in their own homes or force unwilling lovers? That is also the world you want."

"It's got to be better than this," she said, gesturing at the window. "Mindlessly following old rhymes in a book. Saying soft words in large buildings, talking to someone who can't listen? At least before, humanity knew where it stood. Since the Continuance, we have been deaf and blind, hacking away at each other." She started packing up her things. She had already stayed too long. "If I can be an instrument to ending all this suffering, I will do so. And if I die trying, so be it."

Sagar knew this was the end of the conversation. He knew how it would end, but wanted to at least tell himself he had done everything he could to change the outcome.

Checking under the bed to make sure she had gotten everything, Astarte shoved the last few items into her bag. She turned to her friend who had been standing in the circle the entire night and smiled. She knew no one would love her like he did. But now, it was time to say goodbye. "Well, the sun has risen. Its light does not bring me much joy, but I don't really want to stay another minute in this place, so . . ."

Sagar knew this would be the last goodbye, but instead of saying farewell, he said, "I'm going with you."

Astarte looked confused. "Sagar, that isn't possible, but I thank you for the sentiment."

He motioned for her. "My love, come here." She moved closer to him as if to embrace him. Sagar quickly snatched the pendant from around her neck and put it in his left hand. He then smashed the pendant with his right fist and said, "Is adhiniyam ke saath, main apanee aatma deta hoon."

Orange light flashed in his left hand, radiating down his entire body. The light left his body and entered the sand circle she had drawn, and in the same orange light, the sand vanished. Sagar stepped outside of where the circle used to be and hugged Astarte.

Wide-eyed, she asked, "What have you done?"

"What? You're the only one who can do a little magic? It is nice to know that after all this time I can still surprise you."

She leaned back and looked at him eye-to-eye, tears forming in hers. "I know that spell. This is a one-way ticket."

"No stops, exchanges, or refunds. Sadly, also non-transferrable."

"You will be tossed from Existence."

Sagar smiled. "So, let's make it worth it."

CHAPTER 8

"Happy Birthday, Max." Shamsiel placed his hands on Max's head and began his incantation. Sham had done this at least a thousand times. Erasing or altering the minds of mortals was one of his specialties. He had decided to create a story Max would enjoy. Maybe an end of summer party in which Max had a little too much cheer. Max would wake up and maybe give that girl in the coffee shop a call. She had been giving him looks all summer that he'd failed to notice. Definitely no Angie. No Continuance. But Sham would make sure to keep the peace Jude gave his son.

The lights of the basement dimmed, and a bright light erupted around Sham's hands. He could feel the searing heat. If he were a lesser being, his skin may have burned. Sham drew back his hands, and the light formed a hexagram that hovered over Max's forehead, then quietly disappeared.

"Sham, you're wasting your time." The voice that came from behind was familiar, unexpected, and unwelcome. Sham put his hands down, and Max's eyes came open and locked on the stranger that now stood in the room.

"Who are you?" Max asked.

The man stepped forward and placed his finger on Max's lips. "Shhh." Max's eyes closed shut, and he slept while standing. "It would seem this young one is protected from your manipulations. However, while it may seem a kindness to wipe young Mr. Travers's memories of the most recent events, he is going to need what he has learned."

The man was as tall and as handsome as Sham but was dressed in a deep black, three-piece suit with matching long hair. His skin was so perfect, it was as if he had never smiled, or frowned, or had given any expression whatsoever in all his existence.

Making sure Max was stable, Sham turned to the man. "There have been far too many puzzles tonight, but I first want to know what purpose you could possibly have here."

Malhamash did not feel the need to answer Sham's question. He walked around the basement of the necromancer and looked at her collected odds and ends. He picked up a wine goblet that had been knocked over and inspected the residue.

"Your job, Sham, was to save the boy. And you have done admirably. I was tasked with figuring out what was happening here. You have inadvertently helped in that as well."

Sham looked around the room. "Some of this seems pretty clear, Mal. A necromancer was trying to extract this boy's father. Working with Puriel, we mended any rift, saved the boy, and now I was going to wipe his memory clean so he can get on with his life." Sham spoke quickly, hoping his succinct explanation would hasten Mal's leaving. It didn't.

Raising a finger, Mal responded, "And that is where, I believe, you fucked up. You and Puriel opened the Gates to mend this boy and his father. All well and good, but you didn't foresee the consequences."

Sham squinted at the statement. "And what were those?"

Mal didn't answer the question, threw the goblet on the

ground, and inspected a few other items. "So, you say this was a necromancer?"

Sham rolled his eyes. "Clearly."

Mal noticed Sham's human gestures, a talent he had never picked up. "I wouldn't be so dismissive. Necromancers are a dying breed, wouldn't you say?"

"True." Sham hadn't dealt with a necromancer in quite some time, but he knew the information on how to become one was in the world. Much like Prometheus giving fire back to mortals, what had been done was done. "I would assume this person is well studied and has found the proper instructions. Whoever this person is obviously possesses great skill. Skillful enough to evade me, and I am now assuming, skillful enough to escape Jeqon. He has failed in his one task, am I right?"

"Yes. Jeqon is giving chase, but we have already foreseen he will fail in his task. He will meet with a sticky end."

"Then why are you here and not out there helping him?"

Mal shook his head. "Not how it works. Not how I work. Some actions are not meant for me to stop."

Malhamash was the leader of the Memitim, beings tasked with the actual slicing and dicing when it came to immortal retribution. Individually, they all had nicknames. Mal's was 'Poison of God.' Mal's presence was more evidence to Sham that things were much more serious than he'd first assumed.

Mal made one final inspection of the room, making sure he hadn't missed anything. "If this extraction would have been successful, that would have been it for the Continuance." Mal looked at Sham's shocked reaction. "We have been watching this necromancer's work for a long while now."

"So, you know who it is?"

Mal pointed to the goblet and some of the wards. "Same methods. The wine, a special type of home brew. Smell it." Mal tossed the cup to Sham, who obeyed and gave it a deep inhale. "It is a mixture of honey, juniper, storax, and terebinth resins. And an ever so subtle hint of blood. Clearly an old blend. Very specific to a time and place. And very specific to a purpose. This is a brew used specifically, and only, by Astarte. The Necromancer."

Sham forced himself not to give anymore facial cues as to his thoughts, but he was shocked to hear the name. He had heard it countless times over the centuries. Astarte was a legend unto herself. A true boogeyman of Existence. "If you have been watching her for so long, why didn't you swoop in and take her long ago? I would think taking her off the table would have been order number one from Existence."

Mal nodded in agreement. "Not how it works. Not how I work. I do not act without direction. I don't know why Existence didn't make a move until now. I don't question it. But now, Astarte has put certain wheels in motion." Seeing Sham needed more of an explanation, he continued. "When Puriel opened the Gates and allowed Jude Travers to speak to Max, the Gates had to be opened wide—wide enough for this little witch to send her own message. And that is where your little plan fucked up. Everything has a consequence. We don't know what was said, but we know whom it was sent to. We can guess the 'whys' well enough."

It seemed Mal was attempting to guilt Sham, but Sham was beyond such tactics. He knew he could not change what was done. He understood unintended consequences more than most beings, but Sham knew his actions were correct in the moment. Still, he had to know the extent of what damage he may have had a hand in causing. "Who was the message sent to?"

This was the only time Mal's face contorted and looked human. "Sariel the Fallen."

Sham thought about the name he hadn't heard aloud in centuries. If he had to have guessed, he would have said Sariel. But it was best not to throw names like hers around. Not that it was forbidden to say, but there weren't too many beings as abhorred as Sariel. It was clear to Sham why she would be the one Astarte would reach out to. "She needs her old teacher to accomplish her goal."

Mal agreed. "As Memitim, I can go anywhere. I inspected the pit myself to ensure not one atom of light, or cool breeze, or comfort could find Sariel. I assure you she has been kept well wrapped in oblivion. Much has been clouded from me. I suspect meddling, but I cannot see by whom. No matter. I do not doubt if Sariel is called, she will answer. The torment she has been put through in the pit has probably hardened her even more against Existence. I can only hope to stop the end goal. Which is obvious."

Sham nodded. "If Astarte is this close to voiding the Continuance, Sariel would be a great help in that, especially if she becomes aware the Memitim are after her. At the very least, Sariel can help out with that."

Mal retrieved a pack of cigarettes from his inside pocket, pulled one out, and lit it. "I typically wouldn't be that concerned if it was any typical witch. Even if they had Sariel's help. But Astarte…" Mal shook his head and breathed out a cloud of smoke, "she has the power and knowledge to succeed in the task she has been working toward. Tonight's little adventure is proof of that. While I believe Existence has acted too slowly, I am confident I will drain the life from that bitch's eyes myself."

Dark words for a dark deed, thought Sham. But if anyone deserved to be ended, it was this woman. A woman of many names. Astarte. Herrana. Aisha. The Witch of Endor.

Mal continued. "She is brilliant, but we have been able to keep tabs on her over the millennia." He saw Sham smirk. "Maybe not able to track her specifically, but where she has been. Her effects. Meddling here, interfering there. At times, she would always generate too much power and we would investigate." Mal gestured to the room. "All the evidence she would leave in her wake always screamed who it was."

Sham was furious she had been allowed to exist so long. He knew a creature like her on the loose was destruction incarnate. "I have heard rumors she has had her fingers in many pots. Posing as Jezebel, Roxana of Bactria, even Magdalene herself. If any of that is true, she has caused havoc that still reverberates today," Sham seethed.

Mal waited for Sham to stop. "Not rumors. I have confirmed it. We can't be overly certain we know all her incarnations. We know she and Sariel formed their little union sometime at the beginning of the Age of the Prophets."

The Age of the Prophets. A time Sham knew well. Just around the ending of the Greek period, Existence ordered the First and Fourth Gates opened. This ushered in a long time period of various prophets, messiahs, and saviors. Beings like Sham watched and guided when they were instructed to do so, and when the age ended and the Gates were shut, the world had a new set of beings to pray to—beings who were still pretty popular today.

Mal continued. "Astarte posed as men or women, manipulating outcomes that best suited her needs. Well… someone's needs. She turned many good souls away from the right path. She is the mother of apostates. It could be argued not one single person played a bigger part in molding the Age of the Prophets. After Sariel was taken care of, and the Gates were shut, it was hoped that she would just sit back and leave the world alone. Instead, she turned all her focus on the Continuance itself, believing it to be an unjust creation. She has spent her time trying to undo it. Apparently, with this latest act, she has stepped over some line. She has finally been declared anathema to Existence itself. We now have our orders, however delayed they are." Mal breathed in deep, calming himself. "She is very close to her goal. But she will fail."

Sham did not share his companion's optimism. But he was happy some of the pieces had finally come together. That left Max. Sham turned and looked at the sleeping boy. "And what of Max?"

Mal smiled. "I had no idea really what his role in this was until you tried to pry open his mind. Your thoughts?"

Sham knew what the hexagram signified. And it also answered questions he had been asking himself for years. If it were anyone but Mal, he would have kept his revelations to himself. But Mal knew the meaning of the symbol more than most.

"Obviously some sort of trigger spell has been placed on Max. From its makeup, it is tied to his blood and cannot be removed without killing him." Sham was speaking out loud, trying to suss out his next move. The trigger spell on Max sprung forth the moment he'd attempted to magically enter Max's mind. It was nothing Max would even know about. The spell was ingrained in his blood.

"Anything else?" Mal wanted Sham to say it, just to confirm.

Sham nodded. "The Star of David makes it clear who did this and that a signal has been sent. A magical call for help." Sham refused to say who the call had been sent to. He respected her too much to say her name to Mal. Sham turned to look at Max's sleeping face, now seeing he was so much more than first met the eye. "I best get him home. His mom will be worried."

Mal nodded. "Before you leave, I need to give you some instructions of how this next part is going to play out." He put his arm around Sham, who uncomfortably acquiesced. "Now that the House of David is involved, it would be best if we are all on the same page."

CHAPTER 9

A selected excerpt from the unpublished manuscript: <u>A Brave New Bible</u> from Professor Angela Chiseler, PhD in Religious Studies and Theology.

First Samuel 16:

Joseph lived a long while. It is uncertain how many years, but it has been agreed by scholars he lived well into old age. After he died, there was no leader of the Israelites, so each little area of the Israel was controlled by a judge. As you can imagine, in time, most of these men became corrupt, making sacrifices and praying to other gods. Tired of the corruption, the people of Israel asked the prophet Samuel to anoint a king, which he did. His first choice left much to be desired. Bluntly, he did a horrible job. He chose a man named Saul. And the people hated Saul.

It became clear very early Samuel had really dropped the ball and another person needed to be chosen as king, so again, the people asked Samuel to choose. This was despite the fact that he'd done such a shitty job picking Saul in the first place.

One day, King Saul was convinced he was seeing demons sent by his god to attack and vex him. To remedy this, one of Saul's servants brought in a shepherd boy named David, who was known to be very talented in playing the harp. The moment he began to play for Saul, whatever demons Saul saw vanished, and he was soothed.

Seeing this young shepherd boy with such talent, Samuel knew there was something very special about David. He was so impressed with David and his talent, he anointed David as the next king. However, he knew Saul was the jealous type, so he kept the anointing secret.

Years later, David, in single combat, killed a large Philistine named Goliath with a stone, and cut Goliath's head off, which roused the Israelites into victory. After the battle, David took Goliath's sword and gave it to the priests of Nob, in Gibeon, for safekeeping.

It should be noted that while Saul's line ended with him, David and his line ruled Israel for many years to come.

***

Even though life expectancy in the Bronze Age was about 26 years for mortals, Sariel knew Joshua was going to live a long life. Far longer than any normal human had a right to. She had a sense for these things. She could tell he had been touched by otherworldly forces. Fearing any more run-ins with the young warlord, she had Astarte avoid all further contact with him. However, against Sariel's advice, Astarte was always kept abreast of news through correspondence with Sagar. He would give her updates, and she would always know where not to be.

During this time, Sariel taught Astarte about the nature of the Continuance, its purpose, and its function. "Before the Gates were created," she began, "life here in your realm was quite different. Mortals had access to knowledge that has now been cut off from you."

"Why was it taken from us?" Astarte asked.

"I don't know. There is much I am not privy to. But I am also unable to describe it to you. It somehow," Sariel shook her head in bewilderment, "I don't know how to explain. I want to tell you how life was really like before the Rekindling. I can see it in my mind, but the words just won't come." Sariel presumed it was Existence blocking her, but shrugged it off, knowing there was nothing she could do about it."

She told Astarte about how, for the time being, the Gates were open and prophets, demigods, and demons walked among humans.

"The Age of Prophets is what they are calling it," Sariel said as they were travelling the countryside. "I don't know how long it will last, but it will end one day. The First Gate is flooding this land with their minions. You need to do all you can to tilt the world in our favor."

"And how am I supposed to do that?" Astarte asked.

"Do you know what an apostate is?"

"No."

"An apostate is a person who renounces their faith. They must do so willingly. It is a treachery of the soul. That is what you need to do. You need to lead people toward our path. All these foolish rules nowadays. Did Moloch ever demand not to eat certain things on certain days with a specific utensil? Or demand exactly how much land can be used for a certain crop, or how much makeup a woman can wear? Of course not! He wouldn't have dared. Live your life, free from these silly restrictions. That is what you need to show the people. Lead them to a better place."

"Make them apostates."

"Yes. People build their own jails. Why do you think it is a sin for one person to eat pork and not for another? Do you think you should be thrown into the pit because you unrepentantly eat bacon?" Astarte didn't answer. "Of course not, but there will be people cast into the pit for the stupidest of reasons. People, through their choices, build the walls of their damnation. But it doesn't have to be this way."

Astarte was a bit confused. "I thought you wanted people to be damned?"

Sariel smiled. "A common misconception and only part of the story. The Thirteenth Gate isn't hoping for people to do wrong. We only want people to be free to make whatever choices they deem to be good for them. The mortals live a carefree and liberated life, and in the end, their true value is completely understood." Sariel could see Astarte needed a little more instruction in this area. "When a person adorns themselves with a religion and follows all the rules to move on in the afterlife, the question becomes: did they make those choices because they were afraid of some punishment or because they are a truly good person?

Understanding dawned on Astarte. "You are looking for hypocrites."

"Yes, in part. Now, initially, the people you turn will more than likely be given to the Thirteenth Gate, but as you change minds, change perspectives, as people become freer, they will cast off these new gods. This, in turn, will weaken them. The more people you cull from the herd, the weaker the god becomes." Sariel glanced up at the blazing sun. "How many people do you know who still pray to Apollo?"

Astarte squinted up at the sky. "I don't know. Not many anymore."

"Exactly. Apollo was real, and powerful, but as time

marches and new gods come to the forefront, the Greeks cast off their gods, and now Apollo and the whole Pantheon are little more than ghost stories." Sariel made sure Astarte had fully grasped her meaning. "This is what we want from you: free the mortals from these new gods and their childish mandates. You will be our representative on this planet. They need you more than you know."

Astarte considered Sariel's words. "Why me?"

Sariel gave Astarte a warm smile and took her hand. "I was sent to find an innocent. Someone who was in desperate need. A champion for all. All I can tell you is you have been chosen."

Sariel's touch comforted Astarte, and they shared a moment together, looking at each other, hand in hand. "And you will show me how?"

Sariel smiled. "I am here to serve."

As they traveled the land, Sariel taught Astarte different sorcery. Each unique form of magic had a different purpose. For the first lessons, Sariel felt it was best Astarte master deceptions since they naturally came easy to Astarte. This magic focused on a word, a look, or a scent that would ensnare the target, making them more pliable to suggestion. Most of this "magic" came from being silver-tongued, but actual magic could fortify one's deception.

Hand magics came next, which focused on different contortions of the fingers and hands into symbols. With certain gestures, Astarte would be able to break stone or part seas. These spells were great for quick conjuring when one needed a speedy solution to sticky problems.

Then came scrawled magics, which dealt with drawn spells constructed from sand or ash. These spells used ruins and glyphs in which precision was essential. They were primarily used to commune with others over great distances or other realms of existence. And they were the first magics Astarte learned that were deadly to even attempt. Any line out of place, or even smudged, could mean doom to the sorcerer. Astarte was forced to learn various languages, both extinct and not yet created. While exhausting, Astarte's mind became filled with more knowledge than any mortal living.

Astarte had great difficulty with what Sariel called thought magics, which dealt with commanding the elements. Thought magic would allow Astarte to fold the elements to her will. With a thought, she could uproot trees, or fold light into a sword, or command the air to leave her opponent's lungs. It was an extremely high form of magic that demanded quieting one's mind and soul. All the other magics required the sorcerer to put themselves into the spell, pour their love, hate, passion into it for it to ignite. Thought magic was the complete opposite. It needed focus and silence. It was a serene magic. Which was exactly Astarte's issue. Astarte had bottled up so much over her life, she found it difficult to find her center.

"Why do I need to do this?" Astarte shouted. "I can already crush boulders with a hand gesture."

Sariel sighed. "And what will you do when your hands are bound? Or cut off?"

Sariel watched her student grow, and as time passed, she saw Astarte was becoming a formidable master. She was satisfied with how her mission was progressing, but time had softened Sariel. She no longer saw Astarte as a pet to train, but as a partner, and eventually, a friend.

One day, Sariel saw Astarte struggling and told her to sit with her. Sweat beaded along Astarte's brow, so Sariel took a wet cloth and patted her face. Her breathing slowed as she felt the coolness touch her skin.

When Astarte had calmed, Sariel said, "Usually, a mortal focuses on just one discipline, spending their years honing their one craft. After about forty years, if they can avoid being stoned by the village, they become moderately okay at it. You have done so much. You should be proud. I know I am."

Astarte's eyes popped open. "Forty years! Then what the hell am I doing? I have no chance of mastering all this shit in my time. I am basically going to be training until I collapse from age. Thanks for choosing me." She spat the last comment as she pulled away from Sariel.

Sariel considered Astarte for a moment. Astarte was a fully blossomed young woman who had, over their time together, reached her physical peak in beauty and strength. Sariel stood up and faced Astarte. "As I have said, I have been sent here to give you all you need. Come close." Astarte inched closer. Sariel smiled, took her hands, and tilted Astarte's face. Sariel leaned in and gave Astarte a long kiss. Gentle at first, but then she pressed harder. Their lips moved together. Sariel lost herself in the moment, but eventually pulled back. Astarte's eyes were still closed. Sariel saw the red shadow on Astarte's lips flame then disappear.

Astarte's eyes opened, and she grinned. "Not that I haven't wanted to do that, but I have a feeling there was more to that kiss. What was that all about?"

Sariel returned the grin. "You said you needed more time. That is what I have given you."

Troubled, Astarte touched her lips. They were still warm. "You mean I am going to live forever?"

Laughing, Sariel answered, "No, I wouldn't do that to you. I made a covenant with you, and in doing, so I bought you time. You will not age, you will not grow frail. Time will not touch your body. You are tied to my fate. And since things like me exist for eons, you will have all the time you need." Sariel turned to start packing up their things.

Astarte continued to touch her lips. "Covenant spells are two-way streets."

Sariel didn't glance back. "True. You have studied well." Astarte continued to look at Sariel. "Like I said, our lives are tied. Meaning you will not age or die so long as I live. But the moment you die, so do I."

Shocked, Astarte asked, "Why would you do that for me?"

Sariel shrugged. "Why not? Where you go, I go. Now, it is just a little more official." Sariel couldn't bring herself to elaborate further. "We will need to leave. I just drew a great deal of magic from my world. Using that much power will draw things I don't want to deal with."

Astarte was elated. Not just for the gift, but for her bond to Sariel. She laughed, and with a thought, ripped the tree that had been sitting on the bank and threw it into the center of the water. "Let them come. I think we can handle them."

Sariel, impressed by the feat, said, "Astarte, you are not invincible. You may not age, but that won't stop a dagger from putting an end to you, and therefore, me."

Astarte nodded that she understood. "Got it. I will help pack."

This was how it was for what would be many years: Astarte would learn from Sariel, and now and then, Sariel would have Astarte enter a village to right a wrong or wrong a right. When Joshua died, there was no clear leader of his tribes, so Sariel took advantage of the power vacuum. She kept increasing Astarte's presence, who performed grander and grander magics, winning the people's hearts and minds. She began as a wandering medicine woman, but the people eventually regarded her as a messenger from the gods.

All this culminated in an unexpected visitor.

***

Astarte could sense the visitor but did not yet know his purpose. She sat on a downed log, the moon's light shining on her skin, still the embodiment of youth and beauty.

From the shadows, a weary and elderly man approached. He moved as if to avoid the pain in his joints, but he was still graceful. His clothes were well made and showed someone who thought well enough of themselves to buy the best. These clues gave her the answer.

"Sagar?" It could only be him. She had kept in contact with her friend over many years, even elongated his lifespan through various potions. However, it had been decades since she'd last laid eyes on him. The man who stood before her looked as old as the dirt, but his eyes were still bright and wild.

Sagar took in Astarte and marveled at her agelessness. "My Mohini." He bowed deeply, even though his joints fought him every inch. Astarte smiled at his formality, grabbed his arm to help him up, and asked him to sit next to her in the moonlight.

Sariel kept her distance. She knew Sagar did not hold her in high esteem and felt she was leading Astarte astray. Sariel had fought with Astarte over the years about her communications with Sagar and always lost. On the other hand, his devotion to Astarte could not be questioned, so Sariel slipped off into the shadows and allowed the old friends to talk.

"Not wanting the old man to keel over in the road, are we?" He laughed at himself, trying to break the tension, but he sat down next to her and tried to find his breath. "I cannot stay long, dear."

"Why? You can stay as long as you wish. Last I heard, you were out of politics and living the good life by the sea in Tel Dor. No need to rush."

"Well, I cannot stay long because I will not be here long." He looked out over the water and breathed in deep. "The great story of Sagar the Bold is almost over. Just one last adventure." Seeing Astarte's confusion, he added, "I stopped taking your little potions a long time ago."

Shocked, she answered, "Why would you do something like that!"

He put his hand on top of hers to calm her. "Because I am exhausted. I feel as if all I am is hide stretched over bones. People are not supposed to live this long. It takes a toll, deep inside. My spirit has been stained."

Astarte didn't understand. By Sariel's design, she did not feel the passage of time like others did. "Maybe there is something I can give you to bring back your vigor, or make you feel younger. I know I can." She stared off, trying to think of the different spells she could use.

Sagar smiled at her frenzied response. She clearly loved him, and that was almost enough to tempt him to stay longer, but finally, he shook his head. "Nope. No more. You have already given me more than enough. I have fathered many children, who have given me countless grandchildren, who I have now outlived. So much joy and so much heartache. No more." His words were not weak, but bold and final. Astarte knew she would not be changing his mind. "I know you have seen more full moons than any living being now walking. But I feel you still don't understand some things that even the simplest of people know. You don't know what it is to give life. See it blossom, and see it wilt. I will live forever in my progeny. I no longer have to breathe to live on. This, you can't understand. You're still a child, doing your friend's bidding. You have let Sariel's goals become your goals, and that creature has touted you around the world, performing your tricks, disrupting peace, causing wars, breaking marriages. You have allowed her ambition to be your ambition, and you never took any time to just be human."

Even though his tone was grandfatherly, the words stung hard. He had made this argument before when he'd tried to romance her away. But this wasn't like that. This was his last statement to her, she knew that. Therefore, it struck deeper than it ever had before.

He took his hand and cupped her face. "Calm yourself. I don't expect you to change your path right now. Just something to think about when you reminisce about me. For now, you have cast your stones, and I have mine. Let's not waste our time retreading lost arguments. I have come to advise you and Sariel one last time."

Kissing his fingers, she took his hand in hers. "Then advise away, Sagar the Bold." She gave him a teasing look. "Who calls you that?"

"The list is far too long," Sagar said with a sense of pride.

Sariel came out of the shadows and gave Sagar a nod, which he returned.

"I am sorry some of this information is very late. Some time ago, a prophet named Samuel came to this land. He told the people they were being led astray by a false witch god," Sagar looked at Astarte, "who performed false miracles and double-dealt god's children. God asked this Samuel to spend his days searching out a new king and to root out this witch from his land. Even though Samuel has since died, he already poisoned the people against you."

Astarte nodded. "I knew some of this. I remember the time of the judges randomly passing orders and decrees. In the end, many of them fell to me." She gave Sariel a smile. "I am also aware Saul was named king, I am assuming by this Samuel. I guess that makes sense since Saul has been a total prick when it comes to…well, my type of people. It is news to me that I was named a witch god. Cool title." Astarte sounded flippant, but it was to mask the unease of being found out.

Sagar shook his head. "They don't know your name. Well, at least not your true name. Some call you Moloch. Some call you Herrana, which makes me smile. Amazing how a name that was cursed so many years ago is still on people's tongues. But they know for whom they seek."

"Pity," Astarte said as she stretched her back. She knew she had outgrown her little part of the world and would one day be forced to leave. While Astarte could lay waste to an army, it was best if she worked from the shadows.

"All is not lost." Sagar took a long drink from a skin he had carried with him. "Saul has lost favor with his people. He has grown jealous and petty as his power has grown. Yes, he is killing witches and warlocks left and right, but most of them are innocent. The people know he is coming unhinged. Worse still, he knows his time is limited, making him very dangerous."

Astarte smiled. "I have been sending little presents to him in the form of night terrors. Simple incantation, really. They creep into his bedchamber and appear as demons, telling him to kill himself. I am glad they are working."

"Well, you may have broken him. He is attempting to seek answers from the dead." Astarte and Sariel glanced at each other. Joshua had forbidden any dealings with necromancy. Even uttering the word was reason enough to be killed in the most horrible of ways. If Saul, the first king anointed by the god of Joshua, went through with his plan, he would certainly dirty his soul, which would tip the scales nicely for the Thirteenth Gate.

Sariel, excited, asked, "How do you know this?"

Not taking his eyes off Astarte, Sagar responded, "Wanting to talk to the dead is one thing, but finding someone who can, especially discreetly, is another. Over the years, there has been some rumor that I have connections to a darker side of power. No direct accusations, Joshua's protection ensured that. But when he died, I probably fostered these rumors. It kept trouble from looking my way. But if someone wants to reach out to that side of the world, I am still the man they seek."

"And you give me this information, why? Have I ever claimed to know how to raise the dead? Have you ever seen me raise the dead?" scoffed Astarte. Over the years, she had told much to Sagar, and he had given counsel. However, some of the darker arts she had perfected she kept secret from him. He thought the world of her, and she didn't want to dim that perception.

Sagar knew better but played along with his friend. "I just thought you may be able to help him out. Win his favor. Make yourself indispensable to him, then you will have nothing to fear from him or his line. I want my last act to ensure your safety. I know you have the power, why not use it to help him for your own good?"

Astarte liked the sentiment, but thought Sagar was being too hopeful. Astarte had seen glimpses of the future, and Saul's line didn't have much more part to play in it. But Sagar's optimism was from a place of love, so she would not ridicule that.

"Thank you for your counsel, Sagar. Give me a moment." She got up and pulled Sariel with her. It was hard to contain their excitement, but Sariel wanted to remain professional in front of Sagar. They spoke for a moment, then Astarte turned to Sagar. "Please get word to King Saul that I will assist him. Please tell him to meet with me in Endor."

Sagar's eyebrows lifted. "Why so far south?"

"I want some place the Israelites have not conquered. A neutral place. Also, being in the shadow of Mount Tabor, I can draw upon some forces that don't exist in other places."

She left unsaid it was also near the place Saul would meet his end. She wanted to make sure he did this deed very close to his demise, sealing his fate.

CHAPTER 10

Selected excerpts from the unpublished manuscript: <u>A Brave New Bible</u> from Professor Angela Chiseler, PhD in Religious Studies and Theology.

Genesis 4: 1-9:

Kane was Adam's first-born son. Well, that was what Adam had thought, since Eve had told him it was so and Adam had yet to learn the concept of deception. In actuality, Kane was the child of Eve and one of God's angels, making Kane what was known as a Nephilim, a creature of great strength, the creation of which God had expressly forbidden. It wasn't until Kane was grown that Adam noticed he was not of his seed. Adam resented Eve for the fall, and for her infidelity, but took his anger out on Kane, as weak men are apt do to.

Abel, in contrast, was of Adam and Eve, and he'd grown righteous with Adam's loving tutelage. Everything Abel did drew God's praise. Everything Kane did disgraced God.

Frustrated he could find no favor, Kane's heart grew dark and twisted. Denied the love of a father and the love of his God, Kane took his brother out into the field and killed him in a jealous rage. Blind to the fact that it was his actions that had twisted Kane, God still punished Kane and set him apart from the race of man.

First Samuel 28:3-20:

As stated before, Saul was a complete failure as a king. The people turned on him. His army turned on him. His god turned on him. Saul discovered that Samuel the prophet had anointed David the new king, and therefore tried to capture David, but he even failed at this. David fled to the land of Gibeon to seek refuge with the Priests of Nob. He was given the sword of Goliath for his own protection.

When Saul tracked David to Gibeon, he was already gone. Saul had every priest killed for sheltering David. The problem was Gibeon had been given God's protection by Joshua, and Saul's massacre of Gibeon was an ultimate act of treachery. At this moment, Saul was lost.

Saul, while a terrible king, was not a fool. He knew he was damned, so he felt had nothing else to lose by seeking the dark magics of the very witches he had sought to slaughter. He wished to know his next move in order to protect his life and the life of his line. Saul knew that by seeking a necromancer, he would forfeit the right to enter God's kingdom. But living and damned was better than dead and damned.

***

Astarte glared at her face in the water of the basin. She could see by her reflection her face was pockmarked and withered. Her stringy, broken gray hair hung lifelessly. The charm had worked, but the effect was unsettling. By conjuring what her face would look like if she hadn't been touched by Sariel, she added power and realism to the charm, but it unnerved her. She shook her head and told herself it wasn't for much longer.

Reports that Saul's troops were amassing nearby had reached the unassuming hamlet of Endor yesterday. It wouldn't be much longer before she had a visitor.

Necromancy was one of the harder and higher forms of magics. Raising the dead was a simple incantation even some children with a scrying board could muster. The trick was to command the dead, make them talk, and ultimately force them back into the void. That took practice and excessive talent. A complex combination of hand, scrawled, and thought magics.

***

Over the past weeks, Sariel had instructed Astarte on some of the finer points. In the past, Sariel wouldn't allow her to delve too long to avoid detection.

"Messing with the dead causes problems for the Continuance. Trying to communicate with the dead, or worse still, pulling a soul, unbalances, causes irregularities. Death is supposed to be a one-way path. Reversing course is noticed quickly and is summarily dealt with."

Astarte began with only souls of those Sariel deemed particularly detestable. When asked why only the evil were picked, all Sariel would say was any irregularities may not have been noticed as quickly. Sariel never mentioned Dokiel and her hope of him assisting Astarte with pulling souls from the Thirteenth Gate.

For weeks, Astarte would raise a rapist, or murderer, and practice asking questions. She would attempt to make the proper runes in the sand, say the proper incantations, and make the appropriate hand gestures. Only a few times she failed in these first steps. If it had not been for Sariel looking over her, she could have lost her soul to the spell. Astarte began to be more successful with her raisings but always found the conversations were dull in nature, since these people knew nothing she wanted to know. However, putting them back in the void was always a struggle. The dead fought her at every turn, desperate to pierce through to the world of the living. Mostly, though, Astarte put them back in short order. Practice made perfect.

The real problem with necromancy was to perform the spell correctly, the witch had to offer some of her power to the void. That meant, at the point Astarte would try to put the dead back, they would have command of some of her powers. Thankfully, none of these evil souls had the talent to really use it against her. If things got too sticky, Astarte could call upon the guardians of the Thirteenth Gate, but that would put a target on her from the Continuance.

The last lesson, Astarte was to raise a soul with great influence, a kinslayer named Kane. Sariel triple checked all the wards and prepared them to leave for Endor right after the raising, knowing the power Astarte would have to use to meddle with the Continuance would be noticed.

Kane was raised without problem. He was eager to talk to Astarte, who asked basic questions.

"My life sucked," was a common statement he would make. He would go on about all the work he did, how hard he toiled, and how, at the end of each day, his father showered only his brother with praise, while he got nothing. Every now and then, Kane would drift off topic. When Astarte would ask about the murder of his brother, she found he was unwilling to talk about it.

"You must break him to your will," said Sariel. Astarte

nodded, and with some incantations and hand gestures, Kane began wailing in pain. He begged for her to stop and said he would answer any question. Just as Sariel had taught her, Astarte continued torture for just a moment longer than she'd needed. Kane needed to understand he was on her leash and she stopped when she wanted to.

He finally collapsed, the pain receding.

Astarte wasn't wholly cruel, so she allowed him a moment of peace, then asked sweetly, "Please tell me about who you killed."

"I had a half-brother, and my stepfather favored him for his talents and his gifts, leaving me alone and in the dark for so long. Nothing I did bought me any favor. I was only a beast of burden, made to break my back and skin." Kane looked at Sariel and squinted his eyes for a better look. The pain came back, slamming his attention back to Astarte. "I pleaded with my real father for help, and he answered me. Told me to kill my brother. I took a stone and asked my brother to join me by a stream. I coaxed him there with a promise to make peace between us. There, at the river, I finally gained my peace. I walked back from the river, my brother did not."

Sariel was puzzled by Kane's statement about his real father. She whispered into Astarte's ear, and she nodded. "Tell me your father's name." Astarte slammed Kane with even more pain to show she had no intention in hearing his delays.

Struggling through the pain, Kane screamed out, "Malhamash."

Just the sound of the name tore through Sariel. "Holy shit." She turned to Astarte. "Shut it down. Shut it down now!"

Astarte didn't know why, but she had never heard Sariel so frightened. She began the process of putting Kane back. Feeling the pull, Kane fought. He began some incantations

Astarte hadn't heard before, in a tongue that hadn't existed since before the Anunnaki flood. Kane began rolling his hands over and over, then threw them out. Astarte was thrown back and landed face first in the dirt. He moved toward the edge of the glyphs written on the ground.

Astarte shook herself free from whatever spell she had been hit with and looked up to see a warp in reality, a smear in the world. Colors flared and swirled and encircled Kane as he shouted more magics into the din.

Sariel stood, transfixed at the lights, and understood he was on the verge of breaking through. Inwardly, she chastised herself for suggesting Kane. Her ignorance might have doomed them all. She ran over to Astarte and picked her up from the ground. Sariel knew the only way to survive this night was through Astarte. "Concentrate. You have to do this. You brought him forth, it is up to you to put him back."

Blood poured from Astarte's ears and nose, but she shook off her daze and stood. Kane had breached the wall of her drawn spell. She only had moments left before he would be set free upon the world.

With her left arm aloft, she pointed to Kane with her right hand. Astarte dug deep and said, "I call you, Typhon. Someone is escaping your charge. Take him back!" Light erupted between her left fingers, and a hum overtook the noise being made by the warp. "Kane! I throw you back to the pit!"

Kane was momentarily stopped. He let out a howl as a snake-like appendage wrapped around him and dragged him back into the center of the glyphs and through the warp. Astarte watched as Typhon continued to wrap himself around Kane, squeezing like a constrictor around its prey. Kane's bones were crushed and his lungs exploded, which thankfully ended his shrieks. Typhon dragged Kane back into the earth, pulverizing him along the way.

All sounds had ended, and Astarte and Sariel were left in silence.

Sariel gave them only a moment to catch their breath. "We must move. NOW!" Calling one of the keepers of the Gate would bring them visitors they could not hope to defeat.

A handful of hours later, Sariel had stopped looking behind them. She hoped Dokiel was staying true to his word and, at the very least, buying them enough time to get away. Seeing no one coming, she relaxed. "It was my fault," Sariel said apologetically.

"How? I fucked up. He was strong, and I lost focus."

"If I would have known Kane was a Nephilim, I would have never let you call him."

"So, Malhamash? His father?"

"Yes, he is like me, but . . ." Sariel trailed off, trying to find the right words. "Let's just say he is like me, but higher ranking. By a thousand. He is the leader of the Memitim." She whispered the last word.

Astarte hadn't heard the term before. "Who are they?"

Sariel gave one last look behind, just to make sure. "They are Existence's knife. When someone or something is deemed anathema to Existence, there are many ways they can be dealt with. The Memitim are reserved for truly special jobs. It is said they cannot be defeated, and if they ever were defeated, Existence itself would rip apart. They are merciless. If they find you, they do not explain themselves, and there is no pleading with them. They come. You die. They leave."

Astarte felt this was not a subject Sariel felt comfortable discussing, but she couldn't help to ask one more question. "Have you ever seen them work?"

Sariel didn't blanch at the question, but merely glanced

up at the night sky. "Well, we have a long way to go to Endor. I will tell you the story of Mididi and Malhamash and his Memitim."

***

Astarte had cast her glamour and was still looking at herself in the water, marveling at what was or what should be.

"I want to give you something." Sariel's voice startled her out of her thoughts.

Astarte peered up at her companion, who held out a small scroll. "What is it?"

"A gift."

Astarte took the scroll and unrolled it. "It seems like a potion of some sort. Juniper, storax," Astarte continued to read, in silence. "What is this for?"

Sariel's face was determined. "It is an elixir that I wanted you to be able to make if I am not around. You are very talented in your own right, but if we get separated, that potion will keep your strength at its apex until we meet back up. Understand?"

Astarte frowned. "Are my powers tied to you?"

Sariel laughed and said, "I wouldn't phrase it like that. All that you do comes from you. However, with my presence, I can boost your strength. You can do earthshattering magic. Together, we can shatter realms. Understand?"

Astarte nodded and gave a small smile at the thought of them tied together. Sariel pulled out a small box from under her robes and handed it to her. Astarte took the box without asking what it was.

Inspecting it, she saw a black seal had been placed on it, but before she could inspect the symbols, they vanished, allowing her access to the contents. Opening the box, she saw a ring.

"What is this for?" Astarte said, confused. "You have given me much. Why this now?"

"It isn't from me. It is a gift from the one who sent me. He felt at the right time, you would need this. Obviously, the seal being broken, I was right on the timing."

Astarte took the ring out of the box and held it in her hand. It was a burnished silvery metal that seemed to capture the surrounding light. The top of the ring had been flattened and etched with designs. Astarte squinted and studied the ring. She had no intention of putting the ring on before she understood its nature.

She said to Sariel, "I see a hexagram in the center and rays emitting from the star. It's an odd kind of symbol"

Sariel didn't need to see the ring to know what type of star she was seeing. "It is identical to the symbol on the Thirteenth Gate. Where I am from. It is called a unicursal hexagram."

Astarte looked closer and saw runes and read them to herself. Some glyphs were common summoning spells and power intensifiers. She read more. Her eyes became wide. Some of the symbols she recognized as the language of the wicked. Putting the words together, the ring was making various demands. She shook her head. "This doesn't make sense. This isn't possible."

Seeing Astarte's eyes widen, Sariel dryly stated, "It will give you more control over the dead and the damned."

"It says the wearer has control over the Thirteenth Gate." Astarte glanced up at Sariel, trying to understand how such a small item could control otherworldly forces.

"Like I said, you will have absolute control of the dead

who have been cast away. You can call upon certain beings to assist you. Like Typhon. He will come to the ring, not because you ask or because he wants to. He will come because you command it."

The thought of the power blew Astarte away. Instinctively, she wanted bury it a mile deep into the ground and flee, but she was also too frightened to let it go. "How can this be? What is it made of?" The ring, still featherlight, was ice in her hand. So cold, it began to burn.

"I have already told you that when we first shut the Gates to mortals, knowledge of certain things was cut off from you. We also withdrew things that were, at one time, available to you. Knowledge of magic and the ability to commune with other realms were just a few things that were taken. Other things were more practical, more material. One of those substances you now hold in your hand. The Greeks called it adamant, but that is just one of its names."

"Why was it taken away from mortals?" Astarte was personally offended when she learned more and more of what has been denied her by Existence.

"Because adamant can harness powers from other realms, behind other Gates. It is most useful in commanding the…" Sariel tried to explain it but hated using mortal terms, "I guess you could say the darker sides of existence. This ring specifically draws its power from the Thirteenth Gate itself. Other materials, like orichalcum, come from the First Gate."

Astarte gazed at the ring again, thinking of the implications. Then she remembered her battle with Kane and how she'd almost lost it all. Her eyes narrowed. "Why are you just giving me this now?"

Sariel had expected this question. "Well, first, the seals hadn't broken until now, so don't go off yelling at me."

Astarte continued. "But you knew what was in the box."

Sariel sheepishly grinned. "Yes."

"Then why haven't you mentioned it before now? Something I could have at least prepared for. Why spring it on me like this?"

Sariel chose her words carefully. "It does more than help with the dead. It also controls demons. Like me."

Astarte squinted. "And you couldn't stand the thought of some mortal having control over you, could you? I don't see why. You have always done anything I want. What would this ring change?"

Sariel quickly said, "Nothing. And everything. Giving a mortal power over demons is not something that should be done lightly. And it wasn't my idea. I think you can accomplish all your goals without the damn thing, but as I have said, it wasn't my decision. I was to give it to you at the right time. I have taught you all I can. I want you to do wondrous and terrible things on your own two feet. Don't rely on the ring. It's a wonderful tool, but it isn't a replacement for your mind."

Astarte had heard these comments before and gave her a sidelong glance. "I have a feeling there is more to it than that."

Sariel turned away. "I thought about telling you about it earlier on. But as time has gone by, and we have grown close, I wanted more time with just you." Seeing that Astarte didn't see where she was going, Sariel continued. "The ring will change you. It will open up parts of your mind, connect you to other realms. It will make you a stronger, more formidable person, but I fell in love with the person you are, and I just wanted to have a few more moments with you. I don't see you as my student, but as my equal. Once you put that ring on, you're my master. It was foolish of me. Selfish. Especially in light of that Kane business. Forgive me. But know this, ring or not, I will do anything for you. That will not change."

Astarte saw for the first time how deeply Sariel felt for her and was moved. She embraced Sariel and gave her a long kiss. "Like you said, the ring is just a tool. It will not change how I feel for you."

"How we feel for each other. Even if you look like that." Sariel added with a smile. Astarte remembered the glamour spell was in place, making her appear like an old crone of Endor. She laughed and gave her another kiss. She stood back and slipped the ring on her finger. Cold as death at first, the sensation spread throughout her entire body. Astarte could feel the cold enter her head, and it stayed there, like an icy hand had grabbed her brain. From that spot, the ring gave her a quick education in the manner and nature of the Thirteenth Gate, the dead, and demons. Images flooded her mind. Beasts of the pit, princes of the underworld. Names. Places. Secrets. The information overwhelmed her. She went down on her knees, tears of blood streaking her haggard face.

At that moment, one of her wind chimes sounded outside the cave. "They have arrived," said Sariel. She moved to Astarte and placed her hand on her face. "Make me proud."

Astarte nodded and walked out of the cave into the night air.

CHAPTER 11

Quickly, her eyes adjusted, and she saw a hooded man approach. He glanced around quickly before speaking, ensuring there was no one about. "Crone, I need you tonight," he pleaded.

It was clear to Astarte that Saul did not want to be identified, but she had already decided they would be playing this game by her rules.

"My king! What can a wretch like me do for one as high and lofty as you?" Identifying him disturbed Saul. He glanced around again, seeing again if they were alone. "Have no fear," Astarte reassured, "I have seen you coming in my dreams and have prepared a place for you. We will not be bothered by unwanted eyes. It is not as if anyone dare to intrude upon me on a regular day anyway." She gave her best old woman raspy laugh, hoping it didn't come off cartoonish.

"I need your services," Saul said in a hushed tone.

"Your highness, someone like you does not visit someone like me just for giggles. I know there is something you want, so speak plainly to an old woman."

Saul was not used to being spoken to as if he were a mere child. "I need to speak to the dead. I need their guidance. There is going to be a great battle tomorrow, and I feel like all will be lost."

"Well," Astarte said slowly, "have you lost your way, my lord?" She did not wait for him to respond. "As I hear it, even asking me to do this destroys your covenant with your god. Does it not?"

Saul got heated and stammered out, "Just do as I command or…or…I will strike you down." He even heard how hollow his threat had sounded, but he doubled down. "I may be many things, but I will not let a festering sore like you even reference my Lord and my God. I still believe in Him and not your heathen idols." Some of the fire extinguished from his voice. "But I am at my wit's end."

Feigning his insult had cut her, she waved him off and bid him to join her around the circle she had already drawn. All she needed was for Saul to commit to a summoning. Didn't matter who, didn't matter what they said. The act of Saul summoning the dead would be enough to seal his ultimate fate and take another player off the board. She needed to sell it. This was the reason for all the theatrics.

"Your way forward is blocked, you say?" She spun around with her hand in the air. "Spirits speak loud and true today. Assist my king. Help open his path, guide him forward. Do not let him perish on the side of the road, wailing, covered in sores, moaning like a wild animal, blinded by ignorance." Saul was captivated by the images she conjured. He had felt cast aside. As if his time was already over. Of course, Astarte knew this. "Do not pass him over. He is still worthy. Help him. I beseech you."

With another flourish, a gray mist and light enveloped the space above the circle. She had opened the door. Now, she just needed him to give her a name.

"King." She glared at Saul. "Say the name to be brought forward and throw a sacrifice into the mist."

Saul hesitated. "What type of sacrifice?"

Astarte didn't care. It really didn't matter. "Something the dead had owned would be ideal. Call anyone you trust. Your father or brother perhaps?"

Saul considered her words. He pulled a lock of hair from his pocket. He had decided and doomed his soul at the same time. "There is only one I would call to advise me. I want to speak to Samuel." He tossed the hair into the mist.

"Samuel!" she commanded. "Come forth and give counsel." Astarte smiled as the gray mist swirled and the familiar warp formed. Her job was complete. All she needed to do was play this out.

It took her a minute to remember what Sagar had said about a prophet named Samuel.

"Oh shit!" she whispered as a fully formed being emerged from the gray and twisting warp. There was no pain on his face. Unlike the others she had brought forth, he seemed quite confident. And also filled with rage.

Samuel glanced at her only for a moment and turned to Saul. "I knew it. You faithless pig." Samuel spat on the ground in front of Saul as he reeled back. "You were a failure in life. Now, you are a failure in death." Saul went to his knees and pleaded for mercy. "You will get no mercy. Finally, tomorrow, during the battle, you will be slain by your own troops. Cut down like a sick dog. They will deliver your body to the enemy, who will defile it for the next seven years." The warp rose higher, and Samuel appeared as a giant contained in the circle. "Run, cur!" As he said this, flames erupted from inside the warp and lashed out beyond the circle, just barely licking Saul's face.

Saul leapt up and ran off wailing. He was off to meet his fate, knowing all hope was lost.

Astarte looked anxiously at Samuel. She was in full control, but it was wise to approach new situations carefully.

"So, now you're posing as an old hag witch in Endor?" Samuel examined the small cave behind her and at the rest of his surroundings. "This is some life you lead, you nasty bitch. Traveling from hut to hut. Living out of cracks in the earth and off the sorrow of your fellow man."

"Spare me your drivel." She rolled her eyes. "I am truly free. And I set others free, and I always will." She turned to Samuel, making sure he was paying attention. "You know it to be true."

Samuel snapped his fingers, and Astarte's young features returned. "I see you. What did you have to give up for your powers? For your long life?"

"Nothing. I obey no one, nor have arbitrary rules made up by some old fools. I do not kneel to some golden box in the desert."

Samuel hissed and shook against what was confining him in the circle.

Astarte laughed. "Will you go back willingly, or do I need to coax you?" She sent a ribbon of pain through Samuel. It did not register on his face.

"I am not some simple hood or rapist. You have no idea who or what you have raised. I am a prophet of the one Lord. If you had trouble with Kane, you will find me much more vexing." He shot his hand out and pierced the gray mist, hitting the border of the circle.

Astarte, though confident, wanted to end this night and get back to Sariel and pick up where their conversation had started, so she began the dismissal chants. However, that confidence faltered slightly when she watched Samuel emerge from the mist, pounding against the invisible barrier. The wind began to howl around them as she worked. She strained with the effort of the spells as she watched him become whole. Samuel inspected the glyphs of the circle, shut his eyes, and started his own chant. Astarte could hear his words over the din, but she did not recognize the language. Her eyes got wide when the glyphs began to change. A mark here, a downstroke there. Samuel was altering the runes.

Astarte saw shimmers in the barrier. It was failing. She knew she had to act quickly. "I call you, Typ—" She was stopped before she could finish. Samuel was holding his hand out as if to strangle her. Air became harder and harder to draw, thick like porridge in her mouth. She tried to scream out, but only a small wheeze escaped.

Samuel smiled. "So proud. So haughty. Someone has taught you some simple tricks, but it wasn't enough. Now look at you. Writhing on the ground. Alone. No one to hear your last breath."

Astarte tore at her throat, trying to remember any counter spell. The air pushed down the back of her mouth and began to go down her throat. She feared what would happen once it reached her lungs, but she had a pretty good idea. This was intensely powerful thought magic, but there was something different about it. It had a different flavor. Nothing she had dabbled in herself. Dazed, she saw Samuel emerge from the circle, still holding his hand toward her.

"This is the judgement I will set before you." Samuel stepped forward from the circle and breathed deep. "Thou shalt not suffer a witch to live."

Astarte squeezed her eyes shut. She wanted to deny him the pleasure of seeing the light die in them. She tried to will her throat to stop the progression of air, but it was making its way down no matter what protest her body made.

And then, she was breathing again. The hot, deadly air evaporated, and cool air flooded her lungs. She sputtered and coughed as she tried to regain herself. Her eyes popped open, and she took in the new scene. Sariel had put herself in between Astarte and Samuel, hurling various magical blasts and bolts of all different forms. Samuel blocked many, but the few that landed knocked him severely. Sariel was like a wild animal, furiously firing off all types of conjurings. Samuel had escaped the circle, but Sariel's onslaught was pushing him back into it.

"Get up and help me! The runes!" Sariel shouted, but was cut off as Samuel responded to the attack with a volley of repeated blasts. Since Astarte had raised him, Samuel was still channeling her magic. Coupled with his own, he was almost unbeatable.

Astarte understood in an instant. "You got it." Astarte got up and began her work. She began the hand gestures coupled with the incantations, and slowly, the runes Samuel had changed reverted to their original place. Each one locked back into place with a fiery glow.

Sariel redoubled her efforts in an attempt to keep Samuel's attention on her. Seeing her, Samuel screamed, "So, you're the succubus behind this little whelp." He threw his hands, and a slice of light rent the darkness of the night. It slammed into Sariel, who was thrown down in a heap. "I will end you here and now, and maybe erase some of the damage you have wrought through your little abomination." Sariel laid on the ground motionless.

"Get up!" shouted Astarte, but she saw no movement. All she could see was Sariel trying to mouth words, but there was no sound.

Samuel threw his hands out again, bringing another

beam of light down upon Sariel. Before it could hit her, she disappeared.

At the same time, a loud crack emitted, and Samuel looked around at Astarte. She and the air around her glowed in an otherworldly black and green. Her hair floated around her like a halo. The ring on her finger shown forth in a blinding, horrible white light, washing away all of her color. She was like magnesium set afire. It was so intense, it would blind the dead. Samuel rocked back and covered his face.

A shout came from Astarte, "I order you restored. Destroy him," she said without speaking, willing it. Samuel blinked his vision back, realizing he had backed into someone. Turning, he was seized by a fully regenerated, restored, and repowered Sariel. Quickly, she wrapped her arm around Samuel's neck and squeezed. He gasped, but still would not be budged back into the circle. They struggled against each other, but neither would budge. Sariel knew Existence wanted Samuel to win. He was a prophet from his god and would not be easily defeated. Sariel knew this stalemate could not last.

"Call out to the Gate! Do it now!" Sariel shouted over the struggle.

Hearing this, Astarte went to her knees and tried to find her center, a calm place to focus her power. The ring hummed and shone once more as she called forth demons from the Thirteenth Gate. It was a general call for help. And without hesitation, they answered. They emerged from the shadows. In this realm, they had no choice but to obey Astarte. She was their master.

Creatures of all forms, twisted and tortured, surrounded Samuel and Sariel. They sprung up all around and tore at him. He fought back as Sariel maintained her stranglehold. The smell of the Thirteenth Gate was so heavy,

Samuel recoiled at it. He knew he was outmatched, but he gritted his teeth and continued to fight back. Sariel held him fast. Finally, a winged demon Samuel recognized emerged and smiled at the prophet. Samuel opened his mouth in terror and tried to ask his god for his mercy and power, but before even the slightest of sounds could escape, one demon shoved himself into Samuel's mouth, breaking his jaw loose from his skull. Sariel released him as he staggered back into the circle, the various demons dragging his broken form along with them.

Sariel gazed at Astarte in awe. Astarte, in full control of the ring, radiated power. It danced in her eyes.

In that moment, Samuel summoned the last of his energy and the last of Astarte's magics. He threw himself forward, grabbed Sariel, and pulled her back into the circle and the warp with him. The warp folded into itself, and with a loud snap, all the creatures, including Samuel and Sariel, vanished.

With the task accomplished, the ring dimmed.

The silence pushed in on her from all sides. She kept blinking, trying to unsee what had just happened. She crumpled to the ground and began to cry. For the first time in many years, Astarte was alone.

CHAPTER 12

Santa Muerte enjoyed October. Not that time really mattered, but she found the entreaties for her help (that she rarely answered) always increased this time of year. She felt it was always nice to be remembered and wanted. Even though she hated to admit it, her rag-tag group of believers was what kept her going.

She spent most of her time in the gray void. It kept her under the radar. Not that she was a direct threat to Existence, but she knew Existence was as fickle as a small child and it could always change its mind at a moment. It was in her interest not to be exposed.

It would be a mistake, though, to assume that since she kept her head down she therefore was out of the loop. Not by a longshot. After eons of existing, she had found little loopholes that allowed her to listen to the "goings-on," as they say. She loved being in the know. It kept her young, so to speak.

Santa Muerte was the name she went by these days, but in the beginning, her worshipers called her the Queen of Mictian. Her idols had been littered throughout the land. Her people had given her burnt offerings and prayers, and therefore, power. But that had all been before the conquistadors. Those strange looking men in their metal suits had come and thrown down her temples. Scattered her believers. They'd massacred with European efficiency. Even though it had been her people they were cutting down, she was impressed with the men from faraway lands. She knew no matter what the Spaniards did, no matter how many they killed or how many towns they burned, she would survive. Yes, she was a goddess, but also a concept, an idea. It was nearly impossible to kill an idea, especially one that had been ingrained in the mind. She lived through the Spanish Conquest, but just barely. The loss of so many believers made her weak. They were cast out into the wilderness of the rainforest. Shivering in their little huts. But even then, when they had no real reason to, they prayed to her. They kept her alive. But she couldn't thrive. If it had gone on for much longer, she would have eventually gone the way of other legends and gods: a spooky story to tell children and nothing else. At the time, she'd known her days were numbered.

But then, the Roman Church did what it always did with unwanted religions and relics: they adopted her. The Pope's "if you can't beat them, join them" approach had always worked for mother church. The tactic had been used for centuries for things like Easter bunnies and Yule logs. Why not for a washed-up goddess? This cobbling together of old and new world faiths gave birth to the new, and very much improved, Santa Muerte. An added bonus, because her affiliation was mottled at best, some rules laid down by the Rekindling held little sway over her. She had not been not shoved behind one of the Gates but was rather overlooked and allowed to roam the void, and maybe reap a soul or two every now and then.

On this particular day in October, as Santa Muerte drifted through the void, listening intently, she heard some very interesting prayers coming from New Mexico. What was interesting was they all seemed to ask for the same thing, which wasn't typical. She typically kept to old Mexico, but her popularity had been growing as of late, spreading within the dark underbelly of society. She smiled to herself thinking about desperate mortals and their silly little requests.

She listened very hard and concentrated on the strongest voice. It came in soft and scared but bold. Desperate. And from a surprising source. Santa Muerte could have been called the patron saint of the darker side of mortals. Drug dealers, gang leaders, and their families. People who were cornered and deserved to be cornered. But she always listened. She was a beggar, and beggars couldn't be choosers.

But this time, the prayer wasn't coming from a tattooed felon, but rather a man named Father Tomas Florez.

"Dearest Santa Muerte, all is lost. I have made my prayers to all the saints and angels in heaven, and nothing has happened. My church, the people, have all scattered. A darkness has entered our parish and stained our faith. No matter what I do, nothing seems to free us from this sacrilege."

His words were sweet. She could hear his tongue was used to Latin prayers or chanting the rosery. This made his prayer very tempting. Santa Muerte had no problem with temptation. Excitedly, she opened a window in the grey void and peered in at this man who was so desperate. What she saw was a gray-haired man in his fifties, slightly drunk, alone in a bar. His collar was still on, but it looked as if he had worn the same clothes for days.

"I ask you now, holy death, if this is going to be my church's ending, I am pulling out all stops. Please, intercede. I invite you." The priest stopped his prayer and sobbed into his drink.

Santa Muerte considered his appeal. Not the best. No

offerings or sacrifice. Typically, she avoided drunken requests (if she didn't, she'd never get any rest). But there was something intriguing here. She backed up and listened to more people, and a common thread emerged. From what she gathered, it was obvious someone (or thing) had performed a desecration. Specifically, a desecration of Mission San Miguel. That didn't bother her. She, herself, had fouled many holy relics in her time. It was not knowing who was the cause that piqued her interest. Especially since it was in her stomping grounds.

It had been ages since she'd had a mystery in her part of the world that would demand further investigation. Of course, not knowing what she was up against could mean her undoing. She was mighty, but not all powerful. She looked back at the funny little priest and weighed her options. She could just go about her day and stay in the grey, or have a little fun? She thought, *oh what the hell. Why not?* Of course, the reaping of a priest could do her some good.

She emerged from the gray void, right there in the bar, but only visible to Father Florez. She had checked first, of course. No need to make a spectacle of herself. It was late, and most of the patrons were already home in bed. One was sleeping it off in a jail cell. The barkeep was otherwise occupied. The priest was nearly alone. Obviously, this priest had nowhere else to go. But it was important to make the right entrance. Nothing too splashy, but just the right amount.

Father Florez looked up into Santa Muerte's eyes, and at once, he was stricken. She reached out her skeletal hand and held his face, stopping him from making any sound.

"You asked for my assistance. Why are you so shocked to see me?" She feigned being hurt. "Don't try to speak, just focus on my eyes." Father Florez gazed into empty sockets that glowed blue. "I will do what you ask. I will rid you of whatever has blasphemed your little building. Then all your sheep will come back. Yes?" Father Florez made a slight gulping sound. "But I will need something from you to move a little more freely."

Fear exploded in his face.

"Ah-ah-ah," she said, shaking one finger. "Remember, you said, 'I invite you.' This, my good little man, is the price of admission."

The blue glow intensified.

At the other end of the bar, Hector, the bartender, saw nothing seemed that out of sorts. Last call had been announced, but it was now just a matter of babysitting Tomas at the end of the bar, which he had no problem doing. He knew Tomas was a good man, just having a hard time of it right now. Nothing he hadn't heard before, but he never liked to see his friends in such anguish. Which was why he was pouring Tomas's drinks from the top shelf.

He had finished cleaning the bar and heard the crash. He watched as the stool Tomas had been sitting on fell to the ground and Tomas's lifeless body crumbled to the floor.

Santa Muerte, fully emerged from the gray, watched as Hector tried to revive Father Florez. She watched as Hector attempted some sort of sloppy resuscitation. Failing that, he fumbled for his phone to make a call. She turned and started toward the door but had a second thought. If this was going to be her last hurrah, why not go out with a bang?

"Rest easy, Hector," she said to the bartender. He looked up at the voice and saw the robed skeleton towering over him. "Tomas is gone now. Would you like to know where?" Smiling, she saw Hector shake his head. "I think you will like it. Trust me, you won't even know you're dead. You just keep going on. That's the point, we just keep going." With that, a scythe appeared, and in a blink, Hector was cut down and fell next to his friend.

Santa Muerte shuddered as the second soul passed through her to the Continuance. "Thrilling." She then turned out of the bar. There was a mystery to solve.

CHAPTER 13

It took Astarte the better part of a month to completely desecrate Mission San Miguel. The effort had nearly killed her. The Spanish priests who'd put down the original wards had also used relics of the local native tribe of Tlaxcalans. Combining both faiths made for formidable spells.

Sagar had helped with some of the preparations, but the heavy lifting (as it were) had been left up to her. The faster she worked, the faster she could put up her own wards and stave off any Memitim hunting her down. Her speed had paid off. By the last day of October, Mission San Miguel had been completely desecrated and primed for her dark work.

On that night, Astarte rested in one of the abandoned pews. The moment her desecration began, the members of the church could feel it deep in their bones. It would manifest as a chill up the spine or an odd smell, and from there, grow. People started to skip mass and other services. A couple of weddings were cancelled. Funerals were held at the mortuaries as opposed to in the chapel. No one could put a word on it, but they knew something was rotten in the church. By the end of the month, the local priest had spent most of his time in the hospitals or the bar. It would have taken a regular witch the better half of a year to do what Astarte had accomplished. Sagar knew his friend to be talented, but still could not believe the levels of expertise she had gained.

Sagar watched her in the pew as she studied the wood carved alter screen behind the table. Her eyes gave away how exhausted she was. "Tonight is Samhain. Beginning of the dark half of the year."

She stretched to get her blood flowing and gave him a smile, attempting to dispel any idea that she was worn thin. "I am aware. The timing couldn't be better. I could have done this anytime of the year but it should be easier."

Sagar saw through her facade but kept it to himself. He was ride or die. "So, is there anything you need?"

Astarte looked again at the paintings on the screen. All the saints seemed sad and just as tired as she did. "No, don't think so. The ley lines are humming. Samhain is here. The gray void is as thin as it is going to get." She looked around the church at all she had done and shook her head. "I'm crazy, aren't I? This whole thing." She stopped, then added quietly, "Maybe I'm wrong. Maybe the illusion of faith is the best mortals can hope for."

Sagar knew she was in too deep to pull out now. It was time to pep her up. "You can't tell me you're having cold feet now, right when you are this close to the altar?"
She smiled at the reference and gestured to the statute behind the altar. "What would this world look like if the actual Michael stepped in with his righteous sword and smote all the evildoers?"

Sagar looked at the little statue. "I wouldn't be too concerned. I don't believe in him. If he did come to my door, however, I would put my money on Shiva versus this little man with his cute sword."

Astarte wasn't really contemplating quitting, but she needed to say her doubt out loud in the desecrated church.

Just in case anyone was listening. With resolve, she added, "I may be wrong in what I am doing, but I have come too far to stop now. I have no doubt I am damned, so might as well be successful and damned."

Sagar slapped her back. "That's the spirit."

Her momentarily broodiness over, Astarte stood up and went to the table. She drew the runes and glyphs for a summoning, all under the watchful gaze of the Jesus of Nazareth, whose painting was front and center. She had looked at him earlier in the desecration. The painter, as usual, had gotten his look all wrong. White skin. Long, smooth hair. Absolutely none of the humor. She couldn't ever remember him wearing monk robes. On the other hand, his strange looks made her dark work in a church built for him a little easier.

She worked swiftly, saying the accompanying incantations as she went along. Sagar knew not to interfere at this point. She curved the lines to match the intersection of the ley lines that crossed right at the altar. Their power amplified hers, and soon, she was lost in the spell. It was a cool October night, but you wouldn't have guessed it from the sweat that soaked Astarte's clothes. She looked as if she had been working in a blast furnace.

An hour later, her work done, she breathed in deeply and sat back down. Retrieving her bag, she pulled out the bottle with the last of her wine. Sagar looked at it apprehensively.

Noticing this, Astarte said, "No worries, friend. If this works, I won't need it anymore."

"The plan again?"

She had kept some details from Sagar. "I will bring forth Sariel, bring her into our world. Since she is not in the Continuance, it should not be noticed by many, which will buy us time. Sariel can help me with the Memitim, and she can help me finally cast down the Continuance. Two birds. One stone."

"While I have no love for Sariel, I respect her powers. But even she cannot stop the Memitim. If you are on their list, it will take much more than an old teacher."

Astarte knew she would have to spit out the truth, but she resisted. "She can help me get something I lost. Something that will stop the Memitim."

"And what is this wonderous item you have never mentioned before now?" Sagar's eyes narrowed.

Astarte looked at Sagar, weighing her options. "It is a ring. She can help me find it."

"A ring!" Sagar laughed. "Oh my god, please don't tell me you have wrapped your life, my existence, and the future of humanity, on some chase for a magic ring."

The scowl on her face stopped all laughter. "Sagar, this isn't some fairytale. You think I would risk everything on a mere hunch? I know what I need. Sariel will know how to get it. You don't know everything. And that is by my design."

He waved off her anger. "I have never pretended to know everything. I had hoped you would share what you know since I have given my pound of flesh."

She shook her head but removed the heat from her voice. He had given up everything to be with her, and without him, she wouldn't have made it this far. She hated hiding information from him. But some things were beyond her control. "Some things are not for your ears. This is how it has to be."

He bit back his words, knowing fighting with her now would accomplish nothing useful. He was with her until the end. "If you say so, Astarte, I will help see it done."

His words were true, and she let slide any remaining

anger she may have felt.

Sagar had to add, "But why her? Some other being could possibly—"

"Because I love her," Astarte said with clarity, needing to cut through any jealously Sagar may have had.

Sagar grew quiet. "But how do you know she is still alive and had gotten your message?"

Astarte gave a small smile and touched her lips, thinking about that long-ago kiss by the little lake in Canaan. "She is alive, because I am alive."

Even though he didn't understand her statement, Sagar said no more. She nodded at Sagar and drank the remains of the bottle. Astarte stood before the table and centered her mind. The wind began to pick up, tossing her hair. "Come forth, Sariel. I am calling on you. Loosen your shackles and join me."

The familiar gray mist appeared on the table. Undulating gray clouds, swirling like a thunderstorm, filled the alter.

"Whoa, whoa, whoa. Someone's having a party. And I wasn't invited. For shame." The voice bellowed from the back of the church. The voice was raspy but feminine. Sagar turned and saw a hooded figure struggling against some of the wards. They held, but Sagar knew if this being had made it this far inside the church, they had already bypassed perimeter barriers Astarte had put up.

Astarte did not turn, keeping her focus on the altar. "Sariel, I ask you to come to me. Be with me."

The figure struggled more, then stepped through one of the wards. "Save your breath, witch. So, you're trying to free Sariel the Fallen?" The visitor gave a loud, mirthless laugh. "I may not be as in the know as others, but it is common knowledge that bitch is in the deepest of the deep." This much Astarte knew. When Samuel and Sariel were taken into the void, an agreement was struck between the Gates. "Samuel was tarnished for using forbidden magics and walks the void along with me. Not much of a companion, I have to say. But Sariel was locked up in the dark and shadows and was cast down in pain."

Astarte did not react to the words, but Sagar could not contain himself. "Who are you to come here? Name yourself, creature," he commanded.

The figure raised her hand, and a slice of light slammed into a barrier in front of Sagar. "Pity. No worries, little one. I will be through this in a moment." The figure hit the next barrier and struggled again to get through.

Sagar turned to Astarte. "What is going on? I thought the wards would stop Memitim. At least hide you for a while. What the hell is going on?"

Sensing the weakening of the barrier, Astarte finally turned to Sagar and their visitor. "They do hide us from Memitim. But this creature is not Memitim. I should have thought about her. The southwest is her typical stomping ground. This is Santa Muerte. Or, at least, that is what she is going by these days." Astarte turned back to the table. "If you can, please slow her down. I just need more time."

The figure stopped and lowered her hood. Sagar saw the skeletonized face of a woman. He could tell at one time she'd had dark skin and long black hair. Now, the skin that remained was ashen and frayed, and her scalp was a patchwork of bald spots. On top of her skull, she wore a small gold crown with ruby gems.

"You really know how to ruin a dramatic reveal, witch." The figure scrutinized Sagar for a moment. "Listen, pet, you are out of your element. You should leave this to the ladies."

"I am no pet." Sagar threw his hands up into the air, happy to finally be using his knowledge of magic he had learned over his centuries. Erupting from the ground next to Santa Muerte, a Bengal tiger leapt. More light than bone, but his appearance was effective, and Santa Muerte was caught off guard. The tiger pushed her back through the barriers, giving Sagar enough time to fortify it.

Santa Muerte regained her composure and quickly scythed out a blade of light, cutting through the tiger, which disintegrated before it could hit the ground. "Cute trick. Can't wait to see the whole menagerie."

The gray mist swirled faster above the altar. The colors smeared, and an eerie green light shot out. Seeing all she could do was wait, Astarte turned to deal with the unwelcome visitor.

She put a hand on Sagar to put him at ease. "Thank you for the delay. Santa Muerte is a creature who is a hybrid of many different beliefs: Christian, Native, Aztecan, Pagan. When that happens, wards have a hard time holding up against them."

Santa Muerte was halfway through a barrier. "I couldn't help but overhear that you are on the run from the Memitim. Tsk, tsk, young lady, you have pissed off someone important. Since you are damned to die anyway, I might as well help them out. Maybe they would favor me for doing so. I gave my word to an old priest I would reap you myself, but hey, I may come out even better in this deal." She continued to struggle with the wards.

"Will she get through?" Sagar whispered.

"Yes, I just need a moment." Santa Muerte laughed in answer. "Don't worry, old man. I will take you away with your master here. If you promise to stand back, I will kill you quick and painless. I am merciful. Or, if you prefer, I will put you on my leash and you can keep me company for a few eons. Anyway, you and your old world magics have no place here."

Astarte glanced at Sagar. "I have exhausted everything into the summoning. She is right, I can't stop her. We can only hope time is on our side." Astarte looked back at the ever-widening warp over the alter. The green light engorged, casting the whole room with its light.

Sagar did not like the thought of just sitting and waiting to be saved by Sariel, but he would not abandon Astarte.

Santa Muerte had reached the last barrier and began tearing at it. The invisible wall shimmered at every attack. Astarte began some counter spells, but for every tear she repaired, four more appeared. Wind whipped around the warp, and a large black orb appeared in the center of the swirling light. "Just a few more moments," Astarte said as she struggled with the failing ward.

Seeing it was a race against time, Santa Muerte stepped her attacks up on the barrier, shredding it with her scythe. Astarte saw the losing battle and returned to the alter to make the final incantations to give flesh to soul.

Sagar watched as Santa Muerte emerged from the final barrier, which hung in the air like torn gossamer. Sagar let his final magics blossom forth. A Shri Yantra erupted from his hands and sped toward Santa Muerte. The spell enveloped the hooded skeleton and held her in place. Sagar yelled, "Mohini! You're out of time."

Astarte watched as Sariel stepped forward from the warp. Standing on the altar, naked and beautiful. Astarte began the final forms to give Sariel freedom in the mortal realm.

Santa Muerte struggled against the Shri Yantra. "Your cute tricks are endless, little one. But I believe," she paused as she shook loose from Sagar's spell, "they were never going to be enough." She ran to Astarte, screaming, scythe held high. Astarte's back was turned as the blade came down.

Santa Muerte felt the blade hit home and bury deep. She shut her eyes to feel Astarte's spirit go through her and into the Continuance. It was always rapture.

Astarte finished the last of the glyphs and felt something hit her back. She turned and saw Sagar slumped down between her and Santa Muerte, the scythe plunged deeply into his chest. Sagar looked back at Astarte and smiled. "Of course, you would lead me to my destruction. It was set in the stars." Blackness began to flow from his wound. Astarte had seen this before. It was the darkness of non-existence, the price Sagar had to pay for leaving the pendant. Astarte turned to hold her friend one last time.

Santa Muerte's eyes popped open. She was confused. She saw the little man had sacrificed himself, but she had still fully expected Sagar's soul to be reaped into her, adding to her power.

Sagar held onto the scythe with a death grip fortified with his last magics, preventing Santa Muerte from pulling it out. The darkness pooled around him, and he could sense the moment was at hand. Sagar placed his free hand on Astarte's face and said, "Finish it." With an ear-shattering snap and a rending black flash, Sagar was gone.

Santa Muerte, her scythe now free, raised it once more, and gazing at the tear-stained eyes of Astarte, brought her blade down for a second time.

But stopped in midair.

Confused, Santa Muerte looked at the alter and saw Sariel, beautiful, glowing, and in the flesh. Light radiated out from her body. Her eyes bored into Santa Muerte. Hands raised, Sariel closed one and made a fist, and Santa Muerte's blade shattered like glass.

Santa Muerte recoiled as if she had been bitten and tried to run back through the barrier. Another hand gesture by Sariel, and the barrier was reconstituted, blocking Santa Muerte's escape. Sariel opened one fist, and with the other hand, swirled one finger over her open palm. The barrier twisted and rolled itself around Santa Muerte. Sariel then squeezed her fist. Astarte could see Sariel's arm muscles flex and strain.

Santa Muerte shrieked, her robed body now being compressed by the barrier. Slowly, the skeletal bones cracked, then were pulverized by the barrier. Sariel made sure her skull was last so she could see the terror that was now being visited onto Santa Muerte. In a strange language not heard since the conquistadors, Santa Muerte cursed them with the last of her energy. Soon after, her ocular cavities folded in on each other, and she was nothing but a pile of dust on the floor.

Sariel turned to Astarte. She put her hands on either side of her face and ensured she was unharmed. "You look like shit."

Astarte gave a slight smile. "Well, good to see you too." Astarte began to get up, but Sariel kept her hands in place. Confused, Astarte asked, "What? We need to get out of here. The wards are all tattered, the Memitim are on the way, and I am not exactly one hundred percent."

"We have enough time for this." Sariel leaned down, and their lips met. Sariel, buried in the pit, would comfort herself with the memory of their kiss, and promised it would be the first thing she would do.

Astarte had wanted this moment for so long, she had forgotten about all her worries, all the pain. Those feelings were trounced by her joy. They lost each other in that kiss.

For extra measure, Sariel released a thin line of power through her lips and into Astarte. The feeling of the connection elicited a moan from Astarte. She could feel the power mending her cuts and replenishing her reserves.

Astarte's eyes opened. "I love you," she said hurriedly, as if afraid she would forget to say it.

Sariel took in Astarte's green eyes—eyes that had sustained her through countless tortures. She stroked her auburn hair and gently said, "We love each other." Sariel then scanned the area, paranoid of what may be coming, and gestured that it was time to get going. "I would like for that not to be our last kiss. You said the Memitim are after you."

Astarte smiled. "After us now."

Sariel gave out a sigh. "Well, that is a nice welcome home. You know, I can't defeat them."

"I do, which is why we need to leave." Astarte grabbed her things. "Do you have any idea where we can go just to catch our breath and regroup?"

"I have a few ideas." Sariel stopped Astarte one more time and glanced at the dark spot where Sagar last stood. "I am very sorry Sagar is gone. We may not have seen eye to eye, but he loved you. We are going to dearly miss him."

Sagar's loss was too new. Too fresh. Astarte could not bring herself to unpack the pain, but deep down, she knew she had led Sagar to his ultimate fate. Just like he said she would all those years ago. But what was worse was that she'd kept him in the dark. She had used him and their friendship. And that knowledge began to hurt. "I can never replace him or his counsel. The amount of people who give two shits about me has now dwindled." She fell silent for a moment, knelt down and touched the spot where he'd been unmade.

They both left the church wondering how soon they would be joining Sagar in nothingness. Astarte started up the Hellcat.

"Point it north for now. Just go north," said Sariel.

Astarte pressed on the gas, and soon, the fouled Mission San Miguel was a small dot in the background. As they drove, Astarte filled Sariel in on all the information she had to date.

"We need the ring," was all Sariel said.

Astarte nodded. "I was hoping you could help with that."

Sariel smiled. "I would have advised you not to lose it in the first place."

Astarte knew this would be a source of contentious conversation for the rest of her life. "You don't understand."

Leaving this for another time, Sariel continued. "I knew you 'lost' it. Before I left the pit, I put out some feelers. I am waiting for my man on the inside to give us an assist. He owes me one. Actually, he owes me more than that."

They spent the rest of the night driving while Astarte told stories about the past three thousand years.

CHAPTER 14

The Thirteenth Gate opened readily for him. Why wouldn't it? He was a valued and trusted member of Existence and one who maintained the balance of nature.

Here, on the outer rim, the orbs hung gently in the air, nicely spaced. If you traveled further in the scenery changes. The hellscape increases. The air becomes more rancid. The orbs crowd, intermingling one's damnation with another's. This continued until you got to what was affectionally called the Cauldron, where the orbs were boiled together in a large stewing pot. Below the Cauldron were the pits. Which, Dokiel thought, were now missing an inmate. He smiled at the thought of it all.

"Sir? Can be of some assistance to you?" The demon was some sort of paper pusher on the outer rim. Dokiel would imagine this post to be boring, but the young demon seemed content.

"I am here to review some old files. Please bring me the orb of Shlomoh/Solomon 931." The paper pusher paused at the name. "Problem?"

Seeing Dokiel's impatience, he responded, "No, sir. Right away." With a thought, an orb appeared in the paper pusher's hands. "Here you go." Seeing as nothing else was required, he left Dokiel alone.

Holding the orb, Dokiel peered into it, and entered the

world of Solomon.

Dokiel found himself on some dusty road outside the First Temple, which would become known as Solomon's Temple. All an illusion, of course. The First Temple had been destroyed sometime in 500 B.C. by King Nebuchadnezzar. And then, the Second Temple had been built and destroyed by the Romans in 70 A.D. Dokiel would suppose this temple could serve as the Third Temple, but that would be a whole different can of worms.

Solomon was gifted this afterlife. Even though, eventually, he was turned by Astarte, he had many virtues that outweighed his transgressions. But, in the end, Solomon went against his beliefs and truly earned an afterlife here. Just on the outer rim. Not too bad if you asked Dokiel.

"You are a stranger in these parts." The voice was slightly drunk.

Dokiel looked up to see who was speaking and saw his man. He inwardly was very happy the search hadn't taken too long. At a table filled with food and wine sat a drunken Solomon.

Dokiel squinted in the bright sun and walked over. "Do you remember me?"

Solomon studied Dokiel. "Yes, sir, I do. I remember you fought for me. And you won. I believe I have you to thank for placing me here, for all time, outside the Temple, never allowed to go in." Dokiel hoped time would have mellowed him out, but clearly not.

Solomon raised up to strike Dokiel, but his constant drunkenness caused him to stumble, and he sat back down.

Dokiel, seeing his state, sat opposite. He plucked a large grape and put it in his mouth. The gush of juice was exquisite. "I don't know what you're really bitching about. Shall I describe the type of worlds others in the Thirteenth Gate get to live in?"

Solomon waved off the invitation. "Please. I don't need you to tell me your little horror stories. I know you can't threaten me. I am where I am. There is no changing that. After all this time, I have accepted my fate. But it doesn't mean I cannot hold a little grudge, does it, imp?"

Dokiel chewed on another grape. "What if I told you there was a way to change that?"

Solomon ignored the comment and drank deeply. The only thing worse at this point was being sober and tortured. But something inside him stirred. Against all better judgement, a small spark of hope. "You know, I have to say, when it comes to finding out was really tortures a man, you are quite gifted. Imagine if you used your talents for something worthwhile.

Dokiel stared at the Temple, with its white columns that seemed to go on and on, ignoring Solomon's comment. "Man, you really can design them, can't you? Talk about talent. You have it in spades, old man. I bet if you were alive today, you would have chucked that whole king thing and spent your time designing museums or porn sets. They love columns."

Solomon's head was swimming. He didn't have the energy to bandy words with Dokiel all day. Aggravated, he shouted, "Just tell me what you want, beast, so I can tell you to go back to Hell and continue on with my life!"

Dokiel softened his tone and took all the snark out of it. "I want to help you."

Solomon poured another glass. "Sure you do. You know, I have so many demons coming to me these days desperate to help me, I have lost count. So, how can you help me?"

Quickly, Dokiel answered, "What if I changed things a little around here for you? Everything the same for so many centuries, must be tedious after a while, I would imagine."

Solomon took another drink, not wanting to admit anything to anyone.

"How about…" Dokiel looked around, as if searching for an idea, "let me see. What could the great and wise King of the Jews want?" He glanced back at the Temple and snapped his fingers, feigning an epiphany. "I got it! How about if I made it to where you got to go inside your Temple?" Solomon stopped drinking. "Think about it. Kneeling in front of your holy box again. Maybe, if you prayed hard enough, he may hear you and forgive you. Sounds pretty good to me."

Solomon narrowed his eyes, trying to fight back any emotion. "Tell me the catch. What do you want from me?"

Dokiel put up his hands and shook his head. "Nothing much. You don't have to do anything. Don't worry about any weird old man sex stuff or anything like that. I need just some information I think someone as knowledgeable as you can give me."

Solomon sighed. He should have known. He chastised himself for not guessing in the first place. "You want to know about my ring."

"Well," Dokiel scoffed, "I wouldn't call it 'your' ring, necessarily. But yes, I want to know about the ring."

Solomon stared again at the Temple. At the people going in and out. Just ghosts in this world. Mere apparitions meant to give his torture some context. But the look of contentment when they left always made him yearn a little more each day. This torture was masterfully set up. "Who wants it?"

"She is wanting it back."

Astarte, Solomon thought, *is wanting her ring back.*

Part Three: Megiddo

CHAPTER 1

"Yes. I also want to wish you a happy birthday, Max." Malhamash removed his finger from Max's lips. Max hadn't even noticed the hour that had transpired since Mal and Sham had first begun to discuss the recent activities of Astarte.

Max looked around at the two men and the wreck of a basement, completely confused as to what was going on. However, the whole evening had been a complete mindscrew. "Thanks," seemed to be all his mind could muster. Max glanced quickly at his phone, and noticed the time. "Well…again…uh, Sham. . . uh, sir, thank you for what you have done for me and my father. I think I need to be going home." He said the last part as if asking for permission.

Mal smiled. "Sounds good. I am sure your mother is worrying, and we can't have that." He gave a knowing nod to Sham. "Hey, could you give Sham a ride? He took a cab here and you wouldn't believe how hard it is to get service in this one-horse town."

"Sure, Mr…uh?"

"Mal. Just call me Mal."

"Mal. Will do. Have we met before?" Max studied Mal's perfect face, trying to discern if had seen it before.

Mal ignored the question and patted Sham on the back. "You will make sure Max gets home safely. I will finish the clean up here. Tell me if there you hear anything else. Yes?" Sham nodded. "After you, Max." Mal motioned up the stairs. Max bolted up the stairs, never wanting to see the place again. Sham followed but glanced back just in time to see Mal as he vanished into the air.

Getting into Max's car, Sham settled in. Max asked, "Where to, Sham?"

"Actually, just go ahead and drive to your house. I'll walk from there."

With unease at the odd request, Max put the car in drive and pulled out. "You live close by?"

Sham nodded but remained silent. After a few moments in the car, he finally spoke. "Max, there are some things we need to discuss." Max said nothing. "Typically, when people like me, and…uh, 'Mal' get involved in mortal's lives, we don't allow you to remember our meetings. It wouldn't serve a mortal to remember us, it wouldn't allow them to carry on with their little lives." Sham paused to see if Max was listening. "That will not be happening in your case."

Max concentrated on the road but was relieved his mind would be left intact. "Mortal? So, I guess that means you are something other than mortal? Why am I being treated differently?"

Sham didn't want to answer either question right away. "What have you learned from Angie?"

Max shuddered at her name, remembering his time in the gray void. "What do you mean? About everything?"

"Yes. I want to hear what she told you. What you already know."

"We started early in the summer. She would instruct me, and I would study various articles about old beliefs and faiths. They were always focused on either man's relationship with his gods or the nature of death. The way Angie talked about all of it, I could tell there were some aspects she believed and some she scoffed at. I didn't believe any of it."

"Did that change?"

Max nodded. Sham's tone wasn't inquisitive, but more like a priest trying to get him to confess. It felt good to talk to someone about all that had happened. "Around August—that's when she showed me real magic. Real power. We started going into the gray place to find my father."

"Did she explain what the gray place was?"

"She said it was the void between the realms. One of the ways Existence maintains order. She told me that before the Continuance, people enjoyed a close relationship with their gods. People could speak to their gods, and they would answer. Gods would walk among us, some helping, some harming. Then something happened." Max tried to remember what it was called.

"We called it the Rekindling," Sham added.

"Yeah, she said that. And from this Rekindling, the Continuance was created."

"Did she tell you the nature of the Continuance?" Sham asked.

Max nodded, watching a jogger pass in front of the car. "She said the Continuance has two functions. First, when most people die, they are brought to the Continuance to live out the rest of their life. Their worthiness is judged, and if they are deemed good, they move forward. If they are deemed bad, they go somewhere else. She was never very specific about that."

Sham nodded, impressed with Max's retention after tonight traumatic events. "You mostly have the simplistic version down. We don't subscribe to the nice versus naughty dichotomy. This isn't a glorified Santa's list."

Max smiled, "The second function, which Angie told me was the major reason, were the Gates."

Sham took a quick inhale. This part is what he dreaded the most. "And what did she say about the Gates?"

"That they led to other realms. She didn't know how many there were, but each Gate was guarded by the Continuance. There is now no easy passage from our realm to others. She said it isn't that God isn't listening to our prayers, it's that He can't hear our prayers. If we could bring down the Continuance, then the Gates would open, and mortals would be truly free." Max thought about that last statement and how ridiculous it sounded from his mouth while remembering how amazing it sounded from Angie's. "I guess free to be with their god or something."

Sham didn't immediately say anything when Max stopped speaking. Actually, he had most of the information correct. The details were hazy, probably because Astarte didn't feel the need to fill the boy in. Sham would fill in the gaps, and hopefully, Max wouldn't react poorly. Sensing his silence was going on too long, Sham said, "It's most important to remember the Continuance serves as a sorting ground—a place in which Existence can ensure the proper people are in their proper place."

Max nodded. "She said that was the selling point offered at the time of the Rekindling. Angie thought that both sides, somehow, benefitted from the Continuance and it was maintained by both good and evil."

"And she was right, in a way. Most of what she told you has been correct." Max was taken aback by Sham's strategy of agreeing with Astarte on some points. "Did she ever tell you any stories about what had happened when the wrong people were in the wrong place?"

Max thought for a moment on all the conversations he'd had with Angie. Sheepishly, he realized he had mostly believed what Angie had said based on his faith in her alone. He wondered how he could have been so gullible. "No. She just said balance was something that was paramount to the Continuance."

Sham nodded his agreement. "I will not disagree with Angie on some of her points. Before the Continuance, some things were better in ways that are difficult to describe. But neither Angie, you, nor I have any say over the flow of fate. Ultimately, it was decided that everything had to change. Existence had its reasons, and I think it's important for you to hear a story about before the Continuance. One story, among many, that demonstrates the need for the Rekindling and the Continuance itself. I am going to tell you about a very good man who found himself in a very bad place."

Sham began the story of Menes.

CHAPTER 2

CIRCA 3030 BCE:

"Commander, it has happened again." The low-level demon nervously gave Dokiel the paperwork and quickly left the room. He didn't want to stick around to incur any wrath. With Dokiel, messengers usually bore the brunt of bad news.

"How many fucking times is this going to happen?" Dokiel shouted at the closing door.

Reading the report, all he could do was shrug. The numbers didn't lie, but still, he had to check. It was a part of the job description, double checking and triple checking who was being tortured. A sort of quality control for the damned. After a quick scan, Dokiel saw the primary source of the torture was being carried out by an apep, a coiled torment beast sired by Dokiel's most trusted servant. When dealing with torturers, he found it was always best to bring with him their creators. They may not like listening to him, but they always listened to their mommies. With a thought, he summoned her.

"You rang?" Sariel arrived with a flash of fire. Her tone was one of exhaustion. He had been relying on her too often for these mess-ups, but someone had to do the legwork, and it certainly wasn't only going to be him.

"Yes, I have another task for you. Please don't roll your eyes." Dokiel waited until he had her full attention. She was one of his best, so she could get away with a little impunity. "I need you to come with me and review orb Menes 3030. I have just received information that he does not belong with us. And your, ahem, child…" he gave her a look, "is the source of his torture."

Sariel nodded. She knew some of her creations were frowned upon. Existence didn't necessarily appreciate the manner in which she created them. No matter to her, she still prided herself on their usefulness to the abyss. However, she would be the first to admit they could be unruly and in need of a mother's hand to control them.

Dokiel turned his hand over. An orb appeared, black as night. The screams being contained within it were barely muffled. Sariel came closer and placed her hand on the top of the orb. Instantly, they were both transported inside. The room they were in reeked of shit and was as dark as pitch. Four small lanterns illuminated the four corners of the room, giving some dimension to the space. Gruesomely, the lanterns also gave off enough light to see exactly what the apep was doing to the man named Menes.

Sariel's apeps came in different forms. This apep was a multi-headed serpent. It was clear the main body had entered Menes from his rectum, and now the heads had slogged their way through his body. Snakeheads breached out of each of his wrists. One had erupted from his throat and out his mouth, carefully avoiding his trachea, allowing Menes to scream. From the looks of Menes's left eye, another head was about to push through the socket.

Dokiel reviewed the report. Menes had only been here a few moments. He smiled, astonished at how quickly the apep worked. "Enough. Release him!" he said with a smile. The serpent heads that were visible hissed at Dokiel in anger. He turned to Sariel with an arched eyebrow.

She stepped forward, and with a tone of concern and command, said, "Young one, you have done an outstanding job. I am proud of you. We will find you another assignment, but for now, let this one go." The hissing continued. Sariel liked the attitude, but she didn't want to try Dokiel's patience. "Do what I say. Now." The order was enough. Quickly, the serpent recoiled back into Menes's body and exited. From the look on Menes's face, the apep took some final jabs on its way out.

Apparently, the only thing keeping Menes upright was the apep himself. Once it had removed itself, Menes fell to the ground in a heap, wailing in lingering agony.

Dokiel waited for the departed Menes to regain some of his composure. Dokiel could have assisted him, but nothing compelled him to. He didn't have to lift one finger until the report was confirmed. Therefore, he had no intention to do so. He was not in the business of doing favors before they were owed. Anyway, the sound of suffering was far better than the mewing of conversation with departed mortals. In short order, Menes sat up and looked at the two people who stood before him. Scanning the room, he could not see the apep anywhere. Sariel noticed Menes remained ashen, and his wounds were not healing.

"Thank you, sir, for ridding me of my torment," Menes cried and bowed profusely to his two supposed saviors.

Dokiel rolled his eyes. "Enough of the tears. You can continue the bowing if you like, but you do not owe me or my companion any thanks." Menes stopped his crying and looked fearfully at them. Not wanting to hear pleas for mercy, Dokiel quickly continued. "We will not cause you anymore harm once I verify who you are and what you have done in your life." In a businesslike voice, Dokiel began asking his questions, as if he were checking a list.

"Your name?"

Seeing his chance to avoid any more torture, Menes answered quickly. "Menes."

Dokiel nodded. "And you were some sort of ruler?"

"Yes, I led my people. I brought all my people together." Seeing his chance to escape this place, he added, "I don't know why I am here. I spent my life glorifying the gods. I brought worship of the divine to my people. Before me, they only thought of themselves, lived for themselves. Now, they give sacrifice in the name of the gods. How could I have been cast out like this? What have I done to offend Anubis?" Menes wailed, beseeching his various gods for forgiveness.

Dokiel, not wanting to hear anymore, put a hand up, stopping any more words from Menes. Dokiel exchanged a gesture with Sariel.

She nodded. "He's correct. He brought a higher level of worship to his people. One of the first of its kind on Earth. Before him, they were just a bunch of apes chewing and fucking. Now, there are temples and priests and the whole gamut."

Dokiel looked at Menes and smiled. "I think starting organized religion is a pretty good reason to be here." Menes didn't say anything. "Anyway, I am sure Existence thinks you should be lauded. This is odd." Dokiel considered the situation, inspecting Menes with a quizzical eye. "What is going on here? How did you get here?" he asked to himself. Sariel reviewed more of the record and saw what might have been the answer. She turned to Dokiel and shared her discovery, whispering in his ear. "Ah, I see." He turned back to Menes with a smile. "I think we have discovered why you are in this little predicament. Why you have fallen so low. And by the way,

I will try to take no offense that you don't like it here with us. Are you at all familiar with Sobek?"

Hearing the name, Menes got to his knees and began begging for mercy.

Dokiel smiled. "I take that as a yes. Well, it seems your little crocodile god has been quite imprudent. Apparently, in your final hours, you called out for another god's protection. Someone called 'Neith,' or something like that?" Menes continued begging on his knees. "Well, apparently, Sobek, being a jealous little bugger, made sure you came here. Not something he is supposed to do, but…well, no harm, no foul, right?" Dokiel dragged Menes up and turned to Sariel. "Heal him up quickly."

Without examining Menes's wounds, she stated, "I can't."

Dokiel's smile didn't diminish. "Why is that?"

With a matter-of-fact tone, she said, "Apep venom prevents healing from our kind. The poison leaches into the soul, stains it, digests the energy for more effective leaching. It's a new process I came up with. I didn't want anyone to interfere with their work."

"What the fuck!" Dokiel cursed. Nothing could be easy for him.

Sariel didn't react to his shout and calmly added, "I thought it was a good idea. Still do. While not perfect, my spawn have done wonderful things for the abyss." Sariel said the last comment in a huff. She was tired of constantly being judged because her creations were a little unwieldy.

Dokiel regained his businesslike attitude. "Any suggestions?"

She finally smiled, knowing the upcoming reaction. "Of course. I know exactly what to do. You will not like it."

Dokiel knew what she was going to say. In a fury, he grabbed Menes and, in a blink, all three of them were back in Dokiel's office. "I don't want to even—" Dokiel began but was cut off by Sariel.

"I have already called him. It's done." This was happening more and more as of late, and Sariel was not in the mood to debate making the call.

A sound emitted from all directions, heralding an unknown visitor. A man appeared, bathed in white light. He wore a stern and weary countenance, the look of a man who was trying to accomplish a task he found odious. The light diminished, and he stepped forward.

"I have been sent to collect Menes 3030. He apparently was wrongfully given to you. I will take him now." His voice was deep and commanding.

Dokiel, not used to being given such short orders, stepped forward. "And you are? I am just not going to give him up to anyone."

The man looked at Dokiel, and with a scoff, snapped his fingers. Dokiel covered his eyes as white light enveloped the stranger a second time. "Are you asking for my identification? I think it is pretty clear where I am from." Another snap, and the light was gone. Seeing that Dokiel was sufficiently rebuffed, the man added, "I am Puriel, Commander of the Moksha, and I have been informed you have a being who needs help. I am here to offer that help."

"I am Dokiel, *High* Commander of the Abyss. Yes, my companion here, Sariel, has informed me that during the leeching process, we have inflicted damage that we are unable to heal. To…uh, Manes—"

"Menes" interjected Menes.

Dokiel turned to the man and exaggeratedly said, "I

don't care."

Puriel took an empty orb from his pocket and walked toward Menes. Menes flinched at his approach. "Be at ease and calm yourself. I am going to take you home." The words were interlaced with a small charm that calmed Menes. He willingly walked toward Puriel, his hand outstretched. He reached for the orb, touched it, and vanished. The orb became filled with white light. Puriel turned to Dokiel. "There have been too many of these mistakes. I have a terrible feeling we will be seeing more of each other."

Sariel, out of curiosity and not concern, asked, "You think you can fix him?" She was always seeking ways to improve her children's effectiveness.

Sensing her sadistic lack of concern, Puriel simply said, "Unknown."

Dokiel smiled. "So, there are some things you guys can't do. Good to know. This little meeting has been productive." Dokiel couldn't do anything to stop Puriel, but he needed to have the last word. It was a compulsion.

Puriel frowned at Dokiel and knew he was an egomaniac. Bandying words would be fruitless. However, he also knew he would probably have to work with him in the future, so he gave a silent nod, snapped his fingers, and evaporated in a flash of light.

Dokiel watched the spot Puriel had once been and considered the whole situation. This was happening far too often. It was inefficient and time-consuming. Also, Dokiel didn't want to spend any more time with First Gate trash. To himself, more than anyone, Dokiel said quietly, "I don't like that guy."

CHAPTER 3

Max listened as Sham ended his story as they pulled up outside his house. The little stone two story sat on top of a hill and was ringed with oak and maple trees. Even though it was late and his mom was more than likely already in bed, she always kept all the lights on so he wouldn't have to return to a dark house. The lights from the window pushed back the night and were a welcoming sight to his eyes. All he wanted was to crawl into his bed.

He didn't know where Sham was going to go, so he said, "So, Menes…were they able to fix him?" as he shut down the engine and prepared to leave his odd savior behind.

Sham shook his head. "The poison stained his very being. There wasn't much that could be done for him."

Max considered the story a little longer. He knew Sham was going somewhere with this, and he wanted to be courteous. "But what effect did this one guy have? I mean, I have never heard of him. I mean, it's not like you guys lost Jesus or something."

Sham shook his head again. He was desperate for Max to understand. He knew his story wasn't going to do the trick. "Look there, just above the horizon. Tell me what you see."

Sham pointed out the car window to the northwest. Thankfully, it was a clear night and the stars shone bright.

Max could clearly see the handle and the scoop. "That's the Big Dipper."

"Do you see any bright stars at the center of the Dipper?"

Max squinted. "No." He sarcastically added, "Just like always."

Sham leaned back in his seat. "There should have been. A little nebula was supposed to create a star that would have been named Siwel. Bright and blue. And orbiting that star would have been a little planet of Cantis. Little creatures, similar to yourselves, would have lived on it. A good people. Fair. Hardworking. They wouldn't have the hang-ups you people do. They were going to be much more advanced. They wouldn't let little differences among them hold them back. They wouldn't just prattle about their little lives. They were going places."

Max strained again to see anything in the void of the Dipper. Some small specks, but nothing of note.

Sham smiled at Max. "Trust me. They are not there. You mortals are not alone in this realm. You don't know the amount of energy it takes to create life, sustain it, watch it grow, and advance. The universe is infinitely vast, and there are places where creatures inhabit and explore. Some of them are behind you, some are more advanced, but all of you are a monumental effort."

Max marveled at the thought. He always believed in life out there, but to have it confirmed, and somewhat explained, made it more real somehow. He glanced back at Sham. "One man? One man caused the nonexistence of a solar system?"

Sham frowned. "No. That's too simple. But the collective loss of people like Menes, people who couldn't move forward, couldn't grow, couldn't help build the universe, caused the non-existence of Cantis. Shredding Menes's soul, reaping his energy, permanently damaged his potential." Sham knew he was just giving Max the surface but was hoping he would understand. "This may be a little beyond you, Max, but every imbalance to Existence has a toll." He pointed back to the Big Dipper. "We all have a role to play. And when something prevents that, there are consequences."

Max momentarily forgot about his warm bed. "What happened to Menes?"

Sham shifted in his seat. "I was getting to that. The only solution to the problem of these souls that were wrongfully placed, if you will, was to perform a samsara."

The word was familiar to Max through his studies. "That what the Buddhists call reincarnation."

Sham was impressed with the amount of knowledge Max had retained. "Exactly. Running these souls through the mortal realm again and again purified some of the torture they endured in the abyss."

"You turned Menes into a butterfly or something?"

Sham, for the first time, laughed. "No. I know that is what you people think. That, somehow, we can stuff a mortal soul into a bird or alligator. No, a human soul must go into a human form. By the time we figured out we could not heal Menes completely, a great deal of time had passed on Earth. So, when we saw on opportunity to send him back, we did."

Max nodded, accepting this as a completely normal conversation. He'd had odder ones as of late and had seen things that had opened his mind to these concepts. "So, that was that. Menes lived a long life and got put forward, or promoted, or whatever you want to call it."

Sham frowned again. "Sadly, no. It takes a great deal of time to repair a soul. It didn't take just one lifetime. It took many lifetimes. In the end, we never could fully repair all the damage. We realized no matter how many times we sent his soul back, it would never be complete, so, eventually, we moved Menes forward, but he was always . . ." Sham searched for the right word, "diminished? If that makes any sense."

"None whatsoever." Images of his soft pillow crept back into Max's head. He wanted the night over with.

Sham smiled at Max's honesty. "With each samsara, Menes would live out his life without memory of the prior lives, and when he would pass, we would evaluate him. At a certain point, he realized he would never be mended, so he was pushed through the system, never reaching his true potential."

Max nodded. This conversation, while interesting, couldn't override his exhaustion. He was too tired, had seen too much, heard too much, to listen anymore. He took the moment of silence as his opportunity to end his night. "Well, Sham, that was fascinating. Thank you for sharing that with me. I will make sure to keep it in mind."

Sham didn't register Max's comments. "Menes made one request before leaving this realm. He asked that his progeny be watched over." Sham peered over at Max. "In a way, this is the reason your memory wasn't wiped. Why you have Memitim looking after you, killing for you."

The last part terrified Max. "What are you talking about? Who is killing for me? I don't want anybody dead." Max got out of his car and slammed the door shut. "I think we are done here, Sham. Thanks for saving me and my dad. Also, thanks for the nightmares."

Sham stayed in the car but rolled down the window. "Max, we aren't done yet."

"Yeah, we are. I have had one witch bending my ear all summer, and now I have a wizard, or whatever you are, trying to tell me what to do. No thanks. Fool me once, I think is the phrase."

Sham sat in the car as Max opened his front door and closed it behind him.

The sound of the heavy door shutting behind him pleased Max. He was glad to have even a simple door between him and the outside world. He breathed in deep, taking in the familiar and comforting scents. He was home. His mother had changed little in the house since Jude had died. The pictures were still up of smiling faces and better times. Max looked at the most recent picture they had of his father and was again struck by Jude's words from the grey zone. He took comfort in those words. The night hadn't been a total shitfest.

Hearing his mother moving around in the dining room, Max called out. He had decided to tell his mother all he had done, all he had experienced. But not tonight. Tonight, he would hug her and wish her a goodnight.

An hour earlier

Sham knocked on the heavy wooden door belonging to Eva and the late Jude Travers. He knew he would not have to wait too long for an answer, and he was right.

The deadbolt turned, and the door opened. From deep inside the house, Sham heard Eva's voice say, "Come in."

Sham moved into the house and turned to the brightly lit dining room just off the main hallway. Turning the corner, Sham saw Eva Travers sitting patiently at the head of her table. She motioned for him to take the seat opposite her. A hot cup of tea waited for him.

"As I remember, you don't take sugar or cream." She took a sip from her own cup as he sat down.

Sham had been thinking of what exactly to say to her in this moment. They both had a reason to be furious with each other. He couldn't figure out what to say to someone who was just as well armed as he was. She placed her cup down and saved him from having to decide how to start.

"I am assuming you're bringing Max to me?"

Sham nodded. "Once the trigger spell…uh, well, triggered, we realized who Max was and who his mother more than likely was."

Eva smiled comfortably. "I don't know if you can really appreciate the amount of energy I have expended keeping Max and me shielded from Existence."

Sham shook his head. "No, I can't. But I can imagine it must have been quite a trick to flummox us. I guess I can figure out why."

Eva's eyes shone in the light. "Please, Sham. Guess away. Let's see how good your study of mortals has been."

Sham cleared his throat. Not that he needed to, but he knew these little human gestures put people at ease. "After what you went through as a Daughter of David, I assume you wanted nothing like that for Max. You knew it was a possibility that one day, we would come seeking him. I don't know how you did it, but that is why you concealed yourself and Max from our eyes. Because you love your son."

Eva gave him a clap. "Good work, Sham. You almost sound human. Well, I almost pulled it off. The trigger spell is tied to our blood, so there wasn't anything I could do to undo it. I guess I was just hoping no one would try to tinker with his mind. And I was wrong. Now, you are here. Who else was with you tonight?"

Sham didn't want to say. He took the teaspoon that had been sitting next to the cup and struck it against the cup. The ringing from the porcelain cup sounded around the room. Sham looked around as the sound reverberated, revealing the hidden wards Eva had scrawled on the walls. He could see there would be no lying to her. He breathed in deep. "Actually, when I triggered the spell, Mal was on hand."

His statement did not evoke the response he had feared. Eva simply closed her eyes and nodded. "Of course," she finally said. "Makes complete sense. When you perform the magic I did, it comes back to you. And now I have to deal with the worst sort of you beings." She glanced down at her empty cup, and with a thought, it was filled again. This time with something stronger than tea. "So, now that I am revealed, I am assuming there will be no more hiding for me?"

Sham frowned. "I am sorry, Eva. There are too many things going on right now. Too many coincidences that aren't, if you know what I mean. And I am sorry to say, Max is at the center of all of them." She breathed in sharply but didn't interrupt. "If it gives you any comfort, it was not Mal or me or any of us who put Max into play."

She arched an eyebrow. This was news to her. She had assumed Max's bloodline had been found out by the First Gate. "Then who can I thank for my world now being flipped upside down again?"

"It is a long story, and Max will be here soon, so I will fill you in as much as I can before he gets here. The person you need to blame has gone by many names, but for brevity's sake, she is Astarte the Necromancer. And we need your help."

***

"Mom, I'm home. I am happy you're awake. I wanted to say . . ."

Max saw his mother was not alone. Eva Travers put her teacup down and smiled at her son. Sham did the same.

"Max, I'm glad you're home. Sham was just catching me up on the goings-on of your night."

Max was struck at seeing Sham. Max turned to the window and looked out at his car. In the passenger seat, Sham waved at him and motioned for him to turn back around.

"Sorry about the little party trick, Max," Sham said. "Like I said, we weren't done talking. But I think having your mother here would be good for what I have to say next."

Max was infuriated. He had no plans on telling his mom about Angie or the things he had been up to. At least, not tonight. Tonight was for sleep. The morning was for truth. He flushed with the thought of explaining why he had been so easily taken in by the witch.

Seeing his distress, Sham stopped smiling. "Max, it's okay. Your mom understands."

"Completely. I was young once too, Max." Eva tried humor to diffuse the situation. It didn't work.

"Mom, I don't know what Sham has told you, but I am sorry."

"I've told her everything."

Max grimaced at Sham but kept his cool. "Good. Mom you should know everything. I was trying to reach Dad, and it just got out of hand."

Eva got up and hugged her son. "You don't have to explain anything to me. I know losing your father has been hard. It's been hard on all of us," Eva said. "But had I known some hell bitch was strutting about you, I would have been more alert. For that, I am sorry. I failed you this time. I will not let it happen again."

Max was surprised by his mother's language, but more

mystified by her tone. The sincerity of her statement took him by surprise.

Eva examined her son's face. Almost a grown man now, but she still saw the little boy who used to need her. She pushed those thoughts away, but not too far. "What? Why do you look at me like that? I am your mother. Until I cannot draw breath, I am going to look out for you. I am pissed. But not at you." She patted his head. "And honestly, not completely at her." Eva turned to Sham. "I guess you and your kind are also to blame. Who was asleep at the wheel for so long and allowed the Necromancer to get so close to my son?"

Wide-eyed, Max turned from his mom to Sham, who now stood cowed in his dining room.

CHAPTER 4

A small chime sounded.

"Rebecca? Please enter." Puriel was musing over the name of a song and enjoying the feel of a gourd Calabash pipe between his teeth. He couldn't quite remember it. Of course, he could have looked it up, but that would have defeated the point. It was a mental game. He continued his musing as he watched Rebecca enter his office. "Thank god you're here. Do you know the name of the song that begins ba bada badada . . . ba bada?"

Rebecca set down some reports on the messy desk. Even though he could have taken the information in directly with an upload, Puriel enjoyed reading from a page. The tactile touch of the paper made it more real to him. Rebecca silently complied with his little oddities. She had been his girl Friday in the Continuance for at least a millennium, but she wasn't much for conversation. "I have no idea what you're talking about."

The tune bounced around his mind as he reviewed the stacks of paper. The one on top stopped his thoughts dead. It was written on red paper. "What is this?"

"You know what it is." Rebecca turned to leave and blinked out in a white mist.

"Ba bada badada," he whispered as he picked up the paper and read. Red messages were from beyond the Gates and usually meant something had occurred that would ruin his morning. The last time he had gotten one, it had warned that a plague from the Third Gate had been taken. It took him and Dokiel quite some time to recover it, but they had managed to prevent it from being released beyond the Fourth Gate. Puriel smiled remembering the imaginative punishment Dokiel created for the perpetrators.

> *Direct Message from the First Gate to the Continuance: It has been discovered that the abyss has been breached. Sariel the Fallen has escaped. It is believed this is directly related to the rediscovery of the Necromancer in the Fourth Gate. It is unknown what ramifications this may have. It is believed the Continuance should be on high alert.*

After he finished reading, the red paper vanished in a flash. And as if on cue, Puriel saw it out the corner of his eye. It was small, about the size of a small stone. He went over to his bookcase to examine it closer.

It was like the colors of the books had been smudged, and all the colors behind the object swirled into itself. It was what Jude Travers had called a warp.

Not much unsettled Puriel. This set his teeth on edge.

"Rebecca, get in here!"

Before his words could die out, Rebecca appeared. "Yes, boss?"

He pointed to the warp. "Do you see this?"

Rebecca looked at the warp, and it was clear she saw it. "What is that?" she asked worriedly.

Fear seized Puriel. He began pacing his office, trying to figure out what exactly was happening. The big answer he knew: the Continuance was ending. That was the problem. But the other answers of how, why, and what could be done to stop it eluded him. That was what he needed to focus on.

Rebecca, never having seen her boss so unhinged, asked gently, "Is there someone I can call for you?"

Someone? thought Puriel. He could only think of one person. The only person whose fate was also tied to the Continuance.

"Dokiel. Please send for him."

Rebecca nodded, sent a summons, and vanished.

Puriel tried to calm himself. He didn't need to breathe, but he had found long ago the exercise was quite calming and stimulating. He drew in a deep breath and let it out slowly. He didn't want Dokiel to see how unnerved he was. Especially if it was an easy fix. He went over and poured himself a scotch, then went ahead and poured a second glass for his visitor. He then proceeded to sit behind his desk and began drinking as deep as he could. The alcohol had no effect on him, but like breathing, he enjoyed it. It gave him something to do. Kept him occupied. "Ba bada badada," he hummed to himself.

"It's *Shelter from the Storm*." The voice came from nowhere. Before any question could leave his mouth, his office lit up with red and orange undulating light. Searing lava bubbled up on the floor in the center of his office. He knew this was bad news. An ill wind.

From the churning lava, a person emerged. Not just a person, but a woman that exuded lust. She was robed in glowing magma and flame, but in a flash, the flames subsided, leaving her clothed in skintight red leather that left absolutely nothing to the imagination and accentuated every glorious curve. Her hair emerged from the fire, long and red, as if it were still ablaze. The woman turned her head and smiled at

Puriel through perfect white teeth and ample crimson lips. Every part of her screamed lasciviousness. Every part, except her eyes. Black as sackcloth. They only meant torment. No matter how good the artifice, Puriel couldn't be conned. He knew this was no woman, but a beast.

"Puriel," she said as if they were intimate friends. "It's been such a long time." She moved about his office, breathing in the air as if trying to sniff out clues. "When did we last see each other?"

Puriel did not want to seem shocked at her appearance, so he casually said, "Let's see. Mididi, wasn't' it? Just before the Rekindling."

She laughed. "Mididi? Really." She gave a humph as if she didn't recall seeing him there. She started pawing at some of his collection of items. "You really have a thing for these mortals, don't you?"

He didn't feel the need to answer her question. "Not to be rude, Apollyon, but you didn't come all this way, and burn my rug, to discuss my trinkets, did you? Why are you here?"

She gave a look like he had struck her. "Why so rushed? Aren't you going to at least offer a girl a drink?" She saw the second glass.

Even though she had no real powers here in the Continuance, Puriel knew it was always best to oblige a prince of the abyss when you could, especially now when he couldn't be certain how long the Continuance would last. Puriel glanced over at the warp still lingering next to the books. He gestured to the second glass and invited her to drink. "Of course. I assumed you are a very busy lady and didn't have time for pleasantries. The current century has kept you busy."

Apollyon laughed. "Yes. You can always count on the mortals to make the right choices." She grabbed the glass and seductively moved her hip out. "But I always have time to drink with old friends. Maybe even do more than drink."

Puriel didn't respond. Working with Dokiel, he was well trained in not being provoked. He knew creatures from the Thirteenth Gate were masters at torture and temptation. He sat quietly as she finished her drink and watched her pour another.

"Admit it, you would rather bandy words with me for eternity than Dokiel." She drained the second drink. "Speaking of, when was the last time you saw him?" She nonchalantly put the glass back on his desk.

Here it was, Puriel thought. She should know more than anyone where Dokiel was. His eyes widened at the realization. Somehow, the Thirteenth Gate had lost Dokiel. "I don't really recall the last time I saw him. Not too long ago. Don't tell me you lost him? That seems to be a reoccurring theme with you people as of late."

Apollyon continued. "We will get Sariel back in short order. She was such a unique talent. Her beasts still are the best we have. True works of art." She saw Puriel roll his eyes. "No. Honestly, it isn't the mere extraction of energy from a person's soul that is the trick. It's the quality of that extraction. Too fast, and the soul burns and the energy is corrupted. Dirty. A nice, slow, protracted extraction, that's what you need. Takes very talented hands." She looked at her empty glass and contemplated a third pour. "Actually, we blame you two idiots for her escape."

Puriel scoffed. "Blaming others for your failings is the true talent of the Thirteenth Gate. So, let's have it. How do you figure Sariel is my and Dokiel's fault?"

"That petty bullshit with Travers." She returned the scoff and gave a dismissive wave of her hand. "Letting him and his son speak allowed that little witch the perfect opportunity to reach out into the abyss. I am impressed with her knowledge. She knows what she is doing and has obviously been underestimated. Whatever Astarte did, she loosened our grip on Sariel, just a small fraction. But…" she continued in a defeated tone, "it was enough to allow a complete extraction." Seeing the warp, Apollyon smiled and moved over to it and massaged it with her finger. "Yep, it seems like your little fiefdom here is ending. Your good deed is not going unpunished."

"That can't be something you wish for?" Puriel said matter-of-fact.

"It is, and it isn't. Honestly, I'm conflicted. Don't get me wrong, the order is nice. Everything in its proper place. But I have to admit, I do miss the old days. Stalking mortals. Boots on the ground. Real contact. Having souls harvested and brought to me bleeding. Oh, the stench." She closed her eyes. She took in a deep breath, and her body gave a little shiver and jiggled in all the right places. Her eyes snapped back open. "Anyway. No. Ultimately, I am here to help restore order."

Puriel's eyes narrowed. "And why not just let Dokiel and I do it? We don't really need your help. This is something we can take care of."

Apollyon shrugged. "Because Dokiel is no longer with us."

Puriel shook his head. "He may be missing, but he is in the Continuance." What Apollyon was suggesting just wasn't possible.

"Ah, how sweet. Are you worried for your little fat friend? Trust me. Dokiel isn't here. And since you people are for shit when it comes to keeping secrets, I can see you know nothing about it."

"I'm worried more about what the implications are for the Continuance."

Apollyon nodded sarcastically. "Sure. You keep telling yourself that." She walked up behind him, placed her hands on his shoulders, and pressed herself against his back. "I have found that after a few eons, even enemies can become something more."

Puriel extricated himself delicately from her grasp. "You think he has been destroyed? By Sariel?"

Apollyon shrugged. "That is the consensus. It would make the most sense seeing both of you are permanent structures of this place. However, I am uncertain. Some other things have occurred that have caused me certain…" she paused as she continued to inspect Puriel's collection, "suspicions. Do you know Santa Muerte?"

Puriel nodded. "Some mongrel demon. Thinks of herself as some sort of reaper. We get her kills now and then, after she soaks up some of their energy."

"Then it is news to you that, recently, she was destroyed."

That news did surprise him. "When?"

Apollyon continued her inspection. "About the same time Sariel was released. Not long before we lost contact with Dokiel."

"I would suggest the evidence points to Sariel killing Dokiel. If he isn't here in the Continuance, or with you behind the Thirteenth Gate, then he must be dead. As you know, he nor I can leave the Continuance." Puriel looked at the warp, which, thankfully, hadn't grown. "If the Continuance fails, we fail with it. We are tied to it. For better or worse."

Apollyon scoffed. "Sounds like marriage." She thumbed through some paintings Puriel had stacked against a low shelf.

"Or a sinking ship. Anyway, I still don't put it past him to have figured out a work around. Just like that little rat to find an escape, am I right?" Puriel tried to imagine how Dokiel could have managed it when Apollyon shouted, "What's this?"

Puriel looked at the large-framed print Apollyon held up. He could only see the back of it but knew the frame well. "It's from the mid-nineteen-nineties. American. It's called a Magic Eye 3D print. Dokiel got it for me as a running joke when we do the whole psychiatric schtick. I keep it around because I enjoy the irony of it." Apollyon inspected the scattered digital image, trying to see what was so funny. "If you gaze past the image, you will see a 3D sailboat."

The look on Apollyon's face turned from her typical menacing smile to fury. She turned the print to Puriel. He instantly saw what the problem was. The 3D image of the sailboat had been replaced with a 3D middle finger.

Without another word, in a gush of lava and flame, Apollyon vanished from Puriel's office. The print fell to the ground, glass shattering on the hard floor.

Puriel turned from the ruined print to the warp.

"My friend, what have you done?"

CHAPTER 5

"Well, what do you have to say for yourself, Sham? How could you let this bitch get so close to my son?" Eva's question still hung in the air over the dining room table. Max said nothing, as he was still pondering why it seemed his mother knew so much more than he could have imagined.

Sham sunk into the dining chair. "We have no excuse. We are assuming it is Existence itself wanting these things to play out this certain way." Seeing Eva's eyes inflame, Sham quickly added, "But we now believe we have a handle on it. The Memitim have been called forth, and as I have said, Mal himself is leading the charge against the Necromancer."

Hearing Malhamash's name made Eva shiver.

Max saw this. "What? Isn't that good? He seemed like an okay guy."

Eva roughly grabbed Max's shoulder and looked him in the eye. "I have a feeling you are going to hear amazing and wondrous things. Much more fantastic than you already know. But remember, some of these beings," she motioned to Sham, "you can trust more than others. Mal…" she released Max's shoulder and tried to calm herself, "I wouldn't piss on him if he were on fire. Vicious? Yes, he is. Will he kill the Necromancer? Probably. Would he turn around and slice your throat if he could? No doubt."

Max reflexively grabbed his throat. "Then how will I know who to trust? And why will I need to know this information? Why do you know this information? And what the hell is going on right now!" He took in deep breaths, trying not to lose it in front of his mom and Sham.

Eva inwardly chastised herself for losing her temper and nodded at Sham. "Please continue your conversation with Max. I think it would be best if we start there." Eva patted her son's shoulder and took her seat. Max sat next to her and turned to Sham.

Sham cleared his throat. "As I was saying. Existence made an agreement with Menes that we would take care of his progeny. The first person he became after his first reincarnation was the son of a shepherd named Jessie."

Max looked at his mom and knew if he were going to get any answers, they were going to have to come her way. He turned back to Sham and said, "He went from some king to a shepherd? Seems like a demotion."

Eva gently placed her hand over Max's. "Don't be disrespectful." Max considered her words and wondered who he had disrespected and why she cared.

Sham continued. "It was best to put Menes in the body of a common person. His spirit was so full, his energy so powerful after all the treatments we had administered, that if he came back as a king, it would have been too imbalanced. Anyway, his spirit was still overpowered, so even as a shepherd, he became someone much greater. You see, Astarte . . ."

"Who?"

Sham nodded, realizing he had yet to explain that part. "The woman you know as Angie Chiseler has gone by many names. She is a master of deception. She can change her appearance, even her gender if she wishes. But, deep inside her dark heart, she remains a witch named Astarte. Born sometime in the Bronze Age, she has lived many lifetimes, and she has spent that time attempting to influence the mortal realm to her needs and wishes."

Max shook his head and laughed. "That can't be true. There is no way." He looked at his mom, who just stared at him. "Trust me, I know. The way she talks…what she says…"

"Accept it, Max. There is a reason she can do the things she can do." Sham put his cup down. "Max, I have been a Watcher since humans were ooze in a pond. I have conquered beasts of every nature and thrown down titans. I am not easily fooled. And this one did it as easy as breathing." Seeing Max was still hesitant, Sham added, "The evidence was all around the basement. It took Mal to put it all together. It is undeniable at this point. She isn't just some magician, selling tarot and palm readings, making psychic promises to old widows. She is the Necromancer."

Max started to hyperventilate. "You're saying I fell for a four-thousand-year-old woman?"

Sham sighed. "Max, there are bigger issues than that."

"Not to me! Her tongue was down my throat a few hours ago." Max heaved.

Eva, while upset, loved that her son was still worried about young boy concerns. He was still so innocent. She knew that would change all too soon.

Sham waited for Max to settle down. "Okay. As I was saying, Astarte was bewitching a king named Saul. She was sending him images of demons to torment him at night. Anyway, someone told Saul that Jessie the Shepherd's son, David, was talented in music. So talented, he was known to soothe the demons of hell themselves."

Max stopped Sham. "I know this story." Max paused.

"Are you saying Menes was reincarnated and became King David? Like, the King David?"

"Yes. One of his many forms. And he was a successful king. Just like Menes was a successful ruler of Egypt. He brought people together. Changed the world around him. Was a force for good, and trust me, at that time mortals, needed it. Not even Astarte could figure out a way of tainting him. We have no record of her attempting anything against David. It looks like she did whatever she could to avoid his eye, knowing he probably couldn't be beguiled by her."

Eva watched as her son became swept away in the story, much the same way she had been when she first heard it.

Sham continued. "So, as I was saying, by agreement, we, meaning Existence, agreed to look out for Menes's progeny. King David's progeny. A long line of mortals known as the House of David. Which brings me to you." Sham waited a moment.

Max was waiting for Sham to say more. Seeing that he wasn't, Max turned to his mother, who was staring back at him. Then it clicked.

Max stood up. "So, you didn't wipe my mind because I am some great great something or other of King David?"

Sham smiled. "Yes, and others of his line."

Then it hit Max again, and he leapt from his chair. "Jesus Christ!"

"Language," Eva said, smiling.

The gravity of the moment hung in the air. It landed on Max, and he felt the weight sink deep into his body. He felt lightheaded and clamored back to his chair. While the knowledge may not have changed anything, Max felt nothing would be the same. Max looked out the window and up at the stars. He focused on the empty space in the Big Dipper. No one said anything, Sham and Eva clearly waiting for Max to accept what was being said. The silence became deafening.

Max was finally relieved when Sham spoke. "You and Eva are the last of David's line."

Max looked at his mom. She had been there his whole life, yet he now realized he didn't know her at all. She was a stranger to him. She had lied. Anger flared, but he stuffed it down. He didn't want to argue with her in front of Sham. He stared down at his hands. "So, do I have like magical powers."

Sham smirked. "It would be more accurate to say you have certain abilities that can be enhanced with practice and study. You are normal like every other mortal, but you have a certain knowledge engrained in your blood. That knowledge can lead you to understanding. And that unlocks certain powers. Now that we know who you are, we are bound to look after you and assist you in your upcoming tasks. We will get you ready for what you are going to have to do."

Max frowned. "What do you mean? What am I going to have to do?"

Sham looked at Eva, who remained silent. "We feel that while we have every faith the Memitim will find and destroy Astarte, some also feel you also need to be prepared for battle."

"Battle? Who is 'we'?"

"We, meaning the representatives of Existence itself. Beings from every Gate, including the Thirteenth, which you would typically deem more enemies than friends. These beings have deemed it necessary that you be trained in preparation for every contingency. But you won't be alone." Sham nodded to Eva. "It has also been decided that your mother will assist you as a representative from the Fourth Gate."

Max couldn't stand his mother's silence any longer. He turned to her and asked, "How long have you known all this?

Why didn't you tell me? Did Dad know?"

Eva's face was restrained. "I have known about my bloodline since I was seventeen. I didn't tell you because the knowledge is a burden. I just wanted you to grow up like everyone else, because you are just like everyone else. You haven't changed. You're still Max."

"Mom! I am being prepared for some fucking battle! Everything has changed."

She nodded. "I know. I had hoped you wouldn't need to know. You can blame me all you want. You have no idea what it is like to give life and watch it grow, knowing they may be destined for a night like tonight. I had hoped you could live your life in peace. I knew it was foolish for me to hope. But I do not regret trying." She saw the anger still in his face, but she had accepted her decision years ago and wasn't going to second guess it now. "I know you would do the same for your child."

Max saw the stubbornness of his mother and knew yelling at her now would not gain him anything. Finding some calm, he asked quietly, "And Dad?"

The question cut her deeper than she'd thought. She had done her best to get past the loss of Jude, but tonight's events had brought the pain back. "Your father was a good man. The very best. I will never find another like him, and I can't wait to see him again. I know you don't understand this now, but I sent a part of myself with him when he died, just to comfort him, but also a part of me died when he did." Eva thought this division of her being was probably why she was blindsided by tonight's events. She had strained herself too far. "I wouldn't keep anything from him. Jude knew all about me and agreed to keep quiet while striving with me to give you the life you deserved—a normal life. He would have done anything for you."

Max knew she loved his dad, and she loved him. He never doubted that, but it was nice to hear the depths of love. He remembered his dad and his words to him in the void, and his nerves settled. He turned to Sham. "What now?"

"You will spend your time training. Studying. I want you to learn everything you can. If you have to face the Necromancer, you will be ready."

"Why does it have to come to a battle between us? You can't tell me Existence doesn't have some sort of supergun it can use to take her out. Why do they need me?"

Sham shook his head. "I don't know. There is a high possibility the Necromancer will be defeated by Mal and the Memitim, but the other option that is possible is one-on-one combat with the last heir of David. That may bring about her downfall."

From the moment he'd heard the word "battle," a thought had kept coming back into Max's mind. He had to ask. "Is it certain I will win?"

Sham was not one to sugar coat. "No. Nothing is certain."

Eva put her arm around him and squeezed. "When you were born, I prayed nothing like this would ever happen to you. I guess all mothers want their little boys never to grow up. I have to let that go eventually, but I will be with you. Every step." She looked as if she was going to tear up, but she would not allow herself to. She had to be strong for Max. "You will be dealing with things and gaining knowledge I never had nor needed. But I will make sure you're ready."

Max hugged her back and he sat silently considering for a few moments. He turned to Sham. "Okay. I'm in. What's first?"

Relief shown on Sham's face. If Max hadn't volunteered,

Sham would have been out of options. "Well, I guess before we begin, there is just one more thing left to discuss." Sham held out his hands and closed his eyes. Max saw a flash, then, in Sham's hands, laid a sword in its scabbard. It was about four feet long, with a hilt long enough for two hands. The guard was ornate, consisting of twisting sliver metal. The pommel was a flattened silver orb with a gold inlaid six-pointed star. Max recognized it as the Star of David. It was simple, but still beautiful in its simplicity. Sham inspected the sword that had appeared in his hands as if seeing it for the first time and said, "Interesting."

Max had difficulty focusing on anything but the sword. The moment it had appeared, Max felt a warmth roll over him. The hair on his arms stood up as he filled with excitement. It was at that moment Max registered what Sham had said. "Sorry, what's interesting?"

Sham turned the sword over and examined the other side. "This sword has been kept behind the First Gate. That is its home when it's not being used. An object this important must be protected. It's an instrument that can only be wielded by the chosen decedents of David."

Max said, "The House of David?"

Sham was glad Max was paying attention. "Yes, also known as the House of David. Originally it was owned by a Philistine named Goliath. David, before he became king, overpowered Goliath with a mere stone. When Goliath fell to the ground, David ran over to him, stole this sword, and used his own sword to cut off the giant's head. This sword has reappeared over the centuries, always to the children of David. What I find interesting is in each incarnation, the sword changes appearance to suit the user's needs." Sham glanced at Eva, who glanced down. He then held the sword out to Max, who gently took the weapon.

Max took the sword by the hilt. He wanted to see the blade but didn't want to seem too eager. He reverently tried to remove the scabbard. It wouldn't budge. Max, not wanting to seem weak, struggled against the scabbard a second time. "Is there some trick to this? Some trigger I am not seeing?"

Sham shook his head. "I would've been amazed if you had freed the sword on your first night. You are not ready to use it. You must learn how, when, and why to use it."

A little defeated, Max asked, "You said it has come back to the world other times?"

"Yes." Sham looked quickly at Eva and continued. "Not every descendant of David is given the sword. When the world needs a hero, a champion, the sword leaves the First Gate. It is now yours to use and care for until the day you die, when it will go back behind the First Gate, awaiting another champion. Who knows, maybe it will become famous to the world under your use." Sham pointed to the star on the pommel. "That sword in your hands has been called many names. Joyeuse. Caliburn. Hrunting. It has been wielded by great people like the Maid of Orleans and El Cid. And now you, Maxwell Travers. You will join their ranks." Sham looked and saw Max didn't seem to understand the importance of this moment.

Max tried again to release the sword. He failed. "Who?"

Sham rolled his eyes. "These things don't mean anything to you, do they?" Max shrugged. "El Cid was a great Spanish knight who wielded Tizona," Sham tapped Max's sword, "and brought God's justice to his foes." Max glanced back down at his sword. "Joan of Arc, known as the Maid of Orleans, wielded the Sword of Saint Catherine," he tapped the sword again, "and used it to route the English out of France. Don't you see, Max? This is not just a pretty object. It is an instrument of God."

Understanding began to seep into Max. He put the sword down on the table, unsure if he wanted to pick it up ever again.

Sham smiled happy to see humility come over Max. He knew it would serve him well. "It's actually quite ironic you are to use that sword against Astarte."

Max restrained himself from trying again. "What's ironic?"

"After David killed Goliath, this sword was given for safekeeping to the Priests of Nob, who were Gibeonites. As the years rolled on, King Saul became a jealous and evil man. His jealously finally settled on David because he knew David had been anointed the next king. He wanted David dead, and so he sent his soldiers out to kill him. Warned by Saul's son, David fled and found himself in the temple in Nob. Astarte, who hated King Saul, saw an opportunity. She found David hiding in Nob, the land of her childhood, and she entered the temple, posing as the High Priest. David asked her if she had any weapons in the temple he could use against Saul. Using her magics, she imbued the blade of Goliath with enchantments and blood magics. It is uncertain exactly how the magic of the blade works. The knowledge of her enchantments has been lost to time. These magics caused the sword to lock itself to the blood of David, which is why only his decedents can wield it and unlock all its powers. Because it is of her, it is also the perfect weapon to strike her down."

Hearing this, Max picked the sword up and again tried to free it. He failed. "When do we begin?"

Eva rose from her seat and said, "Now."

CHAPTER 6

"The problem, Max, is time," Eva said as she led Max and Sham out of the dining room and toward the back of the house. She reached the end of the hallway that ended in a plain wall. Max looked at the wall he had seen all his life and wondered what they were doing here. "I agree with Sham and the others, and have every faith the Memitim will do their job, and also that you need to be prepared. We just don't know how much time we have." Eva cast her hands over the wall, said a quick enchantment, and a purple door appeared. "However, son, I have a solution to that." She opened the door and gestured for Max to enter. Max peered into the dimly lit doorway and saw stone steps leading down into a non-existent cellar. He made to say something, but Eva just gestured again for him to enter the doorway. With just a slight hesitation, Max went down the steps. Sham began to move forward, but Eva put her hand out. "Not this time, Sham. You can do your lessons out here. This space is for me and Max only. You can either sit patiently or go do some Watcher bullshit somewhere else. Your choice."

Sham gave a grimace but knew not to argue with her. He was in her domain now and could not question her. After all, he was just thankful she had agreed with his and Mal's plan in the first place. "I think I will just sit out here and wait."

"Suit yourself. As you are aware, it won't be long." And with that, Eva began to go down the steps, and the door shut behind her. It vanished with a purple flash, and the plain wall reappeared.

Max walked down the steps and reached a cobblestone floor. He glanced back at his mom, who was following him. He was amazed to see the door and the house above him had disappeared. Looking up, he saw only the open sky with stars twinkling above. He gazed around the room and saw the cobblestone floor extended in all directions without end. He began to have an odd feeling he had been here before. A queasiness overtook him when he realized it. The room reminded him of the gray void between the worlds. Keeping the panic from erupting, he looked at Eva, who stood beside him. "What is this place?"

Eva scanned the room and guessed the otherworldliness was causing Max distress. "How about something a little more pleasant for our purposes?" She closed her eyes and thought of somewhere Max would be more at ease. Smiling, she opened her eyes and snapped her fingers. A violet electric flash emitted from her snapped fingers, and the cobblestones vanished around their feet. Sprouting from the ground, the cobblestones were replaced by manicured green grass. A small brook erupted at the edge of the space and winded its way down the expanse of the room. Large trees erupted from the ground and stood all around Eva and Max. The night was replaced by a light blue sky. Max watched as the blackness of the expanse completely vanished. He found himself and his mother in what looked like a little park. Rolling hills in the distance were covered with wildflowers. The large oak trees swayed with the light breeze that cooled his skin from the heat of the sun. "Come with me," Eva said as she walked out from the little glade of trees onto a large, flat, open space. Max turned around in the wind and the sun and marveled at what he saw. He had almost forgotten he'd been sitting at his dinner table just a moment earlier in the middle of the night. Eva looked around her renovation and nodded. "There. I think that is a little better for our needs, don't you?"

Max reached down and felt the soft grass against his hand. It was real. "What is this place?"

Eva watched him. "If it isn't obvious, this is a training space."

Max walked back to the middle of field and tried to take in the dimensions of the park. The blue sky, the distant hills, the creek that went off into the horizon. It didn't add up. "I don't understand. How is this place even possible? And why didn't I ever notice it?"

Eva scanned the field, making sure everything was ready. "Max, you will find this frustrating, but the answer to most of what you are going to be seeing from here on out is going to be 'magic.' You never saw this place because I didn't want you to. Yes, it is attached to the house, but I have hidden it to where no one can detect it. This will be our training area, just for me and you. Sham will also give you lessons, but those will have to be done outside this space." She made sure he was looking at her when she added, "Seriously, no guests."

Max nodded that he understood. He had been involved with otherworldly magic for the better part of the last few months, so he was used to his questions being only half answered. "You said the problem we were going to have was time. It's a cool place to work out, Mom, but how does it give us more time?"

"I'm glad you asked. It shows you are paying attention. Yes, this place itself is magic, but not just because of the dimensions or its hidden nature. It is in a suspended time loop. I have taken this area out of time. The moment you enter this place, you are suspended. Time does not pass for us in here. It will give you all the time you need to complete your training. To learn all you need to learn before you face the Necromancer, if it is your destiny to do so. The moment you leave, time will start back up."

Max's face scrunched up, trying to digest what Eva had just said. "We can stay in here for days, but when we leave, it will still be my birthday?"

Eva smiled. "Exactly. When we leave, Sham will be waiting, and to him, it will be like we just left."

"Who built this place?"

Eva looked at him like she didn't understand the question. "I did. Who else?" She didn't understand his wide-eyed expression. "One day, I will tell you my story, but just know, I put everything into the spell I had cast to hide you and me from Existence. It nearly killed me. But a spell like that, it has to be maintained secretly, so I needed a place to do that, away from prying eyes. A place just for me and my work. And now, a place for you and yours."

Max marveled at the magic and even more at the fact that it was his mother who'd conjured it. A yellow finch flashed in the sun and zoomed into a nearby tree. "Mom, I had no idea you could do things like this. I mean, not just you. I mean, I had no idea magic could make such wonderful things."

Eva was not used to being complimented on her abilities. For a moment, she blushed with pride. "Thank you. I appreciate that." She pointed to two large chairs that had appeared in the middle of the field. "Take a seat." They both walked over and settled in.

Max thought of another question. "Why would I ever

leave this place if time is not on our side? I mean, can't I stay here for years, train up, then pop out and it is still September?"

Eva pursed her lips, trying to find the right words to make what she had to say make the most sense. She watched her son as his deep blue eyes, just like hers, caught hold of soaring overhead. "There are a few reasons you can't stay here for an extended time. First off, there isn't any food or water in this place."

Max looked at the brook and asked, "Can't you just conjure up a sandwich or something?"

Eva shook her head. "No. This is all an illusion. Extremely real, I'll grant you. But no matter what you are seeing, you are still in the cobblestone room you first saw. There is no water in that stream. There is no bird flying overhead." She didn't let his lip about her making a sandwich go. With another snap of her fingers, a sandwich landed in his lap. "Go ahead. Take a bite."

Max could tell from her tone she hadn't appreciated his statement, so he did as she asked and took a bite. It was delicious. He hadn't realized how hungry he was. "I don't know what you are talking about. This is amazing."

Eva watched as he continued to chew. "Yes, I know. But if you did nothing but eat what is conjured here, you would die of dehydration in about three days. Hunger in about nine." She saw he didn't understand. "Remember, Max. None of this is real. The magic done in this place is just that. Magic. It is shut off from the real world, so no access to water or food or anything like that. Think of this place like a huge VR experience. Can you eat VR food?"

He looked down at the remains of the sandwich as it blipped back into non-existence. "Okay, so every now and then, I will pop out for a burger. Are there any other reasons?"

She smiled seeing he was beginning to take things a little more seriously. "Yes, being time suspended like we are can have unknown effects."

Max became a little anxious. "Like what?"

"I don't want go into it now in great detail because you won't understand half of what I say. When I was taught these types of magic, I was given warnings from someone I trust beyond anyone else. One of the effects I can attest to is a form of sickness. You learn, age, and grow while here, but the word outside stops. If you are in here too long, once you reenter the normal time stream, your mind tries to stretch." She tried to find a better word but couldn't. "I don't know, that's the best way to describe it. I have done it a few times, and I don't recommend it." She could see a look of concern on his face. "Don't worry, Max. I have a good handle on how long to stay. You just focus on our training sessions, then leave when I say so. Trust me, okay?"

He had no reason to doubt her. He was already in for a penny. "Got it, Mom. Train hard, then leave, grab something to eat, and let the real-world soak in."

Eva smiled. "Exactly. Think of it like scuba diving. Can't stay down too long and you need to come back gradually. Now, I wanted this first night to be just us before we involve Sham. I wanted to talk to you about what being in the House of David means."

Any lingering concern Max had evaporated. He had been hoping someone would clue him in. He had been slightly worried he was just going to be given a sword and sent off into the world. "I would really like to know."

Eva eased back. "The history of the House is very interesting, but that is stuff you can look up in any book. Countless stories of heroes and heroines doing great deeds.

That shouldn't be our focus tonight. I think it is important to know what the role of the House of David has in this realm." Her eyes surveyed the little park, giving her a little time to try and find the right place to start. "Do you know what a paladin is?" Max shook his head. "That is what the members of the House of David are. We are paladins, a word coined by Charlemagne. Paladins are warriors of a sort. Not just soldiers, but warriors for all that is right and good. We act outside the laws of man. We are not beholden to any country or group. Our overriding law is to do right. It is a sacred trust that has been given to us by Existence. From David all the way to you."

Max thought about what she said. "Outside the laws of man? I don't understand."

Eva tried to clarify. "You have seen the news." Max nodded. "You have seen terrible things done in the name of the law, correct? Of course you have. Being law abiding and being righteous are not always the same thing. Back in the day, horse thieves were hung and women who lost their virginity were stoned in the street. Those carrying out these executions were following the law. But do you think what they were doing was right?" Max shook his head. "You must do what you think is right at all times. You cannot allow yourself to be tainted or corrupted. *Bireshutt atsemenu.* Law unto ourselves. These are our family's words. It doesn't mean we live outside the law. It means we find the righteous path with or without the law. You are a law unto yourself. Answerable only to yourself. Ultimately, it is a burden."

Eva let that thought set in. Max looked at the sword in his hands and questioned again whether he wanted it anymore.

"It's good that you question using the sword. If you wield it, you will have the knowledge and power of the House of David behind you. But using the blade, destroying in the name of righteousness, is not as easy as you think. Killing, even killing the damned, should not be done easily or with relish."

Max finally asked a question. "And telling me this without Sham?"

Eva knew her son was no fool. He could sense where she might be going with this. "Sham is good. Trust him as much as you want. But…" she leaned over and poked him in the chest, "it is you who holds the sword, you who has to swing it, you who has to bear the burden, when the time comes, if it ever comes, make your own decisions. Understand?"

"Law unto ourselves," Max repeated, now hoping that day would never come.

"On this first night, I also wanted to talk to you about the nature of our family's magic. I think it is generally good you have some knowledge that was taught to you by the Necromancer, but there are going to be some habits we are going to have to break. Witch magic can be unpredictable and spotty. And I have no faith she ever gave you the whole truth of things."

Max had to interrupt. "She didn't really teach me much. Just how to enter the void."

Eva laughed. "'Just.' Well, the discipline to do 'just' that is considerable. I will add to that instruction. There are many different forms of magic, and each can be used for different tasks. Some magic is performed by hand gestures, some by written forms, and some by magic words. The hardest magic to accomplish is performed by thought. Most major conjuring takes a combination of these different magics to perform. Like the door to get in here takes the right words and hand movements. These are the things I will teach you."

Max was excited to begin. "And what will Sham teach?"

"I don't claim to know it all. He will fill you in on

mission specific information, like what creatures you might have to face and different strategies you may have to employ." She moved closer to Max and took his hands. "I need to say this one time. You are going to be dealing with things I never had to. Terrible creatures and terrible decisions. Sham and I will get you ready, I promise you that. But if you want to run, I will help you there too." Eva couldn't help herself. She was a mother first and foremost.

Max could see she was being serious. She would battle anything and everything for him. She was offering an escape, consequences be damned. For a moment, Max was tempted. He glanced down at the sword and thought about what his mother had said. A holy warrior. Doing what was right. That was what his bloodline meant. Max put one hand over hers. "You have no idea what your offer means to me. But you know I can't. I'm already in this, aren't I?"

Eva nodded and finally let a tear well up. "You can't blame me for trying. Trust me, you will do the same," she said again. She gave him a hug. "Okay, enough for one night. You've already had a long day and you will need your sleep. Your world is about to get even harder."

A thought came to Max. "Mom, if we descend from a line that goes back millennia, then why are we the only ones left?"

A pained look struck across Eva's face. "Because being a hero is dangerous work. We are the last. That is a responsibility we both have to accept."

CHAPTER 7

And that was how training began. Max and Eva would spend hours on end in what Max affectionately called "Mom's torture chamber." He had spent the first part of each day perfecting different incantations from his mother. Even though he was a quick study since he had been doing similar work all summer with Angie (he couldn't bring himself to call her Astarte yet), his biggest problem was finding his focus.

Eva kept her patience but still pushed him. "Max, no matter what is going on around you. Angels with torn wings swinging swords to your left. Demons shooting fire out of their mouths to your right. Necromancers and warlocks casting intricate spells ahead—remain focused. It is from that center of calm that our family's power is derived. Thoughtful. Deliberate. Passionless."

Max would practice focusing, but he had trouble. It was similar to what Angie had been teaching him, but that was of little help. With Angie, all she needed was for him to go into the gray place. His mom was demanding much more from him. Spells and counter spells. Shields. Bolts. Elemental magic. Scrawled incantations. A stubborn sword that wouldn't come out. Oh, and a four-thousand-year-old witch he may have to kill. So much was being pumped into his head, it was hard for him to silence the world.

One morning, Eva was teaching Max how to form a shield from magical attacks. The best he could conjure were shields that may have stopped a fly, but just barely. And they definitely wouldn't have stopped anything Astarte would throw at him. After seeing him struggling, Eva suggested, "I want you to tell me a good memory. No, tell me an excellent memory."

Max thought for a moment. He was frustrated. He knew shields were extremely central to any defense he would have against Astarte, and he hated that they were causing him so many problems. "I don't know," he blurted.

Eva rolled her eyes. "You're telling me in all your years of life, you don't have one good memory you can recall? You have to have one. Make it a good one."

Max saw he had insulted his mom. He sat and thought about it and pulled one memory. "It's funny. You would think I would say some vacation we took, or a Christmas morning. But, honestly, before I drift off to sleep, when I need to slow my mind down, I think about being in the backyard with Dad. Playing catch. Just him and me, back and forth. I remember sometimes he was still dressed in his suit from work, but he would always slip on the glove and play with me. Sometimes we would talk. Sometimes we wouldn't. Just the sound of the ball hitting leather. The warm sun. The wind. The fresh cut lawn. It's a memory I keep close."

Eva smiled. "Perfect. Go there. Go back to the yard. Remember the smell of the glove. The feel of the ball. Your father smiling."

Max did what he was told, and the world stopped around him. He tried the spell they had been working on, and it ignited before him. The air bowed and thickened around him. He could feel the shield flex around him and could feel its rigidness. Not much would get to him now, he thought.

Eva cast a simple light spell, and it smashed against his shield, leaving Max unharmed.

"Nicely done, Max. Thought magic demands centering your mind. You are well on your way."

From that morning on, the lessons became easier for him to grasp. Max practiced calming his mind, using his memory to ground himself. Max realized many of the incantations his mother taught him dealt with the surrounding elements.

When he brought this up, Eva nodded. "Every realm in existence is different. We use what is around us as our weapons. Otherworldly creatures are caught off guard and don't know how to handle such an attack." Eva taught him how to weaponize the very air around him, turn heat and light into shields, harness the powers of the mortal realm.

He found his mom to be a good teacher. She was patient with him, but he could sense she was urgent for him to learn as much as he could. She told him by the time she'd had to learn at seventeen, her father had died, so it was left to her uncle to teach her (each time Max had asked why she'd had to learn, his mother had refused to answer). "The House of David is more than a sword. The family has created their own magical forms and chants, unique to the progeny of David. Because of this, they are especially difficult to counter. Another reason we have this area only for us."

One of these lessons dealt specifically with dealing with necromancers. "Max, what you need to understand is a witches' powers are derived from their raw emotions. While it fuels their power, it can also be their undoing. The fury of a witch is something to behold, but if they go too far, it unbalances them, and that is when you can strike. Since you will be dealing with the Necromancer, she will be well trained to keep composure. If you are going to last against her, you need to unhinge her."

"How do I take advantage of that?"

"Oddly, if you have your wits about you, the spell is simple." Eva folded her hands over each other again and again and the air thickened around them. She shot out one hand toward one of the lamps, muttering an incantation. The light fluttered, then was sucked away from the bulb and joined the air around Eva's hands. She swirled her hand in the air. Max felt dry wind brush back his face and could feel all the moisture evaporate into the spell. Eva stopped moving her hands and presented what she had created. It was almost translucent, and the edges were hard to make out, but Max saw a definite shape in the air in front of his mother. It was the shape of an arrowhead.

Max reached out to see if he could touch it.

"I wouldn't do that," Eva warned. "This spell will drive right through the fury of any necromancer, using the fury like a river, straight into the witch's heart. Do it right, and she dies instantly." Eva waved her hand again, and the arrowhead vanished. They spent the rest of that week (which, in suspended time, was considerable) perfecting this spell and discussing the various odd magics of the House of David.

After his hours with Eva, Max would leave the training space and meet Sham, who would be patiently waiting outside the door each day with a lesson about the nature of the various beings and beasts Astarte may conjure. He would also give any updates about Astarte, but those were rare.

Sham tried to give Max as much information as he could. "Exactly how her magics work is a little unknown, but our sources indicate she may be able to conjure demons from the Thirteenth Gate itself. Over the next sessions, I want to explore with you the different types of terrors she could unleash, so at least you won't piss yourself when you see them."

This part, while horrifying, pleased Max since it was almost like story time with Sham. Sham talked about how Max needed to stop thinking of demons from Hell. Not all the demons from the Thirteenth Gate come from fire or dark pits. Some command the air like Andras and his legions of demons riding wyverns.

"What's a wyvern?"

"Oh," Sham thought for the right words, "it is a scaled creature with two legs and two great wings. Most can unleash fire from their breath."

"So, like a dragon?"

"No. Not a dragon. A wyvern."

"Sounds like a dragon."

Exhausted, Sham surrendered. "Fine. Andras and his demons ride dragons. They have various powers, but generally bring fire raining down upon their pray."

Max learned not all beasts used brute force either. Some simply appeared and caused chaos. At first, Max was confused. "Like, what do you mean?"

Sham explained, "Well, for example, Perfidians are a type of demon that, just by their presence, cause people to turn upon each other. Brothers kill brothers. Sons kill mothers. All ties of duty and honor can be undone by one Perfidian. These types of demons cause the most problems because killing the enemy is easy, killing your loved one is a completely different story." Sham always tried to tell a short story to hammer home his point. "You have heard of the city of Belgrade in Serbia?"

Max smiled and said sarcastically, "Oh, of course. Belgrade. Mother, Father, and I would summer in Belgrade almost every year."

If Sham registered Max's tone, he did not say. "Good. In the Third Century BCE, a warring group called the Celts invaded Europe and what is now Serbia. Belgrade, being near the confluence of the Sava and Danube rivers was, even then, an important strategic city. The defenders of Belgrade, the Singi, fought so ferociously, the Celts were pushed back time and time again. After the last push failed, the Celts, being learned in old magics, brought forth three druid priests. Together, they were able to bring forth one Perfidian from the Thirteenth Gate. The creature agreed to perform its evil deeds, but the cost was great. It works swiftly. Just by its presence alone, the Singi destroyed themselves. It began with the men. They didn't slaughter each other but went after the old and the lame. Then they killed their own mothers and wives and sisters. By the dawn, the Celts watched as the children rained down from the tall ramparts of the city, being thrown down by their loving and devoted fathers. Finally, by midday, when the flies were already feasting on the new dead, the Singi men took down each other. Without a sound or a whimper."

The images of children falling and being smashed on the ground turned Max's stomach. When he recovered, he asked, "What was the cost the Celts had to pay for this nightmare?"

Sham, who had been lost in the story, turned back to Max. "Because the actions of the Singi were so depraved and treacherous, Belgrade was accursed by Existence."

Max had heard the term before. "What does that mean?"

"An accursement of a land can take different forms. Some accursed lands won't grow crops or are devoid of life. Some give off noxious fumes and are deadly to even tread. With Belgrade, the curse of the land followed with the people who tried to hold it. This is why Belgrade has been a witness to over one-hundred wars and has been razed over fifty times. The city hasn't seen a lasting and stable peace. And never will." He leaned closer to Max. "Got it."

Max wondered if anything he was going to learn was going to bring him any joy. "Perfidians bad. Avoid at all costs. Got it."

Not all Sham's stories were of monsters and demons. He also told Max the various accounts of the other Sons and Daughters of David. Eva had no problem with this since Sham typically had a firsthand knowledge, having worked with the family for some time.

"It is important for you to know something of your family, since once you unlock the sword, their knowledge will become your knowledge," Sham said, as if it was common knowledge.

Max looked back at Sham. "I don't understand."

Sham tilted his head. "What do you mean?"

"How will their knowledge become mine?"

"Oh…" Sham strained for a way to explain it. "As I have said, the magics Astarte used to make the sword are unique and lost to us. But the blade is a living magical item, tied to your bloodline. And as such, the lessons from all its previous holders are stored in the blade's memory. The sword bearer of the House of David does not go into battle alone but takes an army with him. You will have El Cid and Charlemagne whispering in your ear."

The thought of it made Max's head swim and also creeped him out. "I was wondering about that since no one is teaching me how to swing a sword. I guess you should have told me this earlier. Probably would have put some of my worries to rest."

"Sorry," Sham said sheepishly. "Please understand, Max, typically, I would have been working with you and your family since the day you were born. We are trying to cram a ton of information into you at once. Some things are bound to fall through the cracks. The sword will teach you, and in time, you may teach it some new tricks."

Max tried to pull the sword. Nothing.

Max looked at his mom. "Why didn't you tell me this? I mean, why aren't you showing me how to use the sword? Wouldn't you know better than Sham?"

A pained expression overtook Eva's face, but she composed herself. "Sham has taught the House of David longer than you could ever know. The blade is personal. Unique to its user. My experiences won't help you. In fact, I am certain my experiences would only hinder you. Anyway, a sword never came to me. What I needed to do didn't involve a sword." She said this with a hint of sadness. This was the only clue he had gotten out of her as to the nature of her past mission. She had made it clear she didn't want to talk about what she had done. Max was no fool. He knew whatever she had done had caused her to hide herself and her child from Existence itself. Knowing what he knew now, it was understandable that being in the House of David could leave a person with some deep scars. Eva continued. "The relationship between the blade and the bearer cannot really be taught. It is experienced. When the time is right, it will all fall into place." She started to say something else, but decided against it and got up and left.

The last parts of Max's days were filled with exercises to strengthen his body. Sham warned that, for mortals, the strength of their castings was directly related to their physical power. Also, Eva instructed Max that physical exertion and muscle building would allow him to stay longer in the training space with less negative effects.

No matter what benefit it gave him magically, Max enjoyed this part of the training best. It gave him an opportunity to find calm. Everything he knew had changed, and he needed the time alone to clear his mind. He began with just running in the neighborhood. He had never really been out of shape, but the long runs told him how battle unready he was. With all things, time and pushing himself found he could run longer. Faster.

He went into the garage and uncovered his father's old workout bench. Just one of the many things his mother never got around to getting rid of. The bench was well worn, but nicely maintained. His father's headprint was clearly visible in the soft material. Oddly, it comforted Max. He imagined Jude was beside him while he worked the various weights.

Maxed word hard to build up his stamina and watched as his remaining baby fat burned away, replaced by hard muscle. One night, Eva caught him checking himself in the garage mirror and smiled. "Okay, enough admiring yourself. How about a different workout?"

Max blushed at being caught, but he was always up to a challenge. "Sure. Do you want to arm wrestle, old woman?"

She didn't answer his question. Instead, she turned and led him back into the training area. As always, it was another perfect day in the park, but this time, there was someone waiting for them on the field. A man about his height and build. He had tan skin and dark features. And a large grin.

"Who is that?" Max was on guard until he saw Eva was clearly aware of the stranger.

"It is not a who, Max. Remember, everything here is an illusion. This is a sparring partner I thought could put those newfound muscles to some use."

"Hello, Max," the stranger said.

Max looked at the man, not quite knowing how to respond. "Mom, what is this?"

"I am Multi." The man stretched his hand out, which Max took and shook. "I am here to teach you how to defend yourself in a physical attack."

Max turned to his mom who explained, "Max, I know you have been worried about how you may handle yourself if you have to go out. Magic and education will take you far, but I agree it is probably a good idea you at least know how to throw a punch."

"Or more importantly, how to take one," Multi said, his grin widening.

Eva laughed and turned to Max. "On guard, Max."

At that, Multi's grin disappeared and he took a defensive stance. "It is important in all fighting disciplines that you maintain calm and balance. I know these are traits you are currently working on, so this should be easy." Multi stepped forward. "Try and land a punch, Max."

Max turned back to his mom, who had stepped aside, and gave her an expression to ask whether this was serious. The look on her face showed it was. "Okay," Max said as he stepped forward and threw his first blow. A haymaker. It didn't land. Not only did it not land, Multi countered with a short jab to the gut, and Max instantly found himself crumpled up on his knees, gasping for breath.

"Max," Multi chastised, "you can't just throw a punch and not be ready for a counter." Eva laughed as her son recovered.

"Why are you laughing? What kind of mother are you?" Max was more embarrassed than anything.

Eva stifled her amusement. "The kind of mother who

wants you to survive any attack. I think you have your work cut out for you, Multi."

Multi's grin returned. "I agree, ma'am. I would say every day for at least two hours. I think we need to keep it simple. I would suggest jujutsu if time is an issue."

Eva nodded. "I agree. Start there."

Max was on his feet and glowered at Multi, who did not register how pissed Max was. "Can you also teach me how to use a sword?"

Multi smiled. "Of course. I can teach all forms of fighting with all forms of weapons. Of course, it would be up to you, ma'am." Multi stared at Eva.

Eva didn't hesitate. "Yes, I think that would be fine. Teach him sabre fighting. But do not draw his blood." Multi nodded, and Max was surprised to hear that had even been an option. "I will leave you to it today. No more than two hours, Multi, and then, Max," she turned to her son, "I want you to leave the training area. Two hours tops with Multi, I mean it."

Max smiled at hearing some of his old mother coming through. "Yes, Mom," he said comically.

Eva turned to leave as Max got back onto his feet. He would not stay on them very long during the first thirty matches with Multi.

And this was how his training continued. Every morning, every night, and throughout the day. He learned many spells, listened to many stores, and collected many bruises. Each day, he got stronger and wiser. At the end of each day, he attempted to draw the sword. And each day, he failed.

When his training came to an end, thanks to the magic of his mother, Max was able to condense just shy of a year down to a few weeks.

CHAPTER 8

One evening, sleep had just about found Max when the doorbell rang. His muscles still ached after a particularly difficult session with Multi. But the ache was good. It told him he was still pushing himself. Getting stronger. He found himself staying in the training space longer and longer, and his mom was right, it did play with your mind. But sleep seemed to cure most of his ills. He needed his bed.

The doorbell rang again, and rudely kept ringing.

"Mom! Get the door." Max didn't hear any footsteps and assumed she was outside sitting on the deck. Eva had been working just as hard as Max at times. Honing her fighting skills with Multi, physical training, even hitting the weights. Max never saw her with a blade, and when he asked where hers was, she never answered. All she said was that she was working out to show solidarity. Most nights, she collapsed on the couch from exhaustion.

The doorbell rang.

Max, feeling a little guilt about yelling, slowly got out of bed and trudged down the stairs to the front door. As he passed the dining room on the way to the door, he saw his mother talking with Sham. The look on her face was not good.

The doorbell rang again. But it could wait. "Mom, what is it?"

Eva turned to Max. The expression of her face was resolute. "Get the door, Max. Please."

The doorbell rang again.

Jesus Christ, Max thought as he walked over to the door. He flung open the door, ready to rip whoever kept ringing the bell a new asshole. Max was greeted by three toddlers dressed up as a ghost, a princess, and a firefighter.

"Trick or treat," they all said in unison. Halloween. He had completely forgotten. Still, it was late, and the lack of enthusiasm from the kids was obvious. Obviously, they had been at this a long time. Max could see an irresponsible parent standing off to the side carrying on with another adult.

Max could forgive himself for not knowing the exact date. The time loop was completely to blame. That and the neck breaking pace of his training. The kids noticed he wasn't carrying any treats and started to get impatient. Max scanned around the porch and saw the dish his mom had put out was empty, which explained why he hadn't heard the bell go off until now.

One parent stepped forward. "Sorry, man, we told them not to ring, but we couldn't stop them," the father said sheepishly. The parent's costume makeup was streaking down his face. It had been a long time for him too.

Max relaxed his obviously aggressive posture. "No worries. Let me see what I can find for you three." Ducking back into the house, Max quickly found two bananas and an apple. He had been pretty strict about his diet and knew he didn't have any candy. Even though he knew they would probably end up in a trashcan, he returned to the door and gave them to the kids. They looked at the fruit with some suspicion. Max's impatience flared. "Hey, it's the best I got, kids." Without a word of thanks, they shrugged, put the fruit into their overflowing bags, and left.

Max closed the outside door and looked at his phone. It read 10:15. If he got to bed soon, he could get some good sleep before beginning his training again. Max went back into the dining room to say goodnight. Peering in, he only saw Sham sitting alone in a chair.

The look on Sham's face set his teeth on edge. "What going on, Sham? Where is Mom?"

Sham was clearly troubled and trying to find the right words. At last, he spoke. "Max, please take a seat. There has been a development tonight. It seems Astarte has freed Sariel the Fallen." Max knew from his reading Sariel was the demon who taught Astarte about the Continuance and witchcraft. She also imbued her with power. "Things are progressing much faster now."

Max's heart raced. He'd known he didn't have forever to train, but he had fooled himself into thinking he had much more time. "Do we know where they are?" He tried to sound confident. Fake it until you make it, he thought.

Sham shook his head. "We know where they were. Santa Fe. She spent the past few weeks defiling a church there and brought Sariel back."

Max scowled. "But she isn't there anymore? Why didn't the defiling of a church register on anyone's radar? What the hell are the Memitim doing?"

Sham shook his head. "I don't know. By agreement with Eva, they don't mess with your training, but we also don't mess with their tactics. It has been a gentle peace. But I think it is pretty clear they dropped the ball."

Hearing her name brought his original question back to him. "Where's Mom?"

Sham hated saying this next part. "Max," he said,

scratching his cheek, "it is all hands-on deck now, so to speak. I don't necessarily agree with the call, I need you to know that." Max could see Sham was prepping him for terrible news. "Mal has convinced the powers that be Eva is necessary to the next step. Reports are that the Continuance is already showing signs of disruption." Sham's voice went up higher to show confidence. "And while the Memitim are still on track," Sham stopped, and quietly muttered, "the decision has been made to put you in the field."

Max was furious. He asked again, knowing he was going to hate the answer. "Where is my mom?"

Sham put his hands up as a plea for peace. "Please understand, she is also House of David. Vastly trained. Extremely talented. A credit to your house. Battle-tested and hardened. We need her."

Max closed the distance between him and Sham and shouted, "Need her for what?"

Sham stepped back, allowing him some space. "Max, as she was training you, she was also training herself. You have only learned a quarter of what she knows. She is talented beyond what you know. She has been given her mission, and she is now in play as well."

"You mean she left?" Max began to take in deep breaths. His fury mixed with his pain.

Sham, seeing Max was teetering, explained, "Existence demanded she leave without another word. We knew leaving you was going to be hard enough, but if you pleaded for her to stay with you, she would have. And while that may be good for you, it wouldn't be good for all of us. There are forces here that you, your mom, and even I can't fully understand. You and your mother may not like it, but we are all on the same team, working together for the same goal. Sometimes, we just have to have faith."

"You've betrayed me. You and this 'we' bullshit sent my mom off alone for your own means. Fuck your faith." Anger dripped from Max.

Sham tried to talk himself out of the uncomfortable conversation. "They also learned something we have only theorized. We know why Astarte has been able to live so long. This knowledge is going to give you a leg up if you have to confront her. But, Max, we have to get on the road."

Max barely heard what he said. He only thought of his mom going off into the night alone. "You didn't give me a chance to say goodbye. Or thank you. Or I love you! A decent human would have given us that." Max stepped forward, wondering what would happen if he attacked Sham. He had always been good to Max, had become a trusted teacher, but Max knew he was so much more. Still, the thought of taking his fury out on somebody felt good.

Sham waited a few moments. He knew Max was about to strike, but he wouldn't move against him. If he needed to be a punching bag, he would do it. He watched Max calculate his chances, sizing Sham up. But then he saw Max's rigid jaw slacken. He had decided. Seeing this, he went over to comfort his student. Max pulled away, and without another word, left the room. It took Sham a second to decide to follow him. He didn't know what to say, but before he could think of anything, Sham turned a corner just in time to see the purple door vanish.

Max ran past the glade of trees and into the open field. It, of course, was another perfect day in the park. The wind cooled his face and filled his lungs with perfumed air. He looked around and finally saw Multi sitting on a tuft of grass. He walked over to him and noticed it looked like the multidisciplinary, multifaceted training program had been crying.

"What's wrong with you?" Max asked as he sat down next to him.

Multi didn't turn but gazed towards the hills in the distance. "It was almost impossible for her to leave, you know? She fought against it viciously."

Max snorted. "Apparently not hard enough."

Multi finally turned to Max and glared. "You have no idea what you're talking about."

"Fuck I don't! All that cheap talk of 'we are in this together' and 'I will be right by your side.' Total horseshit."

Max had expected Multi to start screaming at him. Even though Multi was just a training program, Max had learned over time Eva had imbued Multi with human insight and perception. This was why it shocked him a little that Multi just smiled at his comment.

"I forget sometimes you are still a child. You cannot foresee what your mother has done for you. What she is attempting to do for you. You think she left you."

Max asked with trepidation, "Well, hasn't she?"

Multi breathed in deep and closed his eyes. "Just the opposite. Sometimes defending what you love most means going out to destroy the beasts in the shadows. Malhamash came and dangled an opportunity—an opportunity that was irresistible to her."

Max knew, but he had to ask, "And what was that?"

Multi opened his eyes. "To take the weight off her son." The wind kicked up, picking up some leaves that had begun to fall from the oak trees. "I will not say you are ready to face Astarte. But you're as ready as you are going to be."

Max watched the leaves career through the air and

took another moment. Thought of all his parents had done for him. Thought of all that was riding on him. It may not have been fair, but he knew it was time to accept what was, what is, and what may be.

"Thanks, Multi. For everything."

Multi waved a dismissive hand. "You might as well thank an oven for cooking your meal." Multi got up and gave Max a hand. "But if it makes you feel better, you're welcome, and I hope to see you again."

Returning back into the house, time started back up again, Max saw Sham turning the corner from the dining room. Sham approached Max, and thankfully, Max didn't pull away from him. "Max, I am sorry. It wasn't my call. Please remember, the people you are working with, including me, are not human. We don't feel in the same way as you do. All most of us can concern ourselves with is the knowledge that we must win this battle. The Continuance is too important to everyone. To everything. Whatever it takes. You know that. Your mother knows that too."

Sham's words did little to soothe Max. Duty meant little if it also meant you lost the ones you loved. Of course, his words were familiar. Sham was merely quoting his mother after all. Whatever it takes. After all, Max had learned, all she had taught him, how important stopping Astarte was. It was what all this was for.

Sham slapped him on the back. "Also, why are you counting your mother off so soon? Remember, whatever you can do, she can do better." Seeing Max loosen even more, Sham smiled. "Whomever is at the end of her mission, I would not wish to be. Not for anything. And do you know why?" Max shook his head. "Because that person stands between Eva and her son. Actually, I pity that person."

Max had always known this day would come. Looking at Sham, he breathed in deep. In his mind, he went to the backyard. He felt the leather ball hit his glove. Max opened both his hands, and his sword appeared. He tried to draw the sword, and for the first time, the sword came out, but just halfway.

The progress emboldened Max. "Okay, Shammy, where to?"

CHAPTER 9

Apollyon emerged from the fire. Solomon 931 looked much like she'd expected. Tenth Century B.C. Jerusalem had it all: communal toilets, a local bleeder, a place where you could buy fly-covered animal flesh or flavorless bread. She had never visited Solomon's little afterlife. By agreement, his torment was to be incremental and light. Nothing she specialized in. She allowed lesser demons like Dokiel to oversee such things.

The few people who saw her materialize, and saw her true form, fell dead in terror. While this always made her smile, she needed answers, so she quickly changed her appearance to a young, buxom brunette in an attempt to fit in with this world.

Turning the corner, she was greeted by the grand sight of the Temple Solomon had built. She began to walk next to it and its white columns and knew she was on the right track. She had to be close. However, things already seemed off. Aside from the two people when she'd first arrived, she hadn't seen anyone else in the streets or occupying the little shops that dotted the road.

After walking on the deserted road for a while, she finally came to the spot she knew she would find Solomon. The little establishment that had been built by the First Gate as a part of the agreement. This was the place where Solomon would find some sustenance while always having a good view of his Temple. This was the place where he had been eating and drinking his time away in this torture.

Looking at the long wooden table, she saw it was filled with food and drink of all kinds, but immediately saw no Solomon. The chairs were empty.

A short man appeared at the opening of the building. Seeing Apollyon, he gave her a disapproving scowl. "Shoo from here, girl. And keep your eyes to yourself. None of this is for the likes of you."

Apollyon bit back her tongue. "I mean no harm, sir. I was looking for Solomon. Where can I find him?"

The man glanced to the Temple and gave a long smile. "He is in there. Praying for all of us. He is going to deliver us from evil. Deliver us all from this place." The man gestured to the world around him.

His statement gave her pause, but after a moment, she said, "Thank you, sir." Instantly, the man burst into flames, and in a flash, was reduced to a small pile of ashes on the floor. He hadn't even had time to shout. Apollyon knew it was stupid, since no one in here except Solomon was real. Nevertheless, she didn't like to be talked to like that.

However, what the man had said confirmed some of her suspicions. Solomon should not be in the Temple. He could not be in the Temple. But he was. This world was spinning off its axis, and she laid all the blame at Dokiel's feet. Not only was Dokiel at the heart of these problems, but he more than likely had gained the information the Necromancer needed to succeed.

As she turned the corner to the front of the Temple, Apollyon finally saw the majority of the town's inhabitants. They were kneeling all around the opening. On every inch of space of the long steps leading up to the porch, people were genuflecting and making prayers. However, the people had made a clearing right up the middle and into the sanctuary, obviously awaiting someone's exit.

She stood back and debated her next move. She quickly tried to think of all the ramifications of what was happening when she heard her name being called.

"Apollyon, Prince of Fiends, Master of Anguish." The voice was loud and full of authority. The voice paused. She was slightly shook to be called out so brazenly, but even more when all the inhabitants turned to look at her. "Welcome," the voice boomed, but the tone was not welcoming. Not welcoming at all. The people turned and gazed back into the Temple.

First to appear was the golden Ark of the Covenant. The gold shone bright in the sun, and a din of whispered prayers began to rise from the assembled. Solomon appeared behind the box. He wore a sleeveless blue robe fringed with golden bells and a gold breastplate bejeweled with twelve gems. He smiled at the assembly and greeted some men close by who attended the Ark. He'd apparently had it removed from the Holy of the Holies and was putting on a display of power for his people.

Apollyon was on new ground. She watched as Solomon carried on without any care for her. None of this should have been possible. But she was seeing it for herself.

Finally, he turned to look at her. "Do not be distressed, imp. You had to know my God would not abandon me." Solomon outstretched his arms. "Even here, in Solomon 931, my God hears me. And I hear him," he shouted into the sky, and the crowd cheered and wept.

It had been centuries since Apollyon had doubted. Doubted her power. Doubted her situation. Now, for the first time in quite a while, Apollyon was filled with it. She tried to convince herself it couldn't be possible that the Ark would function as it had in the past. Not here, in her realm. Judging from the smirk Solomon gave her, she knew she would not have to wait long for the answers to those questions. She was just hoping she would be prepared for the outcome.

"Greetings, Solomon," she said cheerily as she changed back into her true form. She looked about and saw none of the people were affected by her metamorphosis. She did not let on her surprise. "Let's cut to the chase. I am assuming you have made a deal with Dokiel."

Solomon scowled. "I don't like the usage of that language. I believe the Lord moves mysteriously. And in this way, He moved through your man Dokiel and presented me an opportunity to continue to do His bidding, even here in Sheol. Think of this Temple as a mission in your realm. I am here to spread His word. My Lord is expanding."

Apollyon spat, "Say what you will, old man, you made a deal. Something shiny was dangled in front of you," she motioned to the Temple, "and you grabbed for it. What? Tired of feasting on food and wine? Spare me your complaints. You aren't doing this for your god. You're doing this for you. Your selfishness has been laid bare. Your actions have confirmed that you deserve to be here."

Solomon smiled as he caressed the golden Ark. He rubbed the box lovingly, as if he had been reunited with a long-lost love. "I wouldn't expect something like you to understand."

Apollyon smirked. "I understand human nature better than you do, fool. You gave Dokiel the information that will undo the Rekindling, that will end the Continuance, unbalance Existence. You knew this, but you didn't care. Just as long as you got to go into your little building and stroke your box."

The people shouted at her, calling her a defiler, a blasphemer. She attempted again to destroy them, and again, failed. Solomon smiled. She did her best not to let her fear show, but her doubt was growing into a full out panic.

Even from his high perch, Solomon could smell it on her. "Calm down, please." The crowd settled, and he considered her words a moment longer. "Much of what she says may be correct." As the last of his words echoed out of the hall, the people vanished, leaving Solomon on high, and Apollyon below on the steps, alone. "Astarte will not be brought down by Malhamash and his Memitim, or whatever other creature you can conjure. The question of the Continuance will be decided by single combat. Champion versus champion. I have seen it." Solomon quickly glanced at the Ark. "Obviously, fate has chosen Astarte as one champion. I do so hope the Continuance finds theirs."

"And the ring?" Apollyon shouted. "You told Dokiel where Astarte can find it. That ring belongs here in the Thirteenth Gate. You have tipped the balance in her favor and have unclean hands in this conflict. You alone have made this an unfair contest." Apollyon was trying to appeal to his sense of fair play, for which he was renown, and a little vain about as well.

Solomon considered her words and agreed. With a deep sigh, he nodded. "True. I will also tell you where it is, and then the race is on, and I will wash my hands of this whole affair. But I think it is only fair you give something for the information, much like Dokiel did. I will tell you, then you will leave this world and never return."

Apollyon shook her head. "Listen, old man, you cannot tell me what to do here. This illusion of yours exists in my house."

Solomon shifted the lid of the Ark just an inch. A straight beam of glorious light spilled from the box and would have hit Apollyon if she hadn't dodged quickly to the side. However, the beam bent back and struck her down. She was bathed in a blinding, suffocating light. Horrified, Apollyon tried to vanish out of Solomon 931, but the light held her tight. She felt her body being strained and pulled apart, and for the first time in eons, she began to scream in fear and pain.

Then, it was over.

Solomon had closed the lid. "I will tell you where it is. And then you will leave this world, and you and yours will never return." He waited for an answer.

She was caught. She needed the information and didn't have the time to figure out whatever was happening in this world. The promise was easy enough to make, but she had no plans of honoring it. "Agreed," Apollyon gasped. One problem at a time, she thought. First, the Necromancer, then I will deal with this troublesome old man.

Solomon was relieved he would not have to bandy words with her for much longer. Even he questioned, just a little, if the power of the Word would work here. He was pleased his faith had been rewarded. Also, her caving so easily confirmed his suspicion that these creatures from the Thirteenth Gate had no backbone, and that knowledge may have been very important in the future. "Good." He walked down toward her with no fear and gave her a hand up. "You know, if you would have thought about what I already said, put the pieces together, you probably could have figured out where I put the ring."

Apollyon gave a confused look.

"If there is going to be an all-out battle royale to decide the fate of Existence, between two champions on Earth, where would you guess it would be? Where on Earth could it only be?"

CHAPTER 10

Peeling out of Santa Fe, they headed north, just as Sariel had requested. When they passed Raton and cleared the state line over into Colorado, she told Astarte to turn east at the next highway and to keep driving until the sun came up.

"I guess we have some time now," Astarte said, climbing back into the car after refilling the gas in some shitty little Kansas town.

Sariel shook her head. "For what we have to discuss, it isn't safe to say the words out loud. I can't stress enough how on the cusp of death we both are."

Astarte was hurt. "What do you think I have been doing for the past three millenniums? Knitting? You don't have to say that to me. I have warded the very metal of the car itself. And because it is constantly moving, that, and the wards, makes it a perfect place to talk." Astarte patted the steering wheel. A lot hadn't worked out for her these past few months, but picking up the Hellcat hadn't been one of them.

Sariel inspected the inside the car. While in the pit, she wouldn't have imagined such machinery. She examined the door locks and the window controls. She could see the telltale signs of protection spells Astarte had inlaid into the car and was impressed with the work. There were some glyphs even she was unfamiliar with. Sariel smiled, satisfied with her former student's work. "Forgive me. I was your teacher for so long. It may take a little time for me to accept you know as much," seeing Astarte's smirk, "if not much, much more than me."

Happy with Sariel's begrudging praise, Astarte asked, "How much do you know?"

Sariel thought about the question for only a moment. Creatures like Sariel enjoyed a hive mind with general knowledge of the realm they were in. Once they moved into the mortal realm, they were granted knowledge and understanding of the world they inhabited. Sariel had feared, due to her fallen status, she would not have been granted this benefit of her kind. She closed her eyes and, in her mind, unlocked various histories and world events since the time she had last left the mortal realm. Opening her eyes, she was thrilled Astarte wouldn't have to explain the modern world to her. "Think of me as a recently updated Wikipedia."

Astarte laughed. "Good. And about what I have been up to?"

Scanning her memory for references, she smiled and said, "Thankfully, very little. You have done an excellent job of flying under the radar. I can see your presence in this world. But only now do I truly appreciate how busy you have been. Please, catch me up."

They drove across southern Kansas under a clear night with a slender crescent moon. Astarte filled Sariel in on her adventures, some thrilling, some hilarious. Sariel asked a question here or there, but mainly let Astarte speak. She had missed her voice for so very long, she just sat there and drank in the sound. Astarte would glance over and give her a smile. That alone would give Sariel shivers. She struggled to believe she was actually here, sitting beside her.

Astarte finished her recap. "I basically have spent my

time trying to find a way to destroy the Continuance. Things changed after you left, and I didn't handle it very well. I was so angry." Sariel could sense the pain in Astarte's voice. "I couldn't stand the one-at-a-time. I wanted it all done. All at once. So, that is what I have been seeking." Her tone turned light again as she looked over at Sariel. "Also, I knew this path was a good way of eventually freeing you."

Sariel smiled. "And you never doubted I was gone?"

Astarte looked at Sariel like she was insane. "Look at me! If you had been destroyed, this old sack of skin wouldn't be able to tempt a corpse. I remembered our first kiss. My life is tied to yours. Forever."

Sariel, overjoyed at Astarte's wording, stared at the night sky. The deep black had receded, and she could tell the sun was about to make its appearance.

Astarte was happy to have her back but couldn't shake the thought of what Sariel had endured for her. She knew Existence would have demanded Sariel divulge any information about her. And she never did. "It has killed me that we never said goodbye. And in my nightmares, I can only imagine what you have endured. Would you like to tell me what the pit was like?"

Firmly, Sariel said, "No," ending the conversation. Sariel had promised herself Astarte would never know what happened in the dark and in the smoke. Those ghosts would stay hidden. Forever. She knew Astarte would imagine the worst, but not even Astarte's most imaginative nightmare could give justice to what happened. "That's yesterday. Let's focus on today and tomorrow."

Astarte, sensing the finality of the statement, didn't press any further. She didn't know how long she had left in this world, and she wouldn't spend it prying into areas that would cause Sariel distress.

As the sun crested the horizon, they entered Missouri. The road signs for Springfield began to appear. Remembering the recent events and what was after her, a queasiness took Astarte.

"What's wrong?" Sariel asked.

"Do you think it is wise that we come back here? So close to where this last chapter began? I have a feeling we might be walking back into the hands of the Memitim."

Sariel nodded. "I agree with you, I don't think this is wise, but we really have no viable option at this point. We need to get to an accursed place as soon as possible."

Astarte glanced at her companion with a questioning look. "An accursed place? And you know of one in Missouri?"

Sariel nodded. "It's the closest one for quite some time, so we will have to risk going through the Ozarks. We won't be there for a few hours, but if we are going to accomplish your mission, it is essential we make it there." She left some details unsaid. She still didn't trust she wouldn't be overheard. Trying to distract Astarte from asking more questions, Sariel offered, "Would you like to hear how Pulliam Farm became anathematized?"

Astarte rolled her eyes. She knew when she was being put off, but again, she didn't want to press Sariel so soon. Also, Astarte knew Sariel was chewing at the bit to show off her knowledge again. The teacher in her wouldn't go away. "Story time with Sariel. Please begin."

Sariel smiled and got comfortable in her seat. "In late December 1863, Confederate troops from the Missouri State Guard captured over one-hundred soldiers from the Union Missouri State Militia. The Confederate troops took the prisoners to a place called Pulliam Farm in Ripley County,

Missouri. On December 25, 1863, the commander of the
Confederate troops ordered a dinner to celebrate Christmas.
He invited the townspeople to bring food and drink, and for
that night, he released the Union prisoners, under guard,
to take part in the merriment. He saw both sides as sons
of Missouri and would not allow them to be forgotten on
one of the most holy nights. Union and Confederate troops
were present at the dinner, and all men bowed their heads as
Reverend Timothy Reeves blessed them and their food and
prayed for better days.

"In the middle of the festivities, the crowd was attacked
by two-hundred Union Missouri troops led by Major James
Wilson. The Union prisoners saw their opportunity and turned
on their hosts and began the slaughter. What they did with the
women and children was never written, nor discussed, but you
can guess. But not one Union soldier was harmed. Only one
Confederate survived, Colonel Reverend Timothy Reeves. The
Union soldiers tormented him by forcing him to watch the
destruction. They gouged out one of his eyes and left him to
die. But he did not oblige. Timothy Reeves pulled himself from
that valley and asked for one prayer.

"This blasphemy, this defilement of a sacred trust,
attracted the Thirteenth Gate, and in a rare showing, they
answered his prayer. This accursed the land around Pulliam
Farm. Reverend Reeves' body was mended and fortified, and
his one remaining eye was given the power of singleness of
purpose. Like a guided missile, he set off to find those who
had butchered and raped. He became a living wraith. It took
him until October of 1864, but he finally put a bullet in James
Wilson's head. Wilson being the last, the good Reverend
Reeves dropped dead and was given to the Thirteenth Gate."
Sariel stopped speaking. She smiled at the sound of her own

voice. It had been a while since she'd heard it do anything but scream.

Astarte let silence fill the car. The story didn't surprise her, knowing very well the treachery of men. "I had no idea there was an accursed spot in Missouri. I might have been able to use that." The mile markers flew by. "Can you tell me the reason we need to go there?"

Sariel rolled her eyes. As spellbinding as the story may have been, she'd known it wouldn't be enough to keep Astarte distracted for long. Finally, she said, "For what we will discuss, we need to shield as best as we can."

"I think I already have proved the Hellcat can do all that and more." She revved the engine a little.

Sariel smiled. "Yes, your car is very impressive. But we will also be greeting a friend, and we need a place like Pulliam Farm for that to occur."

Astarte was taken aback by the news of a visitor. Sariel had failed to mention it all throughout Kansas (which seemed like an eternity itself). Even though she was surprised by the information, she trusted Sariel wholeheartedly. If she needed to keep things cryptic, so be it, she thought. They drove the next few hours, telling stories of places and people so long gone, no one under the stars, except them, would have even heard of them.

Eventually, the Hellcat was going around the turns and dips of the Eastern Ozarks with Sariel serving as navigator. Astarte looked at the sky and noticed the sunny All Hallows Day weather had abruptly changed, being replaced by ominous inky clouds. The late autumn scenery lost all of its natural luster, and the trees hung naked, stripped of all signs of life.

Pointing off to the left, Sariel said, "Turn here." Astarte looked and saw a little valley that had a small creek flowing off to the southeast.

The little dirt road hadn't been traveled on in quite some time. Up and down both sides of the road there were no signs of habitation. She realized she hadn't seen a house in miles, but this was not a surprise to her. When an area became accursed, mortals shied away for generations. Crops didn't grow. Animals didn't venture out onto the land. The stain of the defilement was felt in all realms.

Soon enough, the Hellcat was having to negotiate footpaths that would have barely fit a fox, let alone a car. And after about ten more yards, the car could not go any further. Turning the engine off, Astarte said, "Now what?"

Sariel put her hand on Astarte's. "Leave it here. There is a shelter up on the path into the woods." Sariel got out of the car and shut the door. The instant she left the car, she quickly scanned the area, fully expecting the Memitim to appear. She motioned to Astarte. "Quickly please."

The woods they entered were filled with gnarled trees that bowed and scraped in the wind. Astarte saw no squirrel or bird. Other than her breathing, the woods were dead silent. After a short, silent hike, they came upon a stone cabin which, surprisingly, seemed in good repair. The creek swept past the side of the house, but the woods covered all other sides of the building.

Sariel opened the door and ushered Astarte inside.

With a nod from Sariel, Astarte got to work quickly. A few quick spells, a few drawn symbols, and the new wards were up and glowing on the walls. As Astarte worked, Sariel began a fire and opened a few windows, allowing fresh air into the little cottage. Astarte sat down on a block of wood and gave the little cabin a once-over. Seeing that there was a cot in the corner that just wouldn't do, she made a slight gesture and the cot transformed into a comfortable-looking bed. Blushing, she hoped Sariel would not ask her how many times she had used that spell.

Sariel looked at the bed, then back at Astarte's smiling face. "I do not know when our friend is going to be here, so until then, I would like for you to tell me exactly how Solomon got your ring."

A little of the blush left Astarte's face. She'd known this conversation was coming, but dreaded it, nonetheless. She would tell her, but just not yet.

"Before we get to that, I wanted to greet you back to the world of the living. Properly." With a smile, Astarte began to undo her shirt.

CHAPTER 11

A selected excerpt from the unpublished manuscript: <u>A Brave New Bible</u> from Professor Angela Chiseler, PhD in Religious Studies and Theology.

First Kings:

You must remember, Solomon, David's son, was a man whore who couldn't fill his belly or bed fast enough. He was dashing and smart, so accomplishing both tasks was not very difficult.

But he found his existence listless. He wanted more, always more. It would seem nothing could satiate his hunger. Until he met her. His final wife, whose name was Naamah. Strong and cunning in her own right, she took the tempest that was Solomon to task and calmed the storm.

History has relegated her to the dustbin of just another woman who bared a son. But she was a cunning woman who made him a better king. A wiser king. A powerful man, unique among humans. She continued his line by bearing his only true son, Rehoboam. Working together, Solomon and Naamah ushered forth a new peace among the people, in his god's name, and in hers.

Astarte found her clothes crumpled up on the floor at the foot of the bed. She put on her robe and walked out to the large window that overlooked the city. Jerusalem had certainly grown significantly since she first was here. She remembered when it was little more than a dip in the road. Now, with the wealth King David, and then his son, Solomon, had gained, it was the jewel of the kingdom.

"Naamah?" Solomon said as he woke. The night had been filled with wine and sex, consummating their pact and their marriage.

"Yes, husband, I'm here," Astarte said as looked out over the city at the gleaming Temple in the distance. "Would you like me to call for food or drink?"

"No!" shouted Solomon, laughing. "I think I have had enough of both for quite some time. What a wonderful night. And now, Naamah, you are my wife."

One of hundreds, thought Astarte. But the marriage was a part of the plan. A plan Astarte had put into motion months prior. She looked back over the city and remembered all the events that had brought her to this day.

With the loss of Sariel, she had felt listless. Astarte mourned her loss for many years. She had no interest in the original plan of being a temptress. All she wanted to do was fall to the ground and die. But she did not. No matter how many times she begged, her heart kept beating, blood continued to course through her veins.

She had hoped after Sariel left, the aging process would catch up all at once and she would turn to dust on the spot. When that didn't happen, she knew two things: one, Sariel was still alive, and two, she was going to be around for quite some time so she might as well accept it. The thought of Sariel still living warmed her at night and kept her going day in and day out. She had ideas of what her next steps would be, but she didn't yet have the mind to execute any of her plans. She wanted Sariel back, but how to best achieve it? She wanted revenge on Samuel and the whole lot. But how? That was where Solomon came in.

Astarte couldn't believe how small the world really was. Who knew the young man she gave a sword to (hoping it would end up inside Saul) would end up being king? The reign of David had been perilous to her. David wasn't cruel like Saul, but he still sought out any sort of witches, wizards, sorcerers, and the like. Astarte kept her head down for those decades, still mourning her loss. And without her overpowered backup, she was vulnerable until she found her way. In those early days of David's reign, she sought some protection. Therefore, she went to the only person still existing who gave any amount of shit about her. It was the dead of night when she went knocking on his door. When it opened, Sagar looked at his ageless friend. While still the embodiment of beauty in his eyes, he noticed the shine in hers had diminished and her reddish hair hung stringy and lifeless. She seemed as tired as he did, as if she had been dulled by life itself. No matter, he warmly welcomed her into his home.

She stayed in her room for days. Sagar's servants left her food at her door and were instructed never to disrupt their master's guest. After a while, Astarte would venture out and join Sagar at his hearth, and they would spend time in silence staring at the fire or telling small stories that would bring a smile.

One evening, while she was in a particularly good mood, she joined Sagar for a meal at his grand table. It sat forty persons, but that hadn't happened in some time. They comically sat next to each other.

Sagar pushed back from the table and said, "My stomach just can't take much more."

Astarte glanced down at the simple meal with an odd look. "Is there something wrong?"

He smiled. "Yes, but not with the food."

She feigned hurt. "Is it your company?"

Sagar didn't rise to her goading. He clasped his hands together, the old skin on his fingers stretching over the bones. "Watching you these past few weeks has shown me you are still searching. Still uncertain. Not quite the woman I knew back when my hair was jet black and my voice was strong." He paused and took a sip of wine. "You're not yourself, and I feel I have failed you. If I cannot give you counsel like I always have, then what good am I?"

She gestured to her surroundings. "At the very least, you are good enough to offer me your hospitality. And that is what I have truly needed."

He waved off her statement, and in a bold voice, said, "No. That is the bare minimum. What I want is to give you everything. Everything you want, and everything you need." He slumped back into his chair and tried to catch his breath. "But just cannot." After a moment, his smile returned. "Don't listen to me, an old man making old man complaints." He took a long drink of wine. "Well, I cannot help you in my current state, and that is the truth, but the good news is I believe I have figured out a solution to both our problems." Astarte frowned but didn't say anything. "I have already been informed you have a message waiting for you."

"Message?" Astarte stood up. Sagar wouldn't play with her, so she knew to take him deadly serious. "From whom?" she demanded.

Seeing the blood flash in her face gave him joy. Sagar then knew the woman he loved was somewhere in that maudlin body. "Have no idea. I just know a message has been sent. You just need to reach out and get it."

Astarte sat back down and considered her options. She knew any spell to open the Fourth Gate and converse with other realms would need a massive amount of power and would be risky to her. She thought about the ring. She'd never mentioned it to anyone, not even Sagar. She hadn't been able to bear even touching it since the night with Sariel. No matter what her current feeling about the ring was, she didn't see how it could help her here.

The look on her face showed Sagar that she didn't know her next step. "Calm yourself, my love. I have figured a way around your little problem." He unsteadily got to his feet, and after finding his balance, added, "it's such a nice evening, let's go out on the veranda and take in the night air." He offered his arm, and she happily took it.

Astarte gazed out over the plaza on Sagar's veranda and watched the stars appear one by one. She noticed Sagar wasn't leaning into her and seemed to find more strength in the night air. "So, go ahead and tell me, old man, what trick do you have up your sleeve?"

Sagar freed his arms and made a show of demonstrating there was nothing up either of his sleeves much like a carnival magician. He showed her his right hand was empty, closed it, shook it three times, and opened it, revealing the pendant he had given her all those years ago. Astarte reached to her neck and smiled, impressed at how spry the old man still was. "My love, I have one more thing I can give you. No one living can retrieve this message for you, so it is clear someone dead must go." She began to protest, but he silenced her. "Enough. Look at me. I stopped taking your elixirs long ago, but death still alludes me. This way will be quick, sweet, and more importantly, purposeful. As an atman, I can get your message, and if I am tied to some object, say," he peered down at the pendant, "a symbol of my love and fidelity, I can come back and give it to you." He let his words sink in. "This is the two birds one stone scenario people talk about."

Astarte heard his words and didn't feign shock or placate his vanity by imploring him to stay among the living. She respected him too much. Loved him too deeply. All she said was, "When?"

Sagar grinned, excited his plan was now in the works. He ran over to the table, grabbed a goblet, and drained it, wanting one last drink under the night sky. He turned to her and gave her a gentle kiss on her lips. She found his lips warm and flavored with wine. He stepped back from her and saw she was blushing and grinning. "Now, please."

Sagar outlined some of the details of the spell. Since it was his soul that was going to be kept in the pendant, there were some particulars she would need, but all in all, the incantation and various rune-work was simple. After all the preparations were completed, she silenced her mind, made the appropriate gestures, and with a flash that suited his personality, Sagar was bathed in gold light that emitted sparkles all around him, as if his aura was on fire. Soon, his body was taken over by the shimmering, which began to swirl. She beckoned it to come to her and held out the pendant. The gold light shot into the pendant and was gone. "Rest well," was all she said.

Alone in the dark, she watched the moon go slowly across the sky and wondered what the rest of the night would hold for her. Sagar hadn't known how long it would take, but he'd wanted her to wait at least some while. After an hour, she couldn't help herself. To hide herself from the creatures from the other realms, she quickly mixed some herbs and berries into a bottle of wine Sagar had left on the table and took a long drink. The taste was bitter, but without Sariel, the bitterness was something she would need to get used to. Returning to the balcony, with some earth from Sagar's own gardens, she drew a hexagram identical to the one on her ring, encircled it twice, and said, "ana 'astadeik ya Sagar tueal nashni."

Nothing happened for a moment, then the lanterns of the house and all the surrounding candles dimmed and pulsed brightly. The sand of the hexagram began to rise slowly and swirl in the air. A swirling without wind or sound. The sand fell back to the ground, but had formed the crest Sagar had emblazoned on his gate, front door, and all the wine goblets. The crest of his family.

"Well," a voice said, coming from the crest, "this isn't going to work."

Astarte said a small prayer to the pendant, and the sand rose and created a figure of a man. He was wearing the same robes Sagar had just been wearing, but he had the face of her friend from a lifetime ago. From the day she first met him in Joshua's tent.

Sagar looked at himself and nodded in approval. "Fine work, my dear. How long have I been gone?"

Astarte understood time worked differently in other realms and said sheepishly, "About an hour."

Sagar's eyes were wide. "Very interesting. But we can speak on that later. I am sure you are wanting to get down to business."

Astarte loved his directness. "Please. Who is the message from, and what is it, and what am I to do?" Her questions came out in rapid succession, her anxiety in full tilt.

Seeing this, Sagar moved to comfort his friend, but was shoved back by the circles that surrounded him on the ground. He had forgotten there would be limits on what he could do in the mortal realm. "No matter," he said more to himself. "Calm yourself. Just give me a moment. As to your first question, I do not know who the message was from."

Astarte groaned and thought this had all been a waste of time.

"Don't lose heart. Whoever sent it, I believe is a friend, a mighty powerful one I would guess. I am, however, not allowed to know who it is from." Seeing he had her attention back, he continued. "As to the second part, while the message is simple, I do not know the meaning of the words. You are to begin the second phase of your training. Continue what you have started with Sariel, but now focus on taking down the whole system. Crash the Continuance." Sagar didn't grasp the meanings. "Keep pulling as many people out as you can. It may take a lifetime, or ten, but eventually, it will all fall like dominos." Nether Sagar nor Astarte understood the last word, but Astarte got the gist of the message.

Seeing that Sagar seemed finished, she asked, "Is there anything else?" She was hoping there would be something of a more personal nature.

Sagar nodded. "On your road to this goal, you will set free what has been taken. That, I promise you, my child." At the last words, her lips flashed with heat, and the memory of the kiss between her and Sariel burned again in her mind.

Astarte put her hands on her lips as tears formed. Sagar watched her as she began to laugh. Renewed with purpose, she looked at her friend with her bright green eyes with the gold flecks that shined in the moonlight. Sagar didn't understand anything of what was said, but he was happy to have been of service. He yawned and said, "Once more thing before I go back."

Astarte stopped laughing. "Yes, what is it?"

"Start with Solomon." And with that, Sagar turned back into dust and was carried off with the wind.

Astarte stayed at Sagar's house as an honored guest. She had gotten rusty in her arts and spent her time honing her skills. Of course, mindful of what Sariel had taught her, she knew she couldn't stay for very long in one place. After a few weeks, she left under the cover of night. From place to place, she always stayed a step ahead of David's men. She didn't have to work too hard in the long run. David, like most men, no matter how holy, screwed up. He fell for a temptress and had her husband murdered so he could have her for himself. King David fell from grace, and she didn't have to lift a finger. At that point, King David exited the world to answer to his god for his indiscretions.

However, with Solomon, she saw an opportunity. It was clear to her why the message had wanted her to go after him. Early in his reign, he'd exhibited signs of some major vices. He was a glutton. He loved lavish possessions, and he couldn't keep his dick in his pants. The last one she could work with.

Eventually, she got close to Solomon, posing as an Egyptian princess named Naamah. A few flirtations, bottles of wine, and she was in, in a manner of speaking. Their tryst was passionate, full of promises and pledges of love. She swore to him she could give him a son. He swore to her he would give her the world.

However, drunken, lust-filled promises grew into something more. Astarte saw Solomon working with others to keep his kingdom united. He was not cruel or unrelenting like his father. The solutions he had for every type of problem were inspired. He cared for his people, the low and high alike. Even the ones who did not believe in his god, he cared for (something Joshua would not have allowed). He was his father's son in strength and craftiness but surpassed him in intelligence. Astarte respected his mind. Respected the way he thought. This respect grew to the point where she truly hoped he would ultimately ease her path, not obstruct it.

But that wasn't her only want now. The way Solomon would talk about children, about how they were the only way to truly live forever, made her smile. He simply didn't want another worker or another person to call himself king. He wanted his line to grow, flourish, and make the world a better place. The way he talked, so gentle, filled with love, moved something inside her. She realized she'd never thought of motherhood before, but now, it dominated much of her thoughts. A little one to teach, to watch grow tall and strong. Someone who was a part of her. To live forever in someone else. The thought always brought tears of desire. Astarte was going to make sure Solomon's line would not fail, and she would add her blood to it. With Solomon as a guide, motherhood was all she wanted. She allowed herself to believe she could have it all.

***

Solomon coughed to get her attention back. She had drifted off. She turned around and lowered one side of her robe. "Do you want me to reforge our love again?" she said with a lustful smile.

Solomon shook his head. "If we start back up, I don't think I will leave the bed the whole day. And we have a lot to accomplish today. Or do you not want to dedicate your temple today?"

She was happy he was the one who brought it up. She didn't want to sound too eager. "Of course. I love how you have allowed a piece of my past to live here in your kingdom. You honor me."

"Think nothing of it. It makes complete sense to me. How can I ask every person who trods this land to bow only to my god? Everyone should feel close to their gods, no matter where they are. And as my wife, I want you happy. Especially if you give me an heir." He said the last part longingly. No matter how many women he had slept with, they had all come up barren when it came to children. Astarte had been aware of this fact for a long while.

They left their room together and walked past servants and administers, many of whom silently abhorred her presence, but she gave them no mind. Solomon, now and then, would stop and give advice or direction, and people would throw praise on him and scrape and bow.

A carriage took them to the Temple. His Temple. Shining bright and white. She could see the people praying on the steps, and the teachers walking in and out of the porch. Across the road, stood a new temple that would be dedicated to her today by Solomon. It was not as grand as the other, but Solomon ensured just as much craftsmanship had gone into it.

Upon seeing Solomon exit the carriage, his people surrounded him, heaping praise on him for their fortune. When she'd first met him, these displays would sicken Astarte, but over time, she saw in Solomon what his followers saw.

"Thank you, my people, for joining us on this great day. For we are here to bless this temple in honor of my wife." He held out his hand to Astarte, who took it gently and exited the carriage. She could tell no one was there for her glory, but only for Solomon. He wanted this project to proceed, and they made it so, even though they probably built her temple with one hand covering their nose. Nonetheless, she carried on smiling and thanking those who were assembled.

Solomon presented Astarte with a wine-filled terra cotta vessel and walked her to the closest marble pillar. "Please, Naamah, my love, with my permission," he said, loud enough for all to hear.

Astarte took the wine, held it aloft, and said, "To my lord, to my god Moloch, please accept this sacrifice as the first of many to you. Bless these people and my King Solomon." Astarte brought the wine down, shattering the clay for all to see. There was no reaction from the crowd until Solomon turned around, to which they began to cheer.

Astarte was so close to her goal with Solomon, a pang of guilt hit her. She didn't really see it as deceiving him. It was more of an agreement between them. Just not an agreement he knew about. She just needed him to do this act, then she promised herself she would take care of him all his life. "Will you join me inside, my love?" she asked.

Solomon looked as if he hadn't been expecting this. He glanced back at the assembly. For him to be seen entering this temple could cause problems.

Seeing his trepidation, she added quietly, "This will ensure us a son. This one step." The night before, she had made all the proper preparations. She had placed all the right incantations and scrawled spells to ensure she would bear Solomon a son. Her son. It was tricky. She was working against fate. Through her studies, she realized Solomon was destined not to have a son. No matter to her, she had reversed fate many times, but it was more exacting, demanded more sacrifice. But it was done. All that was left to do was for him to come with her. At her words, she saw his want for a progeny burn in his eyes and knew she had him. Solomon, against all better judgement, and against the word of his god, entered the Temple of Moloch.

Seeing him pass the great seal that had been inlaid into the floor gave Astarte chills. To make some spells work, she needed to ensure the seed of her fruit was from a darkened soul. She regretted having to do it to Solomon, but this was the only way to give him a son. In her mind, she justified her actions by saying she was only fulfilling her promise to him. Whatever it took.

Solomon inspected the strange symbols etched into the marble. "I am at a loss, Naamah. What do we do now?"

She led him to the inner chamber, and they stood before the altar. The colossal statue of Moloch towered above them, his horns made from obsidian. Astarte leapt up, sat on the altar, and opened her legs to Solomon.

Solomon, seeing this, knew what he had to do to ensure his line continued. "One thing, Naamah. Before we do this, I am going to need something from you."

Astarte gave him a puzzled look. "Anything. What would that be?"

Solomon didn't relish this part. He had also grown fond of her.

"I know who you are."

Astarte heard the words, but it took a moment for them to register. Solomon said nothing else, just waited for her to react. It finally dawned on her. She tried to rise, to close her legs, but she was paralyzed in place.

"Astarte, please calm yourself."

"Why can't I move?" she asked desperately.

"Because my God wills it." His tone wasn't menacing, more matter-of-fact.

Astarte looked up at Moloch and tried to conjure a counter to whatever was binding her. Her fingers splayed with effort.

"That won't do you any good," Solomon said apologetically. "While you may have made some changes to some of the wards, when I had this place built, I ensured some of your powers would be nullified. Just enough for you to hear me out." She continued to struggle to no avail. "I really need you to calm down."

"What is it you want?" She was desperate. Mentally, she was kicking herself. Why had she thought she could go after a prophet right out of the gate? She was rusty, and she knew it. She had been lulled into thinking Solomon was a means, not an end.

"I want what you want," Solomon said calmly.

"To bathe in your fucking blood!" She mustered all the anger she had and tried to focus her power into her words. He waved them off.

"Please. You want a child. I want a child. Most importantly, I need a son. You can do that. I hold no ill will against you. I admit, I used you, but I think we are both guilty of that."

"That can't be all you want. I was more than willing to give you a child."

"I can tell your spells in this place will ensure you give birth to a strong baby boy. Someone I can teach. Someone who will carry on beyond me in this realm. But I want something else from you. I want power. And you can give it to me."

Astarte calmed down, confused as to what Solomon was getting at. "How can I do that?"

Gently, he said, "Give me the ring."

Understanding dawned on her. While she'd been playing him, she was really the fool. "You don't know what you're asking for."

"The ring from the Thirteenth Gate. The one that commands demons. That will bend them to my will. Force them to do my bidding. Yes, I am well aware of what I am asking for."

"We have slept in the same bed for weeks. You could have slit my throat and taken it at any time. Why all this?"

Solomon shook his head. "Why would I want to do that? Understand, I don't see you as my enemy. I need you now, and will continue to need you for the rest of my days. I don't just want to possess the ring, I want to command it. That can only come from knowledge. Knowledge you can give me. Besides, if I were to take it by force, it would merely return behind the Thirteenth Gate, and that won't serve anybody any good. But you know this."

Astarte was shocked at how much information Solomon had. It shouldn't have surprised her, but it did. "So, I 'give' you the ring, you rape a baby into me, and what? I am chained up until the birth and then beaten with stones until I teach you magic tricks?"

Solomon seemed honestly shocked. "Damn it all, woman. Is that what you think of me? The bindings were only for you to hear me out. I didn't put you up on that altar all spread out." Solomon snapped his fingers, and Astarte found she could move again. She sat up and composed herself. There were things going on she did not understand, so she proceeded forward carefully.

"And if I refuse?" she asked to see if any hatred would flash in his eyes.

"You won't." She was oddly disappointed at how calm Solomon's response was.

"Why do you believe that?"

"Because I can give you what you want. I can give you knowledge you don't understand about the nature of Existence. About the Continuance." He saw her eyes widen slightly. "I know what you want. I don't think you will be successful, but who am I to stop you? I can point you in the right direction." He let the words settle for a moment. "I can also provide you with a wonderful life…well, at least for the length of mine. Our son will grow up strong and powerful under our tutelage. I want a partner in this. But I must have the ring."

Astarte wanted to run out of the temple, no matter how convincing his words were. With the loss of Sariel, she needed direction. She knew she wanted to destroy the Continuance, but honestly, she didn't know how and where to begin. She glanced at the door, then looked back at Solomon.

Solomon gave a calming smile and added, "I will make you another promise." He breathed in deep, knowing he was playing his last card. "When I am done with the ring, when I am done with my life, I will leave the ring to you. So, actually, I am only borrowing it for the span of my life. From here on out. No more lying to each other. We are true partners. Good teachers to our son. King and queen of the land. And when I die, you can go off and do what you wish with the ring."

Astarte had had worse offers in her lifetime. He had grown on her, and he would be an agreeable companion for the next twenty (or so) years.

She extended her hand. "I am Astarte. I have gone by many names, taken many guises, taken many lovers, over many years. But, for you, I will continue to be Naamah, your wife. I agree to your terms."

Solomon took her hand, and she pressed into his the cold metal of the ring.

CHAPTER 12

Sariel listened as Astarte finished her tale. They laid there in the small bed as the November sun heated the little cabin. Sariel didn't have the emotions of mortals, but even she understood making light of the whole Solomon issue may not have been taken very well. "What happened to him?" she asked.

Astarte shrugged. "I don't know the details, which is the current problem. Even though he was king for many years, he still liked to travel and make personal appearances to different parts of his kingdom. One day, he went off and was set upon by some murderers." Astarte attempted to head off questions and heatedly added, "I don't know where he put the ring. But I know he hid it. I just know it."

Sensing her tone, Sariel smiled. "I wasn't asking about Solomon. I wanted to know what happened to your son, Rehoboam?"

At hearing his name, Astarte smiled wide. "I have loved no one like I loved him. We made sure he grew up right and strong. I taught him magics, Solomon taught him kinging. He was such a good boy." Her face became crestfallen. "After Solomon died, I tried to help him transition into his kingship, but even I heard the whispers. As you can imagine. The rumors about me persisted and worsened. To stem off any threat to

Reho, I left him. It was my time anyway. And ageless mother would have resulted in both of us being stoned in the street. But I promised to keep my eye on him. I watched as he grew into a man, had children. I watched them grow up, and have their children, and so on. It became too much for me to just sit and watch my bloodline expand and die. Expand and die. Eventually, I left the land behind." Astarte was amazed that after so many centuries, the pain of the loss still hurt.

"Solomon ended up being good for you." Sariel left all the venom out of her voice, but she wasn't used to the sensation of being jealous.

"Yep," said Astarte, matter-of-fact. "I wanted information. I wanted a child. He could give me both. Ring or not, I do not regret our meeting." Seeing a hint of jealously in Sariel's eyes, Astarte got heated. "We were supposed to do everything together, and I didn't ask you to leave."

Sariel, woundedly, said, "I couldn't have helped that, and as I remember, I was helping you."

Astarte closed her eyes. "I know, and I have been working this entire time to undo what happened. But please see it from my point of view. *Hey, little girl, take down an entire system of Existence. You have your wits and a ring, get to work.*" Astarte paused. "I had no direction. And if you haven't realized, the deal worked. The things Solomon taught me about the Continuance, from his side's perspective, gave me what I needed."

"I am sure it did." Sariel couldn't stop herself.

Astarte smiled at how childish she was being. "You know, this was about three-thousand years ago. Is it the sex that bothers you?"

Sariel shook her head. "Not at all. What bothers me is how you seem to revere him in some manner. You were tricked. And I don't want you ever to be tricked."

Astarte smiled at her teacher. "I understand that. Well, I promise you, no one has gotten the better of me since. And he is long gone, and I am still here."

"And the ring?"

"I can't hold that against him, actually. I know he would have given it to me."

Sariel gave her another scowl of disbelief.

"Don't look at me like that. Look, he would honor our deal. He *will* honor our deal. That is just the way he is. Any other man would have just died with the ring on, which would have made it go right back to the Thirteenth Gate. But no, he took it off and hid it before his death. He must have known death was coming and put the ring somewhere safe. I just need to know where." Astarte moved close to Sariel and embraced her. "I hope you have figured out a way to find it."

"That is what we are waiting for."

"Your friend?"

"Our friend."

A crash from outside cut off their conversation. They both moved over to the open window to see two figures. One was easy to identify. It was the stuff of nightmares. Long features all shrouded in shadow and mist. It stood at least seven feet tall and what body that could be made out was sinewy with undulating muscle that looked like a mixture of tar and asphalt. It was a Memitim, but he seemed to have run into some trouble. Its wings lay broken on the ground, twitching from being recently severed. The creature struggled against an unseen force that kept it on its knees. This was in all in contrast to the person who stood over him. This second person was an odd sight. He was a man, somewhere in his fifties, with tan skin and wearing a priest's cassock.

He smiled at the two women. "If you ladies are done with your little spat, I think there are things we need to discuss."

CHAPTER 13

Astarte opened the front door, and Sariel moved behind her, both of their hands outstretched, ready to cast whatever they may need. Watching the Memitim struggle in the bright sun made it clear to Astarte this man was more than he seemed.

"Who are you?" Astarte demanded.

The priest smiled. "Not here, darlin'. I can't kill these things, I have merely put it in a bubble of time. It thinks it is moving normally, but as you can see, it is moving at a mere creep. However, this little beasty can still hear all we say. Why don't we wait to make our introductions once we're behind your wards, okay?"

Astarte began to object when Sariel interrupted. "How do we know you are the one I am waiting for?"

Instantly, Sariel felt her forearms begin to burn. She glanced down and saw handprints flash like fiery bruises on both her arms. She knew he had come.

"Let him in," she said to Astarte. The priest moved forward. She added, "How long will that creature stay like that?"

The priest pointed back at the creature. "Long enough for us to finish up here and get on our way. Have no worries, my child." Sariel rolled her eyes at the priest's affected tone.

Once inside, Astarte was the first to speak. "Okay, spill it. Who the fuck are you?"

With a bombastic bow, he said, "Well, currently, I am Father Tomas Florez, formerly the Monseigneur of Mission San Miguel of Santa Fe. I think you are familiar with the place, am I correct?"

Before Astarte could say anything else, Sariel butted in. "Enough. It has been a long forty-eight hours. Just be straight with her."

Father Tomas smiled. "Forgive me, Astarte. Sometimes, when it comes to you, I do feel like we are old friends, but I have to remind myself we have actually never met. It is odd, because you could really say I am as close to a father as you have ever had. If not for me, your bones would have turned to dust about one-thousand years ago." He stopped talking, turned to Sariel, and put out his arms for an embrace. She obliged. "You have done well, my child. Not exactly what I thought would happen, but nevertheless, I can't say it has been boring. I will take exciting and suicidal over boring and safe any day." He gave her a kiss on the cheek, and the covenant marks flamed again on his and Sariel's skin. He turned back to Astarte. "Sorry, dear, Sariel and I had little time to talk before she flew the coop. Where was I? Ahhh, yes. May I introduce myself? I am Dokiel, Former High Commander of the Thirteenth Gate. I am extremely pleased to finally meet you, Astarte."

More things were clicking in place for Astarte. "Dokiel? One of the Arbiters of the Continuance, Dokiel?"

Dokiel gave another deep bow. "One and the same."

"How can you be here?" asked Sariel.

Without looking at Sariel, he answered, "It was quite a trick, believe you me. Astarte, you may not be aware of this, but neither me nor my counterpart Puriel the Dull can ever leave the Continuance. If it fails, we fail. Well, I saw what you were doing here in the mortal realm, and I figured there was a slim chance you may succeed." He nodded his head back to Sariel. "And as your lover can attest, I'm not one to go down with the ship. Nope, always leave an out for yourself, girls, listen to Pappy Dokiel." He found a chair, sat down, and stretched his bones.

Astarte looked out the window at the ragged Memitim still struggling and knew no matter how light of a tone Dokiel was using, he was not someone to take lightly. "Then how are you here?"

"I'll tell you, Astarte. It took a very special set of circumstances for me to join you. I needed a soul that was First Gate bound. A real peach of a guy. But I needed him to do something terrible, right at the very end of his life. Something unexpected. Something definitely off script, so to say. Finally, I needed him reaped at the moment he dirtied his spirit. Santa Muerte did her job very well, unbeknownst to her, of course." He moved his face, still uncomfortable in his new skin. "I swear, the more I think about it, I think Existence must be on our side for everything to be working out so. You think?"

Sariel shook her head. "If Existence wanted the Continuance destroyed, it would just be done."

"True. Wishful thinking on my part. Well, anyway, I can parade around the mortal realm with you two as Father Tomas here. Obviously, I have retained all my powers. Which is good."

Sariel wiped some sweat from his brow and showed it to him.

"Ah…well, yes. A sad side effect. These sacks are so gross. All the fluids and oozing. I'm still an all-powerful demon, but inside a weak and easily destructible shell. While I may be able to stop a Memitim, I can also be killed by an old toaster in a bathtub."

Astarte found Dokiel to be an odd mix of clown and serial killer. "Now that you have explained who you are and how you got here, why don't we discuss what you came here to tell us? Unless you couldn't get the information I need?"

"O ye of little faith. I talked to Solomon, greased the skids, as they say, and got the information about the location of the ring." He turned to Astarte. "I don't blame you, young one, for giving it up. Actually, I guess I have myself to blame for putting you on a path to him. Oh well, like I said, no blame on you. I sat and talked to him for a while. He is quite mesmerizing. But, one thing we can count on, he is going to tell anyone else who comes around where we are going. We may have a mortal day lead. At best."

Sariel became impatient. "Then where is it?"

"Megiddo."

Astarte scanned her memory and put two and two together. "Megiddo!" Hearing it now, it seemed obvious.

Dokiel smiled. "Solomon was a prophet and had a flair for the dramatic, which I kind of like. He knew any final battle between you and your enemies needed a suitable location, and what better place than Armageddon? He must have known his days were at an end. On his way to Mount Carmel to settle some disputes in the port city, his caravan was beset by a rouge band of Amorites. Solomon escaped the initial carnage, and long story short, Solomon hid the ring in the temple in Megiddo. He made it so only you could find the ring, if you are looking for it. Of course, putting a ring like that in a holy temple instantly defiled it. The whole town was abandoned shortly thereafter and had remained untouched for centuries."

Relief washed over Astarte. She was right. She knew Solomon, and even with all his faults, knew he wouldn't fail her. They promised each other no more lies for the rest of his life. He kept his part of the bargain.

"Why would he tell anyone who comes along where we are going?" Sariel couldn't understand what Solomon was up to.

Dokiel shrugged. "Fair play. He won't stand in your way of destroying the Continuance, but he also thinks it is only fair that both sides have an opportunity to win. He has given you a head start, but that is all he will do for your side, Astarte." Dokiel began to look around the cabin for something to drink. "Oh, another thing. Something you may like. I have also found out that the other side has picked their champion."

"Who?" Astarte held her breath.

"Your student, Max Travers."

It didn't surprise her. Not really. She'd known it had to be Max. It only made sense. It answered many of her questions about that night back in her basement. His connection to his father. The difficulties in pulling Jude. The Watchers arriving at the last minute. The Memitim on her ass. It had never added up. She had assumed Max or Jude were touched. This confirmed her suspicions. But that really didn't answer why Existence would pick a boy as its champion. "Why him, though?"

Dokiel continued to look through the room for something to drink. "He is a Son of David. So, I guess they think that will be enough to stop you." Astarte was stricken by the information, and Dokiel noticed. "Why do you seem unhappy? I thought you would relish getting another crack at him. Maybe this time you won't be undone by a boy who doesn't have hair one on his balls. And if you're concerned about the sword, let's not forget it was you who created it in the first place. So, that problem is on you."

Astarte knew a thing like Dokiel would never understand. She thought nothing of the sword, but for the boy who now wielded it. Max was a tool to be used, that was all. Whatever slight pain she may have caused him had justified her ends. She had never wanted to destroy him. He had never been her target. But now, more than ever, she did not want to shed his blood. It was her blood. Astarte wondered if even Sariel would understand. Probably not, but she would deal with that later. Donning a resolute look, she said, "So be it. They have chosen. Max cannot stop what I have put in motion." She stared at Dokiel. "But know this, I don't care what powers you may have, no harm is to come to Max. Nothing permanent or disfiguring."

Dokiel was confused and asked a simple, "Why?"

"Because I am not a monster!" she shouted. She had had enough of this little man's games, toying with her for thousands of years. She would have this finale on her own terms. "I don't care how many suns have set. Max is of me, and I won't have him harmed. We can accomplish our task without his blood. Are we clear?" Her command hung in the air. Dokiel turned to Sariel, who nodded in agreement. Seeing this, Dokiel agreed. "Good. Can we make it to Megiddo before Max? What about the Memitim?"

Dokiel gave a dismissive grunt. "That's why I am here. They had their chance and have failed tremendously. Anything to rankle Malhamash is fine with me. Bastard has been playing both sides too long. But, like I said, I cannot kill them, I can only slow them down. I can clear the path all the way to the ring. Once there, with it, you can stop them."

Astarte looked at Sariel, who was already packing up

the small things they had brought with them. With her final destination set, she picked up her bag, and without another word, they all left the cabin. By this time, the Memitim had gotten back on its legs, but its wings were still shattered on the ground.

"Better luck next time, Belkira," Dokiel said as he passed. He couldn't help himself.

They all got into the Hellcat, and Astarte started the engine. "So, I guess we are going to our final battle." Sariel took her hand.

Dokiel shouted, "Fuck yeah!" as "Let's Get Crazy" started playing out of the Hellcat's speakers.

CHAPTER 14

"I just want to say. I think you couldn't have fucked this up any more than you already have. You things talk about yourselves like you are gods. But you are inept infants." Eva Travers seethed in anger, her cool blue eyes boring into Malhamash.

Mal kept his composure. If at any other time a mortal would have talked to him in this manner, he would have peeled off their skin and worn them like a suit. But he was stuck having to take Eva's vitriol. He stood there in her Crown Plaza Hotel room in his perfect black suit. He needed her.

"I understand your frustration, Ms. Travers. I don't really know what more I can add. You are needed to do this. If I or my soldiers were to make another move against Astarte, we feel it will make things worse. Clearly, since we have made several attempts over the past twenty-four hours, all failures, she has someone very talented with her."

"Bring in the mortal to save the day, that's the plan?"

"You said you've never met Astarte, and you will not give off any warning signs like I would. They don't know you. You are mortal. They won't see you coming." Mal picked up the phone and showed Eva the picture once again. "This is Astarte, the woman who wants to undo Existence. This is the woman who tortured your husband. This is the woman who defiled your son. I would assume you would leap at a chance to do this. Especially a woman with your past."

She didn't rise to Mal's digs. She was not some temperamental teenager anymore. "I have no problem doing this. I will probably revel in it. If I can stop her, then Max won't have to. It is as simple as that." She took the phone from him and examined the image, studying the beautiful young woman in the picture. This Astarte was built to ensnare. The hair, the eyes, the body…so disarming. Eva gave a slight smile in the thought that Astarte's attributes wouldn't help her tonight. She turned away from Mal and went to her large penthouse windows. She looked out at JFK airport, lights gleaming. Almost a city unto itself.

Mal could tell from her posture she would do as she was asked. He knew it was a one-way mission, but there was no need to tell her that. Even if she only slowed Astarte down, it may be worth something. To Existence, it was kitchen sink time. He turned to leave, but added, "I have also been instructed that you may use this phone to make a call. Tell him what you wish. No matter how much faith we have in your success, we felt it was prudent to give you this opportunity."

Eva didn't make any indication that she had even heard him. She was not going to give that creature any thanks. Mal got the cue and left the room.

She watched as a few planes landed and took off and thought about the thousands of people going about their day, comfortable in their understanding of things. She wanted that for Max. That was now beyond her power.

She dialed.

"Hello?"

"Max, it's Mom." It had only been a few days since she'd last seen him, but the sting of the way she'd left gnawed at her.

"Mom! What the hell! Why has it taken so long for you to call?"

"This is my first chance I had to call you. What have you been up to?"

Max, uncharacteristically, gave Eva every detail. When she'd left, he'd also left the house with Sham. They didn't quite know where they were going, but they knew nothing was going to happen in Springfield. Sham, at Max's insistence, had stopped with the lessons, feeling he had learned as much as he could in the time he had left.

"So, you have stopped training?"

"No. But I am more just practicing calming my mind. With the way you left, I find it difficult." Max cut off, not knowing how to really explain it.

"Say no more. I understand. And I am sorry." Pain erupted in her chest. She prayed he would understand.

"I know," Max said. He shifted to a different topic. "We found out today where we need to go."

She knew the answer but let him say it. "Where to?"

"A place called Megiddo. It's in Israel. Get this, it is also known as Armageddon. Can you believe that shit? I guess it makes perfect sense. I mean, really, if I am going to conquer the evil of the world, could there be a better place?"

Eva's heart skipped a beat. He sounded excited. Too excited, but Eva didn't want to dampen his spirits.

"Mom?"

"Well, I guess I heard the same thing, Max."

"Where are you?" Max said, realizing he hadn't asked yet.

"In New York. Where are you?"

"We are heading to Atlanta. It's the closest airport with a nonstop. Hey, Mom, Sham said he can get me on the plane without a passport. Do you think that is going to be a problem? Because I didn't bring one."

Eva laughed. "Max, I think Sham can take care of customs and all that for you. You just focus on what you have to do."

"Of course." Max paused. "Mom, what are you doing in New York?"

Eva breathed deep. "I am here to try to stop Astarte from getting on her plane in four hours."

Silence.

Then Max finally spoke. "What do you mean? I don't understand. Isn't that what I have been training for all this time?"

"Yes, and you are still our best bet on winning. But…I don't know, let's say the fates think there is a slight chance another descendant of David can stop her here and now. I have been offered that opportunity, and I am going to take it."

Max sounded panicked. "How small of a chance?"

There was no sugarcoating it. She wouldn't lie to Max. Not now. "Small enough for them to allow me to make this phone call, Max."

Max closed his eyes and remembered what Multi had said. She was going to go destroy the beasts in the shadows. He understood, but he would blame himself forever if he didn't say it just once. "You don't have to do this. You can turn around now and let me do my job."

His tone surprised her. It was not the tone of a pleading boy, but of a man making a simple request. The pain in her chest subsided, having been soothed by her son. An adult request required an adult response. "It means everything that you would ask that. But you know I cannot do that. You have your job. And I have mine. I think you understand that now."

"This is how I lost Dad. He was trying to protect me. And now, I'm going to lose you too?"

"Max, I am so proud of your father. Jude was everything a husband should be. Everything I could hope for in a partner. And in a father to my son. He will be with me tonight. And so will you. I carry you both with me." She began to laugh. "And don't discount your mother so quickly, young man. All these things you have learned over the past months, remember, I am the one who taught you. I'm the teacher here, and I expect to live a long life." Not a lie, she thought. She really did hope to live through this night.

Max wanted to say much more. Try more to convince her to walk away, but there would be no dissuading her. He knew, just like his dad, she would do anything to prevent harm from seeing him. So, Max let all fear and anger go. He wouldn't add to her torment.

They spent the rest of the call just talking. The last thing they wanted to talk about was Astarte and missions. They told stories about Max's first trip on a plane (and all the vomiting), and all the trips they had gone on as a family. Mostly, she told Max how proud of him she was, and he told her how much he loved her.

Time had a manner of spinning away when you didn't want it to. She checked her watch. It was time to go.

"Max. Stick close to Sham. I trust him more than any of the others."

"Yeah, he's cool."

"I will text you when it is done tonight. Maybe I can catch you before you get on the plane. Save you a fourteen-hour flight."

"Okay, Mom. I love you."

"Max, please remember your training. Remember our

words." She had to say one more thing before the lump in her throat caught. "And I love you too."

***

Getting past TSA was easy. No carry-on. No weapons. No little bottles of shampoo or mouthwash. Eva had no intention of getting on the plane, she just needed to get to the gate.

Terminal four was her destination. The red-eye flight to Israel wouldn't depart for another hour, but what worried Eva most was the lack of people. In her mind, she thought a New York airport terminal would always be bustling. But apparently not too many people took advantage of one a.m. flights to the Middle East on a Tuesday. Nothing she could do about that now. She would just have to cast something not too showy. No thunderous lightning orbs or light spells.

She headed to the fourth floor of the terminal where there was a lounge for El Al airlines. Maybe she would get lucky and find her there, put something in her drink, then be back in bed by two-thirty.

There were more people milling around the various lounges on the fourth floor, which gave her comfort. She was able to blend in and just be another nameless person in the crowd. Scanning, looking for her target, she accidentally bumped into a group of nuns.

"I am so sorry, Sister. Forgive me, I wasn't watching where I was going."

The sister shook her head. "Don't think anything about it. This place can be dizzying, can't it? I was telling the group this place might be as wondrous as the Holy Land." The assembled group of nuns and a priest began to laugh.

"But at least here we can drink the water and have all the quilted toilet paper we want," the priest joked. The nuns smiled but shamed him for such talk.

Eva nodded at the group and continued on. She emerged from the crowd and stood outside the lounge. She did a quick scan of the people but saw no Astarte. She started to feel something was off. This had been too easy to get this far, but now she felt as if she was being led to slaughter. She shook off her fears knowing they were natural. *Especially for someone with still a little rust on her*, she thought.

"Are you flying with us tonight?" The bartender smiled at her, hoping she would show her ticket so he wouldn't have to be rude. The distraction was welcome for Eva and chased her doubts away. Showing her boarding pass, he smiled. "Wonderful. As you can see, we have some light refreshments buffet style. Is there anything you would like to drink?"

"Just ice water, please."

He shrugged at the simple order and put the drink on the counter. She nodded and went deeper into the lounge.

Leather chairs lined the wall with large windows that showed off the dark night. She found an empty seat in the corner that faced the rest of the open space. And then she saw her.

It wasn't Astarte, but the other woman she was supposed to keep a look out for. There was no picture of her, but the description matched. Tall, blonde, and painfully beautiful. Clearly either a supermodel or a demon. Sariel. Eva controlled her breathing and kept looking out at the night sky, keeping the woman in her periphery. All she had to do now was wait.

A few moments passed, and the woman was finally joined by Astarte, who was holding two full drinks in her hands. She was smiling, and bent down and whispered something in Sariel's ear, causing them both to laugh. Eva knew it was foolish, but seeing them laugh pissed her off. In her mind, they had no right to laugh. No right to smile. No right to breathe the air.

Eva chastised herself. She had to calm herself. Find her center. There could be no mistakes now. Knowing where Astarte was, and where she would be, was all Eva needed. She quickly got up and left, finding a row of seats in the hallway that had a straight view of the entrance of the lounge. She made her mental preparations. A blade of folded air would be perfect, she thought. Silent. Invisible. No blood. As inconspicuously as she could, she began folding the air in front of her, layer after layer, until she could sense a sharp dagger had been created. All she needed to do was send it on its way home to the bitch's heart and walk away. Sariel would not be fooled, but the people around would suspect some heart attack or stroke. Eva threw Sariel out of her mind. She would deal with her after the mission was completed.

The blade of air hung before her. It struggled against her, desperate to be released. She then saw movement from the lounge and saw her target. She waited for the perfect moment. *Just turn and face me*, she thought. Astarte moved clear and then…

Nothing.

The blade was gone.

A sharp pain pierced her spine. The pain was intense, but she found she couldn't scream out. The air in her mouth would not move. It muffled all sound. She turned to look, and the priest sat down next to her. She tried to mouth words, but nothing.

"Ms. Travers! It is so nice to see you again." The priest

gave a warm smile. He put his arm around her and held her close. "Life is crazy, isn't it? Here we are. You and I have never actually met, but to me, we are old friends." She strained against the air caught in her throat. "You see, actually, Jude and I are good friends. I recently helped him out back in the Continuance. It really is a small world. Seeing you here is crazy."

Eva struggled to move her arms, but the priest embraced her tighter as if to comfort a troubled parishioner.

"There, there now. No need to struggle. You thought you were going up against a witch and maybe her low-ranking celestial friend. You had no idea it was me. Feel no shame. I am no mere milkmaid." He felt her slump every so slightly. "It will be over in a moment. And then, you will be in the Continuance. I am sure Puriel will create a nice story for you. Trust me. Things will be better, while they last, of course." He checked his watch. "I am predicting the end of the Continuance within twenty-four hours. So, enjoy it while you can. I don't exactly know what will happen to you." His sweet breath felt hot on her neck. "But tell you what. I will put a good word in for you. I'll make sure you end up in a fun place. Okay?" He leaned back from her and looked into her face.

He didn't see the expression he'd been hoping for.

She had no fear nor pain.

It was a terrifying calm.

Lighting quick, she scratched his face, drawing blood.

"*Puraturo exercet.*" It came out as barely a whisper, but she did the only thing she could think of. She had given her life over to the spell, forfeiting all the remaining spark she had. The spell ignited.

She fell to the floor dead.

Dokiel grabbed his cheek. He could feel the warmth

of the curse working its magic through him. He cast a few counter curses, but this was a magic he hadn't dealt with before.

"Fucking bitch!" he said as he turned and left her corpse sprawled out on the ground. It took a moment for anyone to see Eva Travers lifeless on the floor, but Dokiel was well away by then, showing his boarding pass to the steward. Dokiel could already smell the festering of his skin on his face.

As he entered the plane, he saw Astarte look at him. Dokiel had never had to deal with mortality before and the terror on his face clued in Astarte that something was amiss. If Eva could have seen it, it would have given her pleasure.

CHAPTER 15

Haifa International Airport was a shitty little airport with one airstrip, but Sham had somehow found a direct flight to it from Atlanta. Max suspected otherworldly powers were at play, but he didn't mention it. Sham had said it would save them a few hours. Max left all the logistics up to Sham, just nodded at all his instructions during the flight. Any other time, the constant talking from a being who didn't sleep would have been grating, but Max spent the whole flight thinking of his mom.

The moment the airplane's doors landed, Max powered up his phone.

"What are you doing?" asked Sham as he stood up, making sure he had all his documents.

"Seeing if my mom has texted me. But I don't have service."

"Of course not."

Then it dawned on Max. His phone wasn't set up for international service. "Damn it." Max stuck the useless phone back into his pocket.

"We will continue as if she wasn't able to accomplish her task until we are advised otherwise." The frown from Max made Sham realize the coldness of his statement. "That is not what I meant. There are many reasons Astarte could still be alive."

Max shook his head and walked off the plane with Sham following behind him. A few moments later, Max handed his false documents to the customs agent. The agent looked at the picture of Max, started to laugh, and said something in Hebrew. He handed the documents back to Max and waved him off.

Max saw nothing odd about his passport, so he shrugged and kept walking.

"What was that all about?" Sham said as he caught up to Max.

Max shrugged. "Have no idea."

They began to make their way to the Hertz car rental. Megiddo was about a half hour drive from Haifa. Max noticed random people pointed at him and laughed as he walked by. Sham noticed it as well.

A janitor dropped his mop on the floor and began to laugh at Max, shouting, "Hu lo yode'a." The other workers standing around joined in with the janitor.

Max turned to Sham. Seeing his stone-faced expression, he asked, "What is going on?"

Sham didn't answer, but approached the janitor and spoke to him. The man continued to laugh and say the same phrase in Hebrew over and over. Sham grabbed the man firmly and said, "Mah zott omerett!" The man did not seem to hear or even recognize that Sham was shaking him. He just continued saying the phrase. Frustrated, Sham released the man. He took his hand and waved it in front of the janitor's face. A sharp light flashed under Sham's hand. The janitor stopped laughing. Everyone stopped laughing and continued on with their day. The janitor asked Sham a question, but Sham only shook his head as he turned away from the janitor. "Let's go, Max. We are already behind."

"I want to know what that was all about." Anxiety was creeping up Max's throat.

"So do I, Max." Seeing that his response wasn't sufficient, he continued. "He was saying 'he doesn't know.' What you don't know is unclear, but I am familiar with the curse these people are under. Someone has cursed your image in these people's mind. All these people know is the preset message and nothing else. It is meant to torture and unnerve you."

"Well . . . mission accomplished," Max admitted. "I guess we can assume Astarte knows I am coming."

"No doubt. But this wasn't her spell. It's too involved, too complex. I can see the strands of it interconnecting all these people. It looks like something that comes from the Thirteenth Gate. Possibly Sariel or cast by the same person keeping the Memitim at bay." Sham noticed none of his musings were of any comfort to Max. He slapped him on the back and quickly said, "At least we know we're on the right track."

They reached the Hertz desk and met with a kind-looking woman. She took one look at Max and began to laugh, but this time, the message was in English. "He doesn't know," she said, peeling with laughter. Sham was about to cleanse her of the spell when she said something new. Max froze. "Max, please know, she died wailing like a stuck pig. I made sure it was slow. The shit I did to her…well, she is going to feel that all the way to the Continuance." She began laughing.

Max couldn't catch his breath.

"No worries, Max. Orphans do well in your world. No more dodging unwanted phone calls or uncomfortable family dinners. I have freed you from all that. Also, 'hey, I just lost my mom' is a great pick-up line," she continued through bursts of laughter. "You could thank me, you know."

She began to repeat the message, but Sham cleansed her, bringing the woman back. She blinked at both of them as if they had just arrived, and asked, "How can I help, you two? Oh my, is there something wrong?" She stared at Max, who had lost all color in his face.

Sham assured her Max was fine, just grieving a loss. She nodded that she understood and went about the business of renting the car to Sham.

Max couldn't find the words. He was in a daze. He just allowed Sham to guide him to the car. Getting in, Sham knew they didn't have any minutes to spare, but whatever part of him that understood humanity told him to wait. He sat there in silence and waited for Max to make the first move.

Max sat in the car and thought about what he had just heard. He knew they could be lies meant to simply deceive him, but he knew. Deep down, a clawing told him his mother had failed at the airport and there would be no message or text from her. Tears welled and fell down his cheeks. Max thought about all those hours training, working, studying. For what? So he could play swords in the desert? He remembered how excited he had been to get on the plane and was shamed that even though he'd thought he'd understood the real risks, it was only now dawning on him.

After about ten minutes, Sham started the car and left the airport behind. Looking at Max and the anguish written on his face, he felt he had to break the silence.

"Max, I know you don't want to hear this, but you have to snap out of it. This is exactly what they want. To knock you off your game, becoming easy pickings."

Max thought about Sham and all he had done. He had

put so much hope into Max, but Max had never felt more out of place than he did in that moment. He was a boy who should be starting his first year in college. Should be trying to get a date or hanging out with friends. Everything just went by so fast, he hadn't had enough time to even think about whether he was good enough. "They're right, Sham, I am easy pickings. Stop the car," Max ordered. Sham slammed on the breaks and turned to the curb.

Max tore out of the car and started hyperventilating. His vision blurred. He collapsed on the ground in a heap. He couldn't catch his breath, couldn't get a hold of himself. The sound of his mother's voice deafened his ears. Their last phone call. The last time he would hear her laugh. Images of his father filled his vision. The shooting. The look on his face as he died. Max began to wail. He was losing it.

Then anger began to blossom. What was his mother playing at? She had to have known this was a possibility and he would just be tossed to the wolves. Max stared up to the sky and screamed, "Why the fuck did you do this to me? To your own son. How could you?" Max screamed until his voice was hoarse. Fury filled him, and he began to remember all the lessons about balance and clearing his mind. About what it meant to be House of David. A paladin.

Walled away, a part of Max's mind unlocked. Righteous anger opened a door. From deep inside, his mother's voice spoke to him and whispered. Max listened. She had warned him about this, every lesson. He could not let his emotions control his actions. He was a law unto himself, and he had to remain focused. Her teachings were all he had of her now. He held them dear. He also recognized the lessons that went unsaid. Sometimes you don't have a choice. Sometimes you must do what is right, even at great cost. Heroes had doubts.

Heroes had fears. Continuing past those doubts and fears was what made them heroes.

Max squeezed his eyes so hard, they began to hurt. He took hold of his mind again. He was back in the backyard, playing catch. His mother was watching from the deck, watching her two loves enjoy the summer sun. The wind whipped, making the corn stalks in the garden sway. Dad, tie loosened around his neck, threw the ball to him, and he watched it all the way into his glove, just like he'd been taught. He felt the ball hit the pocket. Then the glove snapped shut.

Snap.

He understood what was at stake. He had already lost everything, but he could help others. All the people back home, not even knowing they were counting on him, needed him. Needed him to get up. Needed him to be their champion. If not him, who? No one else could.

With a singular mind, Max had one more thought. This witch wouldn't take anything else from him.

Sham came up behind him and watched as Max held out his hand, palm up. The sword of David appeared, gleaming in the sun, almost as if it were happy to be in its homeland. Max held the hilt. Max reached for his center. All sound ended. Time stood still. He counted his heartbeats until they slowed.

He pulled the sword free.

The sound of the sword being released rang out. The double-edged blade shone like a mirror. Sham dropped to his knees and bowed his head at the appearance of the sword.

Max gazed at the blade and saw runes he realized could read. "HE has prepared his deadly weapon." Max recognized it at once from his mother's teachings. Psalm 7:13, written by David. Knowledge flooded into Max. Knowledge gained by the Sons and Daughters of David. Histories. Strategies. Wisdom.

Max laughed. His mother had been right. He wasn't alone. She hadn't left him.

Sham looked at Max, standing there with the sword, and realized Eva's fears had come true: all the traces of the boy named Max Travers had been blown away. The boyish grin was gone, replaced by the hard stare of a man who had already seen too much. One who already knew too much. The boy was gone. What was left was a man chosen to be a hero.

Max returned the blade to the scabbard and noticed Sham kneeling. He smiled. The blade knew Sham. It had seen him serve other children of David before. The sword confirmed what Eva had told Max. Sham was one of the good ones.

With an air of heroic bravado, Max said, "Let's go, Sham. We haven't won yet."

CHAPTER 16

Megiddo was a ruin. Astarte scanned around the desolate valley and wondered why fate had chosen this place to be the site. She hadn't been here in ages but remembered the little fortification on top of a hill. Remembered how full of life it had once been. Thankfully, there had been no drama in finding the ring. The temple had once been the largest in the world, so it had been the only structure time hadn't completely erased. When she'd entered, she'd immediately sensed it. It was hers and hers alone. It called to her. Solomon had been true to his word. She'd held her hand out flat, and the ring had emerged from the rubble, finding itself home.

Now, she was back in the valley, sitting at a makeshift table with Sariel next to her. Waiting.

"I understand your position, but I don't agree with this. You need to put the ring on and be done with this." Sariel was trying to be calm, but current circumstances were very volatile. Astarte knew it was going to be difficult for Sariel to understand what needed to happen.

Astarte shook her head. "Blame Dokiel. I will not have victory his way. We have been doing this his way since the very beginning, and I'm certain you would agree things haven't gone well." Sariel didn't protest. "I will have victory, but not until I have my say." Astarte was furious. When she'd seen

Dokiel on the plane, she knew something was wrong. He had said nothing the entire flight, which had confirmed things were amiss. Her short time with the man had told her you couldn't pay him to shut his mouth. By the time they'd landed, it had been obvious. Dokiel was slowly, and painfully, dying.

The scratch on his cheek had putrefied, giving off the smell of rot. The decay had already spread down his neck and up his right arm. It was well past the muscle tissue, and now invaded the bone. His pain was obvious and excruciating. She'd finally gotten him to explain what had happened.

After listening to his story about Eva and the airport, Astarte had said coldly, "You didn't have to kill her." The information had hit her harder than she'd thought it would. Another child dead. Another small piece of her cast into oblivion.

Dokiel had looked confused. "What do you mean?"

"You didn't have to kill her," Astarte had snapped. "There are a thousand ways to dispatch her without killing. All you needed to do was make sure she didn't prevent us from making a flight."

Dokiel had been agog. He'd looked to Sariel for support, but she'd known to leave well enough alone. "Why do you care?" he'd asked Astarte.

Seething at his blindness, she'd yelled, "First and foremost, she was my blood. You knew that, but you killed her anyway." She'd stopped yelling and calmed herself. "I am about to give birth to a new Existence. I have given everything to it. No more of my blood will be spilled if I have a say. And I will have a say, goddammit." Dokiel hadn't said anything, but had yelled in pain at every bump in the road to Megiddo.

Now, Dokiel sat about fifty yards away. The pain made him more pliable, so he was now taking his orders without complaint. Astarte was happy to see he was making his preparations silently.

Astarte glanced at Sariel. "Max will come. I will settle any disputes. If he cannot accept it," she held out the ring, "I will slip this on and take care of business. But he is my blood, and I want my chance. Now, please go join Dokiel and get ready."

No matter what Astarte thought, Sariel did have an understanding of why she was acting this way. For generations, Sariel had been chastised for her offspring who occupied the pit. Nonetheless, she felt Astarte was being reckless and foolish. But with the ring, Astarte was in command, and Sariel was good at following orders. "You know we can only keep the Memitim at bay for a little while."

Astarte nodded. "Just give me enough time to talk to him. That is all."

***

It was clear where Max needed to go. There wasn't much in the way of buildings in the little ruin of a village, but Astarte wasn't hiding. She sat at a table in the middle of the valley. But that isn't what struck Max at first. It was the dark and twisted creatures who had formed a ring about a hundred yards from her, encircling her. Inky, sinewy bodies, with long, sharp wings. Max didn't have to ask who they were.

"It's the Memitim," Sham said.

Max watched them as they stood there, arms outstretched, hands clawing at the air in front of them in some sort of struggle. "How many are there?"

"One hundred and eight. The full company," Sham said with some awe. He couldn't remember the last time he had seen the full complement.

They approached closer and saw they were being held off by two figures on either side of Astarte, standing half the distance between her and the Memitim. One was a tall blonde woman, the other was a man dressed as a priest. Being the closest to Max, he could see the priest's face was bloated and eaten away in parts, and his arms, while outstretched, were covered in bleeding black blisters.

Max recognized Malhamash, who turned away from the invisible barrier that had been holding him off and walked toward Max and Sham. He had sent the sword away, but the magic of the blade remained. It called to him, screaming silent warnings to Max as Mal approached. Max had presumed this being was no good just from the way his mom had always reacted when he was brought up. The information the sword gave him gave detail as to why. Max gritted his teeth to hold back his tongue.

Mal turned quickly to Max and said, "Good to see you again. I see I was right in sending Shamsiel to take care of you. Sorry to hear about your mother."

With that, his tongue was freed. "Don't talk to me, you fucking monster." It took Max his entire will not to strike Mal down. "You sent my mother on a mission that had no hope. Instead of being here with us to fight, you took her off the field." Mal, usually confident, peered into Max's eyes and blanched. In the mortal realm, Malhamash answered to the House of David. Malhamash answered to Max. "I make you one promise. When this is over, you and I will have words. We have a score to settle."

Sham, while inwardly smiling, knew that in the end, they were all on the same side, so he decided to break the tension. "What is going on here? And how is the mortal keeping you back?" Sham pointed to the rotting priest.

Mal bowed his head, shamed he had to admit his failure. "It's not a mortal. It is Dokiel. He has somehow figured out a way of using a human's husk to leave the Continuance. A barrier has sprung up frustrating out attempts to approach."

"What's wrong with him?" Max asked as he watched the black ooze flood out of Father Florez's face.

"Unclear. He has met with some curse I haven't seen before. Obviously, he is unable to heal himself. He is putting his life force into the wall, which is making it quite unbreakable at the moment. I am assuming he thinks if Astarte is successful, she can restore him in a new Existence."

Sham looked at Astarte, who continued to calmly sit at a table in the middle of the valley as if she were expecting a waiter to bring her tea. He didn't understand why all hell hadn't broken loose. "Obviously they have been here a while. Why hasn't she found the ring?" He asked the question hopefully.

Mal frowned at Sham and dashed any hope. "She has."

Max took in the whole scene and shared Sham's confusion. "Then, why hasn't she used it?"

Mal put his hand out toward the circle. "She isn't speaking to me. I invite you to ask her yourself. If you can." Max noticed the snide sound in his voice and glared at him until he turned away.

Max took a step forward. And then another, fully expecting to feel the barrier. He felt nothing as he took a step further, now farther than any of the Memitim. Max glanced back at Sham. "Be ready." Sham nodded as Max closed the distance to the priest.

Dokiel laughed as he watch Max approach. "Max Travers?"

It was the priest's tone that was odd. It was as if a loved

one had returned from a long trip. As with all things that had been happening, it unnerved Max. "Do I know you?"

The priest's nonchalance continued, even though Max could tell he was exerting a great amount of effort. "Oh, no, we actually have never met. I am a friend of your mom and dad's. Did you get my message at the airport?" Dokiel laughed out of his rotten face, puss flowing from his open mouth.

The smell hit Max's senses first, then he looked closely at the wrecked skin and immediately recognized the curse. A particularly nasty spell his mother had taught him. Only to be used, as she'd said, on the most odious of bastards. "I see you met my mother. It seems like she got the better of you in the end."

Dokiel nodded. "I agree. Talented that one was." Dokiel took on a somber tone. He could feel the mortality of his body. The second life of Father Florez was waning. "Look, Max. Nothing personal. It was business with Eva. You see, this is a gamble for me. All or nothing." Dokiel gave a short laugh that was cut short by a shock of pain that shook him. His barrier weakened momentarily, allowing the Memitim to take another step closer. He mustered what remained of his energy and smiled again at Max. "Anyway, young man, I'm a little busy right now. If you have any questions, please go take a seat at the table and get your answers. I, obviously, am not running this shitshow."

Max nodded and proceeded forward. Any thought of striking him down was dismissed. So far, Astarte hadn't used the ring. He didn't want to give her any reason to change course. This was his job alone. He thought no more of the rotting priest, knowing his mother's curse would not only burn through his flesh, but into his very soul. Dokiel was right about one thing: She was very talented.

Astarte saw Max walking toward her. What struck her was this was not the person she had been expecting. The person who strode toward her, blue eyes locked on hers, was not the same boy she'd known just a handful of months ago. She could see the power emanating from him. Dripping from him. In that moment, he reminded her of Solomon. Wisdom gained by experience personified. His chiseled features and grim face. He had been hardened. Renewed. Reborn. Reforged. She couldn't help herself, but she smiled with some sort of twisted pride.

Sariel had been watching carefully and moved uncomfortably, taking her focus off the Memitim. They took one step further. Sariel knew the House of David had unpredictable and vast powers. While she could overpower most things in Existence, she hated the unknown. And that was exactly what this man was.

Astarte, smiling at Max, motioned for him to sit across from her at the table. Max nodded and sat, quickly taking in the dimensions of the battlefield. Distance between him and her. Distance between Sariel and Dokiel, and them to him. The type of daylight. The moisture in the air. The strength of the breeze. The sword whispered to him suggestions and possible strategies. He did all this while staring at Astarte.

No one had said a word.

Astarte opened her hand and showed Max her ring. The cold metal seemed to glow in an attempt to outshine the daylight. The six-pointed star was clearly visible. Max could see the etchings on the ring, he could discern some of their meanings. She put the ring on the table in front of her, close enough to snatch it back, but clearly meant as some sort of gesture of peace.

Max nodded. He took his eyes off Astarte, looked at the empty table in front of him, and concentrated. The Sword of David appeared before him. It did not give off luster, but rather seemed to absorb the light, snatching it from the very air. Astarte's eyes widened as she glared at the pommel that showed the six-pointed Star of David. A sense of pride flared inside her. She recognized that the Max she once knew was no longer here. This man was a creature she had never met. A man who looked at her through the eyes of generations of men and women who had come before him. She was impressed with her student but felt some guilt for her role.

They both brought their gazes back to each other, still silent.

"You won't believe me. I have given you no cause to believe me, but I wanted to say I am sorry about your mother. I didn't know until after it was done."

Max could hear the honest concern in her voice, but he had been fooled by her before. "Why are we talking? Why haven't you put the ring on and fulfilled your quest for chaos?" His tone was angry, which he regretted. He wanted to sound in control. Disinterested. He failed.

Astarte nodded and did not rise to his tone. "I could have done that. Believe me, my companions did nothing short of forcing the ring onto my finger. And honestly, more than half of me wants nothing more. But that has changed. You changed all that."

"Me?" Max had not expected this. "How?"

"I'm going to win, Max," she said, not snidely, but confidently. "I have seen it. I will stand today with the ring on my finger and bring down the Continuance. Your actions here, while admirable, will not be enough. You haven't trained enough. Haven't learned enough. You aren't ready for me." She waited to see if he would protest, but Max said nothing, only stared. "But I am offering you another path. I wanted a chance to convince you of my position. I used you last summer. I admit that freely."

Regaining his stoicism, he said, "Admitting what you cannot deny is no honorable trait."

"True, but I am still doing it. I admit I wronged you. But all the lessons I taught you were the truth. The Continuance is a lie. It separates us from our gods. From enlightenment. You are lucky. Look around you. You know the truth. You can live the rest of your life now knowing what is beyond. Why deny that relationship with everyone? Bringing it down will open everyone's mind to a new understanding. Yes, it will be chaotic, but only at first. Open all the Gates and accept what may come. It must be better than simply denying the truth."

"I have heard all this before," he said bitingly. "I struggle to believe your intentions are wholesome and honest when you surround yourself with torturers and demons."

Astarte nodded. "I surround myself with those I need. With those who can help me expand knowledge to every living creature. But also, I can say the same for you. If your side is so pure and honest, why is Malhamash and his devils surrounding me? Did anyone tell you anything about Medidi and the horrors he and his Memitim unleased on the people there?" Max didn't respond. "Of course not. I knew he was in New York last night. Why didn't he help your mother? Why did he just offer her up like meat to a wolf?" Max made no comment. "Maintaining the status quo has made for some strange bedfellows for you, Max. But never mind that. Believe me. I want a world in which it doesn't matter who you pray to. In my Existence, there are no sides. It's just people having faith in what they want to believe. On that point, I have never lied to you."

Max considered her words and allowed doubt to enter his mind for the first time.

Seeing no fight from him, she continued, "Allow me this. We can do this together. I know you've been pumped with stories about how great it is to be a Son of David, and therefore you know you're also the child of Solomon?" Max nodded. "That means you are also the son of his wife, Naamah, mother of his only son."

"I know all this." Max didn't know where she was going with this.

Astarte knew they would keep it a secret. Malhamash had to. "They didn't tell you." She waited. "I am Naamah. You are also my son." Max shook his head. He stole a glance at Sham, who'd clearly heard what she had said. Sham quickly darted his eyes to Mal, who merely shrugged. Astarte drew Max's attention back. "It makes our make-out sessions a little creepy, but honestly, I didn't know at the time. Why would your friends keep this a secret from you, I wonder?"

The doubt grew larger in Max's mind. These could be more tricks up the witch's sleeve. One last move. There would be no way to prove anything she said. He would just have to believe her. Max's resolve faltered. What she had said made sense. Mal and his mom. Religion fighting and killing religion. Constant endless war. Max looked around the country he was in and considered what it would be like if religion no longer played a part in the world. Just individual faith. To actually have a connection with other realms of Existence would change the world. He remembered what Sham had said the first night they met. Most of what Angie had told him had been the truth.

He would just have to believe her.

He was tempted. "Tell me what kind of world it would be." Max had to ask.

Astarte didn't smile but was thrilled with the question. "You would make the world a better place. You would help me form an Existence that works for us. Peace to all people. No more strife. No warring over drinking water, or fertile land, or which side you crack your egg. We would usher in a new understanding. With your sword, you are a law unto yourself. You can make a better way. Beyond the laws of men. Justice would rule."

She was making too much sense. His old feelings for her emerged. The way she spoke. So bluntly and honestly. Like impossible things were just right there for him to reach out and grasp. That was what had always drawn him to her. Not her body or her face, but her mind and how it worked. She had never made him think one way or the other, they just simply had so much common ground. Doubt, that had started as a raindrop, poured.

The blade sang out in his mind. But the information was also uncertain. The blade knew how to kill, but these decisions were left up to the bearer of the sword, not the sword itself. He thought about all those back at home. He knew he couldn't fail. He had a duty. To his family. To his mom. Too much was riding on him. On the plan. But is that what I am? he thought. A soldier following orders? Carrying out Mal's demands? Had Existence given him any reason to strike her down other than self-preservation of a system?

Astarte saw he was conflicted. "No matter what happens in these next few moments, Max, I will not strike you down. I have no interest in harming you. If I emerge from this ruin alive, I will make sure you are here to see how right I am. I will try not to draw your blood. It is, after all, my blood."

He wanted to believe her.

Max asked one more question. "You've told a good story of how this world can be made better. Made many promises to me. But I can't be the only one you have made promises too." He gestured back to Dokiel. "What about the promises you have made them?"

"I am a woman of my word. There will be chaos, and it will be painful for many. But from the ashes, you will flourish." She saw Max was searching for a reason, any reason, to carry on with his plan. She changed tactics and put on her best scornful schoolteacher voice. "What do you want, Max? All the kingdoms of the Earth? Then take them, they are yours, if you want. Just reach out and take it. I offer this all to you, just do as I say and bow to me."

Snap.

The ball hit Max's glove. He felt the weight of it in the glove. Max smiled back at Jude and threw the ball back. The corn swayed again. Eva called to her family it was time.

Snap.

Doubt or not, the time had come.

A loud crack came from behind Max, and Sariel staggered to the ground. Sham collapsed on the ground, exhausted from the amount of power he'd emptied into the spell he had cast. To pierce the shield, Sham had to put some of his life into the casting. A selfless act Mal would have never thought of.

Wide-eyed, Astarte screamed, "Sariel!" In her fury, Astarte released her power, blowing the table to the side and clearing her path. The ring fell into the grass. The sword disappeared. Astarte watched Sariel on the ground, unmoving, and knew she had to get to her. Max had been counting on that. He had to do everything he could to prevent that.

Astarte moved toward Sariel, but Max put his body in her way. Max attempted to summon the sword, but instead, had to fend off attacks from Astarte. Astarte began throwing curse after curse against Max. Each one bounced harmlessly off his shield, but with each one, she learned more about the limits of Max's power.

Using both hands, she pushed a ribbon of black lightning at Max. It tore through his shield and hit his shoulder. The pain radiated over his body, but he kept on his feet.

"You are going to have to do better than that, Grandma!"

Astarte sent another bolt. Max had to think quickly. He knew he could no longer just depend on defensive shields. If he did, he would be dead in a matter of seconds. With a quick twist of some of his fingers and a small spell, Max drew the metal out of the ground itself and conjured a lightning rod that snatched the twisting black bolt right out of the air.

"Clever, Max. I'm sure you're pretty good with balloon animals too." Astarte changed her tactics. She cast out her hands, fingers splayed. Blades of air began shredding Max's shield, each one tearing through it. Max felt a sharp cut across his cheek, and the blood began to pour. The pain brought him back into battle. His mind was cool. Remembering the counter, Max put a fist into the air, twirled it, and quickly brought it down hard upon the ground. A small cyclone formed and intensified, pulling the blades harmlessly into the tornado. Astarte watched as her castings were being nullified. She knew Max was reaching his limit. His shield was all but gone. Blood was dripping from his nose and ears from the constant barrage of magic. While the shield had protected him, it was almost like being inside a large brass bell continuously tolling. He only had moments left.

Astarte was conflicted. She watched as Sariel lay motionless on the ground. She could just kill Max, but she was determined she would have her way. She would eat her cake too. Seeing Max weakened, Astarte made another move toward Sariel. Max knew he had to keep her attention and keep her close somehow. He threw a fist of air that smacked her across the face. Not enough to crush bone, but enough to bring her back to him. Astarte was more shocked by Max's abilities than the blow itself.

"Forget about her. She's a goner. You can sense that. I would say that makes us even for my mom, but I don't think she was worth even a fourth of my mom. Some useless little servant of yours. A little bootlicker. A sycophant. Even if you ever cared for her, did you really? You use and you use, with no end in sight. She is just another victim of yours."

Astarte tried to find the right words, but they wouldn't come. Max knew nothing. What could an eighteen-year-old know of anything? Finally, her fury found the right ones. "You don't know what you are talking about. She is everything to me."

Max chortled. "Please. Dime a dozen. You can't tell me you loved her." Max laughed even louder. "Your heart rotted long ago. You are a wasted shell parading around like a human. This act of caring is impressive, but merely an act."

Max's taunts had the effect he'd been hoping for. Astarte had had enough and let loose her fury. A large blast of undulating flame struck what remained of Max's shield. Lava oozed from the holes and landed around Max. The shield shrank against the weight of the blast. Max disappeared in a sphere of fire and brimstone.

Max could sense some of the magics in the flame. Some were elemental. Some were unrecognizable. Inside the shield, Max formed the counter to Astarte's fury. He remembered what his mother had taught him and focused his mind to the task. He began making his arrowhead using elements of the fire. He drew what little air was left into the spell and added the moisture from his very own sweat and blood. The spell struggled against him. It demanded to be released. Max put almost everything he had into it, just kept enough back to keep himself conscious.

He opened his hands, and it was off.

The arrow spliced the river of fire in half and used the stream to home right in on Astarte's heart. In a blink, the fire was extinguished. Max gave a sharp inhale of fresh, cool air. His vision cleared as he stood. He gathered his bearings and saw the arrowhead had struck Astarte down. Max moved toward her body, hoping against hope it was over. And then he saw it. She began to move. He may have done the spell correctly, but he wasn't strong enough to kill her with it. Astarte was clearly stunned, but still alive and deadly.

"*Move!*" The combined voices of the sword screamed at him. If he was going to win, it had to be now.

Max, running toward Astarte, drew his hand up, and the Sword of David appeared in his hands. In a few leaps, he was there. He saw that the arrow had thrown Astarte near the ring. She saw it and reached for it. Max took the sword and whipped it around in an arc. It whistled as it cut the air. Max willed the blade to strike the witch down.

***

Astarte could sense Max right on top of her. She could hear the sword ripping through the air. Max was quick. But Astarte was quicker.

She put the ring on, and in an instant, Max was blown out beyond the circle of Memitim, landing roughly at the feet of Sham, the sword clanging into the brush.

The immense power coursed through her, mending wounds and breathing new life into her. But first things first. Astarte ran to Sariel. Examining her, Astarte saw no wound on her chest. Astarte couldn't imagine the type and nature of the spell that had been cast, but it was of no consequence. Using her ring, she commanded Sariel.

"You are not to die. You are to mend yourself." The star of the ring flashed, and Sariel's body relaxed. Astarte kissed her forehead and watch her love's chest fill with air.

Sariel took another deep breath and looked up at Astarte. Fearing a counterattack, she pushed Astarte away and said hoarsely, "Don't concern yourself with me. We are so close. Complete the mission."

Astarte smiled. "I will only be a moment. I'll get things started, then I will get you out of this place." Astarte laid Sariel down gently and moved toward Dokiel. During her little fracas with Max, he had singlehandedly kept the Memitim away, but at a great cost. Most of the skin on his body was now bubbling with sores.

She laid a hand on his cracked cheek. The ring flashed again, and whatever taint Eva had placed on him was removed. She restored him, not out of any affection, but out of a sense of duty. Dokiel looked at Astarte and bowed his head in gratitude and recognition of her power.

With Dokiel's spell broken, the entire company of

Memitim ran toward Astarte, sensing she was the only true threat.

Astarte didn't make a move and just watched them coming in amusement. She turned to Dokiel. "I think it is time to bring it all down. Do you agree?" She raised her hand to the sky. The power of the ring flowed through her, and she called demons of every type and breed.

The ground shook and tore apart. For the first time in their creation, the Memitim paused their attack. From the depths came a group of apeps that started striking at the Memitims, writhing their coiled forms around their bodies. The Memitim hacked away at the serpent creatures with crude bladed instruments and were successful in ripping them in tatters. But no matter, Sariel herself had made them. The apeps regenerated from the cut pieces and multiplied. In a moment, they had plunged their way into the bodies of their attackers.

From above (as Sham had predicted), the first major demon to answer the call made his appearance. Andras and his seven legions riding wyverns. The beasts shot plumes of fire as they thundered down upon Megiddo and specifically the Memitim. Max, head still ringing from being tossed like a rag doll, looked up, and saw that the creatures riding the beasts had smiling mouths that extended down the sides of their necks. The mouths were filled with rows of large, spiked teeth. A long, snake-like tongue darted through the air. Their proportions were all wrong, unnatural, and unnerving.

Sham came over to Max and shook him from his disbelief. "We have got to get clear of here and regroup. Get your ass up!" Sham roughly pulled Max up, and they both ran behind some ruins of the temple to try to figure out the next move.

"What now?" Max asked. Honestly, they had never

really talked about what would happen if he failed. It was just assumed he would be dead. But Astarte was true to her word: Max had not been seriously harmed. Yet.

Sham looked around and began to hear an oddly familiar popping sound. From nowhere, fire imps appeared, quick and erratic. They didn't seem to have a specific goal except to set everything on fire. No matter what they touched, whether stone or the ground itself, a fiery blaze spouted forth. Sham put his arms up, and a dome of cool water rose up around him and Max. The horrible sounds of battle were muffled behind the wall of water. "Sweet Jesus, Max. I have no idea. The Memitim cannot lose. That is what is written. If they lose, it would go against Existence. Honestly, I'm trying to think of our next move."

Max nodded and allowed Sham to think. Max watched as the Memitim fought against the demons that had been summoned. While the Memitim were clearly outnumbered, they surprisingly held their own. Their only function was to kill, and they were quite skilled. To kill without fail. They pushed the attack toward Astarte, casting spells of their own. Spells in a language Max had never heard. Whatever it was, it seemed to work. Apeps were withering. Andras's warriors fell from the sky, lifeless. Max regained hope, until another creature appeared that seemed to turn the tide away from the Memitim.

To Max, they looked like any average person. They wore tattered white robes and just materialized here and there. They didn't seem to have any weapon or make any aggressive moves. A cold shiver went through Max when he saw Mal's reaction. Upon seeing these new beings appear, Mal's face lost its usual emotionless look. Max saw fear. Mal instantly began shouting orders to his men. But it was too late for some. The

Perfidians worked quickly. A few of the Memitims stopped their attack on the demons and attacked each other, hacking away at their brothers' arms and wings. Being equally matched, the fighting was brutal, and eventually, they simply tore each other apart.

Black lightening fell from above. Fire shot up from everywhere. Bodies of various beasts lay everywhere. While the Memitim had strength on their side, Astarte had numbers. No matter how many of the forces of the Thirteenth Gate fell, more replacements arrived and continued to wreak havoc. Twisted creatures with unknown powers filled the landscape and zeroed in on the remaining Memitim. Like a scene from a Bosch, it was chaos. Sham stood close to Max, taking down any demon that came near, but true to Astarte's word, it appeared as if the demons went out of their way to avoid Max.

Astarte began pulling spirits from a ward she had etched on the ground. Hearing Mal shouting orders over the din, she smiled and yelled. "I have something special for you, Malhamash."

She made some quick hand motions and used the power of the ring to summon a specific creature. They may have had their differences in the past, but now, she commanded the Gate, so she no longer had any fear. He would do as she bid. Mal watched as Astarte pulled Kane from the warp.

Holding the ring before his face, she commanded, "Kane, I give you this gift. Your father." The ring flared again, a brilliant white light, and Kane bowed his head to his master. She put her arm out toward Mal.

Kane turned, and with unworldly speed, charged his father. The two clashed and tore at each other. Astarte knew Kane would not last long, but she wanted Mal to be the one to destroy his own child. She saw it as a fitting punishment.

Watching Mal and Kane battle, Max knew he was on the losing side. He stepped back and turned to Sham. "I'm sorry. I just wasn't fast enough."

Sham put his arm around and hugged him. "Don't worry. Oddly enough, this isn't the worst situation I have been in. But it does seem like we have reached the valley of the shadow of death." Sham smiled as he blasted another demon into bits.

And then the world went white.

A brilliant white. Like staring into the full noonday sun. All were blinded. The good and bad alike. Sham's water dome evaporated from the heat of the radiance. From the light, a high ringing sound peeled out. Like nothing that had been heard on Earth, the vibrations were felt in the marrow of bones. Max fell to the ground again, trying to cover both his eyes and ears. Even with his eyes closed, the light was blinding. He could see the bones of his fingers through his eyelids. It was inescapable. The ringing grew and destroyed his eardrums. Blood flowed from his ears. All fighting ceased. All creatures stopped. There was nothing but the ringing and the light. And odd peace.

Then the world came back. Sham looked around as all the creatures regained themselves. He knew what had just happened. "The Continuance. It's over. All Gates are open." He said this with a smile. With a sense of relief.

Max didn't really know what to expect. Again, they were in uncharted territory. "I wish we wouldn't have put all our apples in the me winning basket," he said to Sham. "We're just standing here with our thumbs up our asses. What do we do?"

Sham smiled. "Who says I am not prepared?" He

gestured to the world around them and said again, "The Continuance is gone. All the Gates are open." He gave Max a knowing look.

Max thought about the implications, all Astarte had said, and he had an epiphany. Max got down on his knees and prayed. He prayed as hard as he could.

The Gates were open. And they were listening.

Thousands of flashes of light appeared at once. One appeared next to Sham and Max. From the light appeared a young Eva Travers wielding twin daggers. Eva looked at her son and smiled. Her eyes were the same cool blue, but she had to only be seventeen years old, the age she had been when she first accepted the responsibility of the House of David. Each light brought forth a Son or Daughter of David, each carrying their blades, ready to battle.

More flashes erupted next to Max. He looked at those who assembled around him. They turned to him and awaited his command. He brought forward his sword. He pointed it in the direction of Astarte. "We cannot do anything about the Continuance. That is not for us to fix. We can only hope to battle back the worst of the hell spawn and keep them at bay. This is our realm, and we must protect it. Here in this valley, we must make this last stand." They all agreed. "Push the attack and send these bastards back to the Thirteenth." Max held his sword up, and they all followed in kind, moving toward the battle.

More demons were arriving to Megiddo, answering the call of the ring. More beings from the First Gate were arriving in answer to prayers. Together, they pressed the attack to Astarte. The Maid of Orleans struck down Andras and cleaved off the head of his wyvern. Others were casting spells with one hand and butchering beasts with the other. Max saw various spells take down Perfidians before they could get too close. Axes hacking off limbs. House of David from all time periods were pushing back the enemy.

Max led the charge realizing the demons were leaving him alone. The tide was turning again. Eva charged forward with Max, slashing and cutting with both hands. They were desperate to reach Astarte and put an end to what she had begun. To fix what she had rent.

A horned beast crept up behind Max. It reached out and seized him by the neck. Max turned, and as his sword entered the creature's belly, Eva, who had jumped on its back, plunged both daggers in either side of his neck. Black blood spurted from the wounds and covered them both. Without another thought, she sprung off the dying beast's back and went back into the fray. She was a whirlwind of death. All fell before her. Max couldn't hide his joy at seeing her.

A Perfidian appeared and began to shamble towards her. She took a step back with a smile, spun, pointed both daggers at it, and yelled, "Decimare!" The demon was instantly sliced into ten even pieces and collapsed in a dust of red blood. She looked at her handiwork with some satisfaction. She glanced back at Max. "Come on, son. Let's end this together." Side by side, they worked their way to Astarte.

Reaching the center of the valley, Max scanned the area, ready for whatever creature Astarte would send him. With Eva, nothing could stand between them. Eva and Max looked at the overturned table and realized they stood alone. Astarte was nowhere to be seen.

***

After the flash of light and ringing, Astarte knew the

job had been done. Pulling Kane had done the trick. Mission accomplished, she ran to Sariel, who had recovered somewhat from the attack.

"Can you move?" she asked hurriedly.

Sariel winced. "Yes. I have survived eons in the pit. I can withstand a little ache."

Astarte moved her behind where the table had been set up. Astarte waved her hand, and the glamor on the ground vanished, revealing, etched in stone, a large hexagram encircled three times. "Come on. We are almost there." She steadied Sariel as they both stood in the center. "You can thank me at any time, you know."

"Are you sure you want to leave?" Sariel said as she saw all the demons gathering. "It seems like it's going to be quite a party."

Astarte shook her head. "Let the kids have their fun. I have what I want right here." Sariel smiled as Astarte leaned down. Their lips met. Astarte's hair fell onto Sariel's face, and for another moment, the world stopped for them both. Their lips parted, and Astarte said, "Let's have a drink." She cast the portal spell. Sariel looked around them, and the valley was replaced by a closet. The hexagram underneath them that had been glowing, dimmed and vanished. Getting up, they opened the door and found themselves on the fourth floor of the JFK airport. Just outside the lounge for El Al airlines.

Sariel, seeing where they were, away from the din, breathed in deep. "Thanks. I need a drink. You know, I have to say, I am impressed with you. Such planning. How did you know I would be thirsty?"

Astarte laughed and pointed to her head. "I am the Necromancer, the Witch of Endor, the Destroyer of the Continuance. I know all."

Astarte continued to hold her as they both entered the lounge. They found two comfortable chairs near the wall, and Astarte motioned for the server to come and take their order. After a moment, they were alone and safe for the first time. Ever. Sariel took in the quiet and shut her eyes. The peace was a new sensation for them both. Astarte looked at her with rapture, thrilled they had gotten away with everything they'd wanted. Sariel opened one eye, realizing she did have one question. "What about Dokiel?"

Astarte grimaced. "Fuck him. He is getting whatever he deserves. We are free. To make our own decisions, set our own path. For the first time, truly free."

The server came over, and they made their orders. "So, where to now?" Sariel asked. Neither of them were even thinking about the distant battle. The outcome didn't matter. They were happy the deed had been done.

Astarte turned to Sariel. "Let's keep things simple. Let's enjoy our drinks, maybe another, and then I say we make our way back to that little cabin in the woods. I think there are some things we can do there to occupy our time for a while at least." She smiled, remembering the short time they'd had alone there.

Sariel was about to say she agreed, but then something caught the edge of her vision. Astarte leaned across the table and gave Sariel another kiss, hungry and passionate. Sariel tried to dismiss what she'd thought she had seen, but when Astarte moved back, she saw it again. Over Astarte's shoulder, Sariel saw Puriel at the bar. He watched the two women, nodded at Sariel, knowingly tipped his drink to her, and vanished.

Sariel understood. They had lost. But in that moment Sariel knew what role she needed to play.

"I love you," said Astarte.

For the first time in her existence, Sariel teared. "We love each other."

CHAPTER 17

Puriel materialized back into his office. In his hand, he held a glowing orb. Apollyon stood up from the couch.

"All set?" she asked.

Puriel nodded. He walked over to his shelves, found an empty spot, and placed the orb named Astarte 2030 in between a rock tumbler and a powdered judge's wig. Puriel stood back and watched the white mist inside the orb undulate, pleased with the outcome. He glanced around the office and answered, "I see no warps. The Continuance has been maintained. I am happy with the outcome, aren't you?"

Apollyon shrugged. "I may come around now and then to see how a world without the Continuance would look, if that is okay with you, love." She got up and read the red paper Puriel handed to her. "How much cleanup will there be in the mortal realm?" She had to rely on Puriel for these questions since she could not contact any of her Watchers on Earth.

"Not much. Shamsiel reported the plan had worked. It was just a matter of time until Max got the upper hand. The boy is quite talented. Just like his mother." Puriel didn't mention Max was taking the whole situation very hard. It was of some concern, but he wasn't going to share that with Apollyon. "The real trick was having her continuance up and running so she wouldn't suspect. I have a feeling Sariel will help us maintain the illusion, don't you think?"

Apollyon nodded. "Why wouldn't she? She gets to live forever with her little witch. Why would she care if it is real or not?"

Puriel poured two drinks and offered her one. "Actually, I am surprised your side had been so willing for this compromise."

Time works differently in the Continuance. In the instant Max had removed Astarte's head, an agreement had been argued over, negotiated, and then struck between the First and Thirteenth Gate. It was felt it would be safer if Astarte never knew she was even dead. And with Sariel there making her ageless, there would be no reason for her to suspect as the decades rolled on. The ring would stay with Astarte, but while inside the orb, it would be rendered useless. The simplest solutions were sometimes the best ones.

Apollyon didn't answer Puriel's question directly. There were things she didn't want him to know, like Solomon and the issues he was causing behind the Thirteenth Gate. Until that was sorted out, it was deemed safer for Astarte to be housed in the Continuance. The ring didn't need to be anywhere Solomon could reach it. Apollyon affected her overly flirtatious nature. "Now that we are going to be working together for the foreseeable future, you will have to get used to me being so reasonable." She got up, took the drink, then moved very close to Puriel. "Trust me, I think we will work very well together."

"And what of Dokiel?" Puriel knew she was hiding something from him, so he pressed. He wanted to see how she would react. It was a little trick he had picked up from his old friend.

Apollyon's black eyes flamed red for a moment. "As you are aware, the body of Father Tomas Florez was found lifeless in Megiddo. As for Dokiel, the curse the Daughter of David used would have also seeped into him. He seems to have escaped Megiddo and the Memitim, but we are optimistic he is wailing in a ditch somewhere in the void. We will collect his husk soon enough."

Puriel hid his smile. "Good."

∗∗∗

Max peered down at the body of Astarte. The spell being broken, her body began to rapidly decompose. After a moment, she was just dust being whipped by the scorching breeze. Next to her laid the Sword of David, blade broken in two. Max fell to his knees. He cradled himself against waves of pain that racked his body, as if he were being torn in two.

Seeing this, Mal smiled, turned, and vanished with the Memitim. Their job was done, and he didn't want to hear any more from the newest Son of David. Broken blade or not, Max was not someone he wanted to deal with.

Sham carefully walked over to Max. Sham looked at the broken blade and knew what it meant. Max had swung the blade and killed. But deep inside himself, he doubted. Max took a life without being certain. He relied on the wisdom of others, not his own heart.

Sham put his hand on Max's shoulder, who abruptly shrugged it off. "Don't touch me, Sham." Max's tone was soft, but it was filled with hatred. Eventually, the pain subsided, but did not completely disappear. It settled in his chest.

Sham stammered, "I had no idea about Astarte and Naamah and Solomon or the whole business. I should have, but I didn't. Please, you have to believe me."

Max said nothing. He did believe him, but that did not

console him. "And if you would have known but had been told not to tell me, what then?" Max glanced quickly over and saw Sham put his head down. Max knew the answer. Sham, for all his wonderful traits, wasn't human. He couldn't understand. "Mom was right, I can't trust anyone but myself. I didn't listen to her, and this is the result."

Sham brought his head up. "I don't know what I would have done, but, Max, I would hope that, in the end, I would have done the right thing. Max, I serve your House. I always will." Seeing Max relax his muscles, Sham attempted to change the conversation. "So," he motioned to the blade, "thoughts as to what to do?"

Max studied Sham and realized he was the only one he had left in this world. Max would be going home to an empty house. The sword was the last thing on his mind. "I used the blade to kill another. Not because I was doing what I thought was right, but because I was doing what I was told. What Mal wanted me to do. What you wanted me to do. I don't see why I should even have it in the first place. I think your dream of me adding to its knowledge is just that. A fucking dream."

Sham disagreed. He knew there was so much more for Max in this world. But he knew now was not the time to say anything. Just nod and agree. "So, now what?"

Max picked up the pieces of his sword, closed his eyes, and sent them away. "I am not certain Astarte was wrong, nor am I certain she was right. I know I will have to live with what I did, so I am going to go home. My champion days are done."

Max began to walk out of the valley, but after a few paces, he stopped and turned to Sham. "Are you coming with me?"

Sham gave a small smile and said, "I serve the House of David," and followed Max out of the valley.

CLAVIS

The following characters have their origins of the original texts of the various Abrahamic religions:

David – King of the United Monarchy of Israel. First of his line. Father to Solomon. Anointed king by the prophet Samuel. He flees King Saul's order for the former's death and takes refuge with the Priests of Nob. Their leader, Ahimelech, gave David the sword of Goliath to defend himself against Saul. Circa 1000 BCE.

Joshua – Follower of Moses. Leader of the Tribes of Israelites during their conquest of the "promised land." Successfully clears most of the land promised to his people by their god. Is tricked into sparing the Canaanite city of Gibeon. Circa. 1240 BCE.

Rehoboam – Son of Solomon and First King of Judah. United Monarchy of Israel dissolved with his ascension to the throne. He fathered over eighty children. Circa 910 BCE.

Samuel – Prophet of the Abrahamic religions. Sent by God to anoint rulers over the Israelites. Chooses Saul as first king. Also anoints the shepherd David as the second king. His soul was raised by the Witch of Endor at the behest of Saul. Circa 1030 BCE.

Saul – First King of the United Monarchy of Israel. Anointed king by the prophet Samuel after the reign of the Judges of the tribes of Israel. Unpopular later in his reign. Saul seeks the counsel of a necromancer in the city of Endor. After hearing of his upcoming fate by the raised soul of Samuel, Saul commits suicide rather than be captured by the Amalekite Army. Circa 1030 BCE.

Solomon – King of the United Monarchy of Israel. Son of David. Considered to be one of the wisest rulers of his time. Builder of the First Temple. Legend tells that Solomon had the power to command demons through the use of the seal of Solomon, which was engraved on a ring. The Seal of Solomon was a precursor to what is known as the Star of David. He married Naamah, an Ammonite woman. Together, they begat Rehoboam. Circa 940 BCE.

Celestial Characters

The origins of the following characters come from various religious texts:

Apollyon – Prince of the Abyss. Leader of the Thirteenth Gate.

Dokiel – Commander of the Thirteenth Gate and Arbiter of the Continuance.

Jeqon – Watcher of the mortal realm from the Thirteenth Gate. Skilled in torture.

Malhamash – Known as "God's Poison," he commands the Memitim. His affiliation is not tied to any Gate.

Memitim – A group of beings tasked with killing for Existence. They either kill those who stand against the Chosen (or guarded) or kill those of the Chosen who have been deemed necessary to eliminate. Led by Malhamash.

Menes – Pharaoh of Egypt. Founder of the First Dynasty. United Upper and Lower Egypt. Upon death, was wrongfully placed in the Thirteenth Realm for extraction. Saved by Existence. Soul placed in multiple incarnations for repair.

Necromancer – One of many names attributed to the being known also as the Witch of Endor. Only mortal that has command over the Thirteenth Realm.

Puriel – Commander of the First Gate and Arbiter of the Continuance.

Santa Muerte – Reaper being who is an amalgam from various religions. Resides in the void between the mortal realm and the Continuance.

Sariel – Under-Commander of the Thirteenth Gate and assistant to Arbiter Dokiel. Creator of various beasts that inhabit the pit.

Shamsiel – Watcher of the mortal realm from the First Gate. Former Commander of the 365 Legions. Friend to the House of David.

As iron sharpens iron, so one person sharpens another. Nothing I have done here would have been possible without the hard work and devotion of others. I have carved out this section to thank them all. Thomas helped me lay down the bones. Anthony, Lisa, and Robert helped with the muscle and the joints. Joseph and Emily showed me how to breathe life into her lungs. Frenchie tore her all to pieces. Carrie wept at the butchering of the English language. But she came back. Better.

So, to all of you, from my deepest parts, thank you.

- I.H.

Please Enjoy a Glimpse Into
Book Two of the Apostate Series:
Kinslayer

\- I.H.

KINSLAYER

PROLOGUE

Max stood at the door of 1337 Escondido, the residence of the late Jude and Eva Travers. He had gotten out of the car under the darkening November sky as the wind whipped at the red oak that struggled to hold on to its leaves, which were more brown than red at this point. As Max pushed aside various packages had been left at the door, it struck him as odd. After all the trials he had recently been through, having to go back to a normal routine seemed disjointed. Get the mail. Rake leaves. Wash clothes. It was all on him this time, and he didn't feel ready. He was desperate to leave Meddigo behind, but was just as desperate to not have life, normal life, lurch forward. He glanced at the red door and remembered the day his mom painted it. He remembered his father wasn't too much of a fan of the color, but Jude pretty much let his wife do what she wanted. Max saw that the red paint was beginning to fade. Someone would have to repaint. Add that to the list, he thought.

Sham easily grabbed what bags they had brought and shouted as he walked to the door, "Go on in and hit the shower. I will take care of these and order dinner."

Turning back to the door, Max paused again. He knew the moment he opened the door reality would somehow be more real. Time would somehow lurch forward, and reality would smack him across the face. Max shook off these thoughts and forced his hand on the cold brass handle and turned the key.

Like always, he kicked his shoes off at the door, but this time he didn't shout any greeting. There wouldn't be any point. Sham shuffled past behind him and went into one of the spare rooms he had been using during Max's training. Max watched his teacher close the door behind him. Thankfully, the journey home had been quiet. Max wasn't interested in any long conversations or any plans for the future; he just wanted to be home, and in his bed. Sham seemed to understand that without asking. Max went upstairs, as he had done countless times, and started the shower.

Taking off his shirt, he examined himself in the mirror for the first time in a long time. All the training had changed him for certain but unlocking the sword had completely altered him. The boy gazed into the mirror and found a grim looking man staring back. He breathed in deep and watched his muscles flex with the inhale and felt the lingering pain from various bruises and pulled tendons. No matter the ache in his arms or legs, they didn't rival the agony that resided deep in his chest. It had sprung up the moment the blade had broken. Max knew that it was there to stay. A physical reminder of his failure. A penance for using the blade not to do what he thought was right, but to accomplish the goals set for him. The pain was the only true souvenir he had brought back from his adventure. Wiping away the steam, glanced at his face one more time and finally smiled, relieved to see that his baby-blues hadn't changed.

The hot water washed away what it could. It wasn't a sadness that had washed over Max, but a feeling of loss. Unleashing the sword, and its power, had awakened something in his blood, and now that had been severed. It was an emptiness he couldn't quite put into words. It continued to dance upon his skin, and as he left the shower, it made Max still feel dirty. He shrugged and knew no amount of soap would absolve him. A little water would not clear him of his deed.

After getting dressed, Max's hunger hit him in the stomach. He couldn't remember the last time he had eaten anything and the smell of freshly arrived pizza wafted from the kitchen. Coming down the stairs, he was about to turn towards the kitchen when something inside him pulled him to a stop. The pain in his chest flared. Max looked down to the end of the hallway to the empty wall. The pain eased. He moved down the hall and stopped. His hands flew up into the air and began to make the summoning gestures. Max whispered the words that had been taught to him and, in a flash, the purple door appeared. Before reaching for the knob, Max glanced back towards the kitchen and imaged Sham leaning against the counter. Sham would probably be trying to figure out what their next move was, or even if there was a next move. Having no interest in that conversation, Max shrugged and opened the door. Because of the magic of the training area, Max knew that Sham wouldn't even know he was gone.

Descending the familiar stone steps, an unfamiliar scene sprung up. The bright park that usually greeted him, with the babbling brook and the winging birds was gone. The eternal spring was replaced by the dead of winter. Large snowflakes steadily fell from gray clouds adding to the blanket had already covered the grass. A few trees still clung on to their leaves, but even those that were left were tossed about in the wind. The cold hit Max's face first. The sharp air seemed to cut down his throat and freeze his lungs. From there, the shock traveled throughout his body causing him to shake. No matter the cold, Max trudged forward through the snow and finally came out of the grove and into the valley.

In the center of the snowy field, Max saw his training program sitting in an armchair, facing away. "Multi!" Max yelled, however the wind whipped down the valley and cut him off. The wind and snow continued to beat upon him from all directions. Whatever the force inside him that compelled him to walk down the hallway, to summon the door, was now beginning to hurt inside him. The pain intensified and he fell to his knees. Max dropped his head. He was tired of it. Of the pain. Of the disappointment. Of loss. He was weak with wary.

The wind stopped. "It is good that you came home." Max stared up and into the eyes of Multi who sat across from him. Max found himself in a matching armchair. The snow had stopped, but the sky remained grim. Multi gave a small smile. "It is good that you suffer. It shows you know you are to blame. I think it is always too easy to lay the fault for our actions on others. Sham. Malhamash. Eva. The onus should always be placed on the person who made the decision. The person who swung the sword, so to say." Multi looked around the park. "It would seem that things did not necessarily work exactly to plan."

Max shook his head. "Not at all. I was an absolute failure."

Multi said, "Nonsense," and leaned in closely and quickly slapped Max across the face. "If you were an absolute failure, you wouldn't be here to feel that."

Heat rushed to Max's face. The pain was minimal, but he was incensed. "Not everything is training, Multi."

Multi set back and considered Max's statement. He was confused. "Whoever said that? Even now, sitting in the snow, comforting your cheek, you are learning."

Max didn't answer, but instead gestured to the park. "I don't understand. What has happened here? What set this off?"

Multi kicked at some snow at his feet, revealing the limp grass below. "Your mother put in place many different, uh," he stammered, "let's call them 'protocols' in an attempt to forecast what you might need in the future. I think it would be best to say this," he gestured to the wintery landscape, "is a hard reset." He smiled. "Eva Travers is dead, but her magic still survives. But where we go from here depends on exactly how much shit you have gotten yourself into." He looked up to Max. "Tell me. From one to ten, how bad is it."

The moment Max conjured the door he knew he would have to answer these questions. He had difficultly exactly finding the right words. Max sighed and closed his eyes. He concentrated and summoned the sword. In a blinding light it appeared in Max's hand, and for a smallest of moments, it seemed to gleam with glory. But that moment passed as the blade split in two and fell to the ground.

Multi reared back as if the broken blade was going to reach up and bite him. "So, an eleven." Before Max could say anything to explain what had happened, Multi put his hand on Max's cheek, gently this time. "I am sorry Max, but she was ready for even this." And then to no one in particular, Multi said, "Accessing Evangeline." With those words Multi began to change. An aura around him began to glow purple and the light intensified until Max had to turn away, but Multi kept his hand on his face. The light cast itself upon the snow and it seemed as if the entire park was nothing but a purple light. And then the world returned. Max opened his eyes to see the person who had replaced Multi.

"Hello Max." A young woman said with a smile. Her

hand was warm against his skin.

Max studied her quickly and knew her. He had seen enough family photos and the old Christmas videos and her face fit perfectly. But his familiarity with the woman didn't put him at ease. He stepped back and she dropped her hand. "I don't understand?"

Eva Travers said, "This was not something I would have ever wished for you to see." She glanced down at the broken blade. "But what's done is done."

Max stammered, "But why do you look like the way you do look?" Max stopped himself when he saw that she was confused. "Why do you look so young? Younger than I have ever seen you. That is what I mean."

Eva glanced down at herself. Her black t-shirt emblazoned with an encircled downward jagged red arrow under a red flannel seemed all to be in place. Her baggy jeans hung comfortably and flowed down to her black Docs. She smiled at Max. "Because I am not really Eva Travers. I am Evangeline Young. I won't become Eva Travers for at least six, maybe seven years. You and I won't meet for a few years after that. So I guess I do become mom. I just appear like she did when she was your age."

Max watched her for a moment as he soaked in the information. It wasn't the craziest thing he had heard this month. He just returned from Israel after killing a four-thousand-year-old witch, who he not only previously made out with, but who also turned out to be his distant ancestor. Not the craziest by a longshot. But still, a modicum of distrust was warranted. "You're my mom at 18?"

Evangeline smiled. "Well, I think it would be more accurate to say I am a representation of your mother at 18-years-old. I was put together by Eva Travers and last updated this past October. When you showed Multi the broken sword, that triggered this protocol to take over."

Max finally looked deep into Evangeline's eyes and found something familiar. Blue as the sky. Just like they always were. Just like his. All his concern melted, and he lurched forward and embraced her. "I know you are not her. But I really need this."

Evangeline returned the hug readily. He was a good head taller than her, but she held him as if he were her baby. She stroked his hair and said nothing, just letting him find some peace.

After a few moments, he let go of her and asked, "Not that it isn't great seeing you but why isn't this protocol something that Multi could run?" She furrowed her brow and he quickly added, "I mean, why all the hocus pocus?"

Evangeline gave a laugh. "Why do you ask?"

"It's just," Max stammered, "it's just not my mom's, or your, or whatever's way. She didn't do things without some sort of purpose. I have no doubt she chose this image for a reason."

"Very good Max. You really have been paying attention." Her smile vanished. "You're right of course. We wanted to start things off a little light, maybe ease you into the next phase, but I will just cut to the chase. Some stories are better told when you can see into each other's eyes. Maybe this way you will better understand what was done. What I had to do."

Max pointed at the broken sword and excitedly said, "Are you going to say something that will help me fix the sword?"

Anguish flared in her face and her eyes darkened. In a calm voice she said, "That is uncertain. I know I am the protocol to run when you have forsaken your calling and have undone the blade. Whether this leads you to remaking it or not is not up to me. Maybe what I have to say will only soothe you and give you some peace." Her face became hopeful. "Would that not be enough for you?"

Max touched his chest and felt the pain subsiding.

Evangeline understood. "I know that pain, Max." She touched her chest. "I lived with it also. But I also know what can soothe it. Hope springing there, from your chest. Hope that not all is lost. I can help you get back on track. At the very least."

Max knew hope was a wonderfully powerful emotion, but also knew one had to be careful of it. It could also torture. Max felt the pain lessen even more and thought about Evangeline's question. "Sham didn't say much to me after the whole Astarte business, but he did say that I had only to focus on the small things. The hour to hour, and then the day to day. To answer your question, yes, just getting through each day would be enough for me."

"Sham is usually right," she said with a wistful smile and shifted in her seat. "I am going to tell you the reason it is snowing."

Max squinted and furrowed his brow. "Multi said it was because my mom died."

Evangeline nodded and said, "That is an oversimplification." Evangeline checked her nails. The black polish was immaculate. "I am assuming that your mother never told you about her time with the House of David and her blades?"

Blades? He thought. "No. She wouldn't say, and I didn't pry."

Evangeline agreed. "Good. You may have found it distracting to your task." Max was going to take issue with that statement, but she put up her hand. "The goal was to make sure you returned home alive. Which you have. Congrats to her. The manner of your return is of no consequence. She was prepared for most scenarios. I am obviously the 'everything got fucked and I broke the blade killing something I knew I probably shouldn't have killed' protocol."

Max was not used to hearing such language from his mother, but he had to remind himself that Evangeline was not her. "Well, I am glad my mother thought of everything. She was pretty smart."

"Not as smart as she wished. She was wise, but that wisdom came at a price." Evangeline statement sounded as cold as the surroundings. She cast her arm out at the surroundings and said, "The winter you see here is a warning. Yes, Multi was right, your mom is dead. Your mom's life, or my life, was keeping something back. And now, it has been set free." She stared hard at Max. "Wisdom comes from doing. And failing. And doing again."

Max met her gaze confidently, but he could do nothing about the growing panic in his gut. "What has been set free?"

Evangeline softened her face seeing that she had made her point. "Let's begin at the beginning."